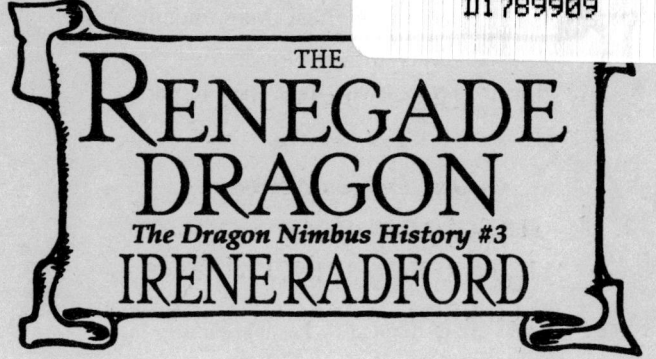

THE RENEGADE DRAGON
The Dragon Nimbus History #3
IRENE RADFORD

DAW BOOKS, INC.
DONALD A. WOLLHEIM, FOUNDER
375 Hudson Street, New York, NY 10014
ELIZABETH R. WOLLHEIM
SHEILA E. GILBERT
PUBLISHERS

Copyright © 1999 by Phyllis Irene Radford Karr.

All Rights Reserved.

Cover art by Yvonne Gilbert.

Interior map by Michael Gilbert.

DAW Book Collectors No. 1138.

DAW Books are distributed by Penguin Putnam Inc.

All characters and events in this book are fictitious.
Any resemblance to persons living or dead is strictly coincidental.

If you purchase this book without a cover you should be aware that this book may have been stolen property and reported as "unsold and destroyed" to the publisher. In such case neither the author nor the publisher has received any payment for this "stripped book."

First Printing, November 1999
1 2 3 4 5 6 7 8 9

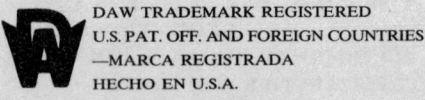

DAW TRADEMARK REGISTERED
U.S. PAT. OFF. AND FOREIGN COUNTRIES
—MARCA REGISTRADA
HECHO EN U.S.A.

PRINTED IN THE U.S.A.

This book is dedicated to the memory of Cindy Carver, Susan Holzworth, Jo Clayton, and Barbara Martin, dear friends who departed this plane of existence too early but left me with a wonderful legacy. Thanks to them I have learned to have faith in myself. Now I just hope I can live up to their expectations.

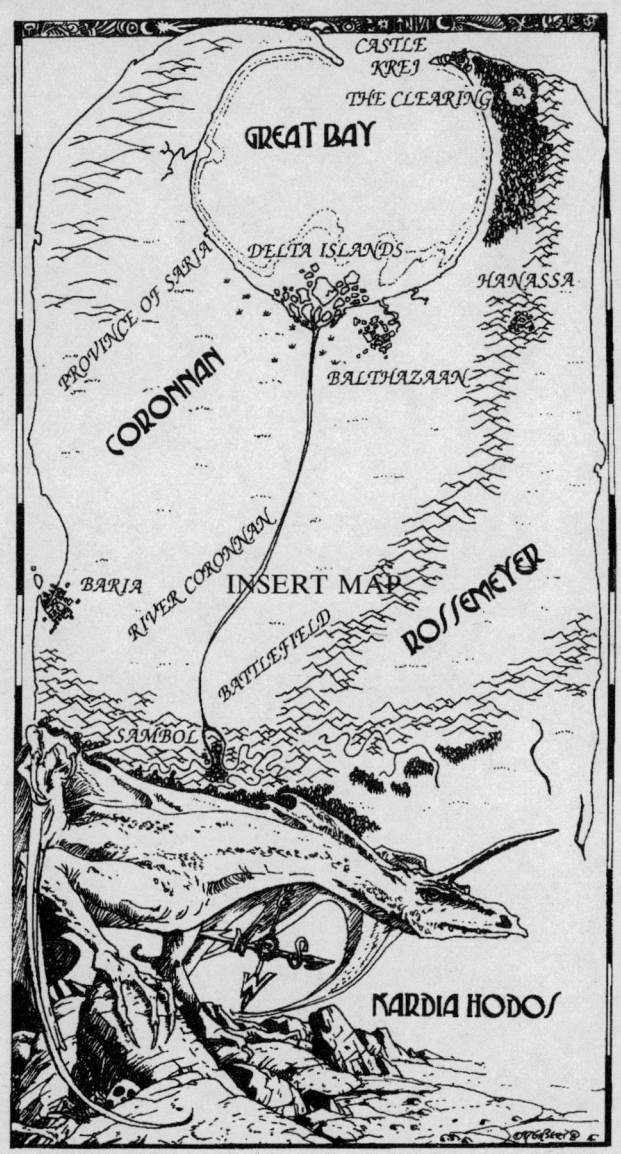

THE VOID BECKONED
TO POWWELL WITH THE SOFT
MUSIC OF THE STARS. . . .

Powwell merged with the blank nothingness of the void. All sense of his body, of direction, of his planetary orientation evaporated. Nothing existed but his mind.

He began to search for his sister, Kalen, expecting her life force to entwine with his own. Suddenly a brighter crystal life danced around Powwell's own life force, just out of reach. Only Shayla, the nearly invisible dragon could be a pure crystal. Powwell relaxed, accepting Shayla as his guide and mentor during this journey.

(What do you seek?)

I search for my sister who is lost to me, Powwell replied.

(Is she truly lost, or do you not know where to look?)

Kalen was thrown into the lava core of Hanassa as the dragongate opened, but before it fully formed. Her companion went into the void. The dragons spat that one out again. I must presume my sister drifts alone in the void as well.

Powwell sensed alarm and wariness in the crystal life force the moment he mentioned Hanassa.

(If the one you seek entered the void from Hanassa, then if she finds her way out again without assistance, she must return to Hanassa. Give up your search. She will not welcome being found.)

I can't. I have to find Kalen. I promised her.

(Look within yourself before you venture into the realm of the renegade dragon. . . .)

Be sure to read these magnificent
DAW Fantasy Novels by
IRENE RADFORD

The Dragon Nimbus:
THE GLASS DRAGON (Book 1)
THE PERFECT PRINCESS (Book 2)
THE LONELIEST MAGICIAN (Book 3)

The Dragon Nimbus History:
THE DRAGON'S TOUCHSTONE (Book 1)
THE LAST BATTLEMAGE (Book 2)
THE RENEGADE DRAGON (Book 3)

Merlin's Descendants:
GUARDIAN OF THE BALANCE (Book 1)
GUARDIAN OF THE TRUST (Book 2)

available in March, 2000

PROLOGUE

Midmorning of Saawheen, the Holy Day of Remembrance, in late Autumn of the second year of the Reign of Quinnault Darville de Draconis, Dragon Blessed King of Coronnan; a meadow west of Coronnan City

Shayla stretched her wings wide, catching a shift in air currents as she cruised the length of the waterway humans call the River Coronnan. Her twelve dragonets had just eaten a bemouth, one of the ferocious fish that inhabited the depths of the Great Bay. Even though her babies drowsed with full tummies, she knew they'd awaken again soon, clamoring for more fresh meat to feed their growing bodies. In the meantime, she took this rare free time to enjoy a few moments of peace and freedom, allowing the air currents to guide her constant search for food.

She scanned the ground for likely game. All of the cows and sheep the humans had set out as a tithe for the dragons looked too scrawny to feed her hungry babies.

The nimbus of dragons had agreed among themselves to allow the herds to increase before culling. Generations of war and privation had taken a toll on both dragons and humans. They would all thrive better if the dragons hunted wild game for a few more years.

Shayla, oh, Shayla, I need your help. A human mind called to the dragon. *Shayla, hurry. I need you.*

Shayla listened closely to the summons. The plea of a woman with a deep problem. A problem dragons couldn't ignore.

She knew the mind calling her away from her leisurely glide around the Great Bay. The female named Maarie Kaathliin, called Katie by those close to her, had mated with dragon-blessed King Quinnault at the same time Shayla had flown a nuptial ritual with five male dragons. Queen Katie had proved to be a formidable woman nearly worthy of leading a dragon nimbus.

(How may I assist?) Shayla banked her wings and circled until she located Katie. The queen stood at the edge of a large field, cradling her baby in her arms. Shayla recognized the other humans who rested nearby after a meal. She grabbed the meaning of their word "picnic" from the mind of King Quinnault. She still didn't understand the difference between eating in the lair or eating in the field. Dragons did both and had no word to separate the two.

She narrowed her telepathic communication so that only the queen could hear her. King Quinnault and his sister Myrilandel were openly receptive to dragon thoughts. Powwell, the fledgling magician who played with Myrilandel's daughter, could hear less. Yaala, a descendant of the renegade dragon—who shall forever more remain nameless—could hear all too much if she opened her mind to her heritage.

Shayla grieved a moment that Nimbulan, Myrilandel's husband, had lost his magic and thus his ability to communicate with dragons. The loss of that magic had aged and saddened him greatly this past year. She had enjoyed his logic and humor—which often mimicked wisdom.

Shayla, I have explained and pleaded with these people for many moons. They refuse to recognize a danger that threatens us all. Can you give them a dragon dream of great import? Katie asked.

(Dragon dreams are dangerous, to yourself and those you hold dear.) Shayla backwinged, puzzled by the request.

I know that, Shayla. I do not ask for a dream that will lead them astray, only teach them a valuable lesson.

(Such as?)

Take a memory from me and make it real to those around me.

Shayla saw the terrible images within Katie's mind and nearly fled to the void between the planes of existence. *(Why do you wish to share this memory? You should flee it as you fled your homeworld.)*

The same danger I fled is on its way to this planet unless we stop it now. We must not destroy this world called Kardia Hodos as my people destroyed Terra.

(Agreed.) Shayla fought her own reluctance to relive the memory in vision form. This was a lesson the foolish humans must learn—now, before they made grave mistakes.

(The dragon spirit within Myrilandel makes her immune to dragon dreams,) Shayla stalled. *(She is influential among many of those you must reach with this lesson. The woman-child, Yaala, needs to live this vision more than most, but her dragon ancestry will make her immune as well. She lives apart from their society and does not know how to value the nimbus of humans.)*

Myri can pluck the memory of this dragon dream from Nimbulan's mind, Katie replied. Her thoughts bordered on frantic. *Powwell, the journeyman magician, will share his knowledge with Yaala, as he shares everything with her. They are friends despite her separateness from others. If Nimbulan, Quinnault, and the journeyman magician experience what terrorizes my people, they will act upon it.*

(For a dragon dream this troubling, I must land.) Shayla worried gravely for the future of her humans should this dragon dream come to pass on Kardia Hodos. She positioned herself so that sunlight arced rainbows through her all color/no color wings as she circled and landed.

The dragonets would nap a while longer. And if they woke, hungry and screaming for more food, they would have to wait. This dragon dream needed to be imparted soon, or it would be too late.

The other humans jumped up, pointing toward her. Joy filled them as they rushed to greet the dragon. Amaranth, Myrilandel's daughter, clapped her hands and crawled toward the pretty display of colored light refracting through the dragon's wings.

"Shayla, I would like to introduce you to Marilell, my daughter." King Quinnault bowed deeply, gesturing to the infant in Katie's arms. "Katie and I ask your dragon blessing on our firstborn." He draped an arm around his mate and female child, pulling them close to his side. With his free hand he caressed Shayla's muzzle.

The dragon allowed her eyelids to droop as she leaned into the he king's caress. She savored his affection, knowing how the dragon dream she was about to give him might frighten him into ending all further communication with dragons.

Myrilandel lifted Amaranth onto Shayla's outstretched forearm. The physical resemblance between Myrilandel and Quinnault had grown stronger since Shayla's daughter had borne a child and forgotten her need to fly with dragons; her silvery-blonde hair had become more golden and her long, sharp facial features had softened with maturity and pregnancy. But Shayla knew that the spirit of a purple-tipped dragon still resided in the body of the king's sister. A spirit that would always demand release. She had survived one such near transformation due only to the love of her mate.

Yaala, too, could experience the need to become a purple-tipped dragon, though a dozen and more generations separated her from her heritage. Was that why the young woman stood back, refusing to approach another dragon?

Shayla peered at the infant Queen Katie held. The new mother bit her lip a little.

"You'll get used to dragons, dear. Their size is intimidating, but their hearts are pure," Quinnault chuckled.

(My daughter calls you friend. The king my nimbus has adopted as one of our own calls you lover. You may trust me with your daughter,) Shayla reassured the queen.

The fledgling magician edged closer. Shayla sensed the man-boy drinking in the magical energy she emitted. She needed him closer yet.

Yaala lingered by the distant tree. So be it. She would not live the vision of a dragon dream whether she stood close or far.

(The child Marilell is worthy of her parents. She will make a strong leader of your nimbus,) Shayla announced to all who could hear her. She kept an eye on Powwell, willing him to draw closer while she chatted with Quinnault and Katie.

Quinnault raised an eyebrow at that suggestion. So did Nimbulan after the dragon message was passed on to him verbally. Shayla allowed herself a moment of humor. One day, humans would learn that females could govern unruly males quite well.

At last Powwell stepped within a dozen talon lengths of the others. Close enough.

Once more Shayla dipped into Katie's mind and wrested the awful memory from her.

Immediately the humans plunged into another world. A stifling world of stale air tainted by artificial materials and chemicals. A filthy haze kept them from seeing the sky. Some kind of unnatural barrier stood between them and the haze. But the barrier trapped clean air, made it stale despite mechanical beasts that scrubbed it and stirred it in imitation of the wind.

More mechanical beasts grunted and whined in a wild cacophony of sound. Humans walked around cautiously, eyes searching every corner for danger. They wore strange clothing, like artificial skin in muddy colors that flattered nothing and highlighted many unattractive features. Across their muzzles they had draped coverings in the same vague colors as their clothing. Each step was listless, hesitant. They kept their arms close to their bodies rather than swinging them freely in confident strides. As they approached buildings or other people, they shied away from the briefest physical contact.

The observers from Coronnan shifted their startled gazes from the drab people to the dazzling buildings made of metal and glass. So much precious glass! Each window represented a Coronnite lord's entire fortune. While the wonder slowly abated, the watchers all wrinkled their noses at the strange-smelling air. They stared at the frightened inhabitants in bewilderment.

An old woman walked a slow, unsteady path between the wondrous buildings. Her wrinkled skin looked waxy and pale with more ailments than just advanced age. She stopped often, swaying with weakness and indecision. Her swollen hands and feet made her progress awkward. A large man with some vivacity still in his step veered sharply to avoid contact with her. He quickened his steps and increased his vigilant watch.

Another man carried his small son as he hastened through the crowd. Despite the urgency in his manner, his feet shuffled as if he had not the strength to lift them clear of the walkway. "Help me find a doctor," he called to one and all. "My son is sick. Someone, anyone, help me find a doctor." The little boy breathed raggedly. The bloating of his extremities had faded, leaving him gaunt and wasted.

His skin stretched too tightly over his facial bones, taking on a waxy, bluish tinge. The father dashed futilely from one person to the next.

An older man whose broad shoulders suggested an earlier athletic build gone to waste screamed, tearing his mask away. He gasped for air. More air. Never enough air. His eyes bulged. Blood seeped from his mouth, nose, and ears. His limbs convulsed. He thrashed at all who came within reach. The pulse in his throat raced until it could beat no more.

Everyone, including the wobbling woman and the man with the sick child, ran away from the hideous sight of the dying man.

Katie wept, burying her face against her husband's shoulder.

Nimbulan reached for the ailing man, needing to help him, offer him whatever healing and comfort he could. He would never reach the phantom man who no longer existed except in Katie's memory. Nimbulan looked for Myrilandel to lend her magic to the healing effort. She couldn't follow him into the dragon vision and didn't see death all around her.

Shayla noted with gratitude that Myrilandel's daughter, Amaranth, also seemed immune to the dragon dream.

Nimbulan beat his fists against the ground in frustration. He didn't realize he touched the clean grass and dirt of Kardia Hodos rather than the smooth, poured-stone surface on the strange and dangerous world of the dragon dream.

Quinnault held Katie back from the vision, needing to shelter her from these unknown dangers. Their daughter slept, dreaming her own dreams, too young to recognize the images.

The fledgling magician backed away from the illusory dying man in horror but couldn't escape the dragon dream. He ran away from the images. His instincts took him toward Yaala, though he could not see her through the dream. Shayla pressed the dream deeper into his mind so that he would never forget and would instantly be aware of the cause of this man's death. He needed every detail imprinted on his mind so that he could relate it accurately to Yaala who stood numbly by his side, clutching his hand.

At last, when the dead man ceased twitching, a machine

looking like a giant square spider emerged from a glass doorway, gliding several talon lengths above the ground. It hummed to itself as it flashed several different colored lights over the victim. Beeping noises followed the lights. One slender arm, clawed like the giant pincer of a bay crawler, poked the man.

The dead man could no longer respond to the probe. Then two metal arms slid out from the machine's belly, scooped him up, and the machine glided off to an unknown destination. A second machine emerged, very similar to the first, but smaller. It sprayed the ground where the dead man had been with a foul-smelling liquid.

Some of the deadly humors that had killed the man died in the obnoxious substance. Most. Not all. Shayla and Katie both knew now that nothing, not even all elixir distilled from the Tambootie tree could kill *all* of that plague.

"Someone has brought the seeds of this plague to Coronnan," Katie announced.

And Shayla knew that she and the other dragons would have to break a centuries-old taboo to prevent the spread of the plague. A member of the dragon nimbus would have to go to Hanassa, the home of the renegade dragon, where the seeds of the plague lay dormant, waiting for a catalyst to bring them to life.

CHAPTER 1

Early afternoon of Saawheen, outside the meeting chamber of the Council of Provinces, Palace Reveta Tristile, Coronnan City

Journeyman Magician Bessel skidded to a halt outside the door to the chamber where the Council of Provinces met in urgent session. He took a moment to steady his ragged breath and straighten his hastily donned formal blue robes. A gravy stain in the middle of his chest refused to stay hidden amongst the folds. He hadn't worn the robe in moons. Master Scarface, head of the Commune of Magicians, usually excluded his Senior Journeyman from every meeting.

"*S'murghit!* I have the right to stand behind Master Magician Scarface's left shoulder, observing, advising," he muttered angrily. Master Nimbulan had never treated his assistants and students as if they did not exist.

Then Bessel straightened his shoulders. "I have to make a good impression on the master today. I can't give him reason to exclude me anymore," he stated firmly as he adjusted the folds one more time, trying to cover the stain. It defied concealment.

He grounded his staff and channeled a touch of magic through it to the stain. His eyes blurred as he found the greasy molecules and loosened their hold on the fabric. In a moment brown flecks dropped to the stone floor.

"While I'm at it, might as well get rid of the wrinkles." A little more magic added crispness to the folds and straightened the line of the robe. But he didn't have time to add fibers to the shoulder seams and neckline to cover the weight he'd gained since he'd worn the robe last. He looked as respectable as possible on such short notice.

Taking one last deep breath that sounded more like a sigh, Bessel calmly opened the door of the large chamber to find all twelve lords, their magician advisers, King Quinnault and Queen Maarie Kaathliin with Scarface as their adviser, seated at the round table in the center of the chamber.

Bessel looked at the forest of magician's staffs standing at regular intervals throughout the room. *My staff will never have those distinguishing twists and whorls within the wood grain,* he moaned to himself. No matter how much magic he channeled through his tool, it remained straight and smooth. *How can I ever fit in, truly belong, if I can't make my own staff behave? Maybe if I search the library again, I can find a trick to get the twisting started.* He sighed longingly as he looked at Scarface's elaborately knotted staff.

Nimbulan and his wife Myrilandel stood against the wall adjacent to the door with Powwell, their adopted son. Those three looked grim, almost frightened. So did the king and queen. Myrilandel, ambassador from the dragon nimbus, should be seated next to her brother, King Quinnault, not standing in near exile against the wall.

But she was the only ambassador present. Whatever had triggered this urgent meeting involved internal matters.

All of the most powerful people in the kingdom had gathered in one room at the same time. That didn't happen often. Bessell couldn't remember it happening since King Quinnault's coronation nearly two years ago, not even his wedding a little over a year ago had brought every lord and magician to the capital city. For both events every ambassador had been present. Now only Myrilandel. Why?

The late afternoon sunlight streamed through the rare glass windows in the chamber. In a few hours, when the last of the light left this bright Autumn day of Saawheen, the Holy Day of Remembrance would begin. All of these people should be at home with their families or preparing for solemn religious rituals. Instead, they crowded into this room, whispering quietly among themselves.

Bessel strained his listening senses to pick up the conversations, but he could not catch more than an occasional word unless he dipped into the speakers' minds. He'd wait for official announcements rather than violate another's privacy.

He took one step to the right, toward Master Scarface. Powwell snagged his sleeve and shook his head slightly. So slightly, Bessel doubted anyone else in the room noticed.

Then Bessel took one look at the Senior Magician's scowl and decided to stand next to Powwell, well away from Scarface. The Senior Magician looked furious even before he noticed Bessel's late entrance. The scar that gave him his nickname stretched whitely from temple to temple across the bridge of his nose; a sure sign of deep concentration or distress. He kept his eyes half closed as if in great pain.

If I had a place to hide where HE couldn't find me, I think I would, Bessel sent to Powwell on a tight telepathic signal so that none of the magicians in the room could overhear—especially Scarface.

So would we. I wonder who is going to end up with kitchen duty for two moons when this is done? Powwell returned on an equally tight line. His eyes looked more haunted than usual and his hollow cheeks seemed almost gaunt with strain. He carried his hedgehog familiar in his hand rather than hidden in his pocket, a sure sign of disquiet. Since having to leave his sister Kalen behind in Hanassa last year, the familiar seemed the only being capable of giving Powwell comfort. Even his friendship with Yaala sometimes failed to help him.

Bessel understood Powwell's sense of emptiness at the loss of his only family.

Kitchen duty is preferable to being thrown out of here with no place to go and no other magician allowed to take us in, Bessel returned, praying that he would not become the victim of Scarface's wrath. Two senior apprentices had lost their place in the University of Magicians last moon for seemingly minor infractions. They'd been with the University almost as long as Bessel, having started under Nimbulan's tutelage.

Where is Yaala? he asked, noting the absence of Powwell's dear friend, the exiled Princess of Hanassa. She should be sitting next to Queen Maarie Kaathliin. The royal couple had practically adopted Yaala as a foster sister and kept her close to them on all official occasions.

Powwell shrugged as if he did not know, but he clenched his fist around his hedgehog familiar, allowing the sharp quills to prick his skin until a drop of bright blood seeped through his fingers.

Who are they waiting on? Bessel tried a different line of questioning. He counted heads.

"Excuse my tardiness. I was detained with important communications," King Kinnsell, the queen's father, said. He stood squarely in the doorway, waiting for acknowledgment from every person in the room.

That didn't take long. The leader from the mysterious land of Terrania dominated any room he graced with his presence. His aura shimmered in tightly controlled layers of color that mimicked a rainbow. No one had that bright array in precisely measured sections. Not normally. Kinnsell used his aura to project authority when realistically he had none. Even the bright sunlight seemed to concentrate on him, making his expensive golden brocade tunic glow.

What is he doing here? Bessel asked Powwell.

The younger magician shrugged again.

Kinnsell moved around the huge table to stand between King Quinnault and Scarface. His posture radiated confidence and authority. He held his right hand beside him as if he curved his fingers over the knob of a short walking stick. As he gazed about the room and nodded to several individuals, he brought his hand back slightly, adjusting the angle of the imaginary stick.

Bessel shook his head at the curious gesture. He was used to watching magicians for a signature gesture to indicate deep thought or information gathering. This hand position was new to him.

Scarface stooped to whisper something to King Quinnault. He had to lean awkwardly around King Kinnsell to do so. The Senior Magician's scowl deepened.

"Now that everyone is gathered, I have unsettling news to relate," King Quinnault announced from his demithrone.

Queen Maarie Kaathliin touched her husband's hand in silent reminder of something. They both searched the room with their eyes, finally resting their gazes on Nimbulan and Myrilandel.

"Where is Yaala?" Quinnault asked. "She is part of this."

"I dismissed the woman," Scarface said succinctly. "Her

information is secondhand and therefore invalid. And so is Ambassador Myrilandel's."

"My sister is ambassador for the dragons. Her presence is required!" Quinnault replied angrily.

Both Myrilandel and Nimbulan remianed quiet, eyes averted from the lords and magicians who stared at her. Perhaps they did not see Quinnault's gesture to make a place for them at his side.

The queen opened her mouth to speak. Before she could utter a sound, King Kinnsell spoke again. "We have enough witnesses to proceed." He smiled and wiggled his fingers as if tapping the imaginary stick.

Who was running this meeting? Bessel tried hard to keep his face bland and unsurprised. He checked with his TrueSight to make sure Kinnsell did not hold an invisible magical tool. He didn't.

"Witnesses, Your Grace?" Lord Hanic asked of Kinnsell and not his king. An edge of defiance tinged his aura.

Bessel didn't expect anything else from the border lord who questioned everything and withheld his vote in Council until he knew which side would win. He sided with Lord Balthazaan against the king more often than not. Hanic's magician, Red Beetle—because his red eyebrows formed an unbroken V on his brow like the beetle with similar markings—whispered encouragement to his lord.

"The dragons have given us a dragon dream of great importance," Quinnault replied, reasserting his authority in the room.

A dragon dream! Bessel stood a little straighter, letting magic enhance all of his senses.

Whispers broke out around the room. Very few humans experienced a dragon dream. Fewer still understood the visions that seemed so real the receiver believed he lived the images generated by a dragon's mind.

"We have decisions to make based on this dragon dream." Quinnault raised his voice above the babble. The attention of those present returned to him. Silence prevailed once more.

Then, slowly and in simple words, the king related how he and the queen had taken a picnic outside the city with their friends. Quinnault related the details of the dream in compelling and minute detail. The sounds of the machines chugging out the filth that provided a breeding ground for the plague dominated his tale. Looks of horror crossed the faces of lords and magicians alike. Bessel felt a tightness in his chest and a heaviness in his gut.

What if that terrible plague came to Coronnan?

"He forgot the smell," Powwell whispered. The hedgehog wiggled his nose in its funny circular motion, emphasizing the unpleasantness of the scent. For the first time, Bessel noticed a rusty coloration on the tip of his spines. Almost like dried blood. He wondered if it were natural or a result of Powwell habitually squeezing his familiar so tightly that he bled onto the spines.

"What smell?" he asked, breathing heavily to shake off the fear of the plague and the smell of Powwell's blood on the hedgehog's spines. He should know if the plague had come to Coronnan. He was Senior Journeyman. He had access to information most mundanes couldn't dream of, but this was the first he'd heard of disease run rampant.

"The smell of the plague," Powwell replied, still whispering. "Metallic, acidic, and yet syrupy sweet. Like nothing born on this world that I know of." The hedgehog hunched and bristled its spines.

"You mentioned glass, fortunes in glass windows," Lord Balthazaan half stood, leaning closer to the king. "If Terrania is so rich and powerful to use glass so carelessly, why haven't we used the queen's connections to exploit their wealth?" He banged his heavy ring bearing the family crest upon the table for emphasis.

Balthazaan's magician adviser, Humpback, waggled his staff as if he used that medium to communicate with his lord. Then he leaned closer to Red Beetle while they consulted secretively.

Bessel wished he could eavesdrop.

Behind the king, Kinnsell smiled in satisfaction. He thrust his broad chest out a little, like a lumbird in a mating display. Bessel nearly forgot how short the man was compared to most of the lords and magicians. Every man in the room—lord and magician alike—kept looking toward King Kinnsell as if needing him to confirm every statement. He had become the natural focus in the room by standing above the royal couple, separating them from their chief adviser. Bessel almost believed the projected image of

Kingsell's political power and importance to the entire kingdom.

Then he remembered Queen Katie's generous dowry. King Kinnsell had worked a miracle last year, creating a port city overnight out of four islands in the Great Bay; he had left Coronnan with a machine to help navigate the mudflats between Coronnan City and the port. Maritime trade in Coronnan had quadrupled since that time. How Terrania benefited from the gift had remained a closely guarded secret.

Would that secret and the true bride price be jeopardized by the removal of that one precious machine from Coronnan?

Get the conversation back to the plague. It's more important than Terrania or glass, Bessel sent to Scarface.

The Senior Magician reared his head back in surprise, glaring at Bessel angrily. *Where did you come from?* his startled thoughts leaked directly into Bessel's mind. Then the Senior Magician calmly folded his hands in front of him, on the big table. *You do not need to remind me of our priorities, young man. I am Senior Magician, you but my assistant.*

Scarface cleared his throat loudly, scanned the room to make certaiun he had everyone's attention, and finally spoke. "Glass and wealth mean nothing if we all die of this mysterious disease."

Kinnsell pushed his hand forward, giving his imaginary stick a new angle as he frowned at Scarface for interrupting.

"True," Quinnault said on a sigh of relief. "We must send dispatches to all parts of Coronnan seeking information. Any unusual illnesses must be reported."

"And the presence of any foreign machines must also be reported," Queen Maarie Kaathliin interjected. "Machines seem to make life easier. But one machine leads to another and another until we are slaves to them and their pollution taints all of our lives. The pollution is the food for the plague, and when it runs out of tainted air, it turns on people. We have loyal magicians who can help us better than any machine. We do not need technology to build a good life, a stable economy, and a healthy populace."

And as long as the magicians served a purpose in Coronnan, Bessel would have the Commune and access to their library. He didn't want to think about a world where impersonal machines replaced a human magician.

"Aren't you overreacting, Daughter?" Kinnsell rested a parental hand on her shoulder. His other hand pushed farther forward. The reprimand in his voice was unmistakable.

Bessel needed to know the origin of Kinnsell's gesture. How could he understand the man and his motives if he didn't know why he held his hand that particular way.

"No," Queen Katie replied. "Our people have lived with the plague so long we no longer know the warning signs. Terrania has become so dependent upon technology her people don't know how, and don't want to live without it, even though the pollution generated by those machines causes many, many deaths," she replied, shaking off his touch.

The two glared at each other a long moment.

Bessel wanted to crawl under the table to avoid this embarrassing family squabble. He'd had enough of those at home—a place he sincerely wanted to forget. The Commune was home now.

"I wish all of you could have personally experienced the dragon dream," King Quinnault said. "But since Shayla only granted this vision of potential disaster to a few of us, then you must accept my word that we face dangerous times, my lords. Very dangerous. Now, please, disperse to your religious and family duties properly warned and forearmed with knowledge."

Attend me, I have tasks for you, Scarface ordered Bessel telepathically.

Bessel nodded his acceptance of the order. So did Powwell.

Behind Quinnault King Kinnsell scowled. He jerked his head several times in brief nods of signal to several people in the room. The gesture happened so fast Bessel missed who replied and who didn't.

He sensed a tension and defiance in the air, almost tasted it like Powwell had tasted the scent of the plague in the dragon dream.

CHAPTER 2

*Two hours before sunset on the Holy Day of
Remembrance, outside the meeting chamber of
the Council of Provinces, Palace Reveta Tristile,
Coronnan City*

Powwell followed Scarface out of the Council chamber. Curiosity burned within him. For the past year, since he had escaped the outlaw city of Hanassa with Scarface and the others, the Senior Magician had gone out of his way to avoid noticing Powwell, or any other student who had come to the University under Nimbulan's tutelage. He wouldn't even allow mention of Rollett, the journeyman magician who had failed to escape the city of outlaws, let alone discuss a rescue attempt.

Powwell was afraid his search for his lost sister Kalen would take him back to Hanassa. The city had almost killed him. If he ever saw the inside of the collapsed volcano again, he was almost glad Rollett would be there to help. If Rollett still lived.

"Powwell, you spend far too much time in the library pursuing your own research. I need you and Bessel to go on a quest together," Scarface said. He refused to meet Powwell's stare of astonishment. "You'll have to lose your dependence upon a familiar to complete the quest, though. Get rid of that nasty little creature."

Powwell tucked Thorny into his tunic pocket as he clenched his jaw against an angry retort. Scarface had no patience or understanding of the unique relationship between a magician and a familiar. If given a choice between working with his familiar or his staff, Powwell had to choose Thorny.

When he could control his words, he replied, "I've only

been a journeyman for a few weeks, sir. The Commune can't send me on a master's quest yet." He had too many things to learn in the library before he embarked on his own quest—one that had nothing to do with Scarface or the welfare of the Commune.

"What kind of quest, sir?" Bessel asked.

Scarface shifted his attention to the older journeyman. "Gilby has been missing six moons in his search for Jaanus, another journeyman magician who has been missing for well over a year. I need you to find them both and bring them back. Coronnan cannot afford to lose any more magicians, especially if a plague threatens us."

"Sound reasoning, Aaddler," Nimbulan said from behind them. "But I think retrieving Rollett from Hanassa would be a more successful quest." His tone left Powwell with the impression he had more to say on the subject. Nimbulan's left hand came up, palm out, fingers slightly curled—his old magical gesture used as an extra sense to gather information or concentrate his thoughts.

Tension flowed out of Powwell at the sound of his adopted father's voice. Nimbulan would look out for his best interests, even if Scarface had forgotten how.

If only the old man could take him into the void to search out Kalen . . .

"We all know your obsession for keeping your students close to you, even though you have nothing left to teach them," Scarface snarled in contempt. "What else do you hesitate to say?"

"Bessel is your Senior Journeyman. He has responsibilities here," Nimbulan replied.

"I have apprentices who can take over his duties."

"Apprentices, sir, not journeymen," Bessel said, his voice and posture quite apologetic. "Apprentices don't have the training yet to help you with the younger students, to prepare your potions for special spells, to monitor your glass for important summons, or to research new spells for you. They aren't mature enough to sit quietly in Council meetings, observing the reactions and whisperings of the lords and ambassadors."

Powwell almost applauded Bessel for speaking up for himself, something the Senior Journeyman rarely did—if you could find him outside the library. Bessel spent more time in the treasure trove of knowledge than Powwell did.

Nimbulan nodded encouragement to Bessel to continue.

"I would be happy to hasten the studies and exercises of some of the older apprentices, sir, so that they are ready for advancement when I am ready for my master's quest."

Powwell almost snorted in disgust at Bessel's humble tone and posture. As usual, Bessel seemed more interested in compromise just to keep his place in the University rather than fight for what he knew to be right.

"It is not your place to question my orders. Either of you." Scarface's clenched lips turned as white as his scar. The anger that always simmered within him seemed ready to explode.

"But it is their place, as the only two journeymen available, to offer observations to help you in your decisions," Nimbulan said. "I trained them to think and not just to obey orders blindly." His face worked as if he held back a big smile.

Powwell wanted to grin, too. Scarface had shown exemplary administrative skills in guiding the Commune this last year. He had stepped into the vacuum left when Nimbulan lost his magic and nearly his life. But Scarface's temper had won him few friends.

"I won't accept your quest, sir," Powwell replied. He stared directly into Scarface's hooded eyes so the man would know his determination. Thorny squirmed within his pocket, suddenly uncomfortable with Powwell's boldness. "I have made no secret that as soon as I figure out where she is, I will leave here to rescue my sister. If no other method exists to find her, I must prepare myself to enter the void to seek out her life force."

Powwell would know her distinctive orange-and-brown signature colors in any guise. Now that he was close to learning a way to find his sister, he wouldn't let Scarface interrupt his quest.

"Powwell, the void is far too dangerous!" Bessel protested. He looked almost as white with fear as Scarface did with anger.

"To enter the void, you must tap illegal magic," Nimbulan reminded him. "Your oath to the Commune prevents you from using those powers."

"You took oaths of obedience to me, young man. You owe me and the Commune." Scarface returned Powwell's stare.

"No, sir. I took an oath of loyalty to the Commune, Coronnan, and my king. I can best fulfill that oath by returning Kalen to the people who love and care for her. She has a valuable talent. If necessary, I'll go to Hanassa to find her. While I'm there, I can investigate what happened to Rollett—a stronger and more experienced magician than either Gilby or Jaanus."

"I do not believe you can assist anyone but yourself on such a wild lumbird chase. If your sister lives, her talent is based upon rogue magic. She must remain in exile from Coronnan. But your sister is dead. We both watched her fall into the pit of boiling lava along with Yaassima, the Kaalipha of Hanassa."

"But Yaassima went into the void between the planes of existence, not the pit. The dragons spat her out again in our presence. Yaassima was thrown into the pit before Kalen. Therefore, I must presume my sister lives."

"You tread on dangerous ground, Powwell. If you flirt with rogue magic to enter the void, then you betray the Commune and me, your master."

"Nimbulan is my master, no other."

Scarface raised his fist as if to strike Powwell.

Powwell reached out with his magic, stopping Scarface's fist in midair.

Thorny bristled, stabbing Powwell through layers of clothing. He absorbed the pain, letting it fuel his magic.

"Consider yourself confined to your rooms except for kitchen duty until further notice. I must think on a proper punishment for this defiance," Scarface ground out, still unable to move his hand against Powwell. The Senior Magician wouldn't think about lowering his hand, only smashing Powwell's restraints.

Powwell turned his back on the Senior Magician and walked away without releasing Scarface's fist. If Scarface had realized that Powwell had tapped illegal powers—through Thorny—retribution would be swift and terrible.

I guess I've severed all my ties to the Commune and Coronnan with that little act of defiance. Severed his access to the library and the information there that might lead him to Kalen as well.

* * *

Inside the meeting chamber of the Council of Provinces

Walk with me, Katie, Quinnault said telepathically, as he rose from the council table. *I need to stretch my legs before my mind will settle and sort through this mess.*

Katie looked quickly around the room to see if any of the magicians present had eavesdropped. She knew that even if they had, they were honor-bound to respect the privacy of the royal couple and wouldn't show awareness of the communication.

Yes, Scarecrow, Katie replied. She slipped her hand into his, surprised by the chill in his fingers. *We both need fresh air and quiet.*

Quiet is something we'll never have while we live in Palace Reveta Tristile. Quinnault chuckled beneath his words. Around them they could hear hammering, stones scraping on each other, as the almost continuous building on the palace and the city within the new capital expanded almost daily.

"Where shall we walk?" Quinnault asked in tones just barely above a whisper.

"Somewhere without a dozen attending guards, courtiers, magicians, and ambassadors," she replied equally quietly.

"Not in this lifetime. We rule, and therefore our lives belong to the masses not ourselves." The king sighed.

"I know. 'Tis the same in my home. I just wish we could have a few moments away from politics."

Katie felt the tension in her husband at her words.

"I wasn't born a politician, Katie. I cannot lie and am always surprised and hurt when others lie to me. No book exists that will teach me how to bend the truth like a politician." A look of bewilderment crossed his face.

"I understand you must select suitable mares to mate with Buan," she announced to the room at large.

Quinnault's eyes lit. *Good idea. Others will follow us, but you have removed the outing from the realm of politics.*

Not entirely. The ambassador from SeLenicca has a mare he wants to breed with your stallion, and so does Jorghe-Rosse from Rossemeyer.

"Buan has enough stamina to satisfy both and more." Quinnault chuckled again. He lengthened his stride as if he couldn't get out of the stuffy chamber fast enough. Katie nearly ran to keep up with him, never letting go of his hand, especially now that it warmed under her touch.

New buildings, many still shrouded in scaffolding, seemed to sprout like stalks of new wheat on every island comprising Coronnan City.

Two years ago, before Katie came to Coronnan as his bride, he had been lord of these islands. His stark defensive tower was now an extensive palace and administrative center. Simple farmhouses and vegetable crops had given way to dwellings and workshops for craftsmen thrown up almost overnight, elegant townhouses for politicians, and temples—dozens and dozens of little temples to serve the growing populace of the new capital of Coronnan.

This city represented her husband's dream of peace for Coronnan and an important place for this country within the world marketplace.

But he'd never planned to be king. She had been raised for her role as a member of a royal family that had ruled a galactic empire for many generations.

Quinnault nodded casually to the city dwellers as he passed them on his way to the nearest bridge. "Time was, I could name them all and their children. Now I know only one out of ten," he muttered.

Katie squeezed his hand in reassurance. "You know more of them than my grandfather ever tried to learn of his immediate household. It's important for us to maintain contact with the people we govern."

Quinnault smiled at her with that special half quirk of his mouth. Her pulse quickened in wonder and awe at her love for him.

They crossed the bridge in the market square. Vendors closing up their booths before the commencement of the holy day and late customers alike stopped to bow or curtsey to the royal couple. Children ran about caring little for the dignity of those who followed the king and queen at a discreet distance.

A flicker of movement in Katie's peripheral vision caught her attention. Just another bystander, propping himself up against the corner of a building. But not just any bystander. She nodded slightly to him and suppressed another smile. Liam Francis, her youngest brother, come to check on her—though they both knew he should not be on planet.

Her father should not be here either, but he was always a law unto himself.

A tiny bit of Katie's homesickness dissolved. She did miss her family. She almost gestured for Liam Francis to join her. At the last instant she dropped her hand. He blew her a kiss and melted into the crowd, one more slim young man among many—though he stood almost a head shorter than most.

One of the ladies rushed to the queen's side and shooed the children away.

"Let them play," Katie said, catching an unsteady toddler trying to follow his older siblings. She cuddled the child close for a moment. "We should have brought Marilell. She needs to get out of the palace more and breathe fresh air."

"We took her on the picnic. She's had enough fresh air for one day and needs a nap." Quinnault brushed a stray curl off Katie's face with his long fingers. "You need a break from constant mothering. We need time together before our next child comes. Any sign of making me a father again."

Katie shook her head regretfully.

The courtiers stepped back one pace, giving them a small illusion of privacy. The guards who hovered around the edges paused as well, surveying the marketplace with restless, wary eyes.

Liam Francis popped up on the other side of the thoroughfare, then vanished again. Her homesickness came back to Katie with a sickening jolt.

Quinnault squeezed her hand this time, as if he sensed her loneliness among this bustling crowd.

She sighed. As long as she had her husband and daughter she had a family. But the only time she and Quinnault were ever truly alone together was in bed. And she wasn't certain the servants didn't listen then, too.

Oh, how she longed to snag Liam Francis and sit quietly

by the fire with a mug of mulled wine while catching up on the latest gossip from home.

The parade of people followed Quinnault and Katie as they crossed a dozen islands between the palace and the mainland. As they stepped up on the last bridge, Katie paused a moment to look back. Their entourage had grown to include a number of curiosity seekers. Some nibbled food and sipped ale from the numerous markets along the route. Musicians played lively tunes in rhythm with their steps—or had they started marching in time with the music? A few people began an impromptu dance, others lifted their voices in songs.

"I've never known a people so ready to turn any event into a party." Katie gazed at them in amazement. Her foot tapped the dancing rhythm. Was that her brother kicking up his heels with a local woman on the fringes of the crowd?

"After three generations of civil war, the common people have learned to grab enjoyment whenever they can, despite the feuds and jockeying for power at court," Quinnault replied. "I want to give my people reasons to rejoice every day. They deserve it."

"Do you suppose it would be beneath our royal dignity to join the dancing?" She would love to maneuver close to Liam Francis and exchange a few words, maybe dance a few steps with him, just like at parties back home.

"Considering that I would tread on your feet and likely slip and fall on my bum, yes, this free-spirited dancing is definitely beneath my dignity." Quinnault chuckled openly. Much of the daily strain of ruling slid from his face, replacing worry lines with youthful humor.

Katie hid a laugh behind her hand. The image of her tall husband sprawling in the mud, long legs tangled in the hem of her skirts presented a decided contrast to his normal public demeanor.

Quinnault's mind tickled hers with silent laughter. He, too, enjoyed the image of himself as the gangling scarecrow of his youth. He still thought of himself as that awkward young man yanked from his quiet life of study in a monastery to govern his family's lands, out of place and bewildered by the enormity of his duty.

"You've never quite grown into your feet, have you?" she asked quietly.

"I'm not familiar with that expression." He continued smiling and nodding his head in time with the music.

"Children and dogs tend to have feet out of proportion to their bodies. They are awkward until their bodies grow to match the feet. Once their proportions match, they become as graceful in mind as in body."

"Ah, yes, they do. Frankly, Katie, I've grown into my feet." He looked down at the monstrous boots that covered them. "But I haven't grown into my role as king."

"Yes, you have, my dear. The people adore you."

"My very minimal magical talent as an empath qualified me for my chosen life path as a priest. I understand what the people endure, and sometimes I can help them heal. But the politicians who make the government work talk circles around me. They lie and hide the truth behind rivers of words. I get lost in the words that mean too many things at the same time."

"Most people are mystified by those wordstorms." Katie gazed lovingly into his eyes, wondering how her alien education might help him deal with the professional wordsmiths.

Shouting in the middle of the crowd disrupted her thoughts. An argument grew around a knot of younger men. She checked to make sure her brother was not one of them. Back home he would be the first to wade into a brawl, fists and feet flying, loving the game of breaking heads to break up the fight. Liam Francis had vanished again. No sign of Sean Michael or Jamie Patrick either.

One of the disputants, clothed in a gaudy orange shirt with purple piping, threw an overripe pear at his neighbor. The fruit splattered the more sober unbleached linen shirt of a dark-haired man who stood a little taller than most of the crowd. He responded by throwing the remains of his ale into Orange-shirt's face.

Both followed through with fists. Their neighbors joined the spreading brawl.

"Guards, go and break this up. Disperse the people before this spreads even further," Quinnault ordered.

Half of the armed escort dispersed through the crowd. Katie clutched her husband's arm, frightened, as the anger spread and engulfed the people standing closest to the bridge. Angry thoughts blasted through her mental armor. The emotions behind the fight made her toes curl and brought lumbird bumps to her spine.

She'd experienced this sensation only once before, when an assassin had crept into her room the night before her wedding. He'd used magic to instill fear in her, a terror so great she lay immobile, defenseless against his attack.

"Come, Your Grace," the sergeant-at-arms suggested. "I'll escort you to the royal stables. You'll be safe there."

"Take Her Grace back to the palace by whatever back routes you can find," Quinnault replied. He patted Katie's hand. "I'll follow by a different route with the others. We'll be safer attracting less attention with smaller parties."

"No, Quinnault," Katie said quietly but with determination. "We both need to stay. Someone is amplifying the crowd's emotions with magic to further their own political agenda. Listen to the argument. Listen hard. We need to stop this here and now!"

"Filthy foreigner!" Orange-shirt yelled. "How dare you think of marrying off your daughter to my son. I'll not taint our bloodline with Rovers."

Strange, Orange-shirt dressed more like a Rover than the man he accused.

"Rovers steal our children as well as our hard-earned dragini." That voice came from a different quarter altogether. The angry emotions swelled, as if being manipulated by a master hand.

The assassin who had used her own emotions against Katie had been a Rover.

Confusion muddled her thoughts. Who was behind this?

"Rovers will rape and control your mind with their magic worse than any Commune Magician." That voice came from an ordinary woman with muddy blonde hair, no Rover coloring in her face or clothing.

"Bad enough we have to put up with a foreign queen and her prancing lumbird father. We don't need Rovers and them desert mercenaries freeloading off our bounty. We don't need a foreign queen controlling our king," Orange-shirt called to the crowd in general.

Katie bristled. Beside her, Quinnault clenched his jaw. A

muscle jumped in his cheek, and the pulse in his neck beat too rapidly.

The few remaining courtiers in their party gasped at the audacity of the crowd voicing these sentiments in front of the royal couple. Most of the dignitaries had dispersed at the first sign of trouble.

"We need a new king," Orange-shirt yelled above the noise of the crowd. "We need a king who doesn't bow to foreign interests."

"Kill all foreigners!"

CHAPTER 3

Late afternoon, Saawheen, on the Long Bridge to the mainland, Coronnan City

"Speak to them, Quinnault. End this before the violence spreads!" Katie tugged at her husband's arm. The moisture on her brow and back turned icy with fear.

The guards surrounded them, swords drawn. Tension made their arms twitch.

If any one of them drew so much as a drop of blood, all hope of exerting calm would disappear.

Quinnault stared at her, gathering his thoughts. Then he nodded his head and took a deep breath.

"My people." Quinnault raised his arms above his head as he spoke the words in a voice that carried to the far reaches of the crowd.

A few people paid heed and ceased their babble.

"Stand higher on the bridge so that more people can see you," Katie urged him. Hope sprouted in her chest at the crowd's initial response to him.

He took two steps back to the center of the arched span. His height and the elevation made him stand well above everyone. "My people, listen to me!" he commanded again in ringing tones worthy of a battlefield—or a pulpit.

Katie immediately felt calmer, more confident. Apparently so did the mob. Quiet spread in gentle ripples.

So this was Quinnault's magic talent. Nothing overt enough for him to be called a magician, but enough—and perhaps the best talent for a man with aspirations to the priesthood or to leading a diverse populace through tribulation.

"Listen to me, please. You must cease this violence!"

Katie saw three men pause with hands upraised, ready to strike. But they didn't complete their blows.

"I understand your fears," Quinnault said. "I lived through the wars, I fought alongside you when rival lords threatened these islands. And when peace came within our grasp, you declared me king. You, the people, decided I should lead you because you knew I would bring the warring factions together in compromise." Quinnault paused a moment to let his words sink in.

"Now we must all work together to maintain that peace. We must fight those who would disrupt that peace from *within* as well as without."

Men and women stared in disbelief at missiles of food and stones and tools and clubs they clutched in their hands. A woman in the front ranks deliberately put down the palm-sized rock she had been ready to lob at the man standing next to her. Her neighbor pocketed the hammer he held poised to defend himself.

Quinnault breathed deeply.

So you noticed that someone manipulated their emotions with magic, Katie commented on a tight mental line. Best if the magician in the crowd did not eavesdrop.

Magic? Quinnault cocked an eyebrow at her. His slightly bemused expression could not hide his unease from her.

Katie searched the crowd for signs of the man with the gaudy orange shirt with purple piping. She should have been able to pick him out in a moment among the more soberly dressed folk.

I sense magic and conspiracy in this brawl. Someone deliberately fed fear into these people.

"Disperse to your homes now to celebrate Sawheen, our Holy Day of Remembrance," Quinnault commanded. "You are good people. You don't need to listen to those who would use you to fight their fears. You need only live your lives in peace. A peace we have fought for. But now the fighting must cease."

"What about the foreigners? What about . . . ?"

Katie searched the crowd for the speaker. It sounded a lot like Orange-shirt, but she couldn't be sure. The voice seemed to come from all directions, followed by ripples of unease. She spotted Liam Francis working his way through the crowd with deliberation. Sean Michael and Jamie Patrick approached from other directions, their bright red hair obvious beacons in the mob. She hoped they honed in on the disruptive magician.

"If you notice people from other lands crowding our city, be assured they bring trade, they bring friendship. I work with their leaders to avoid another war. We all work for peace and prosperity," Quinnault responded.

A mood of calm followed his words, more overwhelming than the anonymous voice.

Katie bit her lip in confusion. Was it right for her husband to use magic to influence the crowd in the same manner another had used magic to bring the crowd to riot?

(Sometimes, Katie, one must fight fire with fire or magic with magic,) a dragon voice reminded her.

"What do we do now, Quinnault?" she asked. Her brothers disappeared again, swallowed up in the mass of people. She had no idea if they found their quarry or not.

"We need to know who started this and why," Quinnault replied. "My investigators must ask questions and keep their eyes and ears open for more signs of trouble. I'm certain there will be more."

* * *

Sunset, neighborhood temple three islands West of Palace Reveta Tristile, Coronnan City

Katie sank to her knees on the cold stone floor of the little neighborhood temple. The last rays of sunlight streamed through the high narrow windows, adding luster to the icon tapestry of the three Stargods descending upon a cloud of silver flame on the back wall of the sanctuary. Beside her, Quinnault bowed his head and murmured the prayers for the dead. Nimbulan, Myri, and Yaala occupied the space just behind the royal couple. Around them—with a buffer zone of empty space out of respect for Quinnault and Katie—the entire congregation recited the same petitions.

A red-robed priest joined Katie in her prayers. She glanced briefly at him. He kept the cowl of his garment over his head, concealing his face. Unusual that anyone not of the royal entourage would come so close.

The priest jostled her elbow slightly as he made a very Terran sign of the cross, touching head, heart, and both shoulders. She'd grown used to the locals using almost the same gesture but with a different invocation from the one she'd learned as an infant back home.

"Almost like being at home," the priest whispered in a Terran accent.

"I should have known you'd show up eventually, Sean Michael," she whispered back to her older brother—the middle one in age of her three siblings. "You aren't supposed to be here. We agreed, no more family contact. We take no more chances contaminating this culture."

"Have to check on my baby sister." He bowed his head again to avoid Quinnault's inquisitive look.

"Liam Francis already did."

"Ah, but our youngest brother has not reported back to us. I suspect he has found a tavern and a lady to entertain him for the evening. Like the dark-eyed beauty over there." He gestured with his chin toward a woman with Rover coloring and Rover-gaudy clothing strung with chains of coins who knelt directly behind Nimbulan.

"Or Liam Francis may have gone looking for a disruptive magician. I thought I saw you and Jamie Patrick following the same psychic scent."

Sean Michael raised a rusty red eyebrow at her. "We found nothing."

"Could you look again?"

He nodded. "And when may I see my favorite niece, the Princess Marilell?"

"In the morning." Katie nudged him sharply with her elbow, a familiar gesture to quiet him during church services.

"Kinnsell is not reporting in to the mother ship either. I really came to haul him back home, but I couldn't resist the opportunity to see you, little sister." He brushed her fingertips gently with his own.

The brief caress filled her with warmth and a longing to hug him close.

A moment later he slipped away, barely noticed by anyone but herself. A void of loneliness opened in her belly.

Someone I should know? Quinnault asked her. He

dropped his hand to clasp hers. His love channeled through the physical contatct.

One of my brothers, she replied. She used to think mind-to-mind communications with her brothers came easily. But compared to the intimate contact with her husband, family telepathy seemed a great effort. No wonder her brother had whispered.

Your family isn't supposed to be here, Quinnault said.

Neither is my father. Sean Michael came to take Kinnsell home.

Odd place to look for your father. I've never known him to show the least interest in our customs.

Kinnsell is only interested in himself.

And causing trouble.

Hush, beloved. Our part is coming up. Katie clasped a spray of bright flowers she had laid on the floor beside her earlier. When the priest signaled her forward, she rose and placed the small bouquet of Autumnal blossoms on the plain stone altar. "In memory of my mother who passed beyond this plane of existence five years ago. May she find peace beyond the void," she recited the ritual.

Quinnault followed her with petitions for a long string of deceased relatives.

Together they bowed to the altar and returned to their places.

Then Nimbulan, Myri, and the rest of the congregation followed suit.

"Who is that woman?" Katie asked, nodding toward the flamboyant woman with a cloud of dark hair and clear ivory skin that her brother had noticed. The two men who placed flowers on the altar, immediately after her, could only be Liam Francis and Sean Michael. Where was Jamie Patrick hiding? And Kinnsell? She was surprised her father hadn't found the exotically beautiful woman yet.

"Her name is Maia. She came out of Hanassa last year with Nimbulan," Quinnault replied quietly. "She has some claim on him. We shelter her here in this sanctuary with magical armor all around so that others of her kind cannot spy on us through her without her knowledge or consent."

"She does not seem happy. What if she decides to leave?"

"I do not know. I only hope that if she chooses to leave,

she will return to her clan and not remain to be manipulated by the Rovers who wish us ill."

A wave of distorted images washed over Katie. Her sense of now and then, up and down, real and unreal, swirled around her in a tornado of bright colors and broken images. Her father, Maia, a shuttlecraft from the mother ship. Dragons, dragons everywhere. And a purple cloud so dark it seemed almost black engulfing them all.

She swayed dizzily.

"Katie!" Quinnault wrapped both arms around her, holding her upright.

"Scarecrow. I see trouble. I've never had a premonition before, but I see trouble surrounding that woman. Disaster cloaks her aura and it centers around my family somehow."

* * *

Saawheen Evening, in the home of Myrilandel, Ambassador for the Dragon Nimbus to Coronnan, Coronnan City

Powwell searched Yaala's eyes for support, compassion, anything but the fear that lingered there.

"This is very dangerous, Powwell," Bessel said quietly from the desk in Nimbulan's study. "Neither of us has much experience with the void. The spell is illegal. I'm not prepared to sacrifice everything to help you find your sister."

"You don't have to work the spell, only monitor me and bring me back if I get into trouble. You're the only magician I trust, Bessel."

"I'll monitor you, Powwell," Yaala said quietly from her window seat. The Autumnal sunset backlit her fair hair and skin giving her the illusion of ethereal fragility. Her heavy brocade gown nearly overwhelmed her slight figure. It reflected the current fashion of muted Kardia tones. Bronze and green flecked the gold fabric. Those colors looked wonderful on Queen Katie with her red hair and green eyes, so everyone at court wore them.

Yaala needed light blues and pinks to flatter her. She also needed a warmer climate. Desert born and bred, she shivered in the drafty window seat. And yet she clung to the light filtering through the oiled parchment pane.

Powwell vowed to take her home again. As soon as he found Kalen. Yaala deserved the best. More than he could give her.

"You don't have the magic to drag me out of the void, Yaala," Powwell replied. He clasped her hand in reassurance. "I'll be all right. I've researched this extensively."

"Shouldn't we wait for Master Nimbulan to return from temple?" Bessel fiddled with one of the master's pens. "He'd be able to monitor you. He knows what you are up against."

"But he has no magic either."

"What if Scarface finds out what we're doing? This spell requires rogue magic. The whole thing is illegal." Bessel began tapping the pen against Nimbulan's desk.

"That's why we're doing it in Myrilandel's house. She's the ambassador for the dragons. This house, the embassy, is foreign territory. We aren't in Coronnan, so the spell isn't illegal here."

Neither Bessel nor Yaala looked reassured by the argument.

"I need you, Bessel. And I'm running out of time. I've wasted moons and moons trying to figure out where to look for Kalen without going into the void. I've tried to abide by the rules of the Commune. Now Scarface has dismissed me from the Commune. He's cut off my access to the library, to the entire University. I'm a magician outside the Commune; therefore I have to either apologize to him or leave Coronnan by midnight. I have to search the void here and now. Either you help me, Bessel, or I do it alone with only Thorny to guide me." He petted the little hedgehog within his tunic pocket.

"Start your trance, Powwell. Best we get this over with before I lose my courage."

Powwell sat cross-legged on the floor, placing Thorny on his right thigh, within easy reach. In an emergency, his familiar could bristle his spines, jabbing Powwell back into his body and this reality. He took a deep breath on three counts, clearing his mind of the room, his companions, every stray thought except his purpose. He let go of the dragon magic he kept stored in his body and found a silvery blue ley line deep within the planet to feed him magical energy. Calm spread through him like warm honey. He took a second breath on the same three counts, holding it three counts, and then releasing it on three counts. The absolute blackness of the void flickered around his peripheral vision. He resisted the urge to plunge into the emptiness between the planes of existence. A third breath took him deeper into his trance. Yaala and Bessel became illusory ghosts to his perceptions. Nothing existed in this reality except Thorny who remained a solid and familiar presence.

The void beckoned him with the soft music of the stars. He almost recognized the melody, needed to hear more to fit the alluring pieces together.

I'll tether you to this existence with the umbilical of your life force while you search, Bessel said directly into his thoughts.

Powwell merged with the blank nothingness of the void. All sense of his body, of direction, of his planetary orientation evaporated. Nothing existed but his mind.

He fought a momentary panic that he might become lost, never find his way back or forward into his next existence. Then Thorny's emotional touch reassured him.

On the heels of the panic came awareness of dozens of bright umbilical cords representing the life forces of all the lives he had encountered. He picked out Nimbulan's blue easily. Though the life force had faded since the last time Powwell had viewed it with his master, the blue still dominated Powwell's life. Myrilandel's crystal and silver wrapped around Nimbulan's blue, essentially binding them together into one being.

Bessel's braid of bright blue and red trailed away from his perceptions, a ladder to climb back into his body if he needed help.

He searched for Kalen, expecting her life force to entwine with his own. An undefined silver cord tinged with lavender wrapped around Powwell with no trace of his sister's orange and brown. Yaala? He looked more closely at the dull silver of his own life, seeking a hint of color. Magicians rarely saw their personal signature colors.

A brighter crystal life danced around Powwell's own life force, just out of reach. Only Shayla, the nearly invisible female dragon could be such a pure crystal. She influenced all the lives in Coronnan without becoming a part of any.

Powwell relaxed, accepting Shayla as his guide and mentor during this journey.

(What do you seek?)

I search for my sister who is lost to me, Powwell replied to the directionless voice that filled the void as well as his mind—perhaps his mind and the void were the same thing. His thoughts threatened to drift into idle speculation. The void invited him to explore each new tangent. Thorny prodded him with a mental jab—like a spine pricking his skin. Powwell yanked himself back to his quest.

(Is she truly lost, or do you not know where to look?) A typically cryptic dragon observation.

Kalen was thrown into the lava core of Hanassa as the dragongate opened, but before it was fully formed. Her companion went into the void. The dragons spat that one out again. I must presume my sister drifts alone in the void as well.

Powwell sensed alarm and wariness in the crystal life force the moment he mentioned Hanassa, the city of outlaws, and the dragongate, the magical portal that could take a traveler away from Hanassa to any number of locations.

(If the one you seek entered the void from Hanassa, then if she finds her way out again without assistance, she must return to Hanassa. Give up your search. She will not welcome being found.)

I have to find her. I am not complete without her. She is my only kin.

(She may be your kin no longer. Seek others to fulfill you. Seek in your heart for the source of the emptiness you feel.)

I can't. I have to find Kalen. I promised her.

(Look within yourself before you venture into the realm of the renegade dragon.)

Powwell fell back into his body with a stomach-wrenching jolt.

A red haze with black sparkles lingered in his vision as Bessel and Yaala solidified before him.

Powwell shook his head to clear his eyes. Deep within the heart of the haze, a shrouded drop of orange and brown lingered and then turned deep purple that darkened into black. A heartbeat later it shrank to nothing. The haze retracted from the others, forming a mist around himself and Thorny, like an aura.

Thorny hummed a welcome and relaxed his hunched spines.

"Wake up, Powwell. Come back, Powwell!" Bessel slapped his face to rouse him. "Leave the void behind you, Powwell."

"Is my magical signature red with black sparkles?" Powwell asked. The words came out slurred. He felt almost drunk with fatigue and light-headedness. He reached out his hand toward Yaala, needing her touch to anchor him.

"You saw your own colors?" Bessel replied. His mouth gaped open in awe.

"Yes, at the last moment as I came back to my body. Yours are a red-and-blue braid."

"I've been told as much," Bessel agreed. "I wish I could see them."

"I saw all of our colors, but I couldn't find Kalen in the void. As I returned, I saw her orange-and-brown life force greatly diminished and shrouded in purple. A purple so dark it was almost black."

"Hanassa," Yaala breathed the word in a frightened hiss.

"Shayla told me I had to beware the renegade dragon. I have to go to Hanassa to find my sister. Did she mean I have to go to the city or to the only dragon exiled from the nimbus?"

"Both," Yaala said. "But first you have to find a way into the city. Land access was destroyed in the kardiaquake as we left the city. The dragongate has either shifted its portals or is broken."

"Scarface has had round-the-clock watches at all the known portals in Coronnan," Bessel reminded him. "None of them have opened in over a year. If the dragongate still exists, you'll have to find a new opening to get into the city."

"I'll find one. Somehow. I hope Rollett is still there to help."

"You'd better hope Rollett is still alive. Hanassa kills outsiders," Yaala reminded him.

"The renegade dragon or the city?"

"Both."

CHAPTER 4

Dawn, after Saawheen, University of Magicians residential wing, Coronnan City

Powell crept out of his cell in the journeyman's section of the University. Fortunately, only one other cell was occupied at this end. Five cells remained empty until more apprentices earned journeyman status. Bessel snored softly in the last room on the corridor, next to the staircase leading up to the masters' suites and down to the kitchen and refectory. Behind Powell, the fifteen apprentice cells were much more crowded, sometimes four or five young men bunking in a single cell smaller than Powell's room. He didn't like leaving Bessel alone, the only journeyman in the complex, the only buffer between Scarface's temper and the vulnerable apprentices.

His mission would not wait, and he would not apologize to Scarface for his disobedience.

The morning air smelled clean and damp, as if it were just awakening to new adventures. Powell yawned briefly and stretched. Longingly he looked back at his rumpled bed. No. He'd come too far. His decisions had been made moons ago when he left his sister in Hanassa.

Resolutely, he shouldered his pack and pulled Thorny out of his tunic pocket. The little hedgehog tried to curl into a tight ball. Normally nocturnal, dawn signaled his preferred sleep time. Powell roused him with a thought. Reluctantly, Thorny uncurled and wiggled his nose. The scent of fresh bread baking, heightened by Thorny's keen nose, made Powell's stomach growl.

Guillia, the cook, housekeeper, and surrogate mother for the University—and also Kalen's mother, but not Powell's—had probably been awake for hours preparing the hearty breakfast required by magicians who burned tremendous amounts of energy working their talents for the good of the kingdom.

Silently, Powwell crept down the stairs. At the bottom of the stairwell, he turned left into the now enclosed corridor, then immediately left again, and stepped down three uneven stairs to the kitchen. When Nimbulan first established the University in the abandoned monastery, this room had been the kitchen where Powwell and two other apprentices gathered with Journeymen Bessel, Rollett, and Master Nimbulan. Jaanus and Gilby, the missing journeymen had been there also, along with Old Lyman the librarian. The cooking fire kept them warm in the drafty abandoned monastery during that first long winter.

Powwell smiled in memory of the bonds of friendship and loyalty they had all formed. His mouth watered for the taste of the Tambootie flavoring his tea. The University would never lace any food or drink with the Tambootie again.

He hated leaving Bessel and Lyman alone with Scarface. Only those two remained from the days when Nimbulan ran the University with a strict but loving paternal air. He'd made the University into a family. Scarface turned it into a stern and unforgiving institution.

"One day you'll learn, Scarface, that the strongest family is one that is bound together by silken cords of love. Some members may leave, but they will return when needed. You prefer to force your fellows to follow you with iron chains of control. Once we escape, we'll never return to you," he muttered as he skirted the long dining tables on his way to the new kitchen, separated from the refectory by a short passage.

Out of long habit, he paused and probed the kitchen with his magic before entering. The years of constant warfare during his youth had made him cautious. The time he had spent as a slave in Hanassa had taught him suspicion. A curious vacancy beyond the door made the hair on his nape stand up. Thorny hunched, all of his spines bristled.

Someone had built a bubble of armor around themselves to keep a conversation very private.

That had never stopped Powwell before. He'd survived war, slavery, Hanassa, and Scarface by learning to eavesdrop. Of course, the armor erected by two magicians using dragon magic might be harder to penetrate than one maintained by a solitary magician. He'd just have to probe deeper.

Powwell opened the door to the kitchen, making sure his magic silenced the hinges and prevented a cool draft from announcing an intruder. He breathed in the welcoming scent of fresh bread, bacon, and dried fruit stewing in wine and spices. Quickly he silenced his growling stomach.

He searched the room, brightened by cooking fires, for any distortions of light. There, to the left of the hearth in the chimney nook, shadows gathered more deeply than they should. Only a light shell of armor surrounded the magicians since the only other person in the room was Guillia who was presumed to have no magic other than her instinct for providing wonderful meals for empty stomachs precisely when needed.

A quick probe of red-and-black light, showing Powwell's unique signature very nicely now that he knew how to see his own colors, and he ducked back into the passageway, leaving the door ajar a tiny crack.

"Bessel was right to refuse the quest! Scarface needs him to help with all the new apprentices he brings in by the sledgeload," Red Beetle hissed.

Powwell heard the click as the middle-aged man snapped his fingers while he talked. He made a sound very like the red beetle he was named for.

Briefly, Powwell wondered if he kept one of the stinky insects in his pocket as a familiar. Wouldn't that set Scarface on his ear if he did! He'd have to outlaw one of his staunchest supporters.

"Bessel is so insecure about being outcast he'll fall under Scarface's total control in no time," Red Beetle finished.

"And I say we cannot take a chance on having any outsiders in the University and Commune. We must purge our membership." A small thud followed Humpback's words. Powwell could almost see the stoop-shouldered magician who advised lord Balthazaan ramming his staff up and down with each word. His awkward posture made him rely on his basic tool of magic as a walking stick as well as a channel for his spells.

"We don't have to worry about Powwell any longer. His

magic is stronger than Bessel's and he's more independent," Red Beetle said.

"Too creative with his spells by half. Powwell always has to be different." Humpback pounded his staff against the flagstones.

"Well, Scarface formally dismissed him. He has to be out of Coronnan in three days or face trial and imprisonment, possibly execution. 'Tis a good law, no magic or magicians without Commune sanction," Red Beetle replied.

So, the removal from the University of everyone who had studied or worked with Nimbulan was an actual conspiracy rather than merely Scarface lashing out at what he could never totally control. Powwell had suspected as much moons ago.

"Once we have total control over all the members of the Commune, the rest of Coronnan will fall into our hands. The ineffective king and Council of Provinces will be obsolete. We will have order governed by dragon magic at last," Humpback said decisively.

Total control of the kingdom? The Commune wasn't supposed to work that way. They provided *neutral* advisers to the king and lords.

What could Powwell do to stop them?

Nothing.

Good thing he was headed to Hanassa as soon as he found an entrance into the closed city deep in an ancient volcanic caldera. If Rollett still lived, Powwell could send him home to help Nimbulan, Lyman, and Bessel fight this conspiracy, too.

Should he warn Bessel?

If Bessel didn't know about the conspiracy now, he would not listen to Powwell's warning.

"Sorry, Bessel, I can't stick around to help you. But you'll land on your feet. You always do, though you might not think so. I'll send Rollett back to help," he whispered to his absent friend, "because I've got to find Kalen and this is the only way to do it."

He listened a few more moments as the magicians planned how they would advise their lords to coincide with Scarface's policies. That wasn't supposed to be the way the system worked. The magician advisers should be neutral observers. Politics should not taint the Commune and the University. But they did.

Then the two master magicians left the kitchen, without glancing at Powwell. They each munched on thick slabs of bread slathered with brambleberry jam.

When he could no longer hear their steps on the flagstone passageway, Powwell slipped into the kitchen.

"I've packed a journey bag for you," Guillia said without preamble. "You'll find my girl."

"I'm going to try," Powwell replied, raising his eyebrows at the woman's perception. He hefted the pack on the worktable, almost as big and heavy as the one he already carried with his books and clothes and tools. How had she known he'd need rations for a long trek on his own.

"She's alive. I can sense that." Guillia removed a large pan full of crisp bacon from the hearthstone.

"Do you have magic after all, Guillia?" Powwell asked, snitching a rasher of bacon. It burned his fingers, and he juggled the hot meat back and forth between his palms until it had cooled enough to eat.

"Just a mother's instinct." She scooped the remaining bacon onto a serving platter with a long-handled fork.

Powwell stole another handful.

"If Yaala asks, tell her I'll meet her in the clearing by Spring. Tell her . . ."

"I know what to tell her, lad. Now, best you be off before *they,*" she jerked her head in the direction Red Beetle and Humpback had walked, "come back and find you still here."

"Did you hear them talking, Guillia?" Powwell asked as he kissed her cheek in thanks.

" 'Course I did. Their paltry armor wouldn't keep out a mouse let alone a woman who needs to know what transpires in this University. They don't like women, so they pretend I'm not here. Though they'll scream loud enough if I'm two heartbeats late with their meals. Now scoot. Just find my girl and make sure she's safe."

"I'll do that, Guillia. For you. For both of us, I'll find Kalen and I'll find Rollett. Then we'll come back and take care of Scarface."

"Just find Kalen. I don't want my little girl left alone without family or friends."

"No one deserves to be without family. I just hope Bessel is as lucky as I am to find both when he's forced to leave here."

"I'll watch over him while he's here, lad. Though I suspect he'll leave, too, 'afore long. All the boys here are like sons to me. As long as Scarface lets me stay, I'll watch over all of them."

* * *

Early Spring, a mining village in Balthasaan, South of Coronnan City

Bessel trudged up the hill toward the mining village and his parents' home. He didn't want to be here. But Scarface had insisted he come. The message from home requesting his presence had been urgent.

Bessel stared hard at his father standing in the open doorway of the family home. Old memories of pain and loneliness clouded his awareness of here and now.

Spring sunshine warmed his back but he might as well be facing the Winter blizzard that had shrouded the village the last time he saw it. The snow had masked the black dust that permeated everything for miles around. But it hadn't hidden the blackness in his father's heart.

Bessel would never think of him as his father again.

"So you've come back," Maydon said tersely. The squarely built man Bessel had once called "Da" blocked the doorway. His stance did not invite Bessel within, despite the urgency of his message.

Maydon balanced his weight on one leg and crutches. He'd lost the left leg from the knee down years ago. Now he looked as if he'd rather use the crutches for weapons than walking aids.

"I was told to come back." Bessel looked toward the path he had just followed to the house, wishing he could reverse directions. New growth of flowers and grasses poked through the pervasive dust. Soon they, too, would be coated in the awful stuff.

Bessel wanted to cough just thinking about the dust.

"And you always obey orders, I suppose," Maydon sneered.

"You ordered me away from your home eight years ago. I obeyed you then. Now I obey the Senior Magician of the Commune of Magicians. He ordered me to visit my mother on her deathbed." Bessel's oath of loyalty and obedience meant a great deal to him.

He'd skirted disobedience in helping Powwell access the void last Winter. No one had heard from Powwell since then, five full moons. Now Bessel followed orders without question rather than risk exile from the fellowship of the magicians.

He couldn't walk away from the home and family the Commune represented as Powwell had.

"Why did you request that the Commune release me from my important studies for this visit?" Bessel asked Maydon after a long moment of hostile silence.

"Book learning never served anyone but greedy magicians. Besides, she asked for you."

"Then I'd best go inside and see her."

Neither man moved.

"Aren't you going to use your *s'murghin'* magic to force me to back up?" the one-legged man challenged his son, never letting his contempt lessen in his voice or posture.

"No."

"Why not?" Surprise loosened Maydon's fierce grip on his crutches a little.

"I won't contaminate my mind or my honor by touching your ugly thoughts," Bessel replied. He wanted to believe that his family had become hostile toward Bessel's magic talent because they didn't understand it. They'd never encountered a magician before, other than the Battlemages attached to the armies that periodically pillaged the mines and the village.

"Watch your mouth, boy. I'm your da, your family."

"You ceased being my father the night you threw me into the teeth of a Winter storm to fend for myself." For the first time, Bessel noticed that his father's stocky frame, formerly rotund, had wasted to tough sinew and bone. His eyes looked too bright, and an unnatural flush rode high on his cheeks and brow. His hands were swollen where he clutched the crutches.

The once substantial stone home looked as frail and neglected as its owner. But then, Maydon had always considered his job as accountant for the mines a poor second to working the mines themselves, even though the job brought in a great deal more money—enough to build this house for the family.

"Did you know I was captured by outlaws?" Bessel continued. Bitterness nearly choked him. "They had a magician of sorts with them who wrapped a spell around me so that I couldn't use my magic to escape. Did you know that those outlaws used me as their toy for two weeks until I was sold at auction." He clung to the warm memory of Nimbulan marching into the outlaw camp and outbidding all the others for the right to exploit Bessel's talent, to enslave him, and abuse him.

But Nimbulan hadn't exploited anything. Instead he'd given Bessel the love and understanding to use his talent wisely. Nimbulan had become more of a father to him than Maydon had ever been.

"Only what you deserve, Magician," Maydon spat the title, staring at Bessel, lips pursed so tightly they lost all color.

"Maydon, come quickly," a woman called from inside the house. "Maydon, she needs you."

Bessel recognized his aunt's voice. Baarben had lived with her brother's family for as long as Bessel could remember. He bit back a cry of welcome for the woman who had been as much a mother to him as his own mother.

Maydon stepped back into the house. His expression of fierce rejection of his son faded into anxiety.

Bessel followed him, being careful not to touch his father. They hadn't touched since the day Bessel had used his magic to free his father from a mine accident. The heavy rocks and timbers that pinned Maydon had cost him his leg. But Bessel had saved his life.

Maydon had declared that without the leg he wasn't certain he had a life. He'd blamed Bessel and the boy's cursed magic talent for saving him.

Every time Bessel remembered what outlaws had done to him, he wished he hadn't levitated beams and rocks from his father's leg, hadn't made it possible for the other miners to rescue him.

The moment Bessel passed the doorframe, a strange smell stopped him short. He should recognize it. What?

The memory escaped him, slipping in and out of his mind like a dragon. One moment it was there, almost tangible, and then the light shifted and it was gone.

He hesitated to enter the house until he understood the smell. Something told him it was dangerous.

The sound of his aunt's loud weeping finally drew him inward.

The smell intensified as he neared the common room. His mother lay on a low bed beside the hearth. She shivered with intense chill in the overly warm room. Fever flushed her skin.

Baarben threw a handful of herbs onto the open fire. Aromatic smoke rose, filling the room. Bessel identified five different herbs that should reduce fever and ease painful joints. Baarben hadn't included the Tambootie in the mixture. It had unique curative powers to anyone with a hint of magical talent but was toxic to mundanes. Should he suggest that she add some? The family must have some magic talent for him to have inherited it.

Maydon seemed more comfortable breathing the astringent essence of the plants. They had no effect on the dying woman by the hearth.

"Did he come, Maydon? Did my baby come home?" Bessel's mother whispered. She gripped her husband's tunic with a wasted, clawlike hand.

"I've come home, M'ma." Bessel knelt beside her. He realized he didn't even know her given name. She'd always been "M'ma," or "Mer Maydon," in his mind.

"Bessel, my baby." Her voice trailed off and a tiny smile touched her lips. Then a fit of coughing grabbed her until unconsciousness claimed her.

"She'll die happy now. You can go," Maydon said. He stared into the flames rather than look at his son.

"She should have a true healer! Why didn't you send to Lord Balthazaan?" Every lord had a magician adviser, a magician healer, and a magician priest assigned to his province. Even if Balthazaan and Humpback were out of the province, the healer and priest should be available.

"There are too many people dying of this strange disease." Aunt Baarben touched Bessel's sleeve in sympathy. "Even the lord's family and household suffer. It takes the old, the young, and pregnant women first. But no one is immune."

"I haven't the healing talent, but I'll see what I can do." Bessel touched his mother's face with exploratory fingers. He wasn't a strong magician. Without illegally tapping a ley line, what could he do other than give his mother a little strength? Even when he'd gathered a full portion of dragon magic, he had trouble joining with the other magicians to increase the power of the joint spell by orders of magnitude. Lately he'd had trouble gathering any dragon magic at all, almost as if there wasn't enough left to go around.

He'd give M'ma all of his strength if he could. That had to be enough until he could summon a healer. She couldn't die. Not yet. Not until he'd made peace with her, made certain she knew that he blamed only his father for his estrangement.

"You'll keep your filthy magic away from her!" Maydon roared, slapping Bessel's hand away. "Let her die in peace and pass to her next existence without interference."

Bessel stared at his left hand a moment, the one his father had slapped away. A dominant left hand had marked him as a potential magician from earliest childhood. Deliberately he closed the offending hand into a fist and drove it into Maydon's jaw.

Maydon reared back. His crutches fell to the slate floor. He flailed clumsily as his body joined the crutches.

"Fewer than half of all left-handers are magicians and less than half of all magicians are left-handed. You condemned me as a magician before you had any true evidence," Bessel said quietly. "And I will help my mother if I can."

"Bessel, your father is a cripple. He can't defend himself. He can't work the mines anymore. You should have compassion." Baarben rushed to help her brother stand.

"He's so crippled he made a small fortune keeping the accounts for the mines after the accident. He's so crippled he fathered five more children on my mother, each one diminishing her strength a little more, making her vulnerable to this hideous disease. Look at her! She's pregnant again. That's why she hasn't the strength to fight it." Bessel returned his attention to what little he knew about healing.

If only he had some Tambootie leaves in his pouch . . . He'd heard rumors that Queen Maarie Kaathliin's father needed the Tambootie to cure a plague in his homeland.

Was this the same plague? The disease caused by machines? He hoped not, but he recalled a grove of Tambootie that grew nearby. He'd stolen some of the leaves as a child and experimented with them until his father had exiled him from the family. Once he eased the fever and strengthened his mother a little, he'd fetch the leaves of the tree of magic.

If he tapped a ley line, he could effect some repairs to her body to buy him more time.

No. The Commune had valid reasons for outlawing rogue magic.

He inhaled deeply on three counts, held it three counts, and exhaled on the same rhythm. His body relaxed. He repeated the exercise, and his mind drifted away from the confines of bone and flesh. A third deep breath brought him within reach of the void between the planes of existence.

(There are lessons to be learned in the void. Do not enter unless you are prepared to expose the truth,) a voice whispered into the back of his mind.

As he hesitated to join with the allure of the void, a ley line filled with magical energy pulsed beneath the ground near the center of the village.

He reached out to tap the line, let it flood him with strength.

Revulsion replaced the magical energy. NO! He couldn't use ley lines and he couldn't access the void. Powwell had had to leave the protection of the Commune in order to use rogue magic in his search for Kalen. Bessel couldn't risk his membership in the Commune.

Dragon magic had limitations, especially when a magician worked alone. But when the Commune worked in concert, their magnified spells could overpower any solitary magician. They could impose rules and regulations, ethics and honor, on all magicians. Rogue magicians had perpetuated civil war in Coronnan for three generations, all in their quest for power, until Nimbulan had discovered dragon magic and created a lasting peace with King Quinnault's help.

Bessel risked the wrath of the Commune and the dragons if he violated their most sacred law. He had to help his mother using only legal magic, no matter how limited.

Breathe in, one, two, three. Hold, one, two, three. Breathe out, one, two, three. This time he concentrated on remaining in contact with the flow of dragon energies within his body. Power tingled in his fingertips. He ran his hand down the length of his mother's wasted body, keeping a thin cushion of energy between his hand and her skin. The heat of her fever, the disintegration and bleeding within her lungs, the irregular rhythm of her heart pulsed at his sensitized hand.

He felt the rupturing of blood vessels deep within her body. His mind saw her internal organs collapsing.

No part of her body was free of the disease.

"Oh, M'ma," he wailed. "I can't help you." If he'd come earlier. If he could tap a ley line to give him the magical energy to repair some of her vital organs . . . But he could not do it. He would not bring rogue magic back into Coronnan—even to help his mother.

CHAPTER 5

Early Spring, the road below Myrilandel's clearing that runs across the pass from Coronnan into Rossemeyer, Southeastern corner of Coronnan

Yaala clutched Powwell's hand in eager anticipation. His palm was as hot and moist as her own.

The long Winter of waiting for the pass to clear had ended. Spring had burst forth in this remote mountain pass a few days ago. The time had come to take the next long step in reclaiming her heritage.

At last she was going home to Hanassa, the only place she belonged. She daydreamed of clearing the city of mercenaries, outlaws, thieves, and murderers, making it a haven for the innocent refugees of war and poverty rather than a lawless haven for those who caused war and poverty. With the help of the machines hidden deep within the lava tube tunnels of the old volcano crater, she could turn Hanassa into a prosperous industrial city with honest work for all. She'd make the people of Hanassa her family.

Quinnault and Katie had taught her that such ideals could exist. It was more than her mother, the late and unlamented Kaalipha of Hanassa, had taught her in her entire life.

"Wait for it," Powwell hissed. "Feel the hot wind? It's opening. I found a new portal for the dragongate!"

"Amazing," Yaala replied. She stared unblinking, mouth slightly agape, at the shimmer of distortion within an arch-shaped shadow.

"We can get into Hanassa now. All these moons of searching are over." Powwell breathed on a deep sigh. "Kalen won't have to wait for rescue any longer."

He hugged Yaala hard. His eagerness to risk his life to

rescue his half sister irritated Yaala. She'd never loved or been loved by anyone with such intensity.

"I can restart my machines and take control of Hanassa," she said, thinking of the only things that mattered to her—other than her friendship with Powwell. "We've had to wait so long, I didn't think this moment would ever come." She refused to believe Powwell's tale of the terrible dragon dream Shayla had given him last Autumn. Yaala's machines used volcanic heat to create steam rather than burning fossil fuels. Her machines did not provide the pollution the disease spores fed upon. She was the engineer. She should know.

Why should she trust a dragon anyway? Shayla and Hanassa the Renegade had been born into the same nimbus, might very well have been part of the same litter. The nimbus had exiled Hanassa—the only dragon in their long history to require such punishment. The once purple dragon had taken human form and founded a city for other renegades. Depredations perpetrated by Hanassa and his followers had plagued the rest of Kardia Hodos for centuries.

She would end their tyranny of terror once and for all.

Yaala pulled her spine away from the outcropping of rock. The jagged stones fit her bizarre spinal structure as if carved for her. In all of her twenty-one years she'd never been able to rest her back against any surface. Her spinal bumps, residual traits of her dragon heritage, had defined her erect posture and set her apart from other humans. Her mother, Yaassima, had treated the minor deformity as a badge of honor. But then, the late Kaalipha of Hanassa had wanted to be more dragon than human.

In the end, both dragons and humans had rejected her.

Yaala didn't want to die like her mother, lost and alone, reviled by one and all. She clung to Powwell's arm as they watched the magical portal take form.

"After the kardiaquakes and partial openings I found these past five moons, I was afraid we'd never be able to use the dragongate to get back into Hanassa." Powwell turned his rare grin on her. His entire face lit with joy. All those hours spent with maps and pins and calculations finally come to fruit."

Yaala returned the smile. "I'm going home. I'll be able

to fire up Old Bertha and get the 'tricity flowing again. I know I can."

"You don't want to do that, Yaala. Remember the dragon dream," Powwell warned.

Yaala ignored him. They'd argued about her machines endlessly since he'd come to her in Myrilandel's clearing where she had waited for him. She *would* restart whatever machines she could repair.

The air shimmered within the arch-shaped shadow created by a rocky overhang and a spreading oak tree heavy with mistletoe. Hot air, born of a volcano, blasted forth from the center of the shadow, replacing the last remnants of Winter chill on this bright day. Colors swirled within the darkness of the shadow. Red, green, blue, black, yellow. More red and even more black.

Between one eye blink and the next, the colors within the shadow solidified into the image of red sandstone cliffs surrounding a murky lake, waters black with a strange substance floating on its surface. In the distance, a volcano belched hot ash in a tall column that reached for the sky.

"It's not Hanassa!" Yaala yelled, hauling Powwell back from stepping through the imagery into the unknown landscape. "We can't go there, Powwell."

"Of course it's Hanassa. The gate always returns to Hanassa and nowhere else. See the path leading up the cliff to the plateau. It's Hanassa. I have to rescue Kalen. We're going now!" The fifteen-year-old journeyman magician grabbed her arm and yanked her forward until she stumbled through the blast of swirling colors toward the alien scene.

"But the path is outside of Hanassa. The dragongate is supposed to take us into the heart of the mountain!" Her words evaporated in the rush of hot wind.

A vortex of spiraling energy caught Yaala. Up and down, right and left, now and then, distorted, blended, became one and shifted. Disorientation lurched in her stomach, then numbed the back of her neck. She needed to curl into a fetal ball but couldn't find her feet.

More hot air hit her in the face. She blinked away the fine grit of volcanic ash that blurred her eyes. She sat on the hot red sand beside the strange black lake.

"This isn't Hanassa. We have to go back." Yaala scrambled for the rapidly fading gateway. Her knees sank into loose sand. She couldn't rise or crawl fast enough. The cool green and brown of a forested road in Coronnan on the other side of the dragongate swirled into a kaleidoscope of colors. The air stilled and around her the temperature rose.

The smell of sulfur intensified; the smell of Hanassa. But this wasn't the city of outlaws her mother had ruled with a bloody fist.

Sweat broke out on Yaala's brow and back, almost as if she was still in the pit beneath the hidden city of outlaws.

Her generators and transformers were in the pit. She had to return to them, get them working again in order to claim her heritage.

"Where are we, Powwell?" she breathed the words, careful not to inhale any of the dust that permeated the air. Her fair scalp beneath her pale hair puckered and she knew she risked sunburn and dehydration even with the heavy ash haze.

"I—I'm not sure where we are." The young magician turned a full circle. He chewed his lower lip and ran a hand through his thick mass of curly dark hair in indecision. His gray eyes took on a cloudy look, mimicking the sky. A flutter of movement within his tunic pocket indicated his hedgehog familiar didn't like this place any better than Yaala did.

She hoped Thorny pricked Powwell deeply with his sharp spines.

"Why did we use that portal? I told you something was wrong." Yaala was also scanning the red-and-black horizon for anything resembling a familiar landscape. A dark speck soared in the distance, near the belching volcano. A dragon? Her dominant spinal bumps prickled, like a dog's ruff standing on end when faced with unknown dangers.

She could see nothing but miles and miles of wind-sculpted sand dunes and baby mountains reaching all the way to the distant horizon where the very active volcano belched again in a shower of spark and more black ash. The dragon disappeared within the dark cloud. Yaala ducked instinctively, even though the hot wind blew the dangerous fumes away from them.

"The dragongate is only supposed to work one way on this end," Powwell mused. "From Hanassa, you can go 'most anywhere if you wait for the right opening. But all of the destinations lead back to Hanassa and nowhere else. We should be in the tunnel overlooking the lava core."

"Well, we found an active volcano. But that's the only resemblance to Hanassa—which blew its top and collapsed into a caldera aeons ago."

"Oh, Kalen, I've failed to find you once again." Powwell beat his fist and his forehead into the hot sand. "How much longer can she hold out in the pit, or the void, or wherever she's hiding?"

"How long can we last here, with only a few journey rations?" Yaala shifted uncomfortably. Ash hazed the sun like a thick fog, but didn't deflect much heat. Nor did it provide any moisture. Her exposed hands and face dried and withered under the burning sun. She wondered if the sand was hot enough to burn through her trews and boots.

"At least we know the gate didn't disappear altogether after the kardiaquake." Yaala touched Powwell's smooth back with tentative fingers.

They had survived a lot together in the last year and a half. He'd been as much a victim of her mother's cruelty as Yaala had in the slave pit below Hanassa.

Thorny poked his nose out of Powwell's tunic pocket. Powwell caressed the hedgehog's relaxed spines and murmured comforting words to the creature.

Yaala knew a moment of painful loneliness. She would never have a familiar. No magic coursed within her veins, no matter how many generations of dragons limbed her family tree. She had no family left. The machines in the volcanic pit beneath the city of Hanassa had been more friendly, predictable, and faithful than her mother. She'd rather study the fascinating intricacies of her machines and the 'tricity they generated than trust a pet for companionship.

Powwell loved the funny little hedgehog so much he kept Thorny's discarded spines. Even on this long journey, Powwell kept the dried spines wrapped in a silk wallet inside his belt pouch.

She shook her head to clear it of the puzzle of magicians and their familiars. She had to think clearly and hopefully.

"Don't give up yet, Powwell. The dragongate may open again in a few moments. We don't know what kind of damage occurred in that kardiaquake just before we left Hanassa."

"What if the dragongate takes weeks to open again at this location? I was sure my calculations were correct. I found the portal. It should open to the pit in Hanassa and nowhere else. So where are we?"

Yaala scanned the land once more. Something about the way the sandy plateau dropped off into a steep cliff, and the narrow valley behind her seemed familiar, but distorted. They sat atop a small mountain. The black lake rippled and shivered. A moment later the land beneath them shifted and quaked. The lake waters rose a few inches and spread. Steam spouted up from the depths. Something . . .

"Maybe we are in Hanassa. But Hanassa of long, long ago, when the volcano was first forming. That lake might lie atop the core of lava at the heart of the mountain."

"But Shayla said that the dragongate only distorts distance, not time. She should know. She's a dragon." Thorny poked his nose out of Powwell's pocket and wiggled it in agreement.

"Dragons don't know everything." Yaala glared at Powwell. "And they don't always tell the truth." Her mother hadn't known how to separate truth from her own desires. Her ancestor, Hanassa, had begun the bloody tradition of reign by terror in the city.

"Dragons know a lot more than they tell."

"Dragons and magicians aren't equal to my machines." Machines couldn't be as evil as Shayla and Queen Maarie Kaathliin pretended in the infamous dragon dream. Resentment of Powwell for ramming two magicians' staffs into the guts of her beloved generator as a diversion for their escape from Hanassa rose sharply within her. She thought she'd forgiven him, understood the necessity of his actions. But now . . . now she wanted to strangle him. Then love him back to life.

What did she truly feel? It didn't matter. She couldn't trust emotions. Especially her own. Machines didn't have emotions.

"Well, I broke the machines with mundane tricks. I didn't even need magic," Powwell replied, sifting the hot sand through his fingers. "And I'm glad I broke them. Machines create pollution that feeds the plague spores. And when they run out of pollution, they turn on people and start eating them from the inside out."

"That's a myth created by the queen to keep technology out of Coronnan. Technology that would replace magicians and give power to every mundane. Besides, Coronnan doesn't have any machines to create pollution, so the plague can't thrive."

Powwell glared at her, then returned his attention to running his fingers through the sand. "Maybe these sands will tell me something. They've been here a long time. A memory of time distortion might be embedded in them." He took three deep, slow breaths, triggering a magical trance. The sand continued to drift through his fingers.

His eyes rolled up and his face took on the blank look of a deep trance. "Fire. Fire burning deep within the Kardia. Fire spreading upward. Fire melting rock. Icy air shattering. Fire. Ice. Time. Time . . ." he chanted in a voice much deeper than his own.

His words sent chills down her spine, despite the heat. "We have to find Rollett and send him back to help Scarface. Don't lose track of Kalen. You came to rescue your sister and Rollett," she interrupted his meditation. Concern for his childhood idol and his half sister should snap him out of the trance.

Powwell didn't reply. He shuddered as he pushed himself back into awareness. He jerked his hand away from the sand as if it burned his skin.

"Rollett can take care of himself. Kalen is much more vulnerable, so young, so untrained. . . ."

His priorities had always centered on Kalen. And yet . . .

Didn't he feel 'tricity shooting through his veins like she did when they touched, even casually?

"Well, we aren't going anywhere until the dragongate opens again." Yaala grimaced as the Kardia shifted beneath her feet again. If they didn't get out of here soon, the volcano might erupt, with them in the middle of the explosion.

"The gate can't open again until the ash clears and the sun creates an arch-shaped shadow for the gate to form in," Powwell reminded her. "The arch is crucial."

"That could take a lifetime or three," she replied.

CHAPTER 6

Ancient plateau of Hanassa, time unknown

Powwell paused before hefting another rock to scan the arid landscape around the plateau. Off in the distance a winged ceature drifted on a rising air current. A dragon?

Help me! he called, trying desperately to contact the being with his mind.

His head remained empty of outside thoughts. Either it wasn't a dragon, or the dragons in this place didn't recognize the need to maintain contact with humans.

The sands, when he sifted them through his fingers, had told him only of fierce eruptions and cyclonic winds over a long period of time. Yaala had interrupted him before he'd had time to sort through the images to see if this had once been Hanassa, or would be at some time in the future. His gut told him the dragongate had returned him to Hanassa, but the portal had destroyed his planetary orientation—or maybe the time shift had. He had no idea where the magnetic poles lay, which was closest, what phase of the moon they entered or which season.

He returned to his self-appointed task and dropped a heavy piece of black rock onto the red sandstone where he thought the dragongate had been. He added a second and third rock to the growing pile that came close to matching the pile two long strides to his left. Maybe, if he could get the piles high enough, he could get something akin to an arch shape for the dragongate to form in.

He couldn't tell for sure, but he thought the portal had to open and close on the exact same coordinates each time. But then again, maybe it only needed to be in the same vicinity.

If the natural shadows wouldn't form an arch, he'd make

one. No matter how long it took. The passage of the sun told him that he and Yaala had only been in this landscape less than one day. His magic senses insisted they had spent a week or more here. Magnetic poles tugged at him from all directions.

To verify his time sense, he'd set up a kind of sundial around the piles of rocks. The sun moved far too slowly.

He and Yaala were trapped here in this alien landscape without food or water beyond their meager journey rations or protection from the merciless sun.

If only he'd had more time to study the dragongate back in his days of slavery in Hanassa. If only he'd kept a tighter hold on Kalen to keep her from running after Wiggles, her ferret familiar, as he and Yaala and the others had escaped Hanassa through the dragonate over a year ago. If only . . .

Guilt and "if onlys" didn't change the fact that he'd made a serious error in judgment when he stepped through the dragongate this time. But the gate had always worked the same way.

(No it hasn't always worked the same. The destinations changed. The frequency of opening changed,) a voice in the back of his head reminded him—a dragon or his conscience? He looked around for the source. Maybe the dragon in the distance had heard his cry for help after all.

The only living being he saw was Yaala. She sat huddled in the tiny shadow of a boulder watching him work. The few large rocks on this plateau offered her scant protection from the diffuse rays pouring through the ash haze.

Powwell's darker skin fared a little better than Yaala's. The backs of his hands had begun to darken and redden, though. They'd both have painful blisters before long.

She had draped a kerchief over her head, knotting it above her left ear, Rover style. She'd worn the same headgear in the pit, protecting herself from the intense heat of the lava core. Now she needed it as a barrier between her fair skin and the pounding rays of light. But the kerchief didn't shade her eyes or protect her face.

He hated the thought of her reverting to the grimy desert rat who had first befriended him in the pit. She'd remained aloof from everyone but him in Coronnan City. Her mother had outlawed her and condemned her to the pit. Yaala had nothing and no one outside of Hanassa. Now he had delayed her return to Hanassa and her beloved machines. Would she ever truly belong anywhere?

Wasn't that a definition of a renegade?

The Kardia shifted beneath Powwell's feet. Not much. A precursor to the main shock. He braced himself for the rolling disturbance, like being aboard a ship in a storm. Just a little quake this time. No new fissures opened in the dry ground. But the movement disrupted his balance. He sat down heavily. Instinctively, he reached with his magic to find the nearest pole for a sense of where and when to reestablish his equilibrium. Nothing. The moon and seasons eluded him as well.

All he knew was the relentless sun. They had to get out of here soon.

Thirst tasted sour in his throat. He sipped a little of his dwindling water supply. They each had a leather container of water and a pack of journey food, enough to take them from one village to the next in Coronnan.

His waterskin seemed far too light. Not enough to last in this searing heat. He thought he'd rationed his water wisely, only taking a few sips each hour as marked on his sundial.

"Powwell, I see shadows!" Yaala called. She rose from her crouched position beside a boulder.

"Shadows? Where?" He peered at the few boulders, willing their shade to expand.

Hot wind sand-blasted his face. The sun seemed brighter. Less ash obscured the horizon. The wind increased, grew hotter yet. It came from his left away from the direction he'd placed his cairns of rocks.

He turned in place, awakening all of his senses for hints of change. A shimmering distortion, like a mirage in a distant heat haze, grew between himself and Yaala within the minuscule puddle of shade cast by the nearest boulder.

"The gate is opening!" Yaala dashed toward him, through the forming gate, and disappeared within the shifting swirls of light! Just like Kalen had when she'd been thrown into the lava core before the dragongate fully formed.

"Yaala!" he screamed and dove after her. He couldn't let her die in the volatile gate. Stargods only knew where she'd end up. They had to complete this quest together.

Loneliness and despair swamped him. He'd not lose another dear one.

* * *

Mining village in Balthazaan Province, south of Coronnan City

Bessel sensed the grief of his gathered siblings. Nine all told counting himself. They stood in a circle around their mother's bed in descending order by age maintaining the ritual death watch.

He watched the grief play over the faces of his oldest brother and two older sisters, the ones he knew from his childhood. They choked back sobs and closed their eyes against tears. He did, too, as much for the lost companionship of his family as for the death of their mother. The fourth young adult in the circle, another sister one year younger than himself, had been only a small child when he left the mining village. He barely remembered her.

The five siblings born after his father's accident in the mine wept openly, darting glances of fear toward their father. Maydon had always ruled the family with a heavy fist and violent temper.

Anger replaced Bessel's grief. Anger that these youngsters had to stand and watch M'ma die. They had said their good-byes to her during her last moments of consciousness. Why did they have to bow to tradition and watch blood trickle from M'ma's mouth and ears while knowing they could do nothing to help? Why couldn't Maydon release them to grieve in quiet privacy until it was all over?

M'ma started coughing again, weakly. Baarben rushed to help her sister-in-law sit up. The children made space for her in the circle. None of them knew how to ease the insistent blockage in their mother's lungs. No one in this mining village learned anything more than their assigned place in life allowed. Maiden aunts were expected to nurse the family's ills. Aunt Baarben was the one who must help M'ma sit up, not the children who stood closer.

But it was late for anyone to help M'ma. She opened her mouth for one last inhalation. Blood streamed from her mouth. She opened her eyes wide, seeing nothing. Then she collapsed. Her life's spirit exited her body.

"Bring her back. You've got to make her live again!" Maydon pounded on Bessel's shoulder. "You're a magician, bring her back to life."

All of Bessel's siblings looked at him, hope brimming in their eyes along with their tears.

"I can't." Bessel bowed his head. "Even if I could, the Stargods forbid reanimating a dead body for any reason."

"I'll get Lord Balthazaan's magicians to compel you to do it. Make your mother live again!" Maydon grabbed Bessel's shoulders and shook him hard, letting his crutches fall to the floor. For a moment, he was entirely dependent upon his estranged son.

Bessel didn't let his small smile of triumph touch his face. Because of the trauma of his experiences in the outlaw camp, no magician had since been able to compel him to do anything he didn't want to do.

"No such spell of reanimation exits. Your ignorance assigns me more power and fewer ethics than any true magician could hope for." Gently, Bessel removed his father's hands from his shoulders, then restored the man's crutches. "If I could have helped her, I would have done it hours ago while she still lived." But he might have helped her, if he'd had the courage to tap a ley line and access the void.

The healer would have come from Lord Balthazaan's castle if Bessel had asked. He'd have come to help another magician. But Bessel wasn't a true magician yet. He hadn't achieved master status.

He was still an outsider looking in. Never more than in this large family that shared his blood but not his talent or his experiences.

"Can't or won't?" Maydon sneered at Bessel. "You can hurt me any way you like, I'm the one who threw you and your cursed talent to the wolves. Kill me if you must, but don't hurt your mother. Bring her back!"

"I can't. No matter what you think, I am not all-powerful. Nor will I break sacred laws."

Bessel walked out of his father's house, not once looking back. Bitterness and regret were his only companions.

S'murghit! The Stargods had taught the first magicians

how to cure a plague. Where was that knowledge when he needed it?

Certainly no one in the village knew the first thing about true healing. Midwives and maiden aunts knew how to use a few herbs and poultices. They could bandage wounds and set broken limbs. None of them knew how to read to learn more. Maydon had taught his children a little ciphering, enough to keep household accounts. Nothing more. Tradition said they needed no more. None of them had ever expressed a dream of achieving anything more than their father had or than Lord Balthazaan expected of them.

And now a plague beset them, and their ignorance was killing them.

The strange scent he had detected in his father's house assailed him again. Stronger, deeper. The village was filled with it along with the black coal dust from the deep mine. Was the dust a kind of pollution for the plague to feed upon?

He stopped in the center of the pathway between houses and turned a full circle. His magic talent bristled a warning deep inside him.

Death stalked this community, just as it had stalked the strangers in the dragon dream Shayla had given Powwell, Master Nimbulan, and the king and queen. Everyone in the Commune had heard of the dream in the minutest detail. Powwell had been most specific about the scent of the plague, relaying it to his classmates in direct telepathic communication. *That* was the familiar smell.

Queen Maarie Kaathliin's plague had come to Coronnan, and no one knew how to cure it.

CHAPTER 7

Midnight, forested knoll outside Coronnan City

Kinnsell O'Hara scanned the forest landscape uncertainly. Why did these primitive bushies always insist upon clandestine meetings in the midst of all of these trees? And they always chose midnight, when civilized men should conduct delicate negotiations over a fine port wine in cozy dens furnished with large, well-padded chairs. Not standing out in the cold wind freezing their arses off.

He felt naked without the protective walls of a building, or his shuttle, or the atmosphere domes of cities back home. But this wasn't home. This was a primitive world where the locals believed that magic worked and dragons were real.

Even the king here was addressed as "Your Grace" because he ruled by the grace of the dragons. Kings should have majesty, as well as grace.

He shuddered in the chill night air. He couldn't leave the country of Coronnan and the planet Kardia Hodos fast enough. Just as soon as he accomplished what he'd come here to do, he'd hightail it away from all this open space and unconfined air and back to civilization.

But his mission would guarantee that he would be the next emperor of the Terran Galactic Empire. None of the other candidates—any of his three siblings and all of their combined children could find themselves elected emperor— knew how to keep the sprawling territories bound together into a cohesive unit. None of them valued the fresh food produced on planets such as this one. They all believed tanked food sufficient to sustain life. None of them understood that truly enjoying life meant unique tastes, unique experiences, and the hope that every citizen might eventually be able to enjoy them. If that hope died—no matter how remote—the citizens had the power to depose the central government. Then the TGE would fracture into dozens of scattered autonomous and warring worlds.

Control would vanish. Briefly, he thrust his right hand forward as if guiding the joystick of a shuttle in atmosphere flight. By dropping the nose a little, he could regain control of airspeed. Then he eased his hand back, control reasserted.

Kinnsell intended to maintain control, starting with the bushie lords and his far too independent daughter.

A rustle of underbrush off to his left told him that someone—or something—large and clumsy approached. His heart climbed into his throat. Suddenly all of the local tales of predatory gray bears, spotted saber cats, and . . . and dragons didn't seem so preposterous.

Something eerie about the place sent his imagination into overdrive, dredging up childhood horror stories of monsters under the bed.

The night breeze chilled his skin despite the heavy layers of protective clothing. He swallowed his fears and checked his scanner. The readings indicated one human, leading some kind of riding beast. Steeds they called them. The locals couldn't even remember the proper name for a horse. Not that Terra had been home to any horses outside natural history museums for many generations.

Kinnsell relaxed. His overactive imagination had tricked him once more. His daughter Katie had the same tendency. Now that she was queen of this backwater, she could give vent to her storytelling without the hindrance of civilized conventions.

She hadn't been on the planet a full day when she started filling his head with tales of dragons.

Imagine, the girl actually claimed she had seen and touched a dragon! A huge beast with crystal fur and telepathic capabilities had "blessed" her marriage to Quinnault. Didn't she know that every myth and legend made dragons—sacred or evil—reptiles with jewel-colored scales?

Even his pragmatic and obedient sons had spouted tales of magical creatures and enchantresses after visiting their sister. Kinnsell had ordered all three of them to remain aboard the mother ship. He hoped Katie's egalitarian attitudes hadn't contaminated them. Otherwise they might all challenge him for the crown of the emperor when Kinnsell's father finally died. The old man was taking his own sweet time about it. The Terran Galactic Empire grew shakier every year. It needed Kinnsell's firm hand on the joystick to guide it back to prosperity.

"Master Varn?" the approaching human spoke confidently, as if he could see in the dark. Maybe he could. The locals constantly surprised Kinnsell with their uncanny abilities.

Kinnsell quickly donned the heavily veiled headdress that kept his identity as a human from a different planet concealed. He hated the costume of layer upon layer of wispy chiffon. But the family insisted. This world must not be tainted by knowledge of its Terran past or by technology and pollution. Soon he'd end the charade. The TGE needed the fresh food produced by this world. But not tonight. He'd not reveal himself or his mission to this bushie noble with delusions of grandeur. Not until Kinnsell had control of the situation.

" 'Tis, I, Chieftain of the Varns," Kinnsell replied in solemn tones suitable to an awesome being of unknown origin and proportions.

"Do you have enough wealth to bribe me to release my entire plantation of the Tambootie?" The man's voice didn't show any sign of deference or awe in the face of one of the legendary Varn traders.

A niggle of disappointment knotted at the base of Kinnsell's spine. His ancestors had started the cult of the Stargods here. His people should appear as gods to these primitives! Instead he was forced by an outdated covenant to effect this ghostly appearance.

But he needed the Tambottie. Lots of it. A lot more than King Quinnault and his own daughter had been willing to give him.

The plague raged throughout the TGE; Tambootie was the only known cure. If he had enough of the weed, he could eliminate the disease forever—as it should have been when genetic scientists first realized their experimental microbe not only ate toxic waste and air pollution, it ate the toxins within human bodies that had built up over generations of uncontrolled industrial waste. And then ate the human hosts.

"I have seeds that will triple your yield of grains," Kinnsell intoned. "Provided the Tambootie is from the Spring harvest, and not fallen leaves from last Autumn."

"Seeds won't do me much good. Most of my land is crags and ravines." The bushie noble spat into the dirt on the forest floor.

"I have sheep embryos that when grown will yield wool so long it will spin almost as fine as silk."

"Embryos? What are they?"

"Fertilized eggs you implant into the uterus of a female sheep."

"Demon spawn!" The man shuddered and made a curious flapping gesture with crossed wrists. His heavy signet ring glinted in the moonlight.

Kinnsell realized the man did not wear a traditional seal set into the ring. Instead, the fine silverwork represented an elaborate and twisted knot reminiscent of his Celtic ancestors on Terra. He suddenly knew lust for that ring. He'd have it on his own hand before he left this backwater for home. His hand thrust forward, reasserting control.

"I'll not impregnate my good sheep with demon spirits." The lord continued. "I'll continue feeding the *s'murghin* dragons my Tambootie rather than deal with demons."

"Can you mine your land?" Kinnsell was running out of options. His hand remained forward, still trying to regain control. He hadn't much left on his mother ship that would help these people—or bribe them.

"My mines were played out generations ago. Not enough iron and copper left to make it worth hauling the slag to the surface." The man's eyes shifted to the side, sure indication he lied.

He had coal. Coal that could fuel industrial plants—here or elsewhere. Kinnsel had smelled the dust the last time he visited Balthazaan.

He smiled and swallowed any lingering loyalty to the anachronistic family covenant. His hand came back in a position of smooth flight. "I can give you tools that will cut through solid rock to the hidden veins of ore."

The lord's eyes opened wide in greed, then narrowed in speculation. "What good are those tools if my miners don't know where the veins are?" He twisted his ring. A sign of agitation or greed?

"I have a second tool that senses the presence of precious metals, iron and coal as well." Kinnsell's mind brightened at the thought of gleaming steel, a commodity of increasing scarcity now that the largest iron-producing colonies had domed their cities and abandoned their mines in favor of full citizenship in the TGE. Now that he'd transgressed a little against the family covenant, he might as well go all the way. "But for the tools, I'll need more than the plantation of the Tambootie trees in trade."

"I haven't got much else. The wars stripped me of everything but a few worthless acres and a bunch of daughters."

"Then with your first profits from the veins of ore *my* tools find for you, you must buy every ton of surplus grain you can find." The Empire needed food more than additional supplies of steel.

"Surpluses are supposed to go to the king. Security against drought, he says." A note of disgust tinged the man's reply. He abandoned twisting his ring to clench his fist and shake it in anger.

Kinnsell got a better look at the ring and coveted it more. He also knew he could exploit the lord's emotion. King Quinnault's foresight in preparing for a drought still five years off—if the normal weather cycle prevailed—had been denounced as ludicrous by his shortsighted nobles. They wanted profit. Now.

"My people suffer from drought now," Kinnsell said. A drought of resources of their own making, not weather induced. He couldn't change a situation created almost a thousand years ago, but he could profit from his society's policy of stripping planets and moving on. "We need the grain now. Your king doesn't need surplus food until a new drought hits you. Droughts are the whims of the Stargods. The next one may never come, or it may be delayed."

"Or it might come tomorrow. I'm not certain incurring the king's wrath by giving up so much Tambootie and selling surplus food is worth a few sledgeloads of ore."

"No mere mortal can tell for sure when a drought will come." Kinnsell fought to keep the desperation out of his voice. These bushies weren't easy to corrupt. Or rather, they were so corrupt already he couldn't turn their vices to his own benefit. The benefit of the TGE, he corrected himself. "You haven't hoarded surpluses before and your people always survived. A year's delay in adhering to the king's new laws won't hurt."

"Give me some reasons not to obey these new laws now. I did just fine in the old days making my own laws and ruling my lands by myself without inference from any king."

Kinnsell swallowed a sharp retort that the lord hadn't done "just fine" during the generations of war. Instead he said, "King Quinnault is like a fanatical priest. He wants everyone to believe as he does without variation and without logical explanations. He doesn't want the good of the country, he wants control of your lives, your resources, your minds." Kinnsell paused a moment to let that thought sink in. "The sooner Quinnault is brought down, the sooner you can go back to making a profit any way you see fit."

"The other lords and I signed agreements to support him. The people love him. Chancy thing to depose him." The bushie lord was back to twisting the ring.

"The people love him now because they don't truly know him. He won't let them see the truth of his need to control every aspect of life in Kardia Hodos—including their thoughts. How do you think he quelled that riot last Autumn if not by mind control? You must show them the truth. Then you will be free to sell your resources for a profit rather than pay the king's useless taxes."

"You'll trade me rock cutting tools and ore finders?" The bushie noble tapped his lip with his forefinger as if mulling over the possibilities.

Kinnsell sincerely wished his telepathy could penetrate the man's mind. The locals like this lord with dark hair and olive skin, similar to the natives of the Mediterranean on Terra, seemed totally impervious to the family talent. The ones with fairer coloring opened easily to telepathic probes—unless they had psi powers that allowed them to pretend to be magicians. He hadn't met anyone with Asian or African features to know how widespread the natural shields were. Each race resided on a different continent here; except for the ones like this lord. They wandered the whole planet like gypsies.

"You Varns always trade in diamonds. If I had some

diamonds, I could buy my neighbor's surplus tomorrow," the bushie lord suggested. "You wouldn't have to wait until I reopened the mines and found a viable vein of ore, then found a market for it and sold it."

"A sudden influx of gems will shout to all of Kardia Hodos that you have traded with Varns. King Quinnault will look closely at your plantations of the Tambootie to see if you have violated your covenant with the dragons."

The noble crossed himself and murmured a prayer. Then he crossed his wrists and flapped his hands.

Kinnsell wished he knew the origin of that bizarre gesture.

"Dragons and magicians have never done me any favors. Don't see why I should give up a tithe of land to the trees of magic, and another tithe of my few sheep to the dragons."

"You shouldn't have to give up anything to charlatan magicians and nonexistent dragons." Kinnsell pressed the man toward a decision. "My mining tools will work better than magic."

The noble's eyes gleamed with greed.

"You get the Tambootie and the grain when I sell the first load of ore."

"I need the Tambootie now."

"I need working capital now."

"Gold. I'll give you gold."

"How much?"

"One hundred coins the size of your thumbnail."

"Coins from where? Merchants don't take every mintage."

"The coins of Varnicia, the spice merchants, are good everywhere." Kinnsell knew how to counterfeit those.

"And hint of Varn origin, just like diamonds."

"Then the coins of Jihab, the jewel merchants."

"Tainted by Maffisto assassins. You guarantee your tools will serve me better than magicians?"

"My tools will eliminate the need for magicians. You and your kind will be free of them once and for all." *And with improved technology, I'll have a planet producing enough food to feed three civilized worlds. We'll export the coal and iron to industrial worlds and leave more men to work the land.*

"Gold bullion will do. I can sell it anywhere."

"Done. I'll take your signet ring as surety..."

"I have neighbors willing to trade grain and Tambootie for freedom from magicians." The lord totally ignored Kinnsell's last request. "They trust me to bargain for them. I have a list of what they need." The bushie pulled a long roll of parchment from his tunic. A very long roll, indeed. "I found a man to write it who failed as a magician apprentice. He stayed at the cursed University long enough to learn to read but not much else."

Kinnsell licked his lips eagerly. He'd have this planet mechanized and shipping massive surpluses within a decade. But he didn't think he'd ever inform the locals of their right to dome their cities and join the Empire as full citizens. Terra needed food, not more citizens. He needed the crown that this world's food could give him. His hand came back, soaring higher in his personal agenda.

Briefly he wondered if he should lift the ban on reading and writing on this world. Not yet. The lcoals might learn too much too fast.

* * *

University of Magicians Library, Coronnan City

Bessel stared at the strange paragraph in the old text. He'd been shelving books for Master Lyman when his talent insisted he open this book and read. The pages had fallen open right where he read and reread the same paragraph.

A person with the healing talent can diminish the effects of disease by symbolically exchanging blood with the patient.

What? How? He had to read further. The three other books he cradled in his arms dropped to the floor with a resounding thud. He ignored the echoes in the normally hushed library. Several apprentices looked up from their studies. Bessel didn't care how much attention he attracted, or about the sniggers of the other students.

He knew his pudgy hands were clumsy. That didn't matter. This book offered a clue to the end of the plague. If he found out how to do this, maybe he could get permission to return to Lord Balthazaan's disease-ridden province. He couldn't save his mother, but he might save some of the others before the plague spread any further. And he wouldn't have to tap a ley line or access the void to do it.

He grabbed the book with both hands and stumbled over the fallen books to the nearest study desk. He was already reading when he plunked down on the stool.

> The healer must first trigger a middling trance being careful not to fall too deep in thrall with the void. While still in contact with his body and his mind, the healer takes his ritual dagger in his left hand and carefully cuts across the right palm of the patient. Then he must repeat the cut on his own left palm. The ritual dagger may then be placed upon a silk scarf to await later cleansing. The healer must place his left palm across the patient's right hand, making sure to align the cuts. With his free hand the healer must bind the hands together with a pristine white bandage, also made of silk.
>
> If the healer has been properly trained and successfully passed the trial by Tambootie smoke, no contagion will spread to his own body, though all mundanes within the room become infected.

Bessel turned the page for the ritual words that would complete the healing spell. The next three pages had been torn from the binding.

He flipped back and forth in the book seeking the missing pages. Ragged edges at irregular intervals testified to several more clumps of pages that had been removed. Whoever had mutilated the book had done it hastily, not taking time to cut the pages cleanly.

Who? Who would damage a precious book?

"Master Lyman?" he asked in a hushed voice. The Master Librarian should be nearby. He rarely left his beloved books. Bessel often wondered if the old man ate and slept in the library as well.

Journeymen whispered legends into the ears of awed apprentices that Old Lyman ate only knowledge and never slept.

"Yes?" Master Lyman peered at Bessel through an opening in the bookshelves. He seemed to have simply moved books aside rather than walk a few feet around the shelving unit.

"Master Lyman, have you read this book?"

"Title and author?" Lyman scrunched up his wizened face in thought.

"*Ceremonies of Symbolic Magic* written by one Kimmer, a scribe from the South. I think this was copied from the original text." Bessel stared at the fine tooling on the leather cover. Traces of gold leaf still clung to the ancient embossed lettering.

"Kimmer? Ah, yes. Kimmer of the South. A fine scholar and one of our most prolific authors. Sadly, I have not had time to read this text." Lyman started to shove books back into place, withdrawing from Bessel's presence.

"Uh, Master Lyman?"

"You have another question?" Lyman poked his head back into the shelf opening. "Two questions in one sitting from the same student? Could it be that one of you is beginning to think enough to ask questions?"

"Master Lyman, someone has torn some pages from this book. Who would do such a thing?" Distress made Bessel's voice rise in pitch and volume. He immediately lowered it to a more appropriate whisper. "I think I've found a reference to early blood magic. It was used for healing rather than power! This is important."

"Hush, boy. You must never say that out loud! I told Powwell the same thing when he read from this text. I also told him to hide this book." Lyman scuttled around the bookshelves and grabbed the book away from Bessel. His funny, old-fashioned tunic that hung to his knees and he'd belted on the outside to hold up his trews made him appear more a harmless gnome than a powerful and wise magician.

Had Powwell removed the crucial pages from the book? Why? Surely he wouldn't need blood magic to rescue his sister. But then, in Hanassa, maybe he would.

The main door to the library banged open. Master Scarface stood framed by the massive double doorway. The scar that gave him his cognomen made a vivid red pathway from temple to temple across the bridge of his nose.

"Out!" he commanded. The scar bleached white, clear evidence of the tension he kept carefully contained. "All of you students out of here now. The masters have important work to do. We cannot be disturbed."

A dozen apprentices gathered up their books, scrolls, and writing implements in preparation for leaving.

"Don't take anything with you. Leave the books behind. Just get out of here. Now."

While I still have the courage to do this. Scarface's stray thought penetrated Bessel's mind. What was the Senior Magician going to do?

"Quickly, boy, hide the book and get yourself away by the postern door." Lyman thrust the book back into Bessel's hands and shoved him toward the back corner of the three-story-high room that filled the entire central wing of the U-shaped University building. "Hide yourself well without magic. He'll smell your magic if you use it."

"Lyman, show yourself," Scarface ordered as he stalked into the library. Three master magicians, all of them new since Scarface had taken over leadership of the Commune a year ago, followed closely upon his heels. All of the master magicians seemed more willing to follow Scarface than make a decision on their own. That was how Scarface had become Senior. No one else wanted to do it.

"Yes, Master Aaddler?" Lyman stepped in front of Bessel, giving the journeyman cover for his quick retreat.

Bessel kept his ears open and his magical senses alert as he sought a dark corner for himself and his book. He knew he needed to hear the truth beneath the spoken words.

The Senior Magician winced at the use of his true name. Since he had taken over, all of the masters had adopted working names and reserved true names for only the most solemn occasions.

"The books must be separated by categories," Scarface said, looking directly into Lyman's eyes rather than at the books. The intensity of his gaze suggested he attempted to influence Lyman with magic.

"They already are cataloged and categorized." Lyman didn't falter or succumb to the mental manipulation.

"For the safety of the Commune and those who seek

knowledge here, a further separation is required. The queen's dragon dream foretells danger in the knowledge contained within these books."

The three satellite magicians moved to flank Scarface, becoming a solid wall of determination.

"I have studied the matter. We can no longer delay in removing dangerous information from the reach of vulnerable apprentices."

"Dangerous as in. . . ?" Lyman remained firmly in place, blocking the other magicians.

"All references to rogue magic must be placed where only master magicians can access them. All references to machines that mimic magic must be set aside for later culling," Scarface announced. "None of my students have need of this forbidden knowledge."

"You are going to ban books?" Lyman asked. For the first time, Bessel watched the old man fumble for a retort that would misdirect or perplex. Lyman stood blinking, mouth agape. He radiated emotional pain.

"We must remove dangerous books from the hands of vulnerable children and those who would misuse the forbidden knowledge secreted therein."

CHAPTER 8

The void between the planes of existence

Pulsing energy jolted through Yaala, the only sensation available to her as numbing darkness enfolded her. She had no body, no perceptions, only thoughts and the rippling currents tingling her mind. Something akin to the 'tricity generated by her beloved machines beneath Hanassa. But different. Unnatural.

(Your 'tricity is unnatural. We belong here,) a voice said inside Yaala's head.

Where am I? she asked. She wanted to speak but had no mouth to form the words. Only her mind existed. Her mind and the voice.

She retained a brief memory of seeing the dragongate start to form and dashing forward to stand beside Powell. Then, before she could reach him, she fell into . . . nothing; nothing but the repeated jolts.

Her thoughts spun, seeking order out of nothing.

(You have found a place where you do not belong and cannot stay.)

I have never belonged anywhere but with my machines. How do I return to them?

(Is that what you truly wish?)

I have no alternative.

(There are always alternatives.)

Then I make the choice to return to Hanassa. With Powwell. The image of underground caverns filled with giant generators and transformers formed slowly in her memory. Gradually, she completed the picture with all of the colors and sulfur smells she had lived with so long. Then she added the memory of Powwell following her about with tools and oil rags.

(That is the one place I cannot send you. Dragons do not venture near the realm of the renegade.)

Abruptly the voice disappeared. And Yaala was left alone in the nothingness, with only her mind and her memories. And the jolting energy.

All energy followed definite currents. She remembered that much from her study of the machines. Even when 'tricity appeared to flare in random directions, it followed some kind of pattern, using the air as a conduit when no wires existed.

Therefore this strange energy had a beginning and an end. She had but to follow it.

She took a moment (if time still existed, which she doubted) to study the patterns of the energy. At first, they seemed random and directionless. Gradually, she tuned her mind to the frequency of the flow. At last, she found a rhythm. It pulsed in her mind almost like music. Haunting and compelling.

(Follow me!) it seemed to say. *(Follow me home.)*

Her mind blended with the pseudo 'tricity and joined the pulsing dance it created out of nothing. A kind of joy filled her. If she'd had a body, she would have laughed.

Laughter. One of many things missing in her life. Yaassima had laughed, but only when cruelty lit her mind. Yaala had never found anything to laugh about in Hanassa, even as a small child. Fear had dominated every aspect of surviving the Kaalipha's strange whims and bloodlust.

Now Yaala laughed and understood that her life could never be complete until she put aside her fears. Yaassima was dead. Yaala's mother could no longer terrorize her. *I am free of her!* She laughed out loud, needing to include others in her mirth. But who?

Powwell, her only friend, was on that lonely desert plateau, lost in time. Nimbulan and Myrilandel were back in the capital. And she was lost in the void.

I don't want to be alone.

The energy swirled in a stronger vortex. Colors erupted around her. Her limbs tingled as they had when she tumbled through the dragongate.

Abruptly she found herself sitting beside a large tree with a rocky overhang sheltering her from a Spring rainstorm.

Evey joint in her intact body ached and rippled with the

residual energy. Especially the base of her spine where she seemed to have landed on her butt on the hard forest floor.

"Was I in the magicians' void?" she asked whoever might be listening.

The tree branches whispered among themselves as the wind rose and the rain intensified. Their conversation meant nothing to her mundane senses.

She crawled to her knees, searching her surroundings for clues to her whereabouts. She needed a drink. The hours she had spent on the desert plateau had evaporated every spare drop of moisture from her.

She knew how to survive. And survive she must. Yaassima had taught her that. The only valuable lesson her mother could impart.

She knew how to survive alone.

The rocky overhang looked promising. Rain ran down the rocks in heavy rivulets. She lapped at them, refreshing her parched throat.

A small measure of strength returned to her with the influx of water. She drank more deeply and filled her waterskin.

Yaala crept deeper beneath the overhang until a large outcropping sheltered her back from the pelting rain and fierce wind. Her prominent spinal bumps fit nicely into the crevices as if made to fit her unique body form.

"Right back where I started from. Only this time I don't have Powwell." A deep ache opened within her, unrelated to the physical distress of her adventures.

"Powwell!" she howled, more alone than she'd ever been before. More alone than when Yaassima, her own mother, had executed Yaala's father and dipped her hands in the still warm blood.

"Oh, Powwell, find me, please. I don't want to be alone."

* * *

The city of Hanassa, home of renegades, dragons, magicians, and mundanes

The Kardia rumbled and rolled beneath Rollett's feet in the hellish volcanic crater called Hanassa, home to mercenaries, political outlaws, thieves, murderers, and exiled rogue magicians.

Stargods? Not again!

"Everyone out! Get out of the tunnel now!" he yelled as he dashed forward. Two dozen men streamed past him, each seeking the exit. Some of them showed signs of panic as they ran. Rollett touched each man on the shoulder, offering reassurance. They calmed down and cleared the tunnel in an orderly fashion.

The confines of the excavation amplified the sensation of motion from the quake. Dirt trickled through cracks in the ceiling of the lava tube passage. Instantly Rollett scanned the partially blocked tunnel with every sense available to him.

He and his crews had almost reached the section where three men had died the last time the only known exit from Hanassa had collapsed on them.

"I won't sacrifice any more men to Piedro's bloodthirsty god Simurgh," he proclaimed to any who might hear. "I won't let this cursed city trap me any longer."

With his last words he slapped his hand onto the most vulnerable crack. Before he'd had the chance to breathe deeply twice, magic coursed through his fingers into the unstable tunnel. On the third breath the calm of a light trance descended in waves upon his muscles. His mind floated free of the restrictions of his body. He followed his magic into the walls of the ancient volcano.

He found the imbalance of broken layers of solidified lava and aeons of dirt. A push here, leverage there, and the tunnel stabilized at the same moment the Kardia ceased quaking.

Rollett returned reluctantly to his sweating and exhausted body.

"Is it safe, Rollett?" one of the masons whispered from the tunnel entrance. Rollett had elevated the man from captive slave to honored workman soon after they began the first digging-out of Hanassa.

"I think so. Give it a moment." He breathed deeply of the hot dry air, willing the air to feed his undernourished body and give him reserves of strength. He'd found no ley lines in this hellhole to replenish his magic. The dragons had deserted this part of the world centuries ago, taking their special magical energy with them. He had only himself to fuel his talent.

He drank deeply from the skin tied to his belt. The sulfur-laden water almost tasted good. He drank again until the rancid flavor made him gag. Then he knew he'd had enough. He'd learned his first week in Hanassa to avoid dehydration at all cost. Water was more precious than food these days.

Both were in short supply.

Without food and fresh water, he didn't have enough of himself left to give at the rate Hanassa used him up. Excavating the tunnel was their only hope to open the city to outside supplies.

"Why don't you just climb up the crater walls and slip through the holes in the fence?" the mason asked. His eyes kept returning to the tumble of dirt and boulders behind Rollett. The mason crossed himself and stepped back into the daylight.

Six moons ago, three men had died in the last cave-in. Rollett hadn't been close enough to stop it with magic then. He and his crew had lost nearly a year's work in a few moments of quaking Kardia.

"You needn't fear the ghosts of those men. They died honestly." Rollett stood up and squared his shoulders. *But they are the last ones to die in this tunnel.*

"You've got the strength and courage to climb the crater," the mason encouraged him, returning to the issue Rollett couldn't explain to himself let alone to one of his crew.

"You have the strength to escape, too, friend. But I made some promises that keep me here. I intend to keep them."

"No one else in this cursed city believes in promises."

"And they have lost their belief in themselves. They have lost control of their lives. Until I finish what I set out to do, we must make do with the few supplies some of our comrades send through those gaps in the barbed fencing. Not enough to make life easy again, but enough to give Hanassa hope that we will burrow out of here."

He remembered the first time he had encountered the fence a year and a half ago. The climb up the outside slopes of the mountain in the desert heat without enough water and food had nearly killed both him and Nimbulan. Then the disappointment of encountering the unbroken line of barbed fencing had nearly ended their mission before it truly began. He and his master had been trying to break into Hanassa to rescue Nimbulan's wife. Now men braved the crater and the fence to break out of Hanassa.

"I hope you succeeded, Old Man," he whispered to his memory of Nimbulan. "I hope you found a way back to Coronnan where you can lead the Commune in the fight for justice and peace. I don't like to think you died in that last battle we fought together in the Justice Hall. Your body should have been among those we carted out and buried, but it wasn't. Though if you escaped, I don't know how."

Scarface, the Battlemage who had become a mercenary, had also disappeared that night. Rollett had never trusted the man, although Nimbulan had. Something about the way the man manipulated the camaraderie of his companions . . .

If you were responsible for making certain I got left behind, Scarface, I'll see that you pay in all of your next existences.

Rollett deliberately separated himself from past grief and suspicions. He needed all of his concentration here and now.

He probed the tunnel one more time with his magical senses. "It's safe to come back in, but you'll need to shore up the walls here and here." He pointed out the weakest spot to the hovering mason.

"I have decided that masonry and mortar require too much precious water," a newcomer said from the tunnel entrance.

"Would you rather watch your city starve, Kaaliph Piedro?" Rollett asked the Rover who had grabbed power the moment the old Kaalipha had died, taking the previous Rover Chieftain and her pet Bloodmage with her.

Piedro's dark eyes narrowed, hardly veiling the animosity behind them. His lithe body betrayed him, he looked more than ready to spring upon Rollett like a legendary spotted saber cat. Then he twisted his head as if listening to a light tune borne on the wind. He shook himself a little and replaced the mask of reasonableness on his face and posture.

"I feed the city. My people work hard at cutting a stairway up the crater walls to the fence. We will have access to the outside world again, when I deem it safe," Piedro replied. "My Rover magic tells me that the outside world is not safe at the moment."

Rollett couldn't penetrate the man's emotions with or without magic. Rovers had strange powers that few outsiders understood or could participate in. One had to have Rover blood to use Rover spells.

"Safe for you or safe for honest workers who were brought here as slaves against their will?" Rollett asked, forcing an air of innocence into his tone. "You don't feed the city, Piedro. You keep us on starvation rations so you can pretend to control the rabble. But you are still sleek and strong. Where do you get your supplies if all the exits are blocked?"

He held back the anger that sent heat through his veins. He hadn't the strength to challenge Piedro openly. And now he'd exhausted himself holding the tunnel together during the kardiaquake.

What do you have hidden in the labyrinth beneath the palace, Piedro? He and the Rover Kaaliph stared at each other for a long moment, assessing, weighing, mutely challenging.

"Mix the mortar," Rollett ordered the mason. The broad man scuttled out of the tunnel. Rollett could taste the man's fear as it permeated the air.

Piedro licked his lips, savoring it.

"Invoking terror only gives an illusion of control," Rollett said, as much to himself as to the upstart Kaaliph. "You don't have Yaassima's cunning or her magic." The late Kaalipha had governed with a bloody fist. Infractions of her few rules met with swift and fatal retribution. But she had rules. Those who broke the rules knew the consequences.

Piedro made and broke his own laws on a whim. No one knew for sure what was legal and what wasn't. Like this tunnel. Yesterday Piedro had welcomed the efforts to dig out. He'd openly told Rollett that the excavation toward the outside world kept troublemakers too busy and tired to wreak havoc within the city—or foment open rebellion.

Rollet wondered why Piedro hadn't assassinated him yet. He'd had many opportunities in the last year and a half.

Perhaps the Kaaliph feared that Rollett's men, who worked and lived as a cohesive unit, protecting each other, might rebel at the loss of their leader. Perhaps Piedro had secret plans to use this crew for something else. Perhaps . . .

The hair on the back of Rollett's neck rose in atavistic fear. He searched first for signs of a ghost. The blocked end of the tunnel remained quiet.

Slowly he turned back to the tunnel entrance, knowing who awaited his notice. A short figure stood beside Peidro. Her head barely reached the Rover's shoulder. A black lace veil covered her from head to toe. The intricate pattern of open and dense thread shifted with each movement, revealing haunting hints of a feminine figure robed in a finely cut black gown. A paler blob indicated the location of her face, but no hint of hair or eye color, distinguishing features, or age filtered through the veil.

She maintained a tighter control of her emotions and her aura than the cadre of Rovers who accompanied Piedro everywhere. Even if Rollett had the energy to spare to probe her, he knew from experience he'd find nothing. The probe would pass right through her.

Rover magic was mysterious. Her magic was unfathomable.

The woman rose up on tiptoe and whispered into Piedro's ear. In the year and a half since the Rover had seized power, no one but Piedro had heard her voice. All that anyone knew of her was that Piedro never went anywhere without her—except the brothels.

"I shall attend you in a moment, my dear." Piedro patted her hand solicitously. She backed away, as if floating in a mist of her veil.

"Leave this excavation, Rollett," Piedro ordered. "The great winged god Simurgh is hungry. His temple—the only temple remaining in all of Kardia Hodos dedicated to him—lies empty within my palace. Don't give me an excuse to feed him your blood. Much as I have enjoyed them, I grow weary of your challenges."

"Who ordered the end of this project, you or your consort?"

"I rule Hanassa. No one else!" Piedro screamed in a voice on the edge of hysteria.

Rollett merely raised one eyebrow in question.

"Guards, post five men here at all times. The work will

cease immediately." Piedro turned on his heel and stalked out. His temper made little ripples in his aura, like watching air distortion around a hot flame.

"Move the next load of dirt to the latrine pit," Rollett ordered his work crew.

The guards looked at their hands. Two masons shouldered them aside, carrying buckets of fresh mortar. Other men followed with shovels and picks ready to attack the blockage.

The Rover guards moved outside and took up assigned posts but did not interfere with the work.

"Rumor has it that Piedro has a new supply of grain and dried fruit. Maybe a load of hams as well," a worker whispered to Rollett as he passed.

Rollett nodded slightly in acknowledgment. Every dark of the moon he heard the same rumor. Always the darkest night of the cycle.

"Tonight," he whispered to the next man who passed him.

"Three hours after midnight," the man mouthed, careful not to let any of Piedro's spies hear.

A presence behind Rollett prickled his senses. He reached over his shoulder and grabbed the first informant by the ear and wrestled him into an armlock.

"Stargods, how do you do that?" the prisoner gasped as he relaxed within the punishing grip.

"Never sneak up on a magician," Rollett warned. "Next time I might kill you with a thought before I check to see if you are friend or foe." Rollett grinned and relaxed his pressure on the man's windpipe enough to let him breath. But not enough to let him go.

"Yeah. Well you'd better be double careful tonight," the informant said, rubbing his throat. "I also heard Piedro started the rumor of new supplies in order to trap you. He's afraid to arrest and execute you, but if you died in honest battle stealing from him . . ."

"I'll remember that." Rollett released the man. Then he shuddered inwardly, keeping all traces of revulsion from his face. He'd spent too many years at Nimbulan's side learning that peace, honor, and justice must bind a society together. Violence came too easy for him these days.

"You'll make a good Kaaliph, Rollett," the mason said

under his breath. "But you aren't ruthless enough to keep the job. You'll need the consort to help."

"Want to make a bet on that?" Rollett slammed the man up against the stone buttress, holding him a foot off the ground by the throat with one hand.

The mason's face began to pulse purple.

Rollett eased his grip enough for the man's feet to touch ground.

"No bets, Rollett," the mason gasped.

"Remember what happens to people who defy me. Now get to work."

He stalked out of the tunnel, disgusted with himself and with life in Hanassa.

CHAPTER 9

Midmorning, Palace Reveta Tristile, Coronnan City

"Be safe, my love," Queen Maarie Kaathliin whispered as she leaned out the nursery window. She pressed her fingertips to her lips and blew a gentle kiss.

In the courtyard below, Quinnault looked up and smiled. He grabbed at the empty air as if catching the kiss. Then he opened his fist against his cheek, planting the caress where it belonged. With a jaunty wave he mounted Buan, his favorite stallion, and rode out the main gate of the palace courtyard.

The waiting company of royal soldiers leaped to their mounts and followed at a canter. They planned to escort a sledge caravan of foodstuffs and firewood to the beleaguered province of Lord Balthazaan. Thrice before, the much-needed supplies had been ambushed by well-organized outlaws and never seen again. The last had happened but days ago. The outlaws should not be quite so greedy for these supplies.

But Katie knew her husband chafed for the chance to confront and punish those thieves.

Quinnault might become lost in the wordstorms of politicians, but when action was called for, he responded readily with a worthy plan.

If only they could find the source of the disquiet in the capital city, she knew he'd form a good plan and act upon it. But vandals tore apart the scaffolding on new buildings, painted anti-foreign slogans on walls, and set fire to pungent offal in the doorways of foreign merchants and ran, leaving no clue to their identity.

Quinnault's dream of justice and peace in Coronnan faded with every act of sabotage.

Rumors gave the troublemakers a dozen different identities and motives. No one presented solid evidence.

The most frequent rumors claimed that the vandals as well as the outlaws attacking caravans were Rovers seeking revenge against Quinnault and the Commune for their exile from Coronnan along with all of the magicians who could not or would not gather dragon magic.

Other rumors spoke of foreign armies. Still others whispered that the dragons stole the food. The latter stories were always accompanied by the strange flapping gesture to ward against evil and a few crosses of the Stargods.

"None of those rumors can be true," Katie said to the air, pounding her fist against the window casement. "A magical border protects all of Coronnan from foreign troops and Rovers. And the dragons have no need for grain and fruit and pickled meat. Do you, Shayla?" She sent the last question telepathically as well as verbally.

But the dragons remained silent. For many weeks they'd been too busy to respond to Katie or Quinnault. She'd heard magicians complain about a lack of dragon magic to gather. Without dragon magic to impose ethics and honor upon magicians, Coronnan might very well dissolve into disastrous civil war once more. What transpired?

Katie moved to stand over her daughter's crib. "I miss the informal clutter of my family." She sighed heavily. Three times this past Winter each of her brothers had visited her clandestinely. Each time she had hugged her sibling close, unwilling to let him go, though she knew she must. They had responsibilities back home.

She had not seen them for two moons. Perhaps they had gone home—taking their father with them. But it was unlike Liam Francis not to risk one final good-bye.

She had chosen her life with Quinnault—her beloved Scarecrow—on this rural planet with clean air and fresh food in exchange for the precious Tambootie to cure a plague. But she still missed her boisterous brothers and their adventures together. She'd never needed friends and lovers until she came here. Her family had filled every emotional need she had.

She must never see them again and must never communicate with them either. The family covenant forbade it. Kardia Hodos must remain free of the taint of technology and the plague.

Still, her brothers bent the covenant to check on her. The bonds of family went deeper than duty.

She gazed lovingly at her daughter, a true miracle of life. This eight-month-old bundle of hungry demands represented the future of this country and her family.

For a few moments, at least, Princess Marilell slept quietly, sucking her fist. Hungry even in sleep.

"Maybe you'll have a baby brother soon," Katie whispered to her daughter. She placed her hand protectively across her belly, hoping. . . .

She shot another question to the dragons. Still no answer. On the night Marilell had been conceived, the dragons had flown a nuptial flight as well. Shayla had told Katie the next morning that both matings had been successful.

Shayla wasn't due to mate again for at least another year. Katie hoped she didn't have to wait until then to become pregnant again.

"Maybe not having enough milk to nurse you, Marilell, is a blessing. Maybe I'll conceive again quickly. Perhaps I already have. No one back home will consider taking the time to nurse their own babies, so they have to resort to drugs and devices to keep from having too many children too soon. But here, children are a blessing rather than an inconvenience necessary for the continuation of the human race."

Or a frightening experience depending on the mother's exposure to the plague. The old, the very young, and pregnant women always contracted the plague first.

No one knew for certain what breakdown in their immune systems triggered a plague spore back into life. The genetically engineered microbes were supposed to eat only toxic waste until they ran out of food, then they should turn cannibalistic until only one remained and it starved to death. But the microbes mutated, turning into dormant spores until more pollution fed them, or they found bacteria and buildups of toxins within the human body a culinary delight.

The reports of illness devastating Lord Balthazaan's province, beginning at the coal mines with their heavy concentrations of mineral dust, had spread to include other regions—city and rural alike. If the problems resulted from privation, the caravan of supplies Quinnault led would help. They needed firsthand reports from the trusted officers with the caravan rather than reliance upon rumor.

Katie read every written report and listened closely to every rumor for similarities between the current illness and the Terran plague. She hoped the symptoms differed enough to rule out the plague. The people of Coronnan succumbed to a choking cough. Terra's plague caused all of the internal organs to hemorrhage. Eventually the patient either bled to death or drowned from blood filling the lungs.

The soldiers had orders to gather fallen branches and limbs along the route to supplement the loads of firewood. Nimbulan had added the request to include the Tambootie for bonfires in the central marketplace of afflicted villages and manors. Scarface had countermanded Nimbulan's request. Smoke from the Tambootie was toxic to mundanes. In this case, the cure could be worse than the disease.

Nimbulan had countered that only eating the raw leaves of the Tambootie had proved lethal to mundanes. Breathing the smoke was such a private ritual of magicians that no record of a mundane reacting to the smoke existed. If a distillation of the Tambootie proved safe to mundanes, then the smoke should be as well.

Who was right? Katie wanted to believe Nimbulan because he was a friend and had proved wise so many times in the past year. But Scarface sounded so logical. . . .

If only they knew for certain that the smoke would *safely* prevent the disease.

The queen traced the baby's cheek with her fingertip. Such soft skin, warm and pink. She vowed that her new home would never know the plague, never live in fear of bearing children lest the plague strike mother and child when most vulnerable.

Silently Katie moved away from the crib to a secret recess in the wall near the outside corner of the room. She pressed and twisted an imperfection in the stonework. The false face of the stone popped open on well-oiled hinges to reveal an opening about twenty centimeters square. Previous queens of Coronnan had secreted jewels and valuable documents here. Katie used the cache for more important equipment.

She withdrew a small computerized box, a vial of test strips, and a lancet. "Do I really need to do this every day?" she asked herself. She dreaded the painful pricks from the lancet more and more. Maybe today she would just put the equipment back in its hiding place. The anxious mother part of her insisted she proceed.

Once brought out of dormancy, the virus spread rapidly by the briefest human contact, devastating entire populations in a matter of weeks. Each carrier caused a mutation of the virus that was resistant to the previous generation of antibiotics. In seven centuries of fighting the plague, Terran scientists had found that only a distillation from the Tambootie tree cured the plague.

In all those generations, Katie's family had never lost a member to the plague. The O'Haras and a few other families had proved strangely immune to the disease. But the microbe mutated so quickly Katie dared not take a chance that the next bug would kill her and devastate her new home.

She had lived on bush worlds for three years before being dispatched to the distant planet known as Kardia Hodos. Aboard the space transport here, she had lived in a special isolation chamber with a different air supply from the rest of the ship. Was that long enough to know she was free of the plague?

No. She had to perform this small chore once every day for ten years to be sure. At least another four years of painful pricks from the tiny needle.

Katie washed her hands with the hard lye soap used by the common populace. She preferred the cleansing properties of this soap to the softer perfumed stuff favored by the local nobility. She winced as the lancet pricked her finger. A bright hanging drop of blood welled up from the minute wound. She touched the surface of the test strip with the blood and slipped the chemically treated slide into the meter.

The tiny computer whirred and hummed to itself as it checked her blood against a thousand tests, including iron levels, thyroid, cholesterol, blood sugar, and hormone levels for pregnancy. In less than a standard minute the machine beeped, satisfied that Katie's blood was clean of the plague, her red and white counts remained normal, and her hormones maintained a satisfactory level. She wasn't pregnant.

This tiny machine should be the only machine that would ever taint Kardia Hodos. And she would destroy it when she no longer needed it.

Except her father had given a sonar unit to the Guild of Bay Pilots. She wished she could sabotage that device. One bit of technology always led to another and another until the entire society was riddled with machines, synthetics, and pollution.

A knock on the door roused her from her silent contemplation.

"Come," she called. Getting servants to respect her privacy had been a long uphill battle, but at least now they knocked and announced themselves when entering. Getting them to leave her alone again was still a problem.

"Your Grace." Kaariin, the queen's personal maid, bobbed a quick curtsy. "King Kinnsell, your father, requests an audience." Her eyes shone wide with awe and a bit of terror.

Kinnsell had that effect on people. Most people. Katie hadn't allowed him to intimidate her since she was twelve and discovered that she had as much right to be elected emperor upon her grandfather's death as her father did.

"What are you doing here, Kinnsell?" she asked the shadowy figure in the hallway. "You left for Terra last Autumn, right after the dragon dream." That had been his announced intention, but she'd seen Sean Michael and Jamie Patrick twice since then and Liam Francis three times. Jamie Patrick, the eldest, had told her Gramps had suffered a third heart attack near the Solstice and they might have to leave for home without notice to attend him.

Kinnsell nodded toward the servant in a gesture requesting privacy.

Katie almost asked Kaariin to stay, just to annoy her father. "I will interview King Kinnsell in the solar," Katie said instead. She caressed her baby one more time and moved toward the inner door that would take her to her private suite.

"You will receive me here, Katie," Kinnsell boomed as he pushed his way past the maid into the nursery, slamming the door in Kaariin's face. He wore a local style of richly brocaded tunic with plain dark trews and boots instead of Varn veils and headdress. He intended to be seen as the King of Terrania.

Marilell whimpered at the disturbance.

"Hush!" Katie commanded her father. "You've awakened the baby."

"Good. About time I had a chance to hold my granddaughter." He reached into the crib and lifted the baby to his shoulder before Katie could intervene. "You know, if you'd let me bring in a monitor, you wouldn't have to spend so much time babysitting. You could get out of this frigid palace, take part in the government, have a life."

"My child is my life!"

"Ah, Katie, all your fine education wasted on this primitive world. They don't even have the wheel, for God's sake."

"Don't forget that at regular intervals this planet provides enough surplus food to feed a civilized world for five years. And never forget that this primitive world is protected by family covenant. I can have you arrested and imprisoned by Gramps and Uncle Ryan if you violate the pact."

"A nice solar heater would make this drafty old barn more comfortable. I don't like the idea of my granddaughter being exposed to constant chill."

Katie sighed. Her father would only hear what he wanted to hear.

"Natives thrive in their natural climate. The strongest survive and build antibodies against *natural* ailments. Besides, the family covenant specifically forbids machines on this planet. We've had this argument before, Kinnsell. Why are you here?"

"I came to see my granddaughter."

"Why aren't you on Terra attending Gramps after his heart attack? You should be delivering a load of much needed Tambootie, that will make enough medicine to cure a million or more people of the plague." She took a deep breath to control her temper. Then she resorted to sarcasm to keep from slapping some sense into him. "You'll never be elected emperor if you don't show your face on the homeworld more than once a decade. No one will remember you as savior of humanity unless you take credit for the cure."

"Pop recovered from his heart surgery quite nicely without me. He'll live another decade or more. Liam Francis and Sean Michael are delivering the Tambootie in my name. About time they made themselves useful."

"I'm happy to hear that Gramps is doing well." And she was. Of all of her vast family, Gramps was her favorite, the one whose ideas about protecting Kardia Hodos agreed most closely with her own. As for her brothers, any one of the three of them might ingratiate himself with the legislature by taking credit for finding a cure for the plague—Jamie Patrick most likely, but he hadn't been sent home. Every one of the family held more moderate views toward expansion and exploitation than Kinnsell. But not as conservative as Katie and Gramps.

"The joint legislature is certain to elect me emperor when I bring Kardia Hodos back into the fold of the Empire. Finders of lost Terran colonies are always highly regarded." Kinnsell preened while holding the baby away from him.

"No!" A wave of vertigo washed over Katie. "This world is protected by the family covenant. We've kept it secret for seven hundred years to protect it from outside influences."

"And I intend to follow another family tradition of bringing lost bush worlds back into the Empire. We need all the agriculture we can get to feed the civilized worlds, the important worlds. Besides, the rest of the Empire needs the Tambootie that only grows here in order to cure the plague once and for all. I think she's wet." He set Marilell back into the crib.

"You'll strip this planet as you've stripped others. You won't be satisfied until every known planet is a desert." The baby could wait a moment, she wasn't fussing.

"Not deserts. Domed and protected from the ravages of climates and natural disasters."

"And unable to produce food, only to consume it. Every domed atmosphere is a potential breeding ground for the plague."

"Not if I harvest the Tambootie." His right hand rode at a comfortable and easy position beside him.

Katie knew she'd not convince him of anything while he felt himself in control of the situation. Still, she had to try.

"Synthetic air and food mutate new viruses. You know that. There isn't enough Tambootie to cure every new mutation. And you'll take it all. I know you, Kinnsell. You'll take all of the Tambootie, right down to the roots. The dragons will die without the Tambootie supplementing their diet. Without dragons, there won't be any magic. Coronnan will perish without magic."

"There isn't any magic. Only psi powers." His hand nudged forward a fraction. Had she broken through his blockheaded opinions, even just a little?

"Little do you know, Kinnsell. Little do you know the miracles this planet offers. I forbid you to take anything from here. Not so much as a grain of dirt. The Commune will back my order and force you to obey. Now get out. Go home. Never darken my door again."

"In my own good time, Daughter. When I've finished what I came here for."

"Over my dead body, Kinnsell!"

"If necessary."

* * *

Library of the University of Magicians, Coronnan City

"Start clearing a space in the gallery for the questionable books, Lyman," Scarface ordered.

Bessel considered slipping out the postern door. The noise of old wood and rusty hinges protesting being opened would alert Scarface to Bessel's presence in the library. The Senior Magician would know he'd been here and hunt down the book. Stargods only knew what he would do to Bessel once caught with a now forbidden book.

"We can block off access with locked gates, and I shall set the magical seal so that only I can open it." Scarface turned his back on the old librarian and pointed out the most inaccessible corners of the library.

"No," Lyman replied quietly. "I will not be a part of this. I am not strong enough to oppose you on my own, but I will not be a part of it."

Bessel sought a hiding place, any hiding place.

What was Scarface thinking, banning books? Nimbulan had made the library the focus of the entire University. Knowledge was valuable, any knowledge, in any form. Magicians keeping secrets had led to intense rivalries and many battles during three generations of civil war.

Now magicians had the responsibility to guide the rest of Coronnan through cooperation and sharing of knowledge. They couldn't do that unless they were the best educated men in the world; educated in all facets of life. How could they combat the dangerous machines if they didn't know their function and design? How could they negate a rogue magician if they did not know the nature of his spells?

Besides, Bessel was certain that information about the plague that had killed his mother could be found in one of these old books.

He couldn't help his mother. A tear threatened to choke him. She had loved him in her own distracted way. His father's prejudice had separated Bessel from the family. Not his mother. His father's prejudice and *ignorance*.

Bessel remembered something Myrilandel had told him about the time she had fled ignorant people who blamed her for all of their ills. People rarely looked up for a fugitive. They always looked down or at eye level.

He climbed. The bookshelves were massive constructions, ten feet high, each shelf a convenient step to the next.

As quietly as possible, he settled himself flat along the very top of the unit. He had only inches to spare between his back and the floor of the first gallery circling the perimeter of the library.

"If you won't help, then move aside, old man." Scarface waved Lyman out of his way. "I didn't expect one of Nimbulan's acolytes to agree with me. Fortunately there are few of you remaining to pester me with outlandish ideas. Coronnan will remain under my control with the blessing of dragon magic."

What? Coronnan would remain under Scarface's control. He hadn't said "the Commune." He'd said "Coronnan." The fine hairs along Bessel's spine tingled in warning.

Lyman hesitated long enough for Scarface's temper to

whiten the scar on his face. At last Lyman bowed his head in submission and stepped aside.

"We must begin putting the forbidden books under the gallery, deeply shadowed," Scarface mused, staring at the upper shelves. "We'll move up into the galleries if we have to."

He waved to his three satellite magicians to begin work at the front of the three-story-high room. They separated and immediately began pulling books off the shelves. They carried each book to the center worktables, making neat stacks of them. They worked rapidly, removing more books than they left shelved. Probably Scarface had decided which books to cull before they began.

Bessel pressed himself deeper into the shadows between the wall and the gallery floor. His squarely-built body barely fit atop the shelving unit.

Scarface brought a ball of witchlight to hand and raised his arm to see deeper into the shadows.

"You there!" Scarface shouted, pointing directly at Bessel. "Why are you hiding up there?"

"Um . . . um . . . I was dusting and I got stuck." Bessel flushed with the awkward lie.

Scarface raised his eyebrows, making the scar white again, a sure sign that he concentrated hard on containing his temper.

"I think not, boy. More likely you sought a hiding place to take a clandestine nap. I knew you were lazy. This proves it. Come down from there. Now."

Bessel looked to Lyman for some kind of direction.

"Don't seek out the old man. He can't tell you what to do. I am Senior Magician. You are oath-bound to obey me without question."

Bessel made the awkward climb down. But as he shifted his legs to dangle over the edge of the shelves, he pushed the precious book deep into the waistband of his trews, covering it with his tunic. He willed it into invisibility. It seemed to shrink and flatten as he continued the climb down the shelves. Scarface wouldn't be able to find it even with his Sight-Beyond-Sight.

CHAPTER 10

A rise overlooking Coronnan City from the South

Kinnsell stood on a slight rise on the South shore mainland overlooking the islands of Coronnan City. The River Coronnan made a natural moat. But enemies had boats, and the inhabitants needed the bridges connecting the various islands to each other and the mainland. The city was vulnerable.

And he planned to take it if Katie and her husband defied him further. "Cursed family covenant is outdated, worthless. The Empire needs this planet. The Empire needs me at its head and this planet will give me the crown. I won't let my renegade daughter keep me from getting it." He spat into the ground. A new sense of freedom lifted a weight from his shoulders. His hand rode easily at his side.

The distances involved in transporting food to the civilized worlds had grown beyond practicality centuries ago. Tanked food kept the Empire fed, but its citizens craved real food and were willing to pay enormous sums for small tastes.

Kardia Hodos was the private storehouse of the emperor.

"What do you see down there that our best generals and Battlemages can't?" his companion asked. The bushie lord continued to twist his heavy ring nervously and had refused several times to part with it, no matter the bribe.

"I see a way for the Guild of Bay Pilots to transport troops into the heart of the city."

"We've tried that. The pilots aren't bribable."

"But they owe me greatly for the depth finding machine." Kinnsell had discarded the Varn costume. His followers needed to know his identity now that he openly worked to establish a power base. Starting with Lord Balthazaan who deeply resented Quinnault and his fakir friend Nimbulan.

"And I owe you for ore finders and rock cutters. What do the others owe you?"

"Five lords in your league of rebellion will discover every one of their ewes will bear twins or triplets that are bigger, healthier, and have longer wool than any beast they've seen before."

"The ones you could persuade to accept your demon magic. If word gets out how those lords became so rich in sheep, no one will buy anything from them. And it will be another full year before the promised wool is available."

"The hybrid wheat will pay off by the middle of Summer." Kinnsell suppressed a cough. Talking dried his throat out. He wasn't used to all this cold raw air. He edged his hand forward.

"If the weather holds, the wheat harvest might be better than average. If the soil hasn't been depleted by overplanting. If the dragons don't burn our fields to dust because we gave you more of the Tambootie than King Quinnault authorized."

"Don't tell me you are so stupid you believe in the dragon myths!" Kinnsell shouted, pushing his hand farther forward. "What is it about this place that makes you all believe that simple psi powers are major magic and that dragons are real? Every contact we have put in Coronnan has forsaken our civilization and gone bush. Even my daughter. And she's supposed to be educated."

"You have obviously never come face-to-face with a dragon or one of the magicians who control them." The bushie lord made the curious flapping gesture with crossed wrists as he looked up. Was he truly scanning the heavens for sight of a dragon?

"None of your magicians will break down my shields and force a dragon illusion on me. I'll prove that the magicians are frauds. Then you won't have to put up with them. You can rely on your own intelligence and my machines." Kinnsell's hand came back to rest easily at his side.

"The lords will follow you if you manage to end the tyranny of the magicians and the dragons. We don't like them any better than you do. But the lords I speak for need proof of your powers before they commit to your cause."

A hot, angry flush burned Kinnsell's cheeks and brow. He was getting very tired of these bushie lords making demands on *him*.

"I set up one of your agents to start the riot that nearly ended all of the foreign treaties. I have given you times and locations and ambush plans for the loads of supplies going to the provinces. You have in turn sold the food on the black market at a tremendous profit. I presume last week's shipment is already on its way to the location of your choice. We can't allow Quinnault to deliver the current load either. Common people all over this hellhole begin to question Quinnault's ability to govern. His only support lies among the city's populace."

"He leads the new shipment with more guards than my soldiers can handle. He'll be seen as the great deliverer."

"Not if I give you a reason to call him and half his troops back before he travels half a day from the capital. The king shall fail in this mission as he has in every other."

"What reason? It will have to be compelling to bring the king back."

"I'll think of something." Like kidnapping Princess Marilell. As the baby's grandfather, he had the right to keep her every other weekend by Terran law. But he wouldn't bother to inform Katie of his plans.

"The lords want action now. They'll need proof of your powers and your sincerity to wait any longer to overthrow Quinnault."

"Like what?" Kinnsell braced himself for the next demand for tools and technology. If he kept this up, he wouldn't have enough left of his ship to fly back to civilization—which couldn't come too soon. He'd hoped to withhold a butane torch hot enough to burn the impurities out of the local sands so they could make decent glass until he'd run out of all other options. Was this the time to offer it?

The sky started to leak an annoying drizzle.

He'd be warm again as soon as he reached civilization. Warm and dry. Maybe then he'd stop coughing.

"The magicians keep a Rover woman prisoner in their University." The bushie lord eyed Kinnsell from beneath heavy black brows. Plots cooked deep within those eyes. Kinnsell wished he could read them.

THE RENEGADE DRAGON 99

"Free the Rover woman, and we will believe your technology is more powerful than magic." *Technology we can use to control you as well as the magicians and the king.*

Kinnsell couldn't help but overhear the man's thoughts. He smiled to himself. Not often did these locals let their natural shields slip. But when they did, he learned a lot.

Best he not let them know his own psi powers were strong and growing stronger.

Something about this planet . . .

"Very well. I will remove the woman from the University tomorrow after I have reconnoitered. Then I will show your craftsmen how to make a spinning wheel to handle all of the wool your new sheep will produce next Spring."

"A Wheel!" the lord touched his head, heart, and each shoulder in the approved cross of the Stargods.

At least Kinnsell's ancestors had gotten something right in teaching these yokels the gesture of protection and prayer.

Then the lord crossed his wrists, left over right and flapped his hands in another ward against evil.

"The Stargods have forbidden the Wheel as well as reading and higher mathematics for all but magicians. Those two things are the keys to all evil." The lord backed away from Kinnsell, repeating the flapping gesture. When ten meters separated them, he turned and ran into the thick trees as fast as his fat legs and long robe allowed.

"Damn!" Kinnsell slammed his fist into the trunk of a tree. "Now I have to start all over again. Unless. . . ."

* * *

Ancient plateau of Hanassa, time unknown

Powwell ran into the dragongate. He banged his forehead against a wall of resistance. Hard. Stars burst behind his eyes. The alluring song of the gate rang in his ears with discordant notes, repulsing him rather than drawing him in.

Yaala had entered the vortex of time and distance while facing him. Her passage must have triggered something, blocking this angle.

He darted around the shadows and approached the swirling distortion from the other side. His eyes tried to follow the shifting landscape within the gate. He lost his focus, and his head swam. The Kardia shifted beneath his feet once more, and he fell headlong into the pulsing spiral of blood red, fire green, and midnight black.

Thorny hunched within Powwell's pocket. The hedgehog's spines jabbed through Powwell's shirt. Thorny's blast of emotional upset followed the sharp pricks. First a plunge from the familiar landscape into the horrible desert. No water. Too much light. Uncertainty. Fear. Now this horrible pulsing energy again.

Thorny was not happy.

Powwell wasn't happy either. He had to find Yaala. Everything else in his life lost importance. He had to stay with Yaala.

Only this opening of the dragongate could lead him to Yaala or Kalen. He didn't know how to find Kalen without Yaala. He couldn't think beyond staying beside Yaala.

He prayed to the Stargods and whatever other forces might hear him that she hadn't triggered the gate too soon and ended up in the void without an anchor.

The colors grew more intense, stabbing into his eyes. Powwell clenched them shut. The pain lessened a little. He concentrated on refinding his planetary orientation, hoping to understand how the dragongate worked. Or where it was taking him.

Energy pulsed around him. He tumbled with it, losing all sense of up and down, right and left. Time and distance became meaningless. He had no idea where or when he traveled, only that he traversed a great distance.

Numbness filled his mind.

The dragongate held him seemingly forever.

Was that a moment of sleep?

He became aware of his body. No longer tumbling. Energy flowing around and with him, heat and light soothed the aches in his joints. And then . . .

And then there was green. Lots and lots of green. He lay in it. Breathed its moisture. Luxuriated in the comfort of being home.

Home! Yes he was home, in Coronnan. The South Pole tugged at his feet, watery sunshine broke through the cloud cover. Sunset was still hours away.

But where was Yaala?

THE RENEGADE DRAGON

He looked around carefully, moving as little as possible. The rocky overhang looked the same as when they'd left it. Hours ago? Days ago?

No, the season hadn't changed by more than a few hours. Early Spring. The dark of the moon tonight. Not quite noon now. The rain shower dissipated quite rapidly as sunshine broke through the clouds. The rain had just begun when they entered the dragongate for the first time at dawn.

So where was Yaala?

Strident voices pierced his ears. Angry men off to his left.

They probably walked the road that ran from Myrilandel's village over the pass into the Southern Mountains. It passed near Hanassa on its way to the desert kingdom of Rossemeyer.

Powwell listened closely.

Men shouted in a language he hadn't heard since before leaving Hanassa. Rovers! Stargods, he had to get out of here.

He heard a heavy sledge scraping the packed dirt of the road.

Powwell opened his senses with magic, striving to understand what was going on. He hoped Yaala wasn't the center of that argument. It sounded as if the men might come to blows in a moment.

"*S'murghin'* four-legged dimwit. Get over here!" a man shouted.

A steed screamed and stamped the ground.

Powwell heard the clang of iron shoes striking rock on the rough road. Not a Rover steed. Rovers didn't shoe their beasts.

A whip cracked. The steed roared in pain. Powwell felt the terror of the high-strung animal. Leather snapped and hooves pounded the road, disappearing in the opposite direction.

"Piedro's going to kill us now. He really wanted that steed," a second man said.

"The Kaaliph refuses to believe steeds are too smart to use the dragongate," the first man muttered.

The import of the words broke through Powwell's mind. Piedro must have taken the title of Kaaliph after all the other contenders had died.

The brief triumph Powwell had felt when he watched Yaassima and her pet Bloodmage murder each other faded to disgust. Hanassa had merely traded one ruthless leader for another.

Piedro now ruled the city; Piedro, the cruel one who had delighted in slamming his fists into Powwell's gut when he kidnapped him along with Kalen and Myrilandel a year and a half ago.

"We have to get these supplies through today. The gate won't open a true path again for another moon," the first man said with a grunt. "Let's move these sledges now. Lord Balthazaan is going to be right on our heels when he discovers how much we've stolen from him. When he hired us, he told us to leave most of this for him to sell on the black market."

"We left the lord extra jewels from Piedro's hoard. The lord can get more supplies from the king. We can't get anything but what we can carry through the dragongate until Rollett digs open the tunnel," the second man grunted as if hauling something very heavy.

"Well, you better hope Magician Rollett never gets the tunnel gate open, or we're out of a job."

"If Piedro wants the tunnel kept closed so he can play benevolent ruler by doling out food at starvation rations, why don't he just execute Rollett as a troublemaker?"

"Because the consort doesn't want Rollett dead yet. And what the consort wants, Piedro orders. Now move it. The dragongate opens in about two hundred heartbeats."

Powwell had to hide. He couldn't let these Rovers catch him at the entrance to the dragongate. But if he went too far, he'd lose the chance to get to Hanassa for another moon.

But where was Yaala? He couldn't go to Hanassa without her.

A light touch on his shoulder jerked him out of his confusing mind loop. Yaala stood over him, a finger to her lips for silence. She motioned for him to follow her.

Powwell scrambled to his feet. He resisted the urge to hug her. They hadn't time to indulge in emotional displays. He followed Yaala behind the outcrop of rock she favored just as the Rovers entered the opening in the trees.

We have to follow them, Powwell sent to his companion.

Yaala shook her head. She had no magic, so she couldn't talk to him mind to mind.

Yes. The gate won't open for another moon.

"Too dangerous," she mouthed. "Rovers."

I know. But if we are very quiet and step through the gate behind them, they won't look back. They never do. We can hide in the tunnels once we get through.

Yaala shook her head again. Tears of disappointment touched the corners of her eyes. She wiped them clear, then straightened her shoulders in determination. One quick jerk of her chin showed her willingness to risk following Powwell.

We're in this together.

"You're in this with me!" the first Rover said, grabbing Powwell by the back of his collar. "Did you forget, boy, that all Rovers have magic? I heard every word you thought. Piedro's gonna like the present we bring him. New victims to execute for his consort. That lady never gets enough blood. She's worse than Yaassima."

CHAPTER 11

Near the Southern Pass between Coronnan and Rossemeyer

"I won't be a Rover slave again!" Powwell screamed.

This time he would return to Hanassa of his own free will and in command of his actions, not the victim of kidnap. He'd rescue Kalen this time or die trying. But he'd never be a slave again.

He slammed his staff into the gut of the man who seemed to be in command of the raiding party.

The Rover countered by grabbing the twisted staff with both hands.

Powwell wrenched it away. His balance shifted back. He stumbled over Yaala. She thrust her hands against his back, pushing him onto the balls of his feet. He swung the staff end for end, clipping the second Rover in the jaw.

Thorny gibbered inside Powwell's pocket, afraid of Powwell's violent reaction. Powwell absorbed the pain from the tips of the hedgehog's sharp spines pricking his skin through his shirt and continued circling with his staff. Thorny wanted to be away from here. Powwell did, too. For different reasons.

Powwell maneuvered his opponent around until the Rover's back was to the overhang and he himself was in the open. The dragongate, when it opened, should be no more than two paces away.

Thorny didn't like that idea at all and hunched. His spines withdrew, then bristled with deeper penetration. Powwell renewed his attack on the Rover with sharpened senses and strength.

A third man and a fourth appeared in the forest opening from the direction of the road.

Yaala flung dirt in their eyes. She swung her pack in a broad circle, catching the first one alongside his temple. He teetered into the men behind, toppling them all.

The Rover leader still menaced Powwell with a knife. Powwell circled the staff one more time and brought it down atop the man's wrist. Wood cracked. Bone snapped. The man howled in pain and dropped his weapon.

"Hurry, Powwell, the dragongate opens," Yaala ducked the man with a bright red weal on his temple. She slid from behind the overhang into the arched shadow.

"Which scene?" Powwell didn't take his eyes off the Rovers. Two of the newcomers staggered upright with clubs and knives at the ready.

"The right scene. The right time," Yaala called back.

Powwell dove after her into the vortex of power that warped distance in an eye blink. He had to trust that Yaala was right this time. All of his instincts screamed to wait and view the other end of the portal himself.

He had to trust Yaala when he hated to trust anyone but himself and Thorny.

* * *

The pit beneath the city of Hanassa

Yaala hit the once-familiar ground running. Her balance reeled in the sudden blackness of the lava tube tunnel. A wall of air heated by the lava core greeted her, nearly searing her lungs. She could barely breathe. Walls pressed against her from all sides, much smaller than she remembered. She needed to clutch the jagged walls for support. She didn't dare. Powwell needed room to pass through the portal directly behind her. Could he use his magic to stop the Rovers from following?

What could she do to help her friend? Not much without tools.

Running footsteps behind her. Powwell. *Stargods, please let it be Powwell.*

The tunnel had changed shape after the kardiaquake. Last time she had been through here, a person could turn around in the narrow confines. Now the walls seemed to grab and block her with every pace. Powwell would have trouble breathing in here. More trouble than usual when underground.

"Duck," she called back over her shoulder, hoping her friend wouldn't knock himself senseless on one of the protruding rocks. At least the tunnel was only ten paces long. It used to be thirty. Or was it a different tunnel? If the dragongate had switched openings, that would explain the changes in its patterns.

A lighter blackness signaled the opening of the tunnel into a huge cavern.

Flickering remnants of yellow light told her that at least one of the generators continued to power the lighting system.

The hulk of Old Bertha, the largest of the machines that generated 'tricity, sat huge and silent within the vast cavern. She looked bigger in the shadowy light, without definite edges and ends. The generator filled nearly the entire cavern with blackened metal and broken conduits. The pipe connecting the machine to an underground lake lay in three broken pieces. Steam erupted from the first open end where the pipe passed above the lava core of the volcano. Upon meeting the comparatively cooler air of the labyrinth, the steam spread out and condensed into water. A new lake formed beneath the pipe, rusting the other sections. Water dripped from every surface, compounding the accumulated rust on Old Bertha.

After only a year and a half, the damage looked beyond repair.

She didn't have time to grieve over the loss of the machine. She needed a tool, a weapon. Powwell had rammed two magician's staffs into the guts of Old Bertha to create a diversion when they escaped from here. The machine was now dead. The staffs served no other purpose now. She grabbed the exposed end of the one that had belonged to Nimbulan, instinctively trusting the tool used and shaped by the honorable old man over the one carried by Scarface.

The seven-foot shaft resisted her tugs. Clumps of rust broke free from the machine around the opening. She pulled again with a downward twist. The wood snapped. She fell backward into a small pool of warm water as four feet of the staff broke free of the machine's grip.

A momentary pang of regret at the destruction of Nimbulan's staff touched her throat. Then she remembered he wouldn't be needing it again. He'd lost his magic in defense of Coronnan. But she needed a weapon. She scrambled to her feet, holding the staff horizontally in front of her.

Powwell erupted from the tunnel mouth and whirled to face whoever might follow.

One Rover pelted through the tight tunnel, screaming his rage. He held his club tight against his chest. The narrow walls and low ceilings hampered his movements.

Powwell drove his own staff straight into the man's eyes. The Rover ducked below the staff, coming up with club extended. Powwell jumped aside. The Rover kept running forward.

Yaala tripped him with the broken staff. He landed facedown in the spreading lake of hot water beneath the broken pipe. Much hotter than the isolated pool she had fallen into. He yelped and rolled to the side, keeping his face free of the steaming liquid.

Mist formed around the splashes. A cold mist. Everything else within the pit was hot. Stifling.

The mist grew, nearly solidified into a human form, but a veiled form without distinct features.

"The wraith!" Yaala said out loud. Chills ran up and down her spine. The fine hairs on her arms and the back of her neck stood on end in atavistic fear.

"With my head and heart and the strength of my shoulders, I renounce this evil." The Rover crossed himself repeatedly, scooting away from the apparition.

A ghostly white arm reached toward Powwell. Entreating. Lonely. Desperate for . . . something.

The Rover reacted first, running back into the tunnel.

He leaped through the dragongate as the inviting green of Coronnan swirled into the wild spiral of closure.

Powwell and Yaala followed their enemy, skidding to a halt on the crumbling ledge overlooking the flaring molten rock of the pit. They looked back over their shoulders.

The wraith approached slowly, still holding out a skeletal arm. The ghostly mist filled the narrow tunnel. Their only escape lay a thousand feet below in the boiling lava.

CHAPTER 12

The pit beneath the city of Hanassa

Shooting flames of boiling rock lulled Powwell into a kind of trance. He needed to step off the ledge, just one step and he would. . . . He deliberately pushed away the allure

(Follow me. Find your destiny in me.) It sang to him like the haunting temptation of the void.

He closed his mind to the temptation and turned away.

The misty wraith stopped its pursuit the moment he turned to face it. But it still held out a ghostly arm entreatingly.

The mist flowed in the small currents and eddies of air around the humanlike figure at the center. The tendrils shaped into the suggestion of a long tail wrapped around the "feet" of the wraith. Other bits and pieces of opaque vapor suggested wings and spines, minus the distinctive single horn sprouting from the forehead like Shayla and her nimbus of dragons.

Powwell dismissed the dragon features and concentrated on the human body within. Yaassima had coveted draconic features. Yaala had inherited a few, like the prominent spinal bumps of vestigial spines, and an extra eyelid. Myrilandel, Shayla's daughter in human form, had the near colorless skin, hair, and eyes of a dragon. None of these women came close to a real dragon in awesome size and power. Nor did the wraith.

Yaala edged closer to him, away from the spectral being. He wrapped his arm around her waist, holding her close to his side. Whatever the wraith did to them, they'd face it together.

He took one step forward. The only way out. The wraith retreated one step as well.

Powwell tucked Yaala behind him, keeping her hand in

his. The tunnel didn't offer enough room for them to walk side by side. She squeezed his hand in silent reassurance. He took another step forward and another.

The wraith flowed backward at an equal pace. The edges of the mist took on a darker hue. Hints of rosy purple? Powwell sensed alarm growing within the bizarre figure.

When they reached the big cavern, where the derelict machine sat like a monstrous spider presiding over the web of tunnels, he breathed a little easier. The wraith hadn't harmed him yet. It seemed almost afraid of him. Or for him?

In the distance he felt more than heard one small machine chugging away. That would explain the dim light. Little Liise, a docile generator who rarely broke down, worked at that particular rhythm. She supplied power to the lights down in the pit and nowhere else. The rest of Hanassa would be in darkness except for natural torches, candles, and oil lamps. Piedro, Kaaliph of Hanassa, wouldn't have enough 'tricity to mimic magic as Yaassima had.

"What do you want of us?" he asked the wraith quietly. His words echoed in the nearly silent cavern. They seemed strangely empty without the machines' constant *yeek kush kush* sounds.

The wraith twisted in upon itself. It raised both thin arms. The vague form suggested that it held its palms up, begging. The tail and wing illusions shrank. Was it writhing in pain? More like indecision or frustration.

"Do you need our help?" Yaala asked, slipping up beside Powwell. She kept her hand in his. The moisture on her palm told him how nervous she was. She should be comfortable here in this labyrinth of tunnels, the only home she had ever really known.

The wraith covered its face with ghostly hands and drifted apart, as mist before sunlight.

"What do you suppose she wanted?" Powwell breathed a sigh of relief.

"She?"

"I guess. I had the suggestion of a female beneath all that haze. I don't know why." He shrugged, not knowing how to examine the feminine feel of the wraith's pleading. He didn't mention the dragon illusion. Most likely it was just that, an illusion meant to trigger a response of respect and awe.

"Let's get out of here." Yaala tugged at his hand.

Powwell followed her slowly, oddly reluctant to leave the wraith that had once haunted him. He never thought he'd be hesitant to depart the inner chambers of the pit and the slavery he'd known here. Suddenly, he became aware of the miles of kardia pressing down upon him.

His breathing became shallow and labored. He needed air. He needed sunshine. He needed OUT! *Stargods, I hope the gate to the palace is open and unguarded.*

Satiric laughter echoed in his mind. A flicker of white tantalized his peripheral vision. Did the wraith taunt him with foreknowledge of the lack of exits?

* * *

Midafternoon, queen's solar, Palace Reveta Tristile, Coronnan City

"Random matings, solely for the sake of conceiving children are no longer appropriate for Spring Festival," Katie stated firmly to the five ladies gathered in her private solar.

"But, your Grace, Spring Festival has always been a time of betrothal. How are our young people to find the right mate if not in the rituals designed by the Stargods?" Lady Balthazaan turned pale with shock.

Katie doubted her Terran ancestors had contrived the ritual dance around a maypole—Festival Pylons they called them here—where the men danced in one direction and the women opposite, changing partners on the whim of the patterns called by village elders. Whichever partner one ended the dance with was their mate for the evening. If that one night together resulted in a child, then the union was blessed by the Stargods and the couple married on or before the Solstice. If no child was conceived, then the couple parted and tried again the next year.

Some of her ancestors probably sanctioned, maybe even participated in the dance. Few of them would have had the imagination to create it.

"The selection of a life mate is too important to leave to young people," Lady Hanic added. Like her husband, she always waited to see what others thought, then formed her opinion to match that of the strongest faction. "Such decisions are best determined by the Stargods."

The remaining three women nodded their heads in vigorous agreement.

"Did you participate in a Festival dance?" Katie asked all of the women.

"Of course not!" Lady Balthazaan gasped. She held her hand to her throat in dismay. "My marriage was a political union. The negotiations between our fathers went on for years."

"I would think a union that important should be left to the Stargods as well," Katie replied quietly, head down.

She played with her needlework a moment to keep her hands busy. All she ever did with her sewing was play and pretend she accomplished something. She'd never learned the fine art before coming to Coronnan. However, her afternoon gatherings with the ladies of the court seemed to demand she join them in the skill.

No one in the room spoke. Katie peeked to see the five women exchanging horrified glances, shaking their heads and biting their lips.

"Spring Festival is a good time to announce betrothals." Katie decided to partially agree with the women. "The dance is even a good way to introduce couples and to celebrate the joy of Spring. But children deserve a stable, loving family with parents who choose to be together rather than those who come together randomly. I do not want Festival in the capital city to degrade into an orgy."

"Our retainers will be most disappointed, Your Grace," Lady Nunio interjected.

"I'm certain young men and women who want to experiment with sex will find a way to do so. But let it be discreet and private."

"What of the young men going off to war? Many do not return. Festival is their only chance to sire a child," Lady Hanic asserted.

Strange that she, of all those present, would present an argument. Like her husband, she usually waited to support whatever side of an argument seemed likely to win.

"We are at peace, Lady Hanic. With luck and diplomacy,

the men will not be marching off to war any time soon." Or did she know something Katie didn't?

"One of the reasons we have clung to Festival for so long is to replenish the unstable population due to generations of civil war," Lady Nunio said mildly. "We may have peace now, but we also have a disease running rampant that is killing as many as any major battle. But we lose women and children as well as men in their prime. We need a good Festival to bring hope back to the people."

Katie stilled in shock. She'd read reports of a few isolated cases of a disease felling many in a single village. A plague running rampant had never been mentioned. Who hid the information and why? Was it *the* plague?

"Your Grace!" Kaariin ran into the solar from the nursery. She wrung her hands in anxiety. Her face looked too pale. "Come quickly, Your Grace, the baby is sick."

Katie dropped her hopeless embroidery as she stood. "How?" she demanded, running toward the inner room.

"She coughs until her skin turns waxy and blue. I'm sorry, Your Grace. I've taken good care of her. I'm not responsible . . ." the girl babbled.

"Send a message for King Quinnault to return immediately." Katie dashed past her maid to her daughter's crib.

Sure enough, little Marilell coughed deeply again and again interspersed with whimpers of pain and bewilderment. Katie picked her up, patting her back in soothing circles. Too tired and weak to hold her head up, Marilell rested her head on her mother's shoulder and continued to cough.

CHAPTER 13

Midafternoon, royal nursery, Palace Reveta Tristile, Coronnan City

Katie looked carefully at her baby, searching for the cause of her illness. "Send for the king immediately, Kaariin," Katie commanded. The maid curtsied and ran down the corridor.

Marilell continued coughing, weaker now, gasping for breath between each spasm.

"Allow me, little sister," Jamie Patrick said emerging from the shadows behind the doorway. "I think I know what ails the child. My own Kevin did the same thing." He held out his arms for the baby.

Katie relinquished her daughter reluctantly. Only the deep love and trust between herself and her brother allowed her to part with her ailing child. He had a little more experience than she with two young children back home with his seldom seen and rarely acknowledged—by her father—wife.

"Thank the Stargods you're here. Is it . . . is it the plague?" she asked, almost afraid that if she voiced her deepest fears they would come true.

"Nothing quite so bizarre," her oldest brother replied. He sat on a nearby stool and draped the little princess over his knee.

Marilell screamed her distress.

"She gets enough air to protest whatever ails her," Nimbulan remarked from the doorway. He held his daughter, Amaranth, easily in the crook of his right arm while raising his left hand, palm outward, fingers slightly curved as if he still gathered magical information with the gesture.

Myrilandel stood beside him. "We were in the palace

and interrupted Kaariin on her errand." She marched to stand over Jamie Patrick and the baby.

Jamie Patrick rapped the baby smartly on the back with the flat of his hand. Marilell gasped and choked, spitting up a thin line of fluid. Another rap brought a whoosh of air from the baby's mouth along with a small metal object that rolled across the floor to land at Katie's feet.

"Lucky for all of us Kaariin noticed her distress so quickly. Much longer and the ring could have pushed farther down her throat and torn delicate tissues or choked her completely," Myrilandel commented as she nodded approval of the way Jamie Patrick rubbed the baby's back.

Katie stooped to pick up a man's ring lying at her feet. Intricately twisted silver strands distinguished it from an ordinary signet ring favored by the men of the court.

"I remember Amaranth trying to swallow a very large chunk of raw yampion when she was that age," Myrilandel said as she relieved Jamie Patrick of his sobbing burden. She cuddled the baby against her shoulder, cooing soothingly to the little princess before handing her over to her mother.

"Thank the Stargods you knew what to do, Jamie Patrick." Katie accepted the precious bundle of sobbing child. She held her daughter tightly against her shoulder as she introduced her friends to her brother.

"Sorry, I can't stay, Sis. Kinnsell doesn't know I'm here and doesn't want me to contact you, but I had to say 'Hi,' one more time before we leave." Jamie Patrick bent slightly to kiss her cheek. Like most Terran men, he stood only half a head taller than Katie, and much shorter than most of the natives of this planet.

"Be careful, Jamie Patrick. Kinnsell is up to something." Katie caressed his lightly bearded cheek. He had sported a dapper little beard since he could grow one, convinced it added maturity and intrigue to his narrow face. His hair was more blond than red, and he'd said he felt washed out in comparison to the rest of the family.

"We'll be in touch, Katie. I wish we could drag Kinnsell out of here now, but our mission isn't complete."

"What mission?"

But he was gone, as quickly as he had come.

"What do we have here?" Nimbulan removed the slobber-covered ring from Katie's grasp. "Unusual design. I have seen something like it before." His graying eyebrows dipped into a sharp V as he frowned in concentration.

Myrilandel studied the entwined strands carefully.

"It looks Rover," she mused. "What do you think, Lan? You lived with Televarn's tribe an entire season."

"Possibly of Rover design. They do very distinctive work. But the memory that tugs at me is older. Much older." He shook his head sharply. "I'll remember at the least likely moment. Forcing the image into my mind won't help."

"Rover?" Katie gulped. "I've heard that the Rovers sometimes steal children. A . . . a kidnapper could have dropped the ring if disturbed in the act." The same legend of stolen children followed Gypsies and Tinkers back home—usually more myth born out of fear of strangers than from any basis in truth. Were the local version of those wanderers guilty of a heinous crime or victims of malicious gossip? She didn't know.

At the beginning of the riot last Autumn, the man in the orange shirt had accused his neighbor of having Rover blood. But Orange-shirt's gaudy clothing more closely resembled Rover preferences than his victim's sober tans and browns.

What was going on here? Was there a connection between the riot and a stranger leaving a potentially lethal object in Marilell's crib, a simple piece of jewelry a teething baby would likely swallow and choke to death on?

"There's been no filthy Rovers in my nursery!" Kaariin protested from the doorway, wringing her hands. "I'd never leave my princess long enough for one of them to sneak in here." She stood straight, fists clenched proudly at her sides.

"No one is accusing you of negligence, child," Nimbulan said soothingly. "A true Rover needs only a heartbeat of time to work mischief."

"Who would do this, Nimbulan? Who would sneak past numerous guards and servants to try to steal my baby?" Katie hugged her daughter closer. Marilell squeaked in protest.

"Someone who wants to hurt you and Quinnault very much. Someone who seeks to control Coronnan by controlling you."

"Kinnsell collects odd bits of unusual jewelry. This is just the sort of thing that would appeal to him. He is also the one man no servant or guard would detain near the royal apartments," Katie whispered.

She had to warn Jamie Patrick. He had to take their father away now, not later, not when their mysterious mission had been completed. Now.

* * *

Late afternoon, on a royal passenger barge in the center of the Great Bay

A fragrant Spring breeze drifted from the mainland toward the passenger barge traversing the Great Bay. Journeyman Magician Bessel inhaled deeply of the clean air colored with salt and new lilies. He stood on the top deck with five ambassadors and their ladies. Below and ahead of them a dozen oarsmen pulled the vessel toward shore by brute strength, helped only a little by a tide nearing its lowest ebb.

Master Scarface had assured Bessel that the deaths in his parents' village were isolated. Lord Balthazaan's greed and mismanagement had left his miners ill nourished. The storms and privations of Winter had weakened the common people, leaving them vulnerable to all manner of diseases. No true plague ravaged Coronnan. Nor would it now that the books with references to technology had been isolated.

The Commune, meaning Scarface, was in control.

The disease that killed his mother couldn't have been the plague. He prayed it wasn't.

The flower-laden air replaced the stink of the plague in Bessel's memory.

Yet the scent, a mere hint of Powwell's telepathic rendition of the dragon dream, but very prevalent at Mama's deathbed, continued to haunt him.

Every time Bessel voiced a doubt, Scarface reminded him that he need not concern himself with plagues and such. His duty to the Commune required he complete his diplomatic training, hence his presence on this barge.

But he still hadn't revealed the hiding place of the little book he'd been reading just before Scarface rearranged the library. A new iron gate with only one key and a personalized magical seal blocked off the now forbidden books. But the book with intriguing references to blood magic was safe in Bessel's room, hidden beneath a loose floor tile.

Scarface had been most generous in reassuring Bessel after the incident in the library. Bessel had expected punishment. Instead, Scarface had assigned him to this luxury barge. As ordered, Bessel listened to and observed five diplomats and their ladies while they toured the new port city at the edge of the deep water in the bay. For an entire day, Bessel had maintained a light trance so that his mind could understand the conversations conducted in five different languages, even if he couldn't understand the words themselves.

Fatigue dragged his shoulders nearly to his elbows and his eyelids drooped heavily. His stomach growled often. Soon he'd be back at the University where he could sleep and eat and then report to Scarface all that had transpired today.

The depth-finding machine at the center of the barge beeped quietly. One little beep every ten heartbeats. Bessel paused in his savoring of the warm breeze to examine the machine with all his senses. The steady beep told him that no hidden submerged obstacles or suddenly changing channels within the mudflats threatened the barge. But what other threats did the machine disguise? How could the Commune be sure the machine did not emit unseen plagues, much as dragons emitted unseen magic?

He wished the Guild of Bay Pilots was not dependent upon the machine to negotiate the mudflats between the port islands and Coronnan City.

But when King Kinnsell of Terrania had magically constructed the port city out of four natural islands as part of the queen's dowry, he had built jetties that changed the pattern of shifting channels within the mudflats of the inner Great Bay. The port city kept cargo vessels, passenger ships, and invading fleets safely in the depths of the outer bay. The Guild of Bay Pilots had the responsibility of ferrying legal cargo and passengers into Coronnan City. They had no way of learning the changes in the channels fast enough to fulfill that responsibility other than with the depth finder.

Queen Maarie Kaathliin would see to it that no other machines were introduced to this planet by her father. But what about this one?

Maybe Scarface had been right to ban certain books. If anyone understood precisely how the depth finder worked, they could duplicate it, adapt it to other uses. . . .

Bessel took a few moments to draw the warm sunshine on his back deep into his bones. In a few moments, when he could master his bouncing stomach, he'd look at the sparkling light on the shifting waters rather than the mysterious machine. The muck of the mudflats might be only a few fathoms below the water here, but the constantly changing waves disguised the depths. He had no focus to anchor his stomach or his magic. The staff in his hand was useless without that focus.

He put up with his queasy stomach and listened to the prattling of the ambassadors and ladies who shared the barge with him. Understanding would be so much easier if he just eavesdropped on their thoughts. But Nimbulan had drilled into him respect for the privacy of others.

Bessel hadn't even invaded his mother's mind to catch her dying wishes. He wished he had. He hadn't felt her love for many years, and he missed her more than he thought possible.

His stomach lurched with a new shift of the currents and tide. Power simmered within the Kardia beneath the waves, begging him to tap it and calm his innards. The power could show him how the depth finder worked. He refused the invitation to rogue magic.

If he had refrained from tapping rogue magic to help his mother, he certainly wouldn't do it to make himself more comfortable.

From the look on the face of the new ambassador from Jihab, he didn't like the rising and lowering of the deck with each new wave any better than Bessel did. The portly man, who had made several fortunes as a jewel trader before turning to politics, blanched and clamped his teeth together. His normally ruddy skin took on the ghastly pallor of green akin to light-shy fungi in the back of a sea cave.

Bessel liked the jovial jeweler. The other four ambassadors, their ladies, and aides on the barge were all too aware of their own self-importance to pay him any attention. But

Heinriiche Smeetsch had greeted Bessel politely and seemed genuinely interested in his studies to become a master magician. Bessel had even confided his secret wish to succeed Master Lyman as librarian.

He could think of no better way to protect the banned books and the knowledge they contained. *S'murghit,* how could Scarface be so sure the disease that felled Lord Balthazaan's province wasn't a plague that needed more than fresh supplies to cure it?

The beeping black box beside the pilot's chair at the exact center of the barge increased the frequency and intensity of its signal. Bessel sensed no change in the mudflats. But dragon magic was Air Based and didn't lend itself to Water-oriented spells. The Kardia-based rogue magic would be able to delve into the mysteries of the bay.

Kardia and Water were teamed as were Air and Fire.

Raanald, the representative from the Guild of Bay Pilots, kicked his arcane machine. "*S'murghit,* I know these waters. There was nothing in this region yesterday to hinder our passage. We should be well beyond the bar. Two degrees starboard," he called to his helmsman. "*S'murghin* machine. Why is it telling me to avoid a clear passage?"

Raanald brushed the folds of his gaudy maroon-and-gold uniform sleeve into a straight line, very aware of his elite calling. He knew the waters better than the machine did.

Or so his attitude indicated. If he knew the waters better than the machine, why risk having the machine at all?

"What does that beeping mean?" Bessel asked.

"The machine does not concern you, Magician." Raanald spat the last word as if it fouled his mouth.

Distrust of the man and the machine rose in Bessel. Maybe that was just his stomach protesting the constant and uneven movement of the barge.

A wave lifted the shallow-bottomed vessel several feet, then dropped it into the trough. Ambassador Smeetsch spun in place, heaving his luncheon over the side.

Ambassador Jorghe-Rosse from Rossemeyer slapped his Jihabian counterpart heartily on the back, making a joke of his squeamishness.

Bessel might have laughed if his own meal rested more easily. Or if the depth-finding machine would stop beeping. It seemed to be getting louder and faster, warning of unseen submerged obstacles. The sandbar that ran parallel to the coastline changed dimensions every Spring as the River Coronnan dumped tons of silt into the bay. It changed again after every storm. Why was Raanald so certain they had navigated beyond it?

He edged closer to the black box, needing to read the arcane symbols and know what dangers it saw beneath the barge.

He ached to tap a ley line and let it fuel his magic senses. Then he'd know for certain what transpired.

No! Bessel reminded himself sternly. That would make him a rogue, an outcast, alone. He'd lose more than just his mother if he succumbed to the allure of rogue magic.

"Three degrees starboard," Raanald called again to the helmsman. Puzzlement creased his brow and clouded his eyes.

Another big wave caught the passenger vessel. The barge had been designed for negotiating very shallow water in calm weather and didn't have enough keel to stabilize it in rough seas.

"*S'murghin'* magicians, can't leave the weather alone!" Raanald glared hard at Bessel as he kicked the machine's black box housing.

The journeyman magician wanted to defend the Commune of Magicians, loudly and vehemently. The Commune didn't mess with the weather. They knew better than to upset the natural balances. The pilot was as ignorant and prejudiced as Bessel's father.

"Is there a problem, Master Pilot?" Ambassador Jorghe-Rosse asked. He stood nearest to Raanald among the passengers milling about the luxury barge.

"Storm coming in. One we didn't know about." The surly pilot looked at Bessel again, affronted. "It's upsetting the tide and wind predictions." One of the duties of the Commune was to keep the local boatmen accurately informed of weather forecasts and changes.

"Pop up storms are not uncommon in Spring and Autumn," Bessel said. "No one can predict them. They do not last long and tend to hit small areas, leaving the coast a few miles away dry and clear." Could the coming storm have changed something in the water to upset the machine?

"Will we reach the docks before this storm hits?" asked

the representative from Jihab. He looked over the side of the barge as if the little left in his stomach might want to join his luncheon.

"I've weathered a lot of these mage—Spring storms," Raanald lectured, covering his word slip with grand gestures. "Especially during the wars." He glared at Bessel as if he were personally responsible for the generations of civil war as well as every storm. "They're tricky. Might pass us altogether and only ruffle the water a little. Like now." He kicked the waist-high black cylinder of the depth finder again.

The machine settled back into its normal calm beep. One every ten heartbeats.

Bessel raised his eyes to the sky in search of some trace of a coming storm. The sky had darkened perceptibly with a complete cloud cover that thickened by the moment.

Dragon magic told him the weather patterns easily, when he had reason to pay attention. Pressure dropped in the air to the immediate East. A rapid change of temperature. Wind rising, driving the storm cell toward land. Right over the top of the barge.

"You gentlemen had best take a seat inside the pavilion." Raanald sniffed the air. His eyes opened wide in alarm. The machine started beeping again, erratically.

Bessel peered over the man's shoulder, eager to know for himself what dangers awaited them.

"Get out of my way, you *s'murghin'* meddler. Wouldn't have anything to worry about if you had kept your weather spells to yourself."

"I did nothing," Bessel finally said in his own defense. He'd had enough of keeping his mouth shut, though he knew his role as diplomatic observer required nothing more of him.

"Maybe not you, but your kind is always messing with the weather. Especially that scar-faced bastard." The pilot spat on the deck at Bessel's feet. "The Guild of Bay Pilots don't need you clogging up our channels and changing our tides. We got machines to take care of us. Royal machines Five degrees a port," he corrected his previous course changes back to their original path.

If the machine is so important, why don't you trust it? Bessel kept his thoughts to himself.

The ambassadors and their ladies took seats on the benches fixed to the deck beneath an awning. The rising wind sent the cloth shelter flapping. Bessel remained at Raanald's shoulder, observing the flashing red lights across the bubble face of the black box. At first he couldn't make sense of the constantly changing display. Then he picked out stylized numbers in red beside the carefully printed words in white against a black background. The words meant nothing to him. Yet.

The numbers decreased on the left and piled up on the right at an alarming rate.

"I said, sit down, Magician," Raanald shouted with curled lip. But the anxiety in his eyes as he looked back to the beeping black box kept Bessel rooted in place. "Hard a port!" Raanald shouted.

The rudder and pole men in the rear quarter of the barge struggled with their tools.

A wave caught them crosswise. The deck tilted sharply to the left. Bessel grabbed the machine housing to brace himself. His staff tangled with his feet. He crossed his ankles to keep his most essential tool within reach.

The dignitaries slid down their benches into the flimsy railing of the luxury barge. Hard wood cracked and splintered. Fine silk gowns and robes flew in the rising wind. Limbs tangled. Ladies screamed and men gasped.

"I said *hard* a port," Raanald screamed.

The rudder man shoved his tiller, hard. Wood snapped as the rudder grounded in the bar. The tiller moved freely, disconnected from the rudder.

The barge swung sideways and leveled. The awning whipped away from its supports, flying toward shore in the rising wind. Another wave slapped across the deck, drenching the tangled passengers. They screamed again. Ambassador Jorghe-Rosse muttered a curse in his desert warrior language.

Bessel didn't need to know the words to understand the meaning. He closed his eyes and concentrated, breathing deeply. At the first deepening of his trance, he sent his magic into the damaged rudder. The wooden mechanism resisted his control. He concentrated harder. His stomach growled with hunger. His legs and back ached from the strain. Sweat broke out on his brow, washed away by the spray of the next huge wave that roared toward shore from the open sea.

If only he could tap a ley line to fuel his magic, he could handle the storm, the rudder, and the passengers. He couldn't. He wouldn't. He had to rely on his weak dragon magic.

Help! he called telepathically to any magician who might hear him. *I need help saving these people.*

A long pause of nothing. Sweat streamed from his brow and down his back as he wrestled with several options. None of them acceptable. He ached for permission to tap the forces he knew could help him. He knew it would never come.

Whatever happens, don't let anything happen to Jorghe-Rosse, Master Scarface returned to him when Bessel thought the emptiness in his head would last forever. *Peace depends upon Rossemeyer's goodwill. They are looking for excuses to invade us again. You must save their ambassador at all costs!*

His master's authoritative tone calmed Bessel a little. Concentration came a little easier. He had to get the barge back under control and into the deeper channel.

The strident beeping of the black box interrupted his thoughts.

"Stay off the bar. *Hard* a port, you *s'murghin* swabbies. I said *HARD!*" Raanald dashed from his station by the precious machine to the rudder. "I knew there was a bar here, but the machine said it was ten yards to port!"

An onerous shudder passed through the barge followed by a jerking halt. The deck canted wildly to the left, upsetting the already disoriented and disgruntled dignitaries again. They landed in a heap against the damaged railing. More of the slender wooden staves that formed the decorative fence broke. Several pieces of wood fell into the churning bay, swirled in the obstacle's eddies, and sank.

Ambassador Jorghe-Rosse bent over his lady, protecting her with his body. The next wave sent him crashing through the decorative wood into the thrashing waves.

CHAPTER 14

Early evening, on the royal passenger barge in the Great Bay

Bessel cast aside his formal magician's robe and heavy boots as he dove after the ambassador. He kept his staff pointed ahead of him, channeling his senses along it for greater awareness.

All of his instincts told him to stay aboard and solve the problem with dragon magic. Nimbulan had taught him problem solving. But he knew he'd not be able to tap enough communal magic to dissipate the obstacle that held the barge, calm the waves, and rescue the ambassador.

A mundane rescue first. Then he'd worry about the other dangers. Thank the Stargods he could swim.

Cold water enfolded him, numbing his thoughts and turning his limbs to jelly. He scanned the turbulent water for any trace of the ambassador's black robe.

Nothing.

With all of those layers of clothing and hidden weapons common to the desert dwelling mercenaries of Rossemeyer, Jorghe-Rosse could easily get dragged to the bottom and stuck in the mudflats.

Bessel dove deep. He forced his eyes open despite the salt sting. Murky water obscured his vision. Crosscurrents assaulted his already heavy limbs. He pushed his concentration into strong strokes that took him toward the obstacle. His planetary orientation kicked in and he "knew" where the buildup of mud, sand, and drifted debris trapped the barge and snared the ambassador.

A year and a half ago, Nimbulan and King Quinnault had fended off an invasion fleet from Rossemeyer by filling the inner bay with felled trees and other obstacles. Now, the rotting remains of one of those defensive trees trapped the ambassador. The barge had grounded on the bar to the side of the snag.

Bessel's lungs burned for air. He'd been down too long.

He poked at the assorted tree limbs and mud with the staff. A long white arm appeared before his red-hazed vision. The currents flattened Jorghe-Rosse against the snag, pining him more effectively than a boulder. Bessel reached out with his hands and his magic. He grabbed hold of cold fingers and wrist with one hand, being careful to stay above the ambassador and the crushing current as he struck out for the surface. He had to abandon the staff, but he knew it would follow him eventually.

Pressure built in his chest. His legs didn't want to kick. The limp hand slipped from his grasp.

He didn't have the strength or air to go back. At last his head broke the surface of the water. Icy needles of rain pelted his face. He closed his eyes against the pain and gulped air. A second deep inhalation and a third.

Without thinking, he triggered a trance and he saw the ley lines glimmering against his inner vision. No dragon magic came to him to replace the enticing power.

Protect the ambassador at all costs. Master Scarface's words pounded into his mind again.

Damn the rules. Peace in Coronnan depends upon this man's safety. I've got to save him any way I can.

Bessel grabbed the power and let it enhance his lungs and heartbeat. Then he dove again. Muddy water, churned by the storm and his own movements, cleared before him. He saw the pattern of the current that pinned the ambassador's body. His staff had grounded in the bar nearby.

Bessel grabbed the staff and wedged it between Jorghe-Rosse and the tree trunk. At the precise moment the current eased the tiniest bit, he thrust all of his weight onto the staff, prying a gap between the snag and the ambassador.

With new strength and agility, and a touch of levitation, Bessel yanked Jorghe-Rosse free.

Suddenly, the magician sensed semi-awareness rippling through the drowning man. Like any drowning victim, Jorghe-Rosse fought the water, his rescuer, and his dimmed consciousness. He whipped his arms into a deadly rotation, seeking to strike whatever pinned him. His left fist connected with Bessel's jaw.

Starbursts exploded behind the magician's eyes. His grasp on the ambassador's wrist slipped. His contact with the ley line and his magic faded. He was lost in the murky, cold water without a sense of up and down.

Jorghe-Rosse gasped for air. But there was none.

Blackness crowded Bessel's vision. The cold numbed his body. He made one last desperate grab for the man he needed to save. His fingers tangled in cloth.

Enough. Aching in every joint, weakened by the blow to his jaw and loss of magic strength he struggled upward.

Finally, after what seemed like forever, he broke the surface. He wasted several moments just breathing. His lungs continued burning, protesting any movement.

Then Bessel struggled for the still trapped barge dragging Jorghe-Rosse behind him.

Anonymous hands reached to relieve him of the ambassador and then pulled Bessel aboard.

"Too late, *Magician*," Raanald sneered. "You drowned the ambassador. Now there'll be war with Rossemeyer. And you caused it."

* * *

The city of Hanassa, before midnight on the dark of the moon

Rollett paused in the shadows around one of the rock outcroppings that littered the caldera floor of the ancient volcano. Shacks and taverns surrounded each jumble of volcanic stone. From here he spied the palace entrance. Fifteen long paces separated him from the arched entrance within the cliff walls that rose from the city proper. The first Kaaliph had built his palace out of an existing cave system. The cool interior of the north wall made it the most desirable location within the natural walls of the city. Other important personages occupied other cave dwellings, like the Rover enclave. Most of the others had to settle for these makeshift dwellings against the massive boulders.

Darkness, darker than the dark night, filled the palace entrance. Yaassima had never allowed shadows anywhere near a vulnerable portal. She had ordered torches shifted every few minutes to illuminate different sectors and her guards firmly fixed in the doorway at all times. In the old days, an assassin or thief had no place to hide and no gaps to penetrate.

Piedro kept his torches stationary and his guards moving. He had Yaassima's ruthlessness but not her cunning. Rollett had discovered in the last year and a half that most Rovers rarely thought beyond "today." They loved the open road and met each day with joy at being alive, and each crisis as it came. Plans for "tomorrow" were useless because "tomorrow" might never come.

The Rovers trapped in Hanassa frequently indulged in violent brawls and self-inflicted wounds. The lack of open roads and a wandering way of life tore at their sanity.

Piedro exhibited the typical shortsightedness of his race. His capricious cruelty could be a sign of his growing loss of reason.

Rollett watched the seemingly random movements of the guards until he saw a pattern. Humans found comfort in routines. Hardened assassins, thieves, and terrorists imposed chaos but worked best within the limits of their own ordered regularity. Within a few moments Rollett knew when and how to walk through the front gate of the palace without challenge.

"One at a time, slide through the doorway on my command. Go all the way to the Justice Hall as quickly and quietly as you can. Don't wait for the rest of us until you get to the Justice Hall," he ordered the line of men hugging the wall behind him. "Now!" he pushed the first man forward.

One by one Rollett's raiders infiltrated the palace. Rollett feared that the prospect of fresh food might make them reckless. Fortunately, the caution bred into them by years of outlawry prevailed. In short order, Rollett was the only man left to enter.

He waited a few more heartbeats to make sure the guards' pattern of movements held true. The man on the left, the one who carried a spear, faltered.

Rollett stopped in mid-step. His balance teetered. As quietly as he could, he planted both feet on the ground and recovered just before he fell flat on his face.

The guard scratched his crotch, belched, and moved on.

But now the guard on the right had turned in his patrol and faced the doorway.

Rollett held his breath, willing the guards to resume their normal pattern. Two more passes and a gap in their vigilance appeared again. Rollett wrapped a shadow around himself and slipped through. He'd only had to use a minor magic trick to divert the guards.

Too easy. He'd made eleven raids on the palace stores. In every one, he'd had to fight for each morsel of food he gained.

The hair on the back of his neck stood up. All the senses available to him jumped to alert. He paused at the first alcove inside the gateway to listen.

Nothing. So far, no one followed. He proceeded toward the rendezvous, watching every flicker of torchlight for signs of a trap.

By the time he had wound his way to the Justice Hall, all his senses tingled with uneasy rawness. Something was wrong. This was too easy.

He paused outside the broad archway leading into the largest chamber in the palace complex, the temple to the winged demon Simurgh—the only one left in all of Kardia Hodos. Locals called it the Justice Hall now. Rollett hadn't observed much justice dispensed from here—only cruel punishments by Yaassima and then her successors.

He listened with his ears and his mind, pinpointing each of his men as they sneezed, shuffled their feet, or murmured a question. So far, none of Piedro's guards shared the huge hall. Where were they? Usually he had to dodge a dozen or more just to get this far.

Slowly he eased around the archway, keeping his shadow cloak close and solid. He'd pay for the magic trick later in hunger and exhaustion. Better to be tired and hungry than dead.

Stargods! He wanted to get home. Ending the Great Wars of Disruption and establishing the Commune of Magicians had been easier than trying to survive in Hanassa. Longing for Nimbulan and his friends in the Commune welled up in his throat, threatening to choke him.

He swallowed the emotion. Any emotion was dangerous

right now. He needed to maintain tight control of himself if he hoped to survive tonight.

Once inside the hall, he remained close to the wall. Only his eyes moved. He peered into every crevice, nook, and shadow.

The hideous stone altar, with its hand and foot manacles at each corner, rested flush with the floor now. Piedro didn't know how to make it rise from its sunken position. The secret had died with Yaassima. The new Kaaliph still executed people, but the bloodletting lacked the aura of a religious ritual without the altar.

If Piedro met an ignominious end in the near future, the worship of Simurgh might very well die with him.

The tapestry behind the dais to Rollett's left hung limp and tattered. Not enough of the peaceful alpine meadow with a waterfall scene remained to conceal an armed guard.

The room seemed empty except for Rollett's raiders.

He signaled quiet to the seven men as he stepped from the shadows. Keeping his back to the walls, he circled the room to the far side where a smaller door lay hidden behind another tapestry—this one portrayed an orgy in vivid and obscene detail.

All of his men waited for him to lead the way. Rollett paused and listened again. The interior corridor remained quiet and empty. He probed it with every mundane and magic sense available to him. But he didn't trust those senses tonight. They should have roused at least ten guards by this time. None of them patrolled their usual routes or slept in their usual hiding places.

Piedro had set a trap. Where?

If his men didn't need fresh food so desperately, he'd abandon the raid right here and now. By tomorrow night the new shipment would be moved somewhere more secure deep in the labyrinth of these caves. Rollett had yet to find that location. They had to steal the food tonight or not at all.

Rollett pointed to his eyes and ears, warning his men to be extra alert. Then he gestured for them to follow him silently.

The corridor sloped gently downward before curving to the right. Three smaller passageways opened on the left before they reached a major junction. The right-hand passageway sloped downward. The left continued straight ahead, level and wide open. From experience, they knew the easy path terminated in a dead end. He'd never explored to the right. The memory of the scent of fresh food drove him up the slope to the center.

Rollett's mouth began to salivate. He needed to run ahead and grab a handful of fruit and nuts. He could devour an entire ham by himself. Caution made him proceed slowly.

As he approached the last twist in the corridor, he held up his hand to halt the men. Once more he listened with every sense available to him. Quiet. Too quiet.

He waited through one hundred heartbeats. Still nothing. He listened for another one hundred heartbeats.

This time he heard what had been missing in the rest of the palace complex, the sound of soft uneven breathing. Several men waited just inside the open door of the storeroom.

Rollett held his breath. Did he dare go through with the raid? His stomach growled. They needed the food stored here.

But something more was wrong than just the presence of the guards lying in wait. The storeroom smelled wrong. It smelled empty of food.

The man just behind him shifted his posture forward. Rollett put out his hand to restrain him. Too late.

"Food!" The three men behind him broke into a howling run, clubs raised.

"Wait," Rollett ordered. They ignored him, too desperate to listen to anything.

He had no choice. He had to follow them into the trap, defend them any way he could. Staff raised, senses alert, he charged after his men. The remaining men in his gang unleashed daggers and boot knives as they, too, joined the fray.

Lights flashed inside the storeroom, blinding the raiders. Rollett resisted the urge to cover his eyes with his hands. He had other senses to compensate for the dazzle blindness. His men didn't have that advantage.

Even before his vision recovered, Rollett knew the battle was hopeless. He heard the screams of dying men as he blocked a sword slash with his staff. The metal bounced off the hardened and twisted wood.

Shadows took on substance before Rollett's eyes. He flipped his staff end for end, catching the attacking guard under the chin. The big man staggered back, flailing his arms.

Rollett's men didn't fare so well. He counted two down, bleeding heavily. The others were sorely pressed and outnumbered two to one.

"Retreat!" he called even as he swung his staff into the belly of a palace guard. "Retreat!"

Rollett followed his own order, backing out of the storeroom. Two guards pursued him closely.

Rollett spun and ran back down the curving corridor. He hated to leave his men. They'd have to fend for themselves. Those were the rules in Hanassa.

Loose sand on the floor turned slippery beneath his hurried footsteps. Rollett skidded into the junction. A wall of new guards blocked the main corridor back to the Justice Hall. He'd never break through them. Even with magic he'd be hard-pressed to battle them all.

And he had no more magic. His limited reserves had gone into shadows and concealment getting into the palace.

He increased his speed and his skid, turning the sharp corner into the unexplored downward slope.

Stargods! I hope this isn't another dead end.

Sweat rolled down Rollett's back. His limbs grew heavy. His lungs labored to draw in the hot air and his heart pounded loudly in his ears. Almost as loud as the heavy footsteps pounding the dirt floor behind him.

The slope increased. The walls became rougher, more like a natural cave, without evidence of being smoothed or enlarged by man-made tools.

His footing grew precarious on the light covering of fine sand. But so did the guards' behind him. A sharp turn appeared before him. He tried to slow his steps and slammed into the wall. The loose sand upset his balance and kept him stumbling forward. He lunged in the new direction, trying to control his momentum. His feet flew out in different directions. He landed heavily on his side.

As he measured his length along the corridor, he rammed his head against the crossed iron bars of a locked gate.

CHAPTER 15

The pit beneath the city of Hanassa, time unknown

"All the caverns lead back to Old Bertha," Powwell said as he kicked one of the rusted pipes strewn about the huge cave. They'd been wandering for hours. Days? He didn't know anymore. Their trips through the dragongate had disrupted his time perception. He needed to eat and sleep before he could restore all of his senses.

"The caverns have always led back here," Yaala replied. Her eyes took on a glazed look of enthrallment. She grabbed the broken pipe and lovingly began to scrape rust off of it with her belt knife. The blade quickly dulled, but she ignored it, completely absorbed in her task and the plight of her machines.

"No, Yaala. The tunnels and caverns all led to the rim of the pit. This cavern only has one or two accesses overlooking the lava core. There are dozens of others. How do we get to them?" Powwell checked the exit tunnel that also gave access to the dragongate. So far, it hadn't opened again while he watched. Something was terribly wrong. The opening and closing had always been random, but rarely more than one hundred to one thousand heartbeats apart.

"Well, we found the living cavern. It's empty of people, but full of food. We'll be all right for now." Yaala continued to clean the broken pipe, frequently comparing the open end with the other pieces.

"Wake up, Yaala. Think. We have to get out of here." He grabbed her shoulders and shook her. She dropped the sections of pipe. Hot water splashed them both.

"We can't do anything without the machines. Old Bertha needs me," she protested when he stopped shaking her.

"Hanassa needs you, Yaala. The city needs a strong

leader. The machines are nothing. They aren't power, they are tools."

She stared at him as if he were the most stupid being on Kardia Hodos.

"I need you, Yaala. I need you to help me find my little sister. I need your strength to keep me from lashing out and murdering everyone in your city until I find Kalen. *We* need to find Rollett and send him home to help Nimbulan. Now stop fussing with Old Bertha and help me find a way out of here."

She turned her head away not answering.

Powwell watched the access tunnel again for signs of the dragongate opening. But he maintained his grasp on her shoulders, needing the physical affirmation that they both still lived, still had quests to keep them going.

"There. That's two pieces together. I bet I can reconstruct the entire pipe. Then I'll clear the tube tunnels of debris and restring the wires to Liise. She doesn't give off much 'tricity, but I should be able to coax enough out of her to control some of the 'motes," Yaala said. "Perhaps we can use Liise to jump-start Old Bertha."

"What good are 'tricity and 'motes that mimic magic if we can't get out of the pit to use them? What use are they in helping me find Kalen? Especially if they carry the seed of the plague. You won't have a city to reclaim if your blasted machines breed a plague that kills everyone. Including us."

"*My* machines would never hurt anyone." Yaala wrestled away from his grasp and resumed her work with the rusted pipe. "I need to know more about 'tricity and Yaassima's gadgets before I reclaim my heritage."

Kalen, with her sullen silences and selfish need to control the people around her seemed more attractive to him now than Yaala obsessed with the generators and transformers.

He longed to tell his sister everything that had happened to him since their separation. She fed his ideas with twists and "what ifs" that gave him new insight into problems, and into life.

Had she grown in the last year? Did she still have Wiggles, her ferret familiar?

"Of course you have to find Kalen," Yaala said after several moments of silence. "You won't be happy until you do. Then you can come back here and help me with the machines."

"No, Yaala. I won't come back here, ever, once Kalen is free."

She didn't seem to hear him. The machines held her attention completely. Almost as if they threw a spell over her.

Becoming Kaalipha and ruling Hanassa was just an excuse to be close to her machines. He should have known this would happen. The machines were her family; she had returned to them. Would Powwell ever return to the Commune? Not without his sister.

"So why have the caverns changed? It takes more than one kardiaquake to move a labyrinth this large." Powwell decided to change the subject.

"Some of the tunnels have collapsed. Yes. Maybe we mistook the way out because of debris blocking the main exit from the living cavern." Yaala's eyes brightened a little as her thought processes moved away from her broken machines.

"Or maybe the wraith has disguised the exit so we can't leave," Powwell mused as he caught another glimpse of drifting white off to the side. He turned to look straight at the place where the wraith had been, but it—she?—had disappeared again.

"You go look, Powwell. I just want to check one thing. . . ."

"We're in this together, Yaala. Come. Now. You can play with your toys after we find a way out." He grabbed her hand and dragged her back toward the cavern that held the food stores. At one time it had been home to several hundred slaves including Yaala and himself. They'd all looked to Yaala for leadership. Had she been this obsessed then?

Powwell stopped at the first tunnel junction. He looked left. If his memory held true, he thought the tunnel narrowed and dead-ended. Then he looked right. The hairs on the back of his neck stood up. Thorny bristled and jabbed Powwell with his spines, urging him left—away from the atavistic sense of dread in the right-hand tunnel. Something nasty awaited them. They needed to turn back, try a different direction. The hedgehog gibbered in panic. Powwell pushed forward through that tunnel anyway. The last three times he'd explored this area, he'd avoided the tunnels that made him too aware of the weight of tons of Kardia pressing down on the flimsy cave system; too aware of the limited supply of air; too aware of his own mortality.

Powwell pressed on, pushing away his fears. He kept telling himself that the wraith wanted him to stay. She was making him and Thorny sense terrors that didn't truly exist.

They passed through the living cavern without pausing to drink from the foul-tasting stream. He'd drunk too much of the sulfurous water a year ago because there was nothing else to keep his body from withering into a pile of dust in the tremendous heat of the caverns. Even Thorny didn't beg for a drink.

At last the tunnels began to slope upward. The air freshened, and the temperature decreased. "I think we've found it, Yaala." He tugged on her hand to hurry. He couldn't get out of the caves too soon.

They slowed on the last slope upward to the gate. Instinctively, they hugged the shadows near the wall. Liise's yellow ceiling lights didn't reach this far, so they had to pick their way carefully over the uneven pathway. The glow behind them blinded them to the darkness in front.

Powwell closed his eyes and stretched his magic senses. He didn't have much dragon magic left. Thorny's sense of smell was probably more accurate than Powwell's TrueSight at this point.

"Thorny smells a human up ahead," he whispered, pausing to share the sense with his familiar. "Blood and sweat and fear."

"Who?" Yaala asked, peering into the darkness.

"Only one way to find out. Keep quiet." Slowly they crept forward, hands linked tightly together. Powwell stretched his other hand in front of him.

At last he grasped one of the metal crossbars of the gate. A glow of light from higher in the tunnel helped him distinguish the interlocking pattern. He found the square plate that housed the lock. Beneath the lock lay an inert figure, more rags than anything else.

Gently he prodded the head region of the lump.

"Huh?" a man shook his head and peered up with bleary eyes.

"Rollett?" Powwell asked. "I'd know those blond streaks

in your black beard any day. Rollett, what are you doing here?"

"I should have died with the others," Rollett mumbled.

* * *

Near midnight at the gate between the pit and the Kaaliph of Hanassa's palace

Yaala stooped to look closer at the bundle of rags that spoke. The little bit of glow from the lower caverns showed lighter streaks in the man's dark beard and hair. By the same light she saw the glimmer of moisture in his eyes.

"I've got to go back. My men are dying up there." Rollett stirred as if he meant to stand, then collapsed against the iron bars of the gate again.

"Where are you hurt?" she asked him.

"I . . . maybe. I hurt all over. But wounds?" He patted his mid region. His hands came up dry. "No blood." He shrugged. Then he winced as if his head hurt at the movement.

"Powwell, give me some light," she ordered.

"You've got to get out of here," Rollett whispered anxiously. "The guards are right behind me. They're out for blood. My blood. They already killed three of my men."

"The corridor is empty," Powwell said. He opened his clenched fist to reveal a ball of witchlight.

"What?" Rollett reared up on one elbow. He looked up the sloping path toward the palace, his aches and pains forgotten.

"Thorny doesn't smell anyone but us, and my magic isn't quivering—except for the wraith," Powwell said. The tiny hedgehog poked his funny head out of Powwell's pocket, wiggling his nose. He stayed out rather than darting back into cover, a sure sign that no one approached them.

"You sure? They were right on my heels, screaming to kill me. Piedro laid a trap for me and my men. My men . . ." He groaned and lay back down again. "I've failed them. And myself."

"Is this the same Piedro who tried to assassinate the queen on the eve of her wedding?" Yaala asked. A gnawing suspicion grew deep within her. Piedro knew how the dragongate worked. He also had a confederate in King Quinnault's palace who helped him escape a magically sealed dungeon.

"What queen?" Rollett turned his piercing gaze on her.

"You haven't heard that King Quinnault married the Princess of Terrania," Powwell replied. "We didn't hear until we got back to Coronnan."

"You've been back? How? When?" Rollett pulled himself to his knees, using the crossbars of the gate for support.

In the last glow of witchlight, Yaala saw a deep bruise forming on the left side of Rollett's face, beginning at the temple. He had to hurt. Any movement would aggravate the pain.

She also couldn't help but notice the clean lines of high cheekbones and straight nose above his trimmed beard. An aristocratic face despite traces of a peasant background in his accent. He might have nothing to wear except rags, but he'd kept himself clean and well groomed. Admirable traits in the foul city above them.

"How did you get out?" Rollett demanded. "You've got to get me out of here. I can't stay here any longer. I've got to get out! I have to find a way to free my men." He shook the gate with all of his strength. The metal remained solidly closed. "I promised. . . ." His quiet words ended in a choke, almost a sob.

Powwell stared at his fellow magician without answering. Rollett had said nothing about Kalen, only about his men. Long moments of silence stretched between them.

"There is an exit near the lava core," Yaala finally said. "It's magic. Every once in a while the mouth of one of the little tunnels becomes a gateway to another part of the world. Within a few heartbeats you can be thousands of miles away. This end opens to myriad destinations, but all of the destinations lead only back to Hanassa. If the dragongate isn't open, you step into the boiling lava."

Rollett nodded in understanding, his eyes wide as he mulled over the possibilities. "That's how Nimbulan and Myri escaped last year. Yaassima must have used it to send her assassins and robbers anywhere in the world. Piedro can bring food and supplies in without going through the city. The dragongate must be why he has repeatedly blocked our attempts to construct exits from above. *He* doesn't need them, so he won't let us have them. But he won't give us access to the dragongate either."

"After the big kardiaquake last year, the dragongate changed," Powwell added. "It won't open again until the next dark of the moon."

"Nooooooo!" Rollett howled. "Don't tell me you came through the gate without the food. We won't be able to continue without the food."

"There is food down here. But we didn't bring anything other than the journey rations in our packs." Yaala thought back to the heavy sledges the Rovers had tried to bring through. Food for a starving city. Her city, if she could reclaim it. Would Rollett help or hinder her quest?

The city was probably more his than hers now. He'd lived and worked among the citizens for a year and a half. He'd helped them rebel against the new Kaaliph. They looked to him for leadership.

All she could claim were a few malfunctioning machines. *Did I risk my life and Powwell's to reclaim Hanassa, or merely to be near my machines?* she asked herself for the first time. She had to think about that for a while.

Who was more important—more like family—Powwell or Old Bertha? The big generator was dead, unrevivable.

Was there anything left of her city to reclaim?

All she knew at the moment was that Rollett triggered emotions in her that made her question everything.

Rollett's eyes brightened a bit, and his face calmed. "What kind of food?"

"The living cavern is full of flour and cereal grains, barrels of salted and pickled meat, dried fruit, root vegetables, and a little wine," she replied.

Powwell searched the ceiling with haunted eyes as the ground rumbled beneath them. He clutched the nearest wall, eyes closed and breathing deeply.

Stargods! What condition was the city in if kardiaquakes rocked it so frequently and Piedro withheld basic food supplies?

The Kardia stopped shifting.

"So that's where Piedro has been hiding his regular stores. All of it is stale and a lot of it is infested with maggots." Rollett closed his eyes. His shoulders drooped. "It's better than nothing, but never enough. Piedro doles it out at starvation rations." He seemed to barely notice the kardiaquake.

"There's water down here, too," Yaala reminded him. She knew how limited the city wells could be if the surrounding mountains had been dry during the Winter. The sweet water of Coronnan seemed too bland after drinking nothing but the heavy mineral and sulfur-laden water of Hanassa all of her life.

"Open this gate. I need to see what's here, what we need most up above." Rollett licked his lips and stared longingly over Yaala's shoulder toward the inner caverns.

"I don't know how to open that gate," Powwell replied. "Yaassima controlled it with 'tricity. No ordinary key can open it."

"Nimbulan broke and reset it when he escaped with Myri and the others," Yaala reminded him. "Piedro has been using it for more than a year."

"I could break it if I had enough strength to use my magic." Rollett shook the gate again.

The murmur of the stream grew louder. Not the stream after all. Voices coming from the upper corridor.

"The guards are coming!" Rollett swung around, his back pressed hard against the gate. "I'm trapped. Piedro will execute me for sure this time. His consort hasn't tasted blood in almost a week."

CHAPTER 16

Near midnight, Great Hall of Palace Reveta Tristile, Coronnan City

Bessel trudged into the Great Hall of King Quinnault's palace. Chill bay water dripped from his trews, and his boots squished with every step. He'd thrown his formal robe back over his everyday trews and tunic, but it was almost as sodden as the rest of him. No amount of emptying his boots and wringing his socks would dry them.

Hours had passed, awaiting rescue and answering questions since he'd dragged Ambassador Jorghe-Rosse from Rossemeyer from the depths of the bay.

Misery dogged his steps as much as the scraggly white mutt with long, curly fur that had followed him from the docks and kept pressing up against him. Bessel wanted to kick it out of the way, but it looked as depressed and lonely as he felt. He let it stay with him as he followed the other refugees from the barge.

Armed guards from both King Quinnault's personal guard and from Rossemeyer had met them as they docked.

Four stern-faced warriors from Rossemeyer led them from the docks into the palace. They carried their dead ambassador on a litter. Another four warriors flanked them protectively. Behind them came the other dignitaries and their ladies, still wet and chilled. The palace guard had given them warm blankets and cloaks. But no one had offered Bessel anything.

Except the dog. When it rubbed against Bessel, he felt a little warmer.

Jorghe-Rosse's lady stood a little apart, dry-eyed and chin jutting with determination. If she grieved, she didn't show it in her posture.

Bessel, the pilot, and the boatmen brought up the rear, along with the bedraggled dog. Bessel didn't need to read the sailors' minds to smell their fear. No one knew for certain how the new widow would avenge her husband's death. Only that she would.

Fires roared in the hearths at either end of the huge hall. The dignitaries gravitated to the bright warmth even at this late hour. Tapestries and flower bouquets gave the room an air of cozy invitation. King Quinnault and Queen Maarie Kaathliin had transformed their major reception area into a home that welcomed petitioners to the court rather than made them afraid of true justice in a cold and forbidding hall.

Bessel didn't think there could be justice as long as Rossemeyer was involved. The entire country of mercenaries made their own rules that had nothing to do with the rest of civilization.

The king and queen entered the hall through a small back door. The king still wore riding leathers flecked with steed foam, as if he'd driven his mount to extremes in his hurry to get here. Queen Maarie Kaathliin clutched her baby tightly as they made their way to the twin thrones on the low dais. She kept looking around anxiously. Usually she left the child with servants while she accompanied her husband on official business. Today she refused the nanny who kept reaching for the child.

Master Scarface and a few of the other master magicians marched into the room, pushing aside the crowd of courtiers. Scarface took up his position between the twin thrones. The other master magicians flanked the royal dais. Bessel tried to catch Scarface's gaze. The Senior Magician scanned every corner of the room except where Bessel stood.

Bessel sent a gentle mental query to his master. Scarface remained impassive and unresponsive.

Wind-drift, the master magician standing just to the right of the queen's throne, a man Bessel barely knew but who had become very close to Scarface in recent weeks, sent an inquisitive mental probe of his own toward Bessel's mind. Bessel saw it as a glowing yellow dart. It sped toward Bessel's right eye. A hair's breadth from contact the energy bolt stopped, turned, and backlashed to the sender at double speed. The magician reared back, clutching his eyes in pain.

Scarface opened his eyes wide in alarm. His scowl deepened.

Bessel shrugged. The magician hadn't asked permission. No magician had been able to read his mind without Bessel's prior consent since his experience with the outlaws as a child.

They'd exile him for sure now and he'd be alone, without the family of the Commune.

The dog plunked down on his foot. Maybe he wouldn't be totally alone. But a dog didn't make up for a family.

May I ask your version of the story? Please? Wind-drift asked politely. His wild red-gray mane, which usually stretched back from his face as if he stood in a strong wind, crackled with the energy of Bessel's backlashed probe.

Since you asked politely. Bessel opened his mind and let his memories of the afternoon pour forth.

Scarface still looked angry and puzzled. Was Wind-drift passing the images along to his Senior or not? Wind-drift hadn't been with Scarface in the library separating the books. Maybe, just maybe, he could be trusted.

"My condolences, Madame," King Quinnault said as he rushed from his throne to take the hands of Lady Jorghe-Rosse. He radiated sympathy. "I, too, have lost many of those I loved. What can we do to show you and your husband the honor and respect due him?" His empathy reached out to include Bessel and the others.

"My husband earned honor as a general on the field of battle as must every man of Rossemeyer," Lady Jorghe-Rosse replied. "He did not die in battle as was his right." Something fanatical burned in the lady's eyes as she stared directly at Bessel.

A chill deeper than the numbing waters of the bay formed a knot in his belly. Senior Magician Scarface's eyes echoed the lady's malevolent gaze.

"A death for a death," Lady Jorghe-Rosse demanded.

The queen gasped and wrapped her arms more completely around her baby. Everyone else in the Great Hall stared in stunned silence. Except the magicians. They nodded in agreement.

"I can't do that, Madame," Quinnault said, meeting the lady's gaze steadfastly.

"Then I must take what is due me." The dark-eyed woman whipped a dagger from the multiple folds of her black cloak. The rippled blade was as long as her forearm. Death at her hands would not be clean or swift. She raised it menacingly at the king.

The warriors dropped the corpse on the ground and drew their own vorpal blades.

Cold sweat broke out on Bessel's face and back.

He didn't want to die.

The dog took a protective stance in front of him, baring his teeth. A growl rumbled from his throat—much deeper and louder than a mutt that size should be able to issue. Bessel bent to touch the matted tangles that hid the animal's eyes. The growl turned to a low moan of pleasure.

If you stay with me, the first chore is a bath, he told the dog with his mind.

It dropped to the ground and buried its head beneath muddy paws. Bessel would have expected a similar reaction if he'd spoken out loud and the creature understood the word "bath."

"There must be no more death!" Queen Maarie Kaathliin gasped. No taller than an adolescent child, she moved beside her tall husband, keeping her gaze firmly on Lady Jorghe-Rosse. She still didn't relinquish the burden of her child to the maid who dogged her steps.

The ambassador's wife didn't put her blade away. She looked down at the red-haired queen, a tall dark lily disdaining a small wild rose.

"I will hear all of the evidence, Lady." Quinnault clamped long fingers over Lady Jorghe-Rosse's wrist. He squeezed until she dropped the blade. It landed among the rushes, clattering loudly in the stunned silence. "I will determine the cause of death. If 'twas murder, then justice will be served. If 'twas an accident, as I was told, then we will take no further action."

"I do not call that justice. I call that cowardice," Lady Jorghe-Rosse screamed, struggling to free her hand from the king's grasp.

"For that I am sorry, Lady. But that is the law."

"A law made by cowards for cowards. My king will go

to war to honor my husband! I will have the death of the one who murdered my husband!"

We will have our justice as well, Scarface reminded Bessel. *You tapped illegal powers. The law will be served.* The magicians of the Commune echoed his thoughts.

* * *

The pit beneath Hanassa, time unknown

Powwell turned his head sharply, trying once again to see the wraith as it flitted about the tunnel, just out of sight, out of reach.

But not out of hearing distance.

She will desert you, the wraith whispered into Powwell's mind. *Look at how she is with this other man. Her eyes linger too long on his face, on his figure. Her hands touch him fondly through the bars. She never touched you like that.*

"Enough!" Powwell shouted, shaking off the insidious voice that had been plaguing him since they approached the gate. His words echoed in the caverns. Rollett and Yaala stared at him. The voices and footsteps farther up the corridor hesitated before thundering forward again.

Scrunching up his eyes and gathering all of his energies, Powwell threw a probe into the lock and shifted the tiny pieces of metal. It opened with an audible click.

Rollett nearly fell through the sudden opening. A misty form oozed through the small opening between the bars.

Thank you, the wraith chuckled and drifted away. *The iron has imprisoned me for too long. Now I can find my body.*

Rollett recovered and scrambled to reclose the gate before the Kaaliph's guards descended upon them. He stared after the misty white form, mouth slightly agape.

The nagging sense of dread in the back of Powwell's neck and the need to hide deep within the caverns evaporated with the wraith. So did his mistrust of Yaala. She'd only shown the other magician concern for his well-being as she had helped Powwell his first few awful hours in the pit.

But Powwell's instinctive fear of being underground returned in full force. He needed all of his concentration to keep from running after the wraith without regard to the guards or the safety of his companions.

Thorny hunched his spines and wiggled uncomfortably in Powwell's pocket.

He swallowed his fears and thanked his familiar for the reminder. He'd lived down here before. He would survive if he kept his gibbering panic under control.

"We'll be safe down here for a while. We can hide," Powwell whispered, gesturing for Yaala and Rollett to follow him.

"We've got to lock the gate," Rollett protested. He moved his fingers trying to make the interior pieces respond to his depleted magic.

"The guards won't cross that barrier as long as it's closed," Yaala replied. "They're more afraid of this place than they are of the Kaaliph. Come on, I know a place to hide."

"I want to hear everything that has happened at home while I've been gone."

"You need to go home as soon as possible, Rollett. Nimbulan needs you to keep Scarface from ruining the Commune," Powwell added. "I can't go until I've found Kalen."

Together they ran back into the living cavern. Yaala searched briefly right and left, orienting herself in the dim light. Powwell kept part of his senses tuned to the curses and stumbles among the guards behind them.

True to Yaala's prediction six men slid to a halt before they collided with the gate. They opened their eyes wide in fear, chewed their lips and looked everywhere but at each other.

"The wraith has Rollett now. We won't get him back," one guard muttered.

"What are we going to tell Piedro?"

Tell him the truth, Powwell whispered into their minds, trying to mimic the wraith's voice. *Tell him his prey is lost in the pit. The dragongate swallowed him as well as the fresh food.*

The guards backed up slowly, keeping their eyes on the gate.

Thorny squirmed within Powwell's pocket. Together, they might have enough energy for one last trick. Slowly the gate opened, creaking ominously.

The guards turned and ran back the way they had come.

"They won't be back any time soon. We have time to rest and eat and plan," Powwell said.

"Plan what? The city is close to starvation. My men need another three moons to dig through the collapsed tunnel—if they'll follow me at all after I failed in this raid. Piedro plays at cutting a staircase up the walls of the crater but mostly blocks all attempts to climb out, and this mysterious dragongate of yours is closed for another moon." Rollett plunked himself down amidst the barrels of salted meat.

"I won't let Piedro have my city," Yaala said, standing with legs slightly apart and hands on hips. "I will do anything to regain control of my city." She thrust out her chin in a gesture highly reminiscent of her mother, the last Kaalipha of Hanassa. Not once did her eyes wander toward the inner caverns and her machines.

"Will you do *anything* to regain your city, Yaala?" Powwell asked, suddenly afraid for her. "Will you murder and exploit just to feel as if you have power over someone else? Will you become as bloodthirsty as your mother?"

Chills ran up and down his spine. The wraith hadn't scared him as much as the thought of Yaala wielding an executioner's sword.

CHAPTER 17

Near midnight, Palace Reveta Tristile, Coronnan City

Bessel held his breath a moment, blocking out the malevolence behind Scarface's telepathic announcement. The long scar running from temple to temple whitened against his ruddy skin. Bessel needed no other communication to know how deeply committed the Senior Magician was to eliminating all use of rogue magic, by whatever means at hand.

Scarface had already started on the library. Possibly he'd used the queen's dragon dream about machines as an excuse to destroy books he'd already chosen as dangerous.

Bessel's execution or exile for using rogue magic was the only option by the law of the land and the law of the Commune. Scarface would make sure the king and Commune would offer no mercy.

He'd have total control of the Commune without interference from anyone who had begun under Nimbulan's benign management. Would control of all Coronnan be his next quest?

A great gulf of emptiness opened in the journeyman magician. Never again would he know the deep satisfaction of sharing magic with the Commune. Never again would the men open their lives and their souls to include him in the circle of magic. He'd almost rather die than live without that intense bond.

The dog sat up and licked Bessel's dangling fingers. Automatically, he scratched its ears. He felt more confident of his future when he touched the animal. *Are you going to be my familiar?* he asked it.

The dog replied with an enthusiastic lick of Bessel's

hand. Together, magician and familiar backed up a step, away from Scarface. The symbolic distance they put between them and the Senior Magician widened immensely.

He couldn't allow Scarface to succeed in his plot to oust anyone in all of Coronnan—magician and mundane—who might oppose him.

Wind-drift smiled slightly. What did the man know? Bessel didn't dare try to read his mind.

A ripple of anticipation and dread passed through the crowd as King Quinnault and Lady Jorghe-Rosse faced each other in determined silence. The desert warriors who accompanied the lady waited patiently, swords drawn, for a signal from her to fight or withdraw.

"Excuse me," said a tall man verging on elderly from the back of the crowd.

Nimbulan! If anyone could sort out this mess, it was the retired Senior Magician.

He'd aged greatly in the year and a half since he'd lost his magic. His skin looked pale, and the wrinkles around his eyes had deepened. But he still stood straight and his step sounded firmly on the flooring stones beneath the rushes. His dark auburn hair had gone almost completely gray. Contentment shone from his eyes. He greatly enjoyed his new role of husband and father. Bessel half expected to see Nimbulan's daughter, Amaranth, toddling along behind him, or tucked under his arm. Certainly, his wife should be close by. The three were inseparable.

But he couldn't see Myrilandel or their child in the crowd. Where was she?

Scarface bowed slightly, barely deferring to Nimbulan. Wind-drift exchanged a curt nod with the retired magician. Quinnault released the widow's hands and also turned his attention to the newcomer. King and magician had become great friends during the long process of bringing peace and stability to Coronnan.

Were these two strong men strong enough and wise enough to keep Scarface under control?

The warriors from Rossemeyer wavered a fraction in their defensive stance as Nimbulan passed them. They reasserted their hostile posture once more when the lady remained firm. They had faced Nimbulan the Battlemage and lost the last time Rossemeyer tried to capture Coronnan's rich resources.

"My condolences, Lady Rosselaara." Nimbulan bowed respectfully to the new widow; the first to grant her an identity other than as the ambassador's wife.

With a Rosse in front of her name, she had to be a royale, a king's sister or daughter, used to having her every whim granted. She'd also have influence with her government. Her family would rally around her.

Would the Commune support Bessel as firmly?

Not while Scarface led them.

Lady Rosselaara bent her head a little in acknowledgment of Nimbulan's greeting. The first indication that her neck didn't have a pole rammed down it.

Nimbulan stepped forward, never taking his eyes off of the widow. "As I understand it, Lady, your husband died fighting the bay and a storm. Worthy adversaries for any warrior. Adversaries that have defeated more good men than I care to remember. He did not die without honor."

"I will have a death for a death. How does one kill a storm?" Lady Rosselaara cocked one eyebrow at Nimbulan.

The aging magician returned the gesture. "Magic will shift a storm elsewhere. Nothing can stop it altogether. But the magicians of Coronnan do not tamper with balances of nature. We strive only to predict storms and prepare for them."

"This magician conjured the storm!" The pilot pointed a finger at Bessel. "I know he did. I saw him ram his staff into the deck and roll up his eyes in a trance. I felt the Kardia shift beneath the bay and move great obstacles that weren't there the day before. Then he spoke demon words. He called up the storm and drove *my* barge onto a bar of his own making."

"Is this true, boy?" Scarface wove his fingers in an intricate pattern—his habitual gesture for seeking information and truth.

"No, it is not true. I maintained a light trance so that I could understand the conversations in five different languages. I would never call up a storm or create a bar of debris. Raanald tried to navigate around the bar, but it caught the rudder and snapped it. Then the waves caught us crosswise and threw the ambassador overboard. I found him plastered against one of the old tree snags from the last sea battle by the currents."

"Then why didn't my depth finder warn of the bar's proximity?" The pilot trembled all over in his anger.

"It did. You kept changing course erratically because you didn't trust it."

Stunned silence filled the room.

Bessel looked from Scarface to Nimbulan and back to the pilot, seeking a response, any kind of response.

"If you do not trust the machine, why should we use it at all?" King Quinnault asked. "Is the machine faulty?" He looked to his queen.

She shrugged her shoulders. The machine had come from her people, from distant and mythical Terrania.

The pilot glared at Bessel, his mouth clamped firmly shut.

"Then perhaps the pilot is the one who must answer for my husband's death," Lady Rosselaara said. "He will speak readily as my blade lops off pieces of his anatomy."

The pilot straightened his shoulders and stared back at her with all of the arrogance of his guild backing him up. He knew himself too valuable to Coronnan for King Quinnault to give him over to foreign justice.

"Answers will be found, Lady," Nimbulan intervened. "But by our methods. If anyone is found negligent in this matter, justice will be served."

"I don't care for justice, Magician. I care only for vengeance."

"Will the death of an innocent bring your husband back to life?"

"The death of a guilty man will give me back my husband's honor."

"Then if any are found guilty, you will be informed of his fate." Nimbulan returned her determined glare. "Go home now, Lady Rosselaara. Go home and grieve. Prepare your husband for his funeral rites."

"You have one day to deliver the guilty man to my door so that he may be buried beneath my husband. If he is not dead at this hour tomorrow, I will kill him." Lady Rosselaara turned on her heel and marched out of the room. The litter bearers exited with her, carrying their fallen ambassador.

Her honor guard sheathed their swords, wheeled as one, and followed her.

No one needed to utter the "Or Else," that followed her final words.

"Now what?" Quinnault asked of no one in particular. "We have conflicting testimony. We have the problem of an untrustworthy depth finder. I am open to suggestions, gentlemen."

"I never liked having to rely on any machine," Queen Maarie Kaathliin said. She shifted the baby to her shoulder, easier now that the foreigners had left. "We should learn to read the mudflats another way."

"Such as?" Scarface intoned, stepping forward to stand beside the king, his rightful place as Senior Magician. The place that Nimbulan resumed all too easily. Wind-drift held back.

"Where is your famous magic, Master Scarface?" The queen turned her gaze to the ugly man who had forsaken life as a Battlemage and mercenary to join the Commune. "Why can't your magicians plumb the depths of the bay and chart the course for the barges?"

"We have tried, Madame." Scarface looked more fierce than regretful. He kept his accusatory gaze upon Bessel.

The young magician wished he could disappear. He tried fading into the background—a trick Nimbulan used often. But he couldn't tell if it worked.

"Again and again, we have tried," Scarface continued, finally looking away from Bessel toward the queen. "But dragon magic, legal magic, is more in tune with the elements of Air and Fire than with Water and Kardia. To delve into Water and Kardia deep enough to chart the channels we need rogue magic. Upon pain of death or exile, we cannot violate our covenant with Coronnan. Only dragon magic can be combined and amplified by many magicians working together. Only dragon magic can be controlled with ethics and honor." The Senior Magician repeated the first rule of the Commune, staring back at Bessel, daring him to admit his lapse in legal magic.

Bessel remembered the day he had taken his oath to king and Commune. At the time he had truly committed himself to obeying the laws of the Commune and Coronnan. Yet today he had violated one of the most basic of those laws. He had tapped a ley line, violated his oath.

Would he violate it further in order to stop Scarface's mad crusade to control all of Coronnan? He'd not be much help to anyone unless he stayed in the Commune.

If he hadn't tapped a ley line to help his mother, surely he would never do it again. Never! Couldn't the Commune give him some kind of probation rather than death or exile?

"Master Scarface, please have one of your magicians take statements from the boatmen and Journeyman Bessel," King Quinnault ordered. "I would know who speaks truth in the matter of the storms and the machine. Then I will need you in my office in one hour to plumb the depths of the diplomatic mess caused by Ambassador Jorghe-Rosse's death."

"Very good, Your Grace." Scarface bowed respectfully along with everyone else in the room as the king exited with his wife. The mundane courtiers and servants filed out of the Great Hall as well.

"I will discuss this matter with Myrilandel, the dragons' ambassador," Nimbulan said. A half smile lit his face. Of course he'd discuss it with Myrilandel, his wife. "There must be a way to read the bay with magic, the same way we . . ." a look of sadness—nearly pain—crossed his face. "The same way the Commune uses magic senses to find veins of ore and tests the fertility of soil." He resumed his normal, dignified demeanor.

"There is another matter that must be discussed in private, among the magicians," Scarface intoned. "Bessel, you will come with me." Scarface beckoned his journeyman to follow him back to University Isle where the Commune would hold court.

Bessel couldn't move. All heat left his body.

"The pilot felt you use rogue magic, Bessel," Scarface reminded all who listened. "You know the punishment for that infraction."

"You will take the word of a mundane and prejudiced witness as truth without so much as letting the boy defend himself?" Nimbulan asked. He shifted to stand beside Bessel.

The dog took up his protective stance in front of Bessel again.

The journeyman appreciated the gesture of support, but knew his case was hopeless. Only the dog truly believed him.

"I, too, felt the Kardia shift as Bessel tapped the power of a ley line," Scarface said. "He has no defense."

CHAPTER 18

Past midnight, the route between Palace Reveta Tristile and the University of Magicians, Coronnan City

Bessel sloshed behind Nimbulan all the way across the bridge to University Isle. The bedraggled mutt kept close to his heels every step of the way. It cringed away from the other magicians as if expecting to be kicked and beaten. Bessel kept close to Nimbulan, his old master, gleaning some measure of temporary safety from his vibrant personality. But nothing could ease the dread eating a hole in his gut. Very soon he would lose the Commune forever. All because he had tapped illegal magic in a failed attempt to save a life.

If he had succeeded, would Master Scarface consider leniency?

Bessel doubted it. The Senior Magician of the Commune was as inflexible in his expectations as Lady Rosselaara of Rossemeyer.

Did he truly want to remain in the Commune with Scarface at its head?

He had nowhere else to go. He needed the Commune more than it needed him.

But someone had to stop Scarface.

More magicians joined the procession from the palace as they neared the University. They closed in around Bessel, excluding the shaggy mutt from their perimeter, as if they knew it would help Bessel escape justice. The dog whined and danced to penetrate the circle.

Bessel missed the creature already.

"Scarface will have trouble gathering enough magic to

implement any punishment," Wind-drift muttered from behind Bessel.

"No one's seen a dragon in days. Not since Scarface removed most of the books from the library," Master Whitehands, head of the healers, replied. "I've got an apprentice watching the skies from atop the tower. He's really talented with FarSight. His reports of dragon activity are dismal. They haven't been seen hunting bemouths in the bay. That's their favorite food and keeps the number of monsters down to tolerable levels. Our fisherfolk will be in trouble if the dragons don't return to hunting."

"We'll be in deeper trouble without any dragon magic to gather," Wind-drift reminded him.

Bessel turned around to ask a question, but the two masters had withdrawn from his proximity. Two potential allies against Scarface. Were there more?

"Did you hear that?" he whispered to Nimbulan as they proceeded through the University. The sound of many boots slapping the flagstone passageway nearly drowned out his words. But it didn't mask the angry barks of the mutt.

Nimbulan merely nodded, holding one finger to his lips to signal silence on the subject.

They proceeded in single file up winding stairs to the tower room above the classrooms. Bessel feared separation from Nimbulan. Behind him, he could hear the dog yipping as he followed the troop. The risers narrowed and steepened each step of the way. Up three flights they climbed. Bessel's heart beat faster, and his legs grew heavier. His drying clothes grew stiff and weighed heavily against his chilled skin. There didn't seem to be enough air in this tight stairwell.

At last Master Scarface passed his left hand over the lock of the tower room. The portal sprang open. Only the Senior Magician could work that spell alone. The other masters needed three different magical signatures to move the lock.

One by one they filed into the working room that was almost filled by a round black glass table. Bessel had been in this private enclave of masters only once before, the day the roof had been finished. Dragons had had to lift the unique and incredibly valuable black glass table onto the roof of the next lower level and then the room was built around it. The tower would have to be destroyed to move the table.

No one else in all of Kardia Hodos possessed any artifact made from so much glass. Only dragon fire burned hot enough to eliminate the impurities in sand turning it into true glass that wasn't so brittle and flawed it shattered at the lightest touch. Dragons had made the table for the Commune. They had given it to Nimbulan in time for the former magician to work his last and greatest spell—protecting Coronnan with a magical border.

But Nimbulan had been forced to leave his magic embedded in the black glass. He'd made his choice, to save the life of his wife, Myrilandel, rather than save his talent.

His magic glowed within the table surface, casting blue highlights within the black glass.

Nimbulan touched the surface with reverent fingers. A look of aching loneliness crossed his face. Then he tucked his hands within the sleeves of his tunic and raised his head. No emotion crossed his face or radiated from his aura.

Bessel grew colder yet, trying to imagine his life without magic. He was about to learn what it felt like. Without the Commune and dragon magic he had nothing, was no one.

The dog whined and scratched at the closed door, reminding him that he had one friend. Bessel closed his ears to the dog's entreaty. He didn't dare trust its offer of faithful companionship. It, too, would desert him if Scarface stripped him of his magic.

Only Master Lyman was missing from the ranks of twenty master magicians come to pass judgment on Bessel. He wondered briefly if the master magicians—all new since Nimbulan's retirement—had shunned the old librarian because he hadn't cooperated with the banning of certain books. Bessel hoped not. The Commune needed Lyman's knowledge, wisdom, and gentle approach to diplomacy.

A measure of resolve replaced Bessel's momentary depression. He had to find a way to stay in the Commune. Coronnan needed him in a position to counter Scarface. He couldn't do that exiled or dead.

Each of the master magicians took a reserved chair placed around the massive table. The chair backs boasted vivid embroidery worked in each magician's signature colors. Every piece of needlework was as unique as the magician who sat in the chair. But together, with hands linked around the glass table, their magic and their souls blended, became one, amplified, and worked miracles.

I'll be a part of that miracle again. Somehow, some way, I've got to stay in the Commune.

"Arbitrary punishment is not our way, Bessel," Scarface said, almost kindly. "Do you have an explanation for your heinous actions?"

A glimmer of hope blossomed in Bessel's heart. "You told me to save the ambassador's life at all costs. The only way I could hope to do that was to see the current that trapped him and drag him free at a moment of slackening. I didn't have the time or strength to do it with mundane skills. Dragon magic did not respond to me beneath the waters of the bay. I used the tools available."

"And still you failed."

"If I had tapped the ley line when I first sensed trouble, I might have been in time. I failed because I hesitated to use solitary magic."

"As well you should. Any use of rogue magic opens the doors to chaos. Only dragon magic allows many magicians to combine their powers and impose ethics, honor, and justice upon *all* magicians."

"I know, Master. And I am sorry for my transgression. It will not happen again." Bessel bowed his head, hoping Scarface would take the gesture of humility into account.

"Once you have tapped rogue powers, there is no going back. You will be tempted again and again. Others will find excuses to do so as well. We must make an example of you." Scarface's voice rose as his scar whitened.

Wind-drift placed a placating hand upon the Senior Magician's arm.

Scarface's jaw tightened and worked side to side as if he ground his teeth in a massive attempt to control his temper.

"Excuse me, Master Aaddler," Nimbulan interrupted. His use of the Senior Magician's true name signified the importance of his words. "There are more important issues before us than Bessel tapping a ley line in a desperate attempt to save a life."

"What more important issue can there be than violation of our most sacred law?" Scarface glared angrily at his former comrade. They'd been friends when they first escaped Hanassa. Now Scarface treated Nimbulan as a distrusted foe.

"There is, first, the issue of the pilot's mistrust of the depth finder. It seems to me he is the party at fault here. If he had listened to the machine's warning and taken precautions immediately, Ambassador Jorghe-Rosse might still be alive and Coronnan would not be facing probable war with Rossemeyer."

"A matter for politicians to decide."

"But we of the Commune are chief advisers to the politicians. *Neutral* advisers. We . . . You need to make decisions, investigate the machine and the Guild, and give all of the information to the king and the Council of Provinces."

"After we have dealt with the transgressions of one of our own. We must police our members so that hysterical and uninformed mundanes do not need to."

"Then you must begin by exiling yourself, Master Aaddler."

"What!" Several of the masters stood, pounding fists against the table. Outrage burst forth from their tightly controlled auras.

But Wind-drift remained calm. Who was this man? More importantly, where did his loyalties truly lie?

The dog yipped outside the door. His bark sounded strangely triumphant.

Hope and bewilderment glowed within Bessel at the same time. He stood a little straighter, grateful that Nimbulan befriended him.

The retired magician waved his hand for them to quiet. The masters obeyed, revealing a measure of respect for Nimbulan that Scarface had yet to earn.

"Continue with your explanation, please, Nimbulan," Scarface ordered, pointedly denying his accuser the right of a title or working name.

"For you to have felt the shift in the Kardia caused by Bessel's tapping of a ley line, you, too, must have been using solitary magic. By your own laws, you also must face death or exile along with the boy you so boldly accuse."

* * *

Past midnight, outside the University of Magicians, Coronnan City

From the supporting buttress of an outside wall, Kinnsell watched the magicians—master frauds more like—wind up the staircase to their private enclave. Now was as good a time as any to rescue the Rover woman. Darkness shrouded the entire complex. He'd never have a better opportunity to avoid detection by the magicians.

He needed to get close enough to the members of the Commune to test the viability of their psi powers. Until then, he had to presume they used sleight of hand and other tricks to convince a gullible populace. But they still held a great deal of political and economic clout on this planet.

Silently, he crept through the long corridors of the ancient buildings. The oldest portion seemed to have been a single story built in a simple U shape around a central courtyard. The corridor that ran along the inside of the U and accessed the individual rooms showed signs of recent enclosure. He had expected to find twisting passageways and hidden staircases here. But each square room abutted the next neatly without unwarranted thickness of walls to accommodate secrets. Four staircases ascended to the recently added second and third stories; one at the end of each of the side wings and one on either end of the central and longest arm of the U. All seemed to have been built on straight lines with quarried stones, neatly squared to fit together. He'd investigate the outbuildings later—all very neat and square as well. Presumably, they housed storage and cooking facilities and nothing more.

Thick stone walls made him feel protected, almost as if he was back in civilization. Almost. These bushies, noble and peasant alike, had not yet discovered climate control, even inside their buildings. A few rooms made use of inefficient fireplaces or even, *shudder,* central hearths that lost more heat than they added. No wonder they wore so many clothes! Nearly a meter of stone between himself and the outside world offered some insulation. But he doubted he'd ever be warm on Kardia Hodos, not even in High Summer.

He wouldn't think about the primitive—meaning nonexistent—plumbing. So far he had managed to trek back to his shuttle at regular intervals to take care of his own personal hygiene, though he'd rather have parked the vessel farther away from the city where it was less likely to be found.

Every room he encountered in the residential and classroom wings of the University seemed to have an overt purpose and no hidden ones. Only the library—which occupied the entire central section of the building—offered the suggestion of places to secrete a prisoner.

Where would they hide the woman the bushie lord insisted must be rescued to prove Kinnsell's technology stronger than the magicians' magic?

He'd watched the comings and goings of this place all day. Other than the cook, there didn't seem to be any women in the University complex. No serving women. No mistresses or wives. And certainly no prostitutes. Where?

In desperation he slid into the library, empty of students at this late hour, although a few lights still glowed. All of the masters had retreated to the tower room—the third story of the classroom wing. Presumably, the apprentices slept. Therefore, there should be no one to hinder his search.

A maze of old-fashioned books tantalized him. The musty smell of learning invaded his nose and spread into his veins like warm insulation gel. Books had been obsolete for storing and dispensing knowledge for almost one thousand Terran years. Yet, still, books persisted as a favored hobby and status symbol among a large majority of the population. Something sensuous about holding a book in your hands, caressing the cover, gazing at the *permanence* of the printed words upon paper (synthetic since the loss of pulp trees after the first doming of Terra).

These books looked to be the genuine thing. Some printed on real paper. Others on parchment. They were bound in embossed leather, carved wood or etched bronze—the latter richly jeweled and engraved.

Kinnsell couldn't help himself. He had to touch the incredible artifacts of a bygone era. He had to open one, read from it, cherish it. Maybe he could steal one and take it home. He could sell it for the price of a bush world. But he'd keep it. He'd honor it. Read from it every day. And when he became emperor, he would return to this library and confiscate as many books as he wanted.

His hand rested comfortably by his side, easy with his control of the situation and his life.

"May I help you, King Kinnsell?" the face of a wizened old man appeared in the gap made by Kinnsell's removal of the tome he held protectively against his chest.

"Who are you?" Kinnsell asked, startled to find anyone hiding in this treasure trove. His right hand edged forward a bit, seeking control. "And how do you know my name?"

Quickly he checked his mental barriers to make sure no one could delve into his mind without his knowing. They seemed intact. But who knew what could happen on this bizarre planet that treasured books but disdained climate control and plumbing?

"Everyone knows the queen's father," the old man replied.

"But not everyone knows you. Who are you?" Kinnsell hated having to repeat himself. He should be able to pluck the man's entire life history from his mind with no effort.

Instead, he found only images of viewing Kardia Hodos from a great height, soaring on strong wings. He reveled in the sensation a moment, recalling glorious moments piloting his shuttle through atmosphere of the many planets he had visited. Cyber controls responded to the briefest thought, but he preferred the sense of control a joystick gave him. Either way, his shuttle gave him the illusion of true flight like a bird—or a dragon.

Then the feeling of hunger for meat dominated the old man's memories.

Yuck. No civilized person survived on a blood diet anymore.

Kinnsell shook himself free of the lingering taint of the old man's perversions.

"Now that you have dipped into my memories, are you any more enlightened than before?" the old man asked. He rearranged some books on his side of the shelf to reveal more of his face and form. Slight, stoop-shouldered with age. Nearsighted, too, from the way he peered at Kinnsell.

"May I please know your name?" Kinnsell asked through gritted teeth. He didn't have time or patience for word games.

"Ah, the magic word. Please. Yes you may know my name. I am called Lyman, Master Librarian in this existence."

"This existence?" Another curious superstition among these people. There had been Terran cultures that believed in multiple incarnations. Bush planets abounded with odd cults. Kinnsell preferred the family tradition of one god, one life, and an afterlife in heaven. That was the accepted philosophy in a large proportion of the civilized worlds. The accepted religion lent itself to a hierarchy of priests who, in turn, could be controlled.

"You didn't come here to debate religion and the purpose of life." Lyman dismissed the subject with the wave of a gnarled hand. "What do you seek? I know all of the books treasured here. I can help you find almost any single volume."

"I'm just browsing."

"Or looking for something not normally found in a library."

"None of your business, Lyman. Just leave me in peace."

"Will you ever know peace?"

"Not until you leave me to my business."

"Your business is my business as long as you seek answers in this library."

Kinnsell wanted to scream in frustration. Instead, he turned abruptly and stalked off through the maze of bookshelves. He thrust his right hand forward and to the right. He'd hardly walked the length of two aisles when the little man appeared before him, blocking the path.

Kinnsell evaluated the now visible little man. He appreciated the fine cloth of the old-fashioned blue tunic that hung nearly to his knees, belted with a silk sash. Most men in Coronnan wore shorter tunics with a leather belt beneath to hold up their trousers—or trews as they called them.

"You won't find what you seek without me," Lyman said.

"I'll find her if I have to tear this building apart, stone by stone." But he'd not harm a single page of the precious books.

"Her? Ah, the only woman you could seek is Maia, the Rover woman."

Kinnsell held his breath a moment. Had he really let slip that vital piece of information? He must be more careful.

"I'm afraid we can't let you take her," Lyman continued. "Out of the question, entirely."

"I didn't expect you people to throw your prisoner at me."

"She's not a prisoner. She remains under our protection of her own free will."

"I've heard that one before."

"You don't understand. She truly wishes to stay under our protection. Strange people, these Rovers. All members of a clan are linked mind to mind. None of them can think or act without all of the others knowing about it. The leader of the clan—usually a powerful magician—directs all of their thoughts and actions, just like a political dictator but more effective because of the magic. They have no freedom as we understand it. We have managed to shield Maia from the manipulations of her wandering relatives. As long as she stays here, she is free of them."

"This entire planet has truly bizarre beliefs. That is the most outrageous yet."

"Is it? Why else would one of her relatives have coerced you into an impossible rescue attempt? They don't need her. They fear her position here because they cannot monitor or manipulate her actions. She does not spy upon us for her clan. Therefore, they believe she must be returned to them or be killed. You, King Kinnsell, are their tool for that purpose."

"I serve no man but myself."

"That's what you think. If you will excuse me, I must consult with the Commune about your uninvited wanderings." The old man grinned, ambled off among his beloved books, and was soon lost from Kinnsell's sight.

CHAPTER 19

*Past midnight in the tower room reserved for
Master Magicians in the University of Magicians,
Coronnan City*

"Impossible!" Scarface screamed. He half stood from his thronelike chair. "I could never violate my oath to the Commune and revert to rogue magic. I am Senior Magician. I am in control of myself and this Commune at all times." He sat back again, composing his face.

But Bessel saw the tension in his shoulders and the whitening of the ugly scar.

"There is no other way you could have sensed a shift in the energies of the Kardia when Bessel tapped a ley line. You must have been working rogue magic at the same time," Nimbulan replied blandly. A twinkle grew in the old man's eyes. He sucked in his cheeks as if suppressing a laugh. He was enjoying himself.

Bessel, however, didn't dare relax. His life and his career were still in jeopardy.

"Explain your outrageous accusation, Nimbulan." Scarface stared at the former Senior Magician.

All of the other master magicians remained absolutely silent. Only their eyes moved, shifting from Scarface to Nimbulan and over to Bessel, then back again.

"You put forth the theory yourself last year in a very learned document," Nimbulan continued. "Communal magic is tuned to Air and Fire much like a harp and flute can be tuned to blend their music together. Kardia and Water are similarly tuned—but to a different harmony that does not blend well with Air and Fire. For you to sense the changes in the Kardia energies, you must have been in tune with them. What were you doing in the first moments of the storm? The moment when, under orders, Bessel grabbed the only magical energy available to him in a mad attempt to rescue Ambassador Jorghe-Rosse."

Bessel watched Nimbulan cock one eyebrow in question. Then the former magician raised his left hand, palm outward, fingers slightly curved.

"I was . . . I was . . ." Scarface stammered. He glanced at each magician around the table, as if seeking inspiration. At last he looked Nimbulan directly in the eye and spoke. "I am not on trial here, Nimbulan. Journeyman Bessel is. If I was tuned to the Kardia, I was not aware of it. Bessel knew precisely what he did and why."

The man lied. Bessel knew it in his gut as surely as he knew the dog waited for him outside the door.

"The why is important, too," Nimbulan reminded them all. "You told him to do whatever was necessary to save the ambassador."

"And he failed," Scarface concluded.

"At least I tried. And I almost drowned trying. None of you offered me any assistance or advice," Bessel accused. "Did you want the ambassador to die so that you could prove your superiority in another war?"

The chill of his wet clothes had penetrated to his bones hours ago. None of these judgmental masters had even offered him a towel, or a chair, or a hot drink. Yet here they sat, fat and warm and comfortable and dry.

"Would you have jumped into the storm-tossed bay to rescue a foreign ambassador?" Nimbulan asked everyone in the room.

"I can't swim," Scarface whispered.

"Then how would you have carried out your own orders to save the ambassador at all costs?"

Silence rang around the room.

"Masters, come. We have a situation," Lyman called from the doorway. He breathed heavily as if he had run up all three flights of stairs to the workroom. A sparkle in his eyes indicated he had left much unsaid and that amused him.

The dog dashed between Lyman's legs to jump against Bessel. He whined and yipped for attention until Bessel picked up the smelly bundle of tangled curls. Warmth began to penetrate his body immediately.

"What, Lyman?" Scarface demanded. Every muscle in his body radiated his angry frustration.

"I have interrupted an attempt to free Maia from our custody. The Rovers have hired a professional to do their dirty work."

"Rovers in the capital? We cannot allow Rovers anywhere near Maia," Scarface said.

As one, the masters rose and rushed toward the door. They appeared all too anxious to separate themselves from the uncomfortable questions and accusations that had been flung about.

Scarface grabbed Nimbulan and Bessel by their arms to stay their retreat.

"This business is not finished. For now, Bessel is in your custody, Nimbulan. See that he breaks no more laws. And keep him away from me!"

"And what of yourself, Aaddler?" Nimbulan asked. His left eyebrow rose again in query. "What laws will you break before this business is finished.'

Bessel wished he had the confidence to confront the Senior Magician with his true name. But then, Nimbulan had little to lose. He'd already lost his magic.

Bessel could lose everything. The dog licked his face.

Well maybe he wouldn't lose everything.

* * *

The pit beneath the city of Hanassa, time undetermined

Noise pressed on Rollett's ears as he followed Yaala and Powwell deep into the labyrinth of caverns. Yaala intrigued him and irritated him. Something about her made the hairs on his arms and his nape stand on end. He'd seen a lot of horror this last year that did not make him as suspicious as this.

He took a moment to study her in detail as she led the way. She had the long face, straight nose, and wide set eyes of Yaassima and Myrilandel. But her small stature and golden-blonde hair did not suggest a relationship to the deceased Kaalipha of Hanassa. He'd heard enough horrific tales about Yaassima's need for blood to hope the young woman hadn't inherited that single trait from her mother. She had survived when everyone thought her executed.

How had she managed that?

By taking refuge in this hidden sanctuary with the machines. She moved through the labyrinth of caverns easily, familiarly. Every step took them deeper into the inner caverns and the source of the annoying *yeek kush kush* noise. Yaala's posture and stride loosened the closer they came.

He was reminded of how he had sought a kind of refuge with Nimbulan the Battlemage during the wars. Once he'd found relative safety, companionship, and comfort with the magicians, he hadn't wanted to venture out into the real world at all. For many years he'd found it difficult to even go into the markets for supplies on his own.

Then one day, a year and a half ago, Nimbulan had set out on the long journey to Hanassa in search of his kidnapped wife, Myrilandel, and their two adopted children, Powwell and Kalen. Rollett couldn't let him go alone. He could not let his fears confine him within the safe walls of the University of magicians when Nimbulan needed him. Then Scarface had entered the picture and forced or coerced Nimbulan into leaving Rollett behind in Hanassa.

Powwell and Myrilandel had escaped with Nimbulan and Scarface, but not Rollett. And presumably not Kalen.

Powwell had confirmed Rollett's suspicions in his tale of Nimbulan's retirement and Scarface's elevation to Senior. Scarface, ex-Battlemage and ex-mercenary, wouldn't be happy until he controlled every aspect of every life around him.

Rollett needed to go home. Now. But he also had a duty to his men here in Hanassa. They relied upon him, trusted him with their lives.

"Show me the machines," Rollett said grimly.

"Why?" Yaala asked. Suspicion darkened her pale blue eyes. They weren't as colorless as Yaassima's and were much more expressive. Dared he read her mind?

He couldn't afford to waste his magic. He'd wait until she did something threatening. Then he'd invade her mind and strip it of every bit of knowledge he needed to escape Hanassa once and for all. With his men.

"Show me the machines and how they work. I need to understand everything about them if I'm to overpower Piedro and get us out of here. The city won't last another moon until your dragongate opens and food can come through," Rollett finally said.

"I'm not leaving until I find Kalen." Powwell placed his hands on his hips and jutted his chin in the most decisive posture Rollett had seen in the boy.

"She's not in the city, Powwell. I'd know if she got left behind."

"You didn't know about the pit and the dragongate. You don't know the palace," Powwell replied. "She's here somewhere. I sense her presence." He lifted his nose almost as if sniffing for her distinctive scent. The hedgehog poked his head out of Powwell's pocket and mimicked his action.

Strange, Rollett always thought of familiars as belonging to women's magic. He'd found so much satisfaction working with the men in the Commune he'd needed no companion but his staff. He couldn't remember if Powwell was particularly gifted with dragon magic or not. The boy—almost a man now—had spent so little time at the University with the other apprentices and journeymen, that Rollett hadn't had enough time to truly know anything about him except his unusual attachment to the girl Kalen, his half sister.

"I'll show you what I can," Yaala finally said after spending a long moment looking longingly toward the machines and back toward the passageway into the city.

Which did she prefer, the machines or the power of the Kaalipha? He wished he could trust her. Or at least understand her motives. Later. He'd know everything about her before he put his next plan into action.

Rollett listened carefully to her detailed explanation of generators, transformers, resistors, and currents. Her rather plain face glowed with a special beauty when she spoke—almost like a proud mama showing off her numerous children.

A piece of him wanted to reach out and teach her how to trust again. But he didn't dare trust her, so why should she trust him?

He shook off the emotion and concentrated on her lecture—sermon?

Generators made the mysterious 'tricity from steam. Transformers changed the raw energy into a usable form, as a magician transformed dragon magic. Currents flowed through the wires. Magic flowed through a man's blood.

"I've used ley line magic to power my talent, and I've used dragon magic. 'Tricity isn't so different," he said.

"I thought the same thing," Powwell agreed. "But I've touched this power, and I don't think it's safe for men to use."

"Yaassima's tricks with lights, making the altar stone disappear, and her sudden appearances on the dais were all illusions powered by this 'tricity." Rollett confirmed Yaala's lesson.

"Yes." Yaala nodded slowly. She kept her eyes on Rollett, searching his face for something.

"Then we don't need magic, we need 'tricity to overpower Piedro and reclaim the city." Rollett mulled over a number of possibilities in his mind. Magic and 'tricity. 'Tricity and magic. Where did one end and the other begin?

Ideas begin to awaken in his brain. With ideas came plans and hope. But first he needed more information.

"I wonder if we can use 'motes to stabilize the dragongate?" he muttered.

Powwell's eyes went wide with speculation. "The gate worked often and well while the generators ran continuously. Now the dragongate has shifted, stalled. Maybe it doesn't have enough power to open more frequently, and it doesn't have the power to keep it locked in one time span."

Yaala shook her head in dismissal of the argument. "Yaassima had 'motes—triggers—hidden all over the palace, some in her jewelry," Yaala continued. "The 'tricity never touched her body, only the 'motes. She used them to channel the 'tricity into specific chores. The hollow rods used on the gate lock and to stun people at the entrance to the palace were also a kind of 'mote."

Rollett had experienced those hollow rods. The guards struck a special rock with the wand to make them emit an ear-piercing sound that froze mundanes for long moments—but only made magicians uncomfortable. The guards used that time to search suspects and those who wished to enter Hanassa. They also used the wands as a kind of detector for metal weapons. An effective security device.

Yaassima's guards must have had some kind of protection from the sounds. Rollett wondered how to mimic that for his men.

"None of these tricks will help us get out of Hanassa," he sighed in resignation. There had to be another way; 'tricity was the key. "We can't slap a wand to stun the guards. Half of them are Rovers and immune to the sound." With their mind-to-mind connections, all Rovers had the possibility of magic even without the specific talent. "We need a dragon to dig us free or fly us over the rim of the crater."

"None of the dragons will come near Hanassa," Powwell reminded him.

"Yeah, I know. They say that Hanassa, the renegade dragon, still rules here," Rollett replied.

"How can that be?" Yaala looked at them both, eyes wide with wonder. But her pointed chin trembled with a touch of fear. "My ancestor took human form and founded this city over seven hundred years ago. Once in human form, he had to live and die a normal life span."

"Dragons are very long-lived. Lyman told me that a dragon can live a thousand years or more." Rollett began to pace. He circled the generator, the one Yaala called Liise, touching it occasionally, trying to understand the how and why of Hanassa the renegade dragon. Hanassa had stolen the machines from the Stargods and used them to mimic the magic of the three divine brothers.

"Dragons live a long time in dragon form," Powwell corrected him. "When they take human bodies, like Myrilandel did, then they are limited to the life span of the body."

"But Myrilandel borrowed an existing human body. She didn't shapechange," Rollett argued. "When her body dies, her spirit could move to a new body if she chooses."

Stunned silence greeted that statement.

"Couldn't she?" Rollett repeated.

"Yes, she could," Yaala whispered. "I don't think she would want to, though, because she has embraced the limitations of humanity."

"What if Hanassa never accepted his human body as anything but a temporary host?" Bizarre thoughts plunged into

Rollett's mind faster than he could assimilate them all. "What if Hanassa's spirit hides in these caverns waiting for a likely body to inhabit, then steals the body until he no longer needs it or it dies?"

"The wraith," Powwell and Yaala said together.

CHAPTER 20

Before dawn, Library in the University of Magicians, Coronnan City

Kinnsell walked to the back of the library. He stretched his stride, covering the twenty-five meters in short order. He ignored the tantalizing shelves of books along the way. He didn't have time to dawdle and read titles, caress bindings, or smell the unique combination of old paper, ink, and leather.

Iron bars blocked his exit. Behind the locked cage stood another library, as large or larger than the front portion. The stairway to the gallery and more books also lay behind the gate. Deep shadows hid these books from casual view. Kinnsell needed a lot more light to read the spines of even the closest volumes.

"More secrets?" he asked the books. They didn't reply. Not that he expected them to. He shook his head. Of course the magicians had to lock away most of their knowledge. The only way they could maintain control of the populace was to keep them ignorant.

"Education will be the first thing I introduce to these people once I am in control. Then the wheel. After that, progress will be unlimited. They'll thank me in the end."

He pulled a small, zippered wallet from inside his tunic. He brushed a dozen tiny tools made of the finest alloys with his fingertips. A hooked probe about the size of a toothpick seemed the proper piece to pick the lock. He could have used his telekinetic powers to manipulate the lock, but those skills didn't come as easily to him as telepathy. He might need his strength later, to free the woman.

The hair on the back of his wrist stood up in alarm as he inserted the probe. What? Cautiously, he channeled a little of his psi powers along the probe and met a wall of resistance.

"Aha!" He smiled. The master magicians had set the lock with telekinetic powers. Only stronger powers would release it. Presuming, of course, the opener used his mind instead of a key.

Kinnsell swallowed the atavistic fear that shot along the probe and up his arm. Merely the power of suggestion. His technology had to be stronger than the magicians' psi powers. This was just the first test of his skills.

With a little fiddling, the lock tumblers shifted under the probe. The gate swung open on well-oiled hinges. Kinnsell slipped through the opening and relocked the gate with the probe. He shook off the lingering tingle of distaste that infected his fingertips. The next person through here would find the lock much easier to manipulate.

Thousands of books lay between himself and whatever exit he might find back here. He wanted to linger and learn from them. Not enough time today.

"I'll be back," he promised himself. "I'll own all of you before I'm done with this planet. And I'll know why the magicians hide you. When I am emperor, I shall make books a priority. E-readers are efficient, but books are life." He caressed a book spine and moved on.

Half the wealthy merchants, nobility, and financiers in the Empire collected books. They would lobby for his election on that proclamation alone.

Sure enough, a small postern door lay secluded in a dark corner, almost hidden among the shadows between the stacks of shelves. He thought he'd spotted it during his search of the exterior grounds of the University. He bent low to lift the antiquated latch. The little door refused to budge.

"Mere locks won't stop me." But the mechanism resisted his tools. He turned his concentration on the lock. This was a trick his family didn't know about. No one in the O'Hara family had been able to use telekinesis since the first Mary Kathleen seven hundred years ago. But Kinnsell could. He'd kept his talent hidden all his life, using it to keep a competitive edge over the other contenders to the imperial throne.

The lock yielded to his mental touch after only a few

moments of concentration. He should be panting and sweating with fatigue. Instead he felt as if he'd opened the lock using only mundane means.

Curious. What was it with this planet? He could eavesdrop on mundanes with little or no effort—except the bushie lord. And now locks moved at the merest thought. But magicians, men who merely had strong psi talents, could block out his strongest efforts to read their minds.

He had a glimmer of an idea of why his family went bush so readily on Kardia Hodos. Would the augmented powers stay with him after he returned to Terra? No one could oppose his election to the imperial crown if it did. And if he met opposition, he'd just change their minds for them.

He slipped through the doorway—so small and narrow even he had to duck, and he was several inches shorter than the bushie natives. As he straightened his back and drew a deep breath, he caught sight of the cook running from the kitchen building behind the residential wing to his right. The only woman allowed on University Island, and now she was running away in the middle of the night. She should be busy fixing the next meal for the hundred or more magicians and apprentices. Curious.

Well, he searched for a woman who should be secreted in the University but wasn't. Why not follow the only woman who did live here?

Guillia. He plucked her name from her mind quite easily. She was mundane, then. Her thoughts were more chaotic than most women suffering PMS. Something about a conspiracy . . .

More curious. A conspiracy within the Commune might serve him well. "A house divided . . ."

The woman led him along a convoluted path across several bridges and down streets that were barely wide enough to call alleys. During the day, these streets were crowded enough to be called major thoroughfares.

Even at this early hour numerous people moved about, finishing up late business in the taverns, the end of gatherings, and parties in the homes of the wealthy, getting ready for morning trade. Kinnsell felt comfortable for the first time since coming to this disgusting planet. His rapid pace stirred his blood until he was quite warm. Crowds pressed in on him. Wonderful crowds of people. That's what he missed about the bush. Civilized planets were crowded. No one was ever truly alone in a domed city. He heard a thousand different hearts beating the staccato rhythm of life and sighed with relief.

Guillia almost slipped away from him in shadows cast by torches and candle lanterns. But he'd touched her mind. She couldn't elude him long. There, two blocks ahead, she turned into a tidy little stone building with a tall steeple reaching toward the heavens.

A church? Ah, yes. His esteemed ancestors had started the cult of the Stargods here. They'd modeled it after their own beloved faith, merely substituting the three O'Hara brothers for the Holy Trinity of the Father, Son, and Holy Spirit. Of course the churches would have steeples and the natives would make the sign of the cross as a ward against evil.

Kinnsell stepped into the nave of the church. He paused a moment, waiting for his eyes to adjust to the dim interior and to catch his breath. One of the many things he intended to change on this planet was the minuscule windows in the churches. They deserved tall stained glass panels. He would definitely leave the augmented butane torch with his bushie lord. He'd make a fortune melting local sands into fine glass. The limited capacity of the fuel tank would make him greedy and eager to serve Kinnsell again in return for a refill.

Kinnsell moved from the dim porch into the nave where a hundred candles lit the worship space. Out of long habit, Kinnsell touched his head, heart, and both shoulders then bent one knee in obeisance to the altar. So what if he worshiped a different god than the ones revered here? The intent was the same.

He searched the open space for signs of Guillia. If the natives used pews, they had cleared them away after their last worship service. He saw no hiding places in the square room. Not even pillars to support the roof.

His skin prickled as if someone looked over his shoulder. He looked in all directions. Something more than pews was missing from this church: Crosses. No crucifix hung above the altar, no wings extended from the nave to make the building into a cross. The icons on the walls, too, were devoid of crosses. How could these people believe in an afterlife—which he knew they did—without the dominant symbol of faith?

But then they didn't believe their god had died for them and then resurrected to a new life. They knew only that their Stargods had cured a plague and given a select few psi powers—what they called magic.

He shuddered and crossed himself again and again to make up for the lack of religious symbols and for the blasphemy of his ancestors.

The sense of being watched increased. He needed to get out of here.

"Are you looking for someone?" a woman asked quietly from behind him.

Kinnsell whirled to confront her. A short woman looked up at him through liquid black eyes. Her thick black hair was bound into a neat bun at the back of her head. A delicate mole lay just to the right of her mouth, enticing him to kiss her.

She looked so small and lonely he needed to enfold her in his arms, protect her, love her. . . .

Kinnsell checked his lustful response to her. He'd met women like her before. They used their minor psi talent to entice men, mold them to their will. Once alerted to their mental entrapment, he knew how to build barriers against it.

Then he noticed the olive tones of her skin and the bright red, purple, and black of her clothing. She wore large hoops in her ears and a dozen bangles on each arm. Just like the gypsies back home on Terra.

"Are you Maia?" He spoke as quietly as she had. His heart beat double time in excitement. This task was proving easier than he expected. He hadn't even had to rouse the woman from sleep. The bushie lord would have his captive and Kinnsell would have the entire planet at his disposal.

He needed to cough and control his breathing.

"Who are you?" She backed up, looking about for an avenue of escape, or to make certain he had brought no accomplices with him. She looked like a frightened deer he'd seen in pictures of old Terra. Another ruse.

"I won't hurt you, Maia. I've come to help. I'll take you home if you want." He held out a hand to her, inviting her to trust him. He used his own talent to persuade her.

THE RENEGADE DRAGON 177

"Who are you?" she asked again. Her shoulders relaxed a little, but she did not take his hand.

Kinnsell tried a light mind probe. She was as well armored as the bushie lord. No wonder she didn't fall for her own tricks used against her.

"I am an emissary from the Stargods come to rescue you." He swallowed the lie as easily as every other lie he told in and out of church.

* * *

Before dawn, tower room reserved for Master Magicians, University of Magicians, Coronnan City

Bessel clutched the wet dog against his chest, almost as a talisman. Nimbulan led the way down the three flights of stairs to the University courtyard.

"What's going to happen to me now, Master Nimbulan?" he asked as the other master magicians angled off toward the library.

"Nothing, I hope," Nimbulan replied, proceeding into the open air. He headed across the circle of the courtyard. His long stride seemed shorter than usual and his feet dragged a little. Was that a trace of puffiness in his fingers?

Bessel had known the former magician for most of his life. They had survived together through years of hard living during the Great Wars of Disruption. Huge armies had protected them then, but only because Nimbulan had been the strongest, most cunning Battlemage of his generation. The tremendous effort of working great battle magic had depleted his energies and life force time and again.

He deserved his retirement. But could Coronnan afford to let him retire as long as Scarface ran the Commune?

A few clouds scudded away in the brisk wind. No other traces of the storm lingered.

The dog licked his face and squirmed to be let down. Bessel placed him on the damp stones reluctantly. Already he missed the reassuring warmth of the dog.

"Master Scarface entrusted me to you until the matter is settled," Bessel reminded the older man. He petted the dog, trying to postpone separation as well as decision.

"Then you will continue your studies from my home rather than here at the University. We have plenty of room in that great barn of a house Myri inherited from the dragons, especially now that Powwell is gone." Nimbulan paused to stare at the mongrel. He wrinkled his nose at the smell of wet dog. "I hope you aren't planning to bring *that* with you." He pointed accusingly at the dog.

"I don't know. It followed me when we left the docks." Bessel stooped to continue caressing the dog. In a way it seemed they belonged together. The bedraggled mutt looked up at him adoringly and licked his hand.

"Myri won't let it in her house until it has had a bath. I'm not sure I want the thing around. I've never had a use for familiars. My staff was always enough. . . ." He looked up at the sky and gulped back his emotions.

"My familiar." Suddenly Bessel knew that by announcing the bond between himself and the dog he had completed the process of adoption. They belonged together like the family he'd never truly had. Even the Commune had not offered him the trust and companionship this scruffy mutt did.

Bessel looked at the dog in a new light. "I wonder why it waited until now to adopt me? Not many magicians have familiars anymore." Perhaps the dog had sensed his magic only when he tapped the ley line. Perhaps the relationship of magician and familiar depended upon rogue magic.

"That's a question we can puzzle out later, along with other matters. Gather your things and meet me at the house in the morning, after you've cleaned up yourself and the dog. I wonder if the dragons have replaced familiars . . . ?" Nimbulan turned and wandered off into the city. He kept his left hand up, palm out while he pondered whatever great thoughts filled his head.

No matter how depleted Nimbulan's body, his mind obviously continued as bright and active as ever.

"Come on, dog. Do you have a name? I can't keep calling you dog." Bessel beckoned the animal to follow him.

Mopplewogger. The word came clearly into Bessel's head.

"That is a bizarre name. Mopplewogger. I wonder what it means."

Pictures of a long-legged and sleek water dog standing in the prow of a fishing boat filled his vision.

"Sorry, dog. You don't quite fit the picture."

The dog sat abruptly with a depressed look, if a face truly existed beneath the tangled ropes of muddy curls.

The mind picture the dog sent Bessel abruptly switched to show an even larger dog jumping from the boat to assist a fisherman battling a bemouth, one of the voracious giants that inhabited the outer depths of the bay.

"If you say so, Mopplewogger," he chuckled. "That's how you see yourself. Maybe you are as brave and loyal as those dogs even though you're less than half the size and all that wet fur would weigh you down in the water. C'mon, we both need a bath, some sleep, and something to eat before we present ourselves to Master Nimbulan and Ambassador Myrilandel. She talks to dragons. Maybe she can answer some questions for me."

CHAPTER 21

*Before dawn, neighborhood temple near the
University of Magicians, Coronnan City*

"Home? You'll take me back to Televarn?" Maia bounced into Kinnsell's arms.

"Whatever you wish, my dear." *Whoever Televarn is, he's a lucky man.* He held the young woman close against his chest a moment, breathing in her delicious feminine scent. He hadn't been with a woman for quite a while. Surely his current wife would forgive him one lapse considering the wealth and prestige he would take home to Terra. It was not as if he were replacing his wife with a younger woman with a bigger dowry and better political connections.

He'd done that three times before and was tired of the game. His current wife suited him fine. She'd make an elegant empress.

Then the significance of the name Maia had given her man at home hit him between the eyes. Televarn: one who speaks to Varns. He'd run into a swarthy man of that name once on a mission to Kardia Hodos about a decade ago. The man was incapable of telling the truth, would betray anyone for the right coins, and drove a hard bargain, harder than any other trader Kinnsell had come across anywhere in the galaxy. He was also one of the most beautiful men Kinnsell had ever seen. No wonder Maia wanted to return to him.

Kinnsell certainly wouldn't take this delicious woman anywhere near Televarn until he'd finished with her.

"Do you have possessions you must gather? We must leave immediately." He'd take her to his ship, just outside the city. They'd have privacy for a while and then he'd move the little shuttle to make her think they traveled where she wished. But he'd take her only as far as the home of the bushie lord who bargained almost as fiercely as Televarn had.

"Possessions?" Maia laughed. She shook her head, setting the hoop earrings to bouncing. Her breasts strained against her black bodice.

Kinnsell wanted to rip the restrictive cloth away and free those full, ripe breasts. They'd fill his hands nicely.

He clenched his hands into fists and kept them firmly at his sides. She must have strong psi powers to go along with her allure. He swore to himself not to fall victim to her. He'd use her the way she wanted to use him.

"I am a Rover," Maia announced proudly. "Rovers wear their wealth. There is nothing more valuable than my freedom. Ah, to wander the roads of the world again. Televarn will wish to rove again after so many years in Hanassa. He was never truly meant to remain in the city of outlaws as their Kaaliph. I will remind him of the wonders of the road." She closed her eyes and smiled dreamily.

"Then we will leave now." Kinnsell grabbed Maia's hand, caressing her palm with his thumb. He drew her fingers to his lips, drinking in the lush smell and taste of her, telling himself that this was what she expected, so why not enjoy flirting with her. His breathing went ragged again, and he coughed to steady it.

Finally, he set his left hand to the back of her waist while keeping her hand bound in his right and headed out of the church.

"We can't go that way." Maia held back. She tugged his hand rather than releasing it. "*They* watch me. We must use a different door. And then find a place to hide until sunset tomorrow. The dawn comes, and with the light their power increases." Her eyes went wide with fear.

"Who prevents you from leaving a church?"

"The magicians. They watch every move I make while they claim to protect me from my own people. They invade my privacy worse than Televarn ever did with his mind in my mind all of the time. The magicians hate women and will kill me if they catch me outside the sanctuary of this building." She hissed as if her words, like the magicians, were tainted with venom.

"Is there another way out of here?" Kinnsell didn't trust

his psychic shields to hide them from a truly powerful magician. He should have noticed a spy with psi powers lingering around the outside of the church. He'd have to learn the trick of extending mental invisibility to another person, something the magicians used all the time in protecting their king—the compromising weakling Katie had married.

"Of course there is another way out. The priests and magicians think it secret, but I found it." She seemed to include priests within the same category as magicians, both menacing and dirty.

"Then why haven't you left before this? You have friends and allies waiting for you."

"Getting out of this sanctuary is one thing. Staying hidden while I escape the city is another. But you will protect me." She caressed his cheek and pursed her lips as if expecting to be kissed.

Kinnsell leaned closer, more than willing to oblige. She smiled so very sweet, promised so much. . . .

He shook himself free of her spell.

"We must be quiet." Maia pressed a finger to her full lips. Her eyes sparkled with mischief. "The priest consoles the cook from the University. She comes here often, supposedly to check on me, but mostly to confess to the very handsome priest. I would confess to him, too, but he prefers his women fair and docile. We can learn something the magicians do not wish the world to know." She tiptoed toward the altar and a small postern door.

"Eavesdrop on a confession?" Kinnsell gulped back his sudden apprehension. He had to keep reminding himself these people didn't believe in the faith that had sustained his family for more generations than anyone could count.

"Knowledge is power, and power is more valuable than any wealth," Maia reminded him.

"That is a concept I can appreciate." A concept his sons could never comprehend. He'd hoped that Katie had learned it. But she, too, had opted to hide on this bush world rather than seek political power. True power.

Thankfully, his current wife understood. She'd forgive his lapse in fidelity for the sake of knowledge and power.

Together, he and Maia moved toward the altar. A large tapestry showing the three Stargod brothers descending to Kardia Hodos upon a silver flame covered the area immediately behind the slab of blue marble. The cold flames in the woven picture looked amazingly like an antique space shuttle. The murmur of quiet voices filtered through the beautiful needlework. Kinnsell looked closer and realized the tapestry separated the main worship area from another room.

The feminine voice became tearful. The masculine voice whispered soothing comfort.

Kinnsell and Maia listened closer.

"Scarface threw me out! I'm not to return to his island again. Not even to visit my husband," the woman wailed.

"He must have had a reason. Have you been remiss in your duties as cook?" The priest kept his voice neutral.

"I provide amply for my boys at the University. I feed the Masters even better, but does he appreciate my efforts, my talents. No. He says that women distract his magicians from their true calling. He says that women represent the old magic and that all traces of it must be eradicated. He told me to be gone before dawn."

"That is a serious change from what I was taught in my early training as a magician, before I opted for the priesthood."

Kinnsell remembered that all the priests and healers in this world must first be magicians. Their first loyalty would always be to the Commune. The woman Guillia might have made a mistake taking her problem to a priest.

"I am not to return to the island again, not even to retrieve my belongings or kiss my husband good-bye. I have lived there three years. It is my home! And my mundane children must leave, too. Nimbulan promised them an education. They can't learn to read and cipher anywhere but at the University. What is to become of us? We have no place to go!"

"Guillia, only magicians may learn to read. That is the law of the Stargods. Scarface is correct in removing your sons from the school. But surely your husband will support you? He can buy you and the children a house on another island. He can live there and work at the University."

"You don't know Stuuvart very well." The woman snorted in disgust. "He's more interested in counting his crates and barrels in the storeroom than in the welfare of his family."

Kinnsell had heard enough. The Senior Magician sought to consolidate his power by evicting all the women from the University, in the name of removing all traces of the old magic—whatever that was. He'd condemned a journeyman magician for using that old magic in an effort to save a drowning man. What would be his next step in controlling everything in this miserable country?

The library. The storehouse of all knowledge accumulated since the Stargods had left the family book collection here seven hundred years ago. Over half of it was locked away already. How long before its existence—even protected by iron bars and telekinetic locks—proved too dangerous and Scarface destroyed the wonderful treasure trove of books?

Kinnsell had to go back and save all of those wonderful books. *His books!* But he had to get Maia away from here in order to win the support of the lords. How much time did he have?

* * *

Near dawn the morning after the dark of the moon, the pit beneath the city of Hanassa

"The spirit of Hanassa used my mother's body!" Yaala exclaimed. That explained why Yaassima had executed her consort for no reason and exiled her own daughter—her only child and heir. Hanassa controlled the city and thirsted only for blood and more blood. Hanassa didn't need an heir, he would simply invade the next convenient body.

Did the spirit displaced by Hanassa become the next wraith that haunted the pit?

Relief made Yaala's knees tremble and her head light. She need not fear falling into the pattern of her mother's ruthlessness because the Yaassima she knew hadn't been her mother.

"But the wraith was here in the pit before Yaassima died, Yaala," Powwell argued.

"The wraith we knew was my mother's spirit. And now it is someone else's." Yaala glared at Powwell as if begging him not to shatter her brief moment of looking toward her future with something akin to confidence and hope.

"Who is the wraith now? We have to know who, so we can deal with Hanassa in that person's body," Rollett reminded them. "Neither the wraith, nor Piedro is going to allow us to just walk out of Hanassa."

Powwell's face looked bland and empty. Thorny retreated deep into his pocket. Both sure signs that he knew more than he told. Yaala knew from experience he wouldn't tell until he was ready.

"This is all very interesting. But I need food and sleep before I can think any further." Rollett yawned.

Yaala heard his jaw crack as he repeated the yawn and scrunched up his eyes. He opened them again reluctantly.

Suddenly he looked vulnerable and young. The last year in Hanassa had aged him beyond his twenty or so years. At first glance, she had thought him closer to thirty. But he couldn't be that old and still a journeyman. Young men either progressed to master or left the University while still quite young.

"Take what you need from the living cavern. There are pallets there, too. Don't forget to drink," Yaala reminded Rollett. She fell back into the attitude of authority. For years, the denizens of the pit had obeyed her without question. Her mother's guards had respected her and feared the accidents she arranged for those who defied her. Yaala pushed aside the notion that she could be as ruthless as the late Kaalipha of Hanassa.

"I need you healthy and strong when we go above," she added to her orders to Rollett. Once we have deposed Piedro, I'll do all I can to help you return to Coronnan. Hanassa needs Coronnan's strength and resources to become truly independent again."

"Do what you can to fix those blasted machines, Yaala," Rollett said over his shoulder as he stumbled toward the large living cavern. "I think I know how to make use of them. I'll need your machines to end the tyranny of Piedro and the consort. They probably sabotaged the tunnel every time we came close to the exit."

"Yes." Warmth began to glow in the pit of Yaala's stomach. With the machines operating again, she could do anything. She could resume control of her life as long as she had the machines.

She turned to speak to Powwell. Her words died in her

open mouth as the wraith flew into the cavern, circling them again and again.

I want my body back. I want it back now! He can't have it. It's mine! The wraith's hysterical gibbering invaded Yaala's mind, driving out all coherent thought.

CHAPTER 22

Neighborhood temple near Palace Reveta Tristile, Coronnan City

True to her word, Maia led Kinnsell to a small ventilation grate in an outside wall of the church. She tugged on the metal bars. They came loose with little effort.

Kinnsell saw places where the hinges had been scraped clean of rust. She must have been planning her escape for some time.

The young woman wriggled through the small opening with little effort. The sight of her enticing bottom squirming about made his blood pressure rise. He swallowed his desire and concentrated on following her.

He had trouble getting his wide shoulders clear of the metal framework. The small opening pressed against his back and chest. He had to cough several times to relieve the pressure in his lungs. At last he squirmed free. A coughing fit made him stagger until he'd relieved the ache.

His elegant brocade tunic suffered almost as much as his breathing. Well, he wouldn't need it once he got back to his ship and resumed his heavy Varn costume. At least then he'd be warm. The layers and layers of thin veils insulated better than the fur lining of his bushie clothes.

"Where is Televarn now?" Maia asked in a hushed whisper.

"I'm not certain. He moves around a lot," Kinnsell twisted the truth as he knew it only a little. Why did he feel uncomfortable lying to this woman? Making the truth fit his own needs had never bothered him before. "We'll have to go to my ship and contact him from there." The shadows grew long. He didn't have a portable torch to light the way to his hiding place. They'd have to hole up somewhere tonight. Unless Maia could see in the dark like the bushie lord and half the population of this cursed planet.

Wherever they spent the remainder of the night, Kinnsell intended to spend it in Maia's arms. Her posture, her attitude, her very being promised him many exotic delights; things his wife had forgotten as soon as she said "I do."

"You will work a summons spell at your ship?" Maia's eyes grew wide. "Then you are a Master Magician, too!"

"Y . . . yes. What do you mean 'too'? Who else do you know that is also a magician?"

"Why, Televarn, of course." She sucked on her cheeks and avoided his gaze.

She was lying. Someone else very close to her was a magician.

Kinnsell crept behind her on tiptoe until they had put several streets and alleys between them and the church. The sensation of being watched grew stronger with each step he took. He searched the area with his eyes and ears as well as his psychic senses. Nothing. He couldn't find anyone watching them, not even the few remaining people on the streets at this chill quiet hour before dawn.

He had to concentrate hard to see where he placed his feet. Maia kept darting in and out of his view as she slipped from shadow to shadow—just like a magician—an illusionist. He had to keep reminding himself that the magicians here, just like the entertainment magicians back home were merely actors who specialized in tricking their audiences.

When he could no longer see the church or its tall spire among the jumble of rooftops, he breathed a little easier. But the chill of unease wouldn't leave him. He still felt as if someone spied upon his every move. A less determined person would have gone back to the church to end the disquieting sensations.

He prided himself on his determination and kept walking.

Kinnsell stumbled over an uneven paving stone. Maia stepped confidently ahead, surefooted and swift.

The darkness intensified. The hair on Kinnsell's nape stood up in atavistic fear. If he didn't find shelter soon, he'd start prattling about dragons just like Katie.

By the time they reached the last bridge out of the city onto the Southern mainland, Kinnsell breathed heavily.

Sweat rolled down his back and under his arms, but he didn't feel warm. The tightness in his chest increased with each step. He'd have to let a cough loose soon. But the noise would echo loudly through these empty streets, betraying their position to any watcher. If he could only hang on until they crossed this last bridge.

The night breeze increased. Kinnsell began to shiver. He prayed that shelter awaited him close by.

New storm clouds built up in the outer bay. The air temperature seemed to drop dramatically. He didn't make it beyond the center span of the bridge before an explosive bark erupted from deep within his lungs. Again and again his lungs tried to expel building fluid and failed. He couldn't drag in enough air. He clung weakly to the bridge railing. His knees wobbled and dizziness assailed him.

Thankfully, this wasn't the plague. His family had always been immune through countless mutations, as were several other clans. Scientists hadn't yet found the genetic code that allowed them to combat the dreaded disease.

This must be some obnoxious ailment caused by exposure to the elements. He hoped the antibiotics he had aboard the shuttle would counter it.

"You are ill, Master Kinnsell?" Maia stood beside him, one hand on his shoulder.

Warmth invaded his system from that hand. The cough eased enough for him to breathe.

"I'm all right now. I'm just not used to the air here."

"Yes, the city is filthy. Better we take to the road where we can breathe free." She tugged on his sleeve. "But the road will wait for tomorrow or the next day. The road will always be there, we have but to set foot on it. For tonight, I know an inn."

Slowly, Kinnsell followed her across the last few steps to the shore. Up ahead, rushlights sparkled in the growing darkness. The cold, damp river mist hadn't reached the lights yet.

He paused to look up at the stars, as bright as the torches. Humans on Terra hadn't been able to see stars from their homeworld for many centuries. Long before the first domes went up, pollution had obscured the night sky. He wished he could see Terra's sun from here; know that he was still a part of the Empire and civilization.

"What will the inn cost us for a room and a hot meal?" he asked, as the thatch of a roof showed black against the dark night sky. He fingered the stash of local coins he carried. He had no idea what each one represented in the true value of goods and labor.

"He will charge you nothing." Maia skipped lightly, twitching her bottom. The movement sent her petticoats swaying.

Kinnsell watched her with growing interest. She hadn't objected to the idea of one room for the two of them. Perhaps she flirted as seriously as he.

One hundred long and wearying paces later, Maia pushed open the drooping gate into the inn courtyard. Kinnsell followed her into the open space, too weary to handle the heavy wooden gate. A painted sign showing a green-haired and seaweed-clothed water witch swung in the breeze, creaking on rusted hinges.

"The Bay Hag Inn," Maia said, sweeping a hand in the direction of the sign.

Kinnsell peered closer for any indication of written words on the creaking slab of wood that swayed in the predawn breeze. Only the picture stared back at him. Maia had read the picture. Only magicians on this world had the knowledge to read words.

A few listless stable hands groomed shabby, knock-kneed steeds. The cook yelled from the kitchen, something about evicting witch cats. Kinnsell couldn't make out all of her words through her thick peasant accent. Guests sang a drunken ditty quite loudly in the common room, with total disregard for key and tone—or the hour.

The stench of unwashed bodies, crowded horses, and stale chamber pots sent Kinnsell into a new coughing fit. He bent over, clutching his knees in an effort to remain on his feet.

"You have to stop this, Master." Maia rubbed his back solicitously. "The innkeeper won't let you stay here if he thinks you carry the plague that ravages the interior provinces."

"I don't have the bloody plague, Maia. Believe me, I'd know if I did." A niggle of doubt tried to insert itself in his mind. He pushed it away. In these filthy conditions, disease must run rampant. But whatever felled the populace, they couldn't have the same plague that decimated the civilized worlds. Local conditions wouldn't support that plague. Anything else, he could cure with a few antibiotics once he reached his ship. Tomorrow. They'd walk there first thing in the morning.

"Tomorrow we hire steeds to take us to your ship," Maia continued. "They will travel much faster than walking."

"I'll be damned if I bruise my backside on one of those beasts!" Kinnsell straightened from his coughing crouch. "If the inn can't provide anything better than those nags, I'll walk." The energy of anger and insulted pride gave him the strength to walk into the inn.

"I'll do the asking, Master Kinnsell. The innkeeper will not refuse me." Maia stepped in front of him as a paunchy, middle-aged man wearing a stained apron approached. He reeked of meat and stale ale.

Kinnsell almost gagged. He had to remind himself that on bush worlds people had to eat meat to survive. The prejudice of civilized cultures against blood diets was only valid on civilized planets.

Maia sidled up to the innkeeper. She draped herself around him, clutching his shoulder as she caressed his cheek with delicate fingertips.

"A private room and a meal for the gentleman?" The innkeeper eyed Kinnsell briefly, then turned his attention back to Maia's lips that hovered much too close to his own. "And for you, my lady, clean sheets and mulled wine in my cot." He grabbed the Rover woman around the waist, pulled her close, and kissed her soundly.

"But, but . . ." Kinnsell gasped. How could she pay for their bed and board by . . . by . . . She owed him—Kinnsell. He'd rescued her. She had no right to peddle her body to this filthy commoner.

Kinnsell narrowed his eyes seeking a suitable revenge. He pushed his right hand forward striving to gain control of the situation and his emotions.

"Do not worry, Master Kinnsell. I will join you later. When you are rested." Maia smiled at him.

Kinnsell relaxed his posture. Let them think him placated.

She and the innkeeper ambled away, arms draped around

each other familiarly, hands exploring bottoms and breasts already.

"But . . . but . . ." Kinnsell continued protesting for their benefit. Frankly he was relieved he would not have to perform just yet. This nagging cough left him tired and weak-kneed.

A very young blonde maid took his hand and led him up rickety stairs to the private room tucked under the steeply sloping eaves.

"I'll stay with you, Master," she offered, staring at him with huge blue eyes.

She couldn't be more than fourteen, a child. Barbarians!

He rammed his hand all the way forward. For once the gesture did nothing to help him.

Kinnsell slammed the door in the girl's face. The walls shook and the tiny shuttered window rattled from the force of his blow on the door panels. A mouse and loose straw dropped on his head from the thatch. He coughed again from the dust that filled his nose and mouth.

* * *

Noon, the University of Magicians, Coronnan City

Bessel and Mopplewogger slept until noon. They grabbed a handful of bacon and bread as they ducked out the back door. After an easy trip through the bustling city, they passed Jorghe-Rosse's embassy on the way to their new abode. Already blood-red mourning wreaths adorned all the doors. Cloth banners of the same blood red were draped from every window. Warriors from Rossemeyer expected to die in battle, therefore the color of freshly spilled blood represented death.

The dog scuttled past the house. Bessel followed as rapidly. Mopplewogger radiated fear that invaded Bessel. Just as they passed the dwelling, a man clad in the voluminous black robes and tall turban of Rossemeyer stepped onto the front stoop. The long strand of black cloth that normally draped from the turban across the man's face hung limply to his shoulder. A fierce frown drew the man's mouth into an expression of malevolence. He watched Bessel and his familiar through eyes narrowed in calculation.

Then he unsheathed his serrated short sword from the depths of his robe.

Bessel willed himself invisible.

You are dead, the warrior mouthed the words and stepped down to the street level. He maintained eye contact with each step.

Mopplewogger yipped and scooted forward, his bobbed tail tucked down.

Bessel ran after him.

The warrior didn't follow. Lady Rosselaara had given King Quinnault one day to produce a suitable victim for her harsh justice. Bessel had until midnight—if the desert mercenaries counted time the same way the rest of the world did. Somehow, Bessel knew they counted time to fit their own desires. They would wait for King Quinnault's justice only if it suited them.

Still looking over his shoulder, Bessel scuttled around an imposing townhouse half an island away. He knocked on Myrilandel's and Nimbulan's kitchen door with more urgency than was probably necessary. He wanted to be indoors and out of sight of any potential assassins. Since he could not fade from view with magic, he'd hide behind mundane walls.

Most of the houses on this island belonged to various ambassadorial parties. A few foreign merchants with enough wealth to buy one of these tall narrow dwellings had settled near their ambassadors. Dragon gold had purchased one of the slate-fronted houses for Myrilandel, their ambassador to the humans.

Nimbulan, Myrilandel, and their daughter Amaranth lived somewhat more modestly than their neighbors, with few if any servants, rarely giving lavish parties or hosting large retinues of their followers. Dragons didn't need to court favor with politically powerful people. People needed to keep the dragons happy.

But if no dragons had been seen in several days, did that mean the dragons were not happy with humans right now?

At last Myrilandel opened her kitchen door to Bessel's rapid knock. He continued looking over his shoulder for signs of pursuit.

The dragon's ambassador carried a broom and wore a simple peasant gown with a kerchief hiding her white-blonde hair. Nimbulan was nowhere in sight. Bessel ducked into the warm room with the dog tangling his feet.

"I will not have dogs fouling my clean kitchen," Myrilandel announced, herding Mopplewogger back toward the door with the broom. He scooted around the broom and hid under the long worktable.

"He's not just a dog!" Bessel defended his new friend. "He's my familiar."

"Well, a familiar is different," Myrilandel peered at the dog through slitted eyes, as if assessing him with her magic. "I lost my Amaranth over a year ago, and I still miss him. Even naming my baby girl after my familiar didn't fill all of the gap his death left. What's this one's name?"

"He calls himself Mopplewogger."

"What in this existence is a Mopplewogger?" Nimbulan asked, coming into the kitchen with his daughter tucked under his arm. The little girl giggled around a damp thumb stuck into her mouth.

"Some kind of water dog," Bessel replied.

"Looks more like a dust mop with a nose and tail." Myrilandel shook her head. "Mopsie, I think."

The dog looked up at the shortening of his name, wiggling from nose to tail and back again.

"Pick a bedroom for yourself and Mopsie." Nimbulan gestured toward the stairs. "Then join me in the study, I'd like to assess your progress before we commence on new courses."

"Pick a room close to an exit for the dog," Myrilandel added. "You'll have to open doors for him, and you'll get tired of walking up and down those stairs in the middle of the night. Believe me, I know what it's like to be owned by a familiar."

"Uh, sir, I think I might need to learn something about self-defense and disguises." Bessel paused in his retreat toward the back stairs—the servants' stairs in any other household. If Myrilandel made use of any servant except an occasional nanny, Bessel had never seen them.

"Why?" Nimbulan dropped the arm he'd been gesturing with. "Has someone from the University threatened you?"

"No, sir. I had to pass the Rossemeyerian Embassy on the way here. One of their warriors came outside and watched me very closely. He unsheathed his sword and said something, but I couldn't hear the words."

Why didn't he admit that he knew what the man had said? Maybe the man hadn't said the words, only thought them.

"Did you read his intentions in his mind?"

"No, sir. I won't eavesdrop unless invited." An embarrassing flush heated Bessel's face.

"Even to save your life?" Nimbulan raised one eyebrow in question.

"I . . . I don't know. I've never been that desperate."

"Think about it while you settle in. And think about invisibility spells. I used to be quite good at hiding myself while in full view of those I wished to escape. Sometimes I didn't even need magic." The elderly man chuckled as he set his daughter onto her feet. He knelt before her and tousled her hair. "But I'll never escape you, Ammie."

The little girl laughed wildly.

Bessel wondered how much Nimbulan could teach him now that he'd replaced his magic with a loving family. Then his old teacher stood, slowly unbending his limbs. A grimace of pain crossed his face and he coughed.

CHAPTER 23

Afternoon, the pit beneath the city of Hanassa

"Are you sure this thing will work?" Powwell asked as he eyed the little black 'mote suspiciously. He held the box so the wraith could view it, too. The misty apparition hadn't left him for more than a few seconds since she'd returned, not even while they slept and ate. The iron gate had remained opened after the guards left. She could come and go as she pleased. So why didn't she go?

At least she'd ceased her wailing.

"I'm not sure of anything," Yaala replied. She repeatedly touched various parts of Little Liise, the generator that chugged happily along converting steam to 'tricity. Mostly Yaala fiddled with a control panel she had exposed on one end of the machine. "Touch the left button and see what happens."

Powwell held his finger over the button she indicated. Sometime in the past it had been painted red. Generations of use had worn the paint off and there were only a few wisps of color left to suggest its purpose. He closed his eyes and pushed hard on the button.

"Nothing's happening." Rollett scanned the caverns, holding out his staff as a sensor. He seemed unaware of the wraith hovering right in front of him.

"Wait a moment," Yaala advised as she fussed with buttons and switches on the nearby transformer. "Push it again."

Powwell pushed the button.

Still nothing.

"Point the 'mote toward the light control panel embedded in the wall." Yaala heaved a sigh of resignation. "I thought you knew a 'mote had to have a purpose and line-of-sight contact with its objective."

"Now we know," Rollett replied with a grin. "Just like FarSight. The magic lets you see farther than your eyes alone, but you have to be in line of sight."

Powwell and Rollett looked at each other. They both shrugged. More and more, 'tricity sounded like magic. But Powwell knew it wasn't magic. It was dangerous to touch, dangerous to any but the most expert engineer—Yaala.

And the machines would let the plague into Coronnan. He knew that the moment he smelled the metallic/chemical taint in the air beneath the pervasive sulfur when they arrived by the dragongate. He'd never forget the smell of the plague in the dragon dream.

The wraith wrinkled the part of its face that might be a nose, mimicking his own action.

Powwell pushed the button again, trying to ignore the wraith. The lights dimmed to a faint glow. Heavy darkness crept closer to him. His senses started adding up the grains of dirt and piles of rock in the mountain above him.

The wraith cooed gentle comfort into his mind, just like Kalen had.

"Now push the green button, the one on the right," Yaala instructed, before he succumbed to panic.

She looked happy, so Powwell guessed the 'mote and the machines behaved as she expected. He obeyed her instructions, remembering to keep the 'mote pointed at the control panel. The lights gradually brightened. He continued to hold the button. More lights flickered on.

For the first time, Powwell felt a lightening of the weight on his chest that came from being underground in the dim caverns. The wraith hadn't helped him as Kalen had.

"Will this 'mote do anything else?" Rollett asked, inspecting the device.

"What do you want it to do?" Yaala turned to look at him, hands on hips.

Powwell wondered why she looked so exasperated, so confrontational with Rollett. She loved talking about 'tricity and her machines. But she seemed almost afraid to give Rollett any more information than she had to.

Afraid of Rollett? They were on the same side, weren't they?

"Will it make the altar stone rise up from the floor of the Justice Hall?"

"Probably."

"Will it allow me to appear on the dais without prior warning?"

"No. But I think it is tuned to a bank of lights in the ceiling to create a blinding flash in front of the dais so you can get through the tapestry of the waterfall before dazzle-blindness wears off anyone in the Justice Hall." Yaala took the 'mote back from Powwell and fiddled with it. "Yaassima liked all her 'motes tuned to the same frequency so she could use them interchangeably. This one should work on everything."

"Then let's go above," Powwell said. He started walking toward the exit before he finished speaking. He couldn't get out of the pit soon enough. The wraith floated close by.

You'll help me get my body back now. He can't have it. I'll do my best.

Yaala's 'motes wouldn't help him evict Hanassa from Kalen's body. He needed magic, strong magic. Only magic would save Kalen and get them all out again. He'd make Yaala come back to Coronnan with him and Rollett. She didn't really belong in Hanassa. No honest person did.

The next few hours could get very messy. Probably bloody, too.

* * *

Afternoon, the pit beneath the city of Hanassa

"This is just a reconnaissance mission," Rollett stated firmly. "We don't take any chances and we stay hidden as much as possible." He fixed a stern gaze on Powwell and Yaala in turn. The men of Hanassa usually flinched in fear when he stared at them like that.

Powwell and Yaala returned his gaze steadily. Each nodded briefly, decisively. They'd obey him this time because his plans coincided with their own.

"At the first hint of trouble, or if anyone recognizes you, head back here immediately. Don't wait. Don't try anything. Just come back here where it's safe."

"We know, Rollett. You've repeated it a dozen times,"

Powwell said impatiently. "Repeating it isn't going to help me find Kalen."

Rollett almost grabbed Powwell by the throat to intimidate some respect into him.

And hated himself for his instinctive reliance upon violence. What good could he do back home if he had truly succumbed to the violence inherent in Hanassa?

"Let's go. No sense wasting any more time with old instructions and older arguments." Yaala moved between the two. She placed a restraining hand on the chest of each man.

Rollett mastered his violent reaction. New respect for the woman cooled his temper further. She'd make an admirable leader in a civilized land. But here, among the lawless, she'd need help. His help. Should he stay?

He indulged in a closer examination of Yaala's face. She had washed off some of the journey grime and combed her blonde hair, leaving it flowing free and soft rather than hiding behind the ugly kerchief knotted Rover style over one ear. Striking rather than beautiful with her long features and pale skin. He looked forward to seeing her dressed as a woman rather than a sexless ruffian. And hoped his desire would fade with the realization she had little or no figure to entice a man.

He didn't have the time or energy to waste on a woman.

He didn't know how much longer he could tolerate the city or the way the city had shaped him this past year.

"Our first task is to try the 'mote on the gate." Rollett marched forward, holding the 'mote in the palm of his hand. "Is there a way we can keep Piedro from opening the gate with magic or a key, Yaala? If he can't get to the food, he'll be in big trouble in the city. That will shift the balance of power. Food and escape are the only currencies in Hanassa." He aimed the little black box at various control panels as they passed. Lights came on and diminished as he pressed the buttons.

"I'll be interested to see who the veiled consort sides with if we manage that shift of power," Powwell mused. He kept looking over his shoulder as if he saw something or someone the other two couldn't perceive.

"So will I," Yaala joined in. "From what you've said, Rollett, she's the one who directs Piedro's every move. He strikes me as a man with ambition but not a lot of forethought. If we take out the consort, he'll be indecisive."

"The consort is the one I plan to watch most closely on this mission. Remember we just watch and learn this time." Rollett approached the gate slowly. He listened with all of his senses for evidence of Piedro's Rover guards.

He heard a mouse scuttle through the dust. A snake slithered behind it. The corridor remained quiet except for those tiny sounds. He checked the light quality for evidence of body heat or auras—though Rovers managed to suppress the visible radiation of heat and energy from their bodies. Last of all, he opened his mind to stray thoughts. Rovers had great armor around their minds when they traveled to places where they were a persecuted minority. But here in Hanassa, where one of their own ruled, the tribe had become lazy.

Silence except for the small rustlings of creatures who belonged down here and the subtle shift of rock and dirt.

The hair on the back of his neck stood up, and his stomach lurched in apprehension. "Kardiaquake coming," he warned the others, grabbing a wall well clear of the gate.

Powwell and Yaala pressed themselves against the wall of solid rock beside him. Interestingly, Yaala faced the rock while he and Powwell instinctively faced outward so they could watch for falling hazards and dodge them if necessary. He edged closer to Yaala so that he could shove her away from danger if necessary.

The ground beneath his feet seemed to roll. The corridor wall across from him rippled. Then quiet descended. He waited for the crash of a passageway collapsing. A few rocks rolled together, nothing bigger.

"How'd you know about that?" Powwell asked, pushing himself away from the wall. He touched Yaala's shoulder gently as a signal for safety.

"I was listening for evidence of the guards. I heard the shift in the Kardia," Rollett replied, still listening to the Kardia for an aftershock.

"If we could maintain a light listening trance, we could predict all of the kardiaquakes. We could awe the populace into obeying us rather than Piedro." Powwell bit his lower lip and ran his hand through his hair in thought.

"Takes too much energy without a dragon or ley lines.

I've tried it," Rollett dismissed the notion. "Come on. We've wasted enough time. Let's see what Piedro is up to."

When they had passed through the gate and closed it behind them, Yaala pulled a new 'mote from her inside tunic pocket. How many did she have? "When you use magic to open a lock, you just move the inside pieces around until they fit a pattern that releases it. Right?"

Puzzled, Rollett looked to Powwell. How did she know so much about the process of magic? He thought those secrets were kept from mundanes. Powwell shrugged and grimaced.

"Correct," Rollett replied, looking over Yaala's shoulder as she flipped open the black casing with a tool she kept hidden in a pouch tied to her waist.

"That's what a key does. And that's what a 'mote does." Yaala fussed with the insides a little. "So what we have to do is make the closure a puzzle."

"Rovers are canny with puzzles. They don't think in straight lines," Rollett said, watching her closely.

"If I reverse the polarity, and retune the resonance . . ."

Rollett felt more than heard a high-pitched hum in the back of his head. He tried duplicating it in the back of his throat. Too deep. He moved the vibration higher into his sinuses. Closer.

"There. Now we can open the gate with this 'mote and only this one, but Piedro will probably exhaust himself trying to manipulate the lock with magic and there is no mechanical keyhole.

"Will the wands the guards used to carry work on it?" Powwell ran his fingertips over the metal plate that housed the lock. A faint red aura followed his hand.

"Not anymore. They are tuned differently." Yaala pocketed the 'mote and marched up the corridor with quick, decisive steps.

Rollett had to stretch his stride to catch up to her. He hadn't had time to fix the exact pitch of the hum in his mind.

At the junction, Rollett paused. He wanted to dash into the Justice Hall and confront Piedro but knew that course would only lead to more trouble than he could handle.

"Storeroom first," he mouthed. His two comrades followed him up the slope to the site of last night's ambush.

The room echoed emptily. If any foodstuffs had been stored here, they were gone now. Someone had even wiped the room clean of remnant aura traces. No telling who had been here and who hadn't.

He closed down his magic senses quickly, ruthlessly conserving his energy.

Silently he motioned the others to follow him. At the junction again, Yaala stepped into the dead-end tunnel. "Dead end," Rollett whispered. He waved her back along the main corridor.

"Hidden staircase behind a door. I can open the door with your 'mote," she returned.

"Next trip. I need to see what is happening among the guards first." Rollett clamped down on his curiosity. Everything of import happened in the Justice Hall. Everyone in the city passed through there at some point of almost every day.

"I think you need to see what is up there," Yaala replied, stepping resolutely into the corridor.

"Wait, Yaala," Powwell said as he chased after her. His aura seemed to detach from him and follow like a ghost. The wraith?

Stargods! Was the wraith trying to steal Powwell's body?

Then Rollett paused and smiled. The wraith was Kalen, Powwell's sister, almost his alter ego. That meant that Hanassa was in Kalen's body, the consort. He knew he'd never trusted the veiled woman for more reasons than the obvious. Kalen was immature, self-centered, manipulative, and sneaky. A prime candidate for the renegade dragon to use.

"We're supposed to stay together!" Rollett rushed to keep up.

"Then follow me. I know what I'm doing." Yaala threw the last words over her shoulder as a challenge.

Gritting his teeth, Rollett marched behind her that last two dozen paces to the dead end. He searched the apparently blank wall with all of his senses and found nothing. Powwell shrugged at him in confusion. He probably couldn't find anything there either.

Yaala grinned at him in sarcastic triumph as she held up a 'mote and pointed it at the top right corner of the end wall.

Slowly the rocks behind him groaned and protested. The

noise became louder as rust and inertia fought with the overwhelming command of the 'mote.

Rollett resisted the urge to cross himself. Yaassima could have hidden any number of dead bodies behind that stone door.

Instead, the weak light from the corridor behind them revealed a narrow staircase that wound upward. "How far up does it go?" he asked when he'd found the nerve to speak again. A tiny bit of respect replaced some of his distrust of her.

"Nearly to the top of the crater wall," Yaala replied, setting her foot on the first step.

"I've seen small openings up there. I thought they were windows to parts of the palace." Rollett followed her as closely as he could without stepping on her.

"Windows, yes. But this is the only entrance to that part of the palace. I don't know that Yaassima knew of the treasure hidden up there."

"Treasure? Don't let Piedro or his people hear about this or we'll be dead in a moment for the knowledge." This time Rollett did cross himself. Piedro's greed for power would kill the entire city. In the Rover culture, money and jewels represented power to be hoarded.

"Not this treasure."

Yaala paused for breath on the first landing, fifteen steps above the corridor. At the next landing, twenty steps above the first, the passage narrowed. Rollett had to slide up the steps sideways. At the fourth landing they all bent double, gasping for breath in the rarified air.

And then finally, after the sixth landing, sunlight filtered down from the top.

Rollett squeezed past Yaala to greet the refreshing light of dawn. Dazzle-blinded at first by the natural light after the dim stairwell, he couldn't see anything beyond the five narrow windows cut into the stone walls. His magic sensed openness around him. He closed his eyes and let the light bathe him a few moments. Then, slowly, he opened them again to better awareness of his surroundings.

"Books!" Powwell gasped from behind him.

"Almost as many books as the library back at the University," Yaala said. "This is the true legacy of Hanassa."

CHAPTER 24

Early morning the next day, queen's solar, Palace Reveta Tristile, Coronnan City

"Nimbulan, Scarface, I need Bessel to escort me into the country on a quest," Queen Maarie Kaathliin said to her dear friend and the Senior Magician. She had summoned them to her private solar at first light. Now the sun hovered barely an hour above the horizon. She couldn't wait any longer to counter her father's manipulations. Discovery of the ring that had nearly choked Marilell had been followed closely by the diplomatic crises over the death of Ambassador Jorghe-Rosse. Katie had spent the entire next day with Quinnault and his Council investigating the incident. They had concluded the accident and death were caused by the storm.

Now she had to take action to end Kinnsell's manipulations for his own gain. She had no doubt the kidnapping attempt was tied to her father's quest to become the next emperor of the Terran Galactic Empire.

The Rover ring that had nearly killed Marilell could have slipped off his hand or he could have put it there deliberately. He loved exotic jewelry and picked up new trinkets wherever he traveled. Kinnsell was perfectly capable of kidnapping his own granddaughter and using her as hostage to his ambitions.

"Bessel may not leave the confines of Myrilandel's home," Scarface replied. He looked steadily at the wall behind Katie's right shoulder rather than at her.

"Look at me and tell me that," Katie demanded. She didn't like acting the authoritative queen among her friends, but Scarface had ceased acting like a friend several moons ago.

The Senior Magician glanced briefly at her face then turned his gaze back to the wall. "Bessel is under suspicion for several crimes. He may not leave Myrilandel's home until my investigation is complete, Your Grace."

"Then release him to my custody." Only Bessel would do. He was the only young magician left who had begun his training with Nimbulan; the only magician she trusted to be uninfluenced by Scarface's surly attitude. Scarface was so like her father when he needed to control everything and everyone around him.

She needed Nimbulan to pressure Scarface into giving his permission for Bessel to join her. Nimbulan seemed the only man left who could influence Scarface. If a way existed for the king and Council of Provinces to oust the Senior Magician, Katie could not find it in the written laws of the land. The Commune was independent from the government. They had to work with Scarface no matter how stubborn and prejudiced he became.

"Impossible. I will not release Bessel from confinement until this matter is settled," Scarface replied, just as authoritative as she. And just as inflexible.

"Nothing is impossible. I need that journeyman and only him." She'd be damned if she'd explain herself to the Senior Magician. Of late, his good-natured ability to organize and lead had turned sour and demanding. What was wrong with him? One would almost think that the Commune and University resisted his control. . . .

Hmm. Maybe. Something to think about. Later.

"The only reason Bessel remains alive and in Coronnan is because *I* have granted him probation until my investigation is complete," Scarface continued. "He worked rogue magic. By law he may not leave his sanctuary until judgment is handed down."

Katie looked to Nimbulan for confirmation. He nodded the truth of his replacement's statement. Scarface only looked more sour and determined to defy her. Very well, she'd maneuver around the Senior Magician and his blasted Commune.

"Bessel has knowledge that I require. I will interview him." And then convince Quinnault to grant him a pardon if necessary to keep him close to her on her quest. Powwell would have been a better choice, he had actually lived the dragon dream with them. But he had disappeared the day after the dragon dream. Yaala had never returned to court from Myrilandel's clearing last Winter. Presumably, she followed Powwell (or led him) into Hanassa.

Frustration gnawed at Katie. If she knew her father, she hadn't much time to thwart his plans. She couldn't do anything while cooped up here at court. And she dared not venture out without the protection of at least one magician. Was frail Old Lyman hearty enough to ride with her?

"Then, I fear, Your Grace, you must wait until I have completed my investigation to interview him," Scarface replied. He looked as if he intended to stalk out of the solar without waiting for permission to withdraw from the royal presence.

"You'd best hurry your investigation, then. I intend to ride on my mission within the hour with Bessel at my side."

"At your own risk, madam." Scarface deigned to glance briefly at her, then back at the wall behind her left shoulder.

Katie tilted her head in question but didn't dignify the remark with words.

Scarface sighed and then explained. "Bessel is out of control."

"I thought he exercised admirable control," Katie remarked. "His testimony in Council yesterday was most concise and logical." She needed to draw Scarface out, get him to say something, anything, that would give her a clue as to why he had become so implacable of late. Then she'd know how to appeal to his better judgment and have him release the journeyman magician.

"You cannot know, Your Grace, the evil in the power that tempts him."

"Explain it to me, then."

Scarface shuddered deeply. Then he looked to the door and to Nimbulan for some kind of reprieve. Resignedly, he turned back to Katie.

"Imagine, if you can, being forced to watch renegade soldiers torturing your closest family for information they did not have. Imagine yourself bound and gagged by magic so powerful you cannot even close your eyes to the carnage wrought in the name of justice. Then picture the glee on the faces of those same magicians as they revel in the pain of their victims, draw power from their screams of agony. And nothing could stop them except another magician more powerful than they. These magicians forced me to become a Battlemage. As soon as I had enough power to escape them, I ran to Hanassa to become a mercenary rather than continue to wreck havoc in their employ. Nothing could control the terror these men brought to Kardia Hodos until the dragons blessed us with their magic. Dragon magic allows—no, demands—that many magicians with honor in their souls combine their powers and amplify them beyond the dreams of the most powerful solitary magicians and control them. I must control Bessel. I must control all solitary magicians who attempt to bring down the Commune."

"Don't you mean that the Commune must control those who attempt to bring down the Commune?" Katie raised her eyebrows and stared at Scarface, daring him to countermand her.

Scarface did not look away as he spoke again. "I lead the Commune. The responsibility for its failures and its successes are mine."

"Bessel is one young man who respects both you and the Commune," Nimbulan protested. "He would never . . ."

"He used rogue magic once. He will use it again. The lure of the ley lines is addicting. He will learn to fear the Commune because we must prevent him from tapping illegal sources of power. With fear comes hatred and the need to destroy. I have seen the pattern before." Scarface sighed deeply as if Bessel's one action was a deep personal insult.

"The Commune can control Bessel. He is more valuable as an ally than an enemy," Nimbulan argued.

"I have no choice. The young man must remain in his sanctuary or be declared a fugitive from justice, subject to immediate execution by any who can capture him."

"I have requested an interview with Bessel as part of the investigation, Master Aaddler. I am your queen. You may interpret that request as an order." By invoking his true name, Katie hoped to force him to answer. She'd use every trick at her disposal to have Bessel as her escort, but she wouldn't stoop to reading Scarface's mind, even if she were able to penetrate his personal armor—which she doubted she could.

Scarface merely stared at the wall, not intimidated in the least by her.

Nimbulan stared at Scarface, jaw slightly agape. Then he closed it with an audible click of his teeth. The silent tension among them grew almost like a living thing that squeezed the air out of the room.

"I will bring Bessel to you, Your Grace," Nimbulan said defiantly.

"I could force you into exile for violating the law of the Commune," Scarface snarled at Nimbulan.

"No, you can't. I'm not a magician anymore."

For the first time since he'd lost his magic, Nimbulan didn't shrink from admitting it. Katie wanted to applaud him.

"You have taken binding oaths. Be warned, Nimbulan, you are in contempt of the Commune. Both you and Bessel had best watch yourselves." Scarface stalked out without even bowing to his queen. "I refuse Bessel permission to leave his sanctuary. If he flees my authority, he announces to one and all his guilt in the matter of Ambassador Jorghe-Rosse's death. If he steps outside of Myrilandel's home, he is fugitive," he added as he disappeared through the doorway.

"Is there any way I can have that man demoted to the scullery?" Katie asked.

"Not without a major mutiny within the Commune," Nimbulan replied with a smile that more closely resembled a grimace. His skin looked too pale, almost clammy. She knew from experience he'd never admit to pain.

"I don't know what has gotten into Scarface. He used to be so pleasant to work with," she said rather than acknowledge infirmity in stalwart Nimbulan.

"Responsibility weighs heavily on Scarface's shoulders. Guilt, too, I guess. His past is full of contradictions."

"Enough of that man, Nimbulan. I need your journeyman on this mission."

"Does this have something to do with the dragon dream you had Shayla impose upon us last Autumn?"

"Yes, it does." How much more did she dare reveal to him? Telling him her father's plans for bringing Kardia Hodos into the Terran Empire felt very much like betrayal of her family. But her family as a whole would not accept

Kinnsell's actions. Surely her brothers could see through their father's plans and intervene?

And after that? Though her heart ached to hold Liam Francis, Sean Michael, and Jamie Patrick close against her heart one more time, she knew she had to give them up.

She had come to Kardia Hodos hoping for safety from the plague. She had found love and friendship beyond her hopes.

She couldn't help but smile at her love for Quinnault which grew daily beyond her wildest expectation.

"Scarface has sent all of the magicians who came to the Commune as my friends into retirement. My journeymen and apprentices have been dispatched on meaningless quests and never returned. Now he condemns Bessel without trial for an offense that Scarface himself is guilty of." Nimbulan bowed his head sadly.

"What?"

"Yes." Nimbulan nodded. "I don't know how or why, but Scarface was in deep communion with rogue magic at the time of the storm. He couldn't have sensed Bessel's tapping a ley line otherwise. And there was something strange about that storm. . . ."

"Could Scarface have manipulated the storm for reasons we cannot guess?"

"Possibly. He wants to exile or execute Bessel without a trial, but that seems very out of character considering the story he just told us. Something strange is going on here. We must watch him very carefully." Nimbulan paused while he looked out the window. "I presume you need a magician as bodyguard on this quest of yours?"

"Yes."

"Bessel is threatened by both the Commune and Rossemeyer. I will defy Scarface and send the boy with you. But he is not a strong magician. You need someone else as well."

"Someone I trust, and I no longer trust anyone under Scarface's influence."

"Myrilandel does not use her magic often, but she is strong when she needs to be. With the diplomatic immunity you granted her, she may use her solitary magic to protect you."

"I couldn't take her away from you, Nimbulan."

"Then I must go with you as well. Amaranth is old enough to be left with some trusted friends. The cheese maker in our market square has many children of her own and always welcomes Amaranth into her household. How long will we be gone?"

"I don't know. A few hours, perhaps a day or two." Her father wouldn't have parked his shuttle very far from the capital. He didn't enjoy walking and hated riding steeds.

"Is your husband in agreement with your plan? And what of your young daughter, Queen Maarie Kaathliin?"

"My husband will agree when he learns you will join us. I just wish he could come, too. I need his strength and clear sight where my emotions might get the better of me." One of them had to stay with Marilell, to protect her from Kinnsell or whoever threatened her.

"Now is not a good time for Quinnault to be absent from the capital. Leave the expedition with me. I will make the arrangements and see to it that Scarface gives Bessel permission to leave the city. Do you know which direction we will travel?"

"We head South, I think."

"Just what are we searching for?"

"Once before, many generations ago, three O'Hara brothers came to Kardia Hodos and cured a virulent disease. I just hope my brothers can arrive in time to prevent the next plague."

* * *

Early morning, the hidden library in Hanassa's palace

"Books, the knowledge of the ages," Rollett whispered, too awestruck to raise his voice. He reached a tentative hand to brush his fingertips across the spine of the nearest volume.

The faintest whisper of power tingled against his skin.

"Books," Powwell repeated. He rushed into the room and started reading titles. He pulled volume after volume from the shelves. Dust rose in massive swirls like columns of smoke.

Rollett choked back a cough. Powwell barked from deep in his lungs, stirring the dust into a wilder storm.

"Have you read these books?" Rollett asked Yaala.

"I . . . ah . . . I don't know how to read. Yaassima didn't think it a skill I would find valuable. But the last engineer taught me to read diagrams. Each engineer has passed on the knowledge of this library to his successor." She pulled a tall volume from a shelf just to the right of the entrance—easily grabbed by a person who had only a stolen moment to get in and get out. She opened the well-worn book to a page in the middle. Lines snaked around the pages in geometric patterns. At certain intervals blobs and crosses indicated something important. Yaala traced the pattern with her finger.

"This is a circuit board inside one of the 'motes."

Rollett looked at her blankly.

"The lines are wires. This is a resistor, and this a switch," she explained, pointing out the various symbols. "This diagram is greatly magnified so I can learn the exact pattern and find broken places in the 'mote."

"Look, Rollett, this is an herbal remedy book compiled by Kimmer—he's the scribe who wrote so many of the books in the University library." Powwell thumbed through the small volume quickly. "And this is a . . . *Stargods*! This is a journal of one of the Stargods. In the original hand! Do you know how valuable this information is? We have to get these books back to the University."

"No!" Yaala protested, much too loudly. "These books are *mine*. Hanassa stole them from the Stargods along with the machines and willed them to his descendants. They are mine!"

"To what purpose?" Powwell returned angrily. "The books serve no one but you, and you can't even read. The world needs this information."

"The books remain here, protected and secure. The only people who can come here revere the books. They don't burn or ban them." Yaala faced him, hands on hips, lips pursed in determination.

Rollett stared at her a moment, struck by the intensity of her commitment.

"Who is burning and banning books?" Rollett asked.

"No one," Powwell answered.

"Scarface has talked in the Council of Provinces about putting certain books behind locked doors to keep the knowledge contained within them from falling into the wrong hands," Yaala answered. "He'll destroy them, mark my words, I know that man. He'll destroy anything he can't control. I will never allow him to control these books."

"These books must remain hidden a while longer," Rollett agreed. He'd discuss ownership of the books with her later. She must see that knowledge and, therefore, the books belonged to all. "We can't move this many books until we know how we are going to escape Hanassa." *If we escape Hanassa.* "We have to scout the city better, we have to know what we are up against. That is knowledge more immediately valuable than this entire library of collected learning."

I have to save these books as well as my people in the city, Rollett thought to himself.

For this treasure I might agree to stay in Hanassa. With Yaala at his side if she wouldn't yield to him?

That thought brought him up short. He wanted nothing more than to be gone from this city with or without the daughter of the late, unlamented Yaassima. But if he opened the city to the outside world, then the library would be available to all magicians, priests, and healers. He could rule the library—but he'd have to rule Hanassa as well.

The image of Yaala standing by his side, helping him govern, kept replacing the image of him presiding over the library. He pushed it aside, concentrating on the here and now. He had to depose the current ruler of Hanassa and make an escape route—or open an entrance.

"Let's go find out what Piedro is up to." He turned his back on the wonderful treasure and marched back down the turret stair. When he reached the first landing, he heard Yaala's and Powwell's footsteps following him sluggishly—reluctantly?

Back in the main corridor, Rollett waited for his companions to catch up. He noted a rectangular book-sized bulge in Powwell's tunic, right below the pocket occupied by Thorny. Rollett decided to ignore the theft temporarily.

A little farther along, they found the wall of tapestries that hid the side entrance to the Justice Hall. The last time Rollett had been through this doorway, he'd led a dozen men on a raid. How many of them had survived the trap laid by Piedro?

He held back an obscene tapestry while Powwell poked his head and his magic sense through the doorway. The younger man stopped short, gagging.

"What?" Yaala pushed her way past him. She turned back to Rollett, eyes wide, throat working convulsively, skin pale and sweating.

Rollett swallowed his sudden fear and looked as well. He immediately wished he hadn't.

The severed heads of two of his informers lay atop the raised altar stone, still dripping blood.

CHAPTER 25

Early morning, the second day after the dark of the moon, in the home of Myrilandel, Ambassador from the Nimbus of Dragons

Bessel slipped out of Myrilandel's house early. He needed to retrieve a few more personal belongings, and he wanted another look in the library. No one had told him he had to stay in the house, just out of Scarface's way, and the day looked too warm and fair to spend it indoors.

After the full day of testifying before the Council of Provinces or being locked in Nimbulan's study reviewing his magical education, both he and Mopsie were ready for some fresh air and exercise.

He'd broken his fast alone on some mixed grains that had stewed into a wonderful cereal overnight. A little dried fruit and thick cream in the bowl had filled his belly nicely. Even Guillia at the University—wonderful cook though she was—didn't have quite the right touch with cereal that Myrilandel did.

Mopsie hadn't liked the cereal, but he'd loved the juicy bone Myri had given him last night, and he'd lapped up a bowl of cream this morning as if he hadn't eaten in a moon or more.

Myri and Nimbulan had stayed up late last night talking over Bessel's report of Scarface's removal of books from library circulation, the investigation of Jorghe-Rosse's death, Scarface's increasingly fanatical policies, and the seeming absence of the dragons. Myrilandel had commented that the dragons still spoke to her but from a great distance. They gave no explanation for wandering farther afield than usual in their hunting. Bessel hadn't been able to stay awake until they came to some conclusion. He presumed they still slept this morning. He and Mopsie had had the kitchen to themselves.

The dog ran a little ahead of Bessel and back again along the road. "Are you scouting ahead for me, Mopsie?" The dog wiggled his hind end and extended his pink tongue in a happy grin. Bessel drew a scent picture from the dog's mind of all the other dogs who had passed this way, piddling on appropriate marking spots. He was amazed at the varied information carried with each scent. "You are a terrible gossip, Mopsie."

The dog agreed and ran off again.

They headed away from Ambassador Jorghe-Rosse's home. The trip to the University would take at least half an hour longer this way, but Bessel wasn't about to risk attracting the attention of the vindictive warriors again. He hoped Lady Rosselaara had accepted the Council's verdict of death by accident.

The city came to life as they walked. Merchants emerged from their homes setting up booths along the major thoroughfares. Smells of cooking meats, baking bread, and stewing fruits tantalized Bessel. Mopsie enhanced each scent and noise for him. Bessel's other senses of sight and touch amplified as well. He turned circles as he walked, appreciating life as he hadn't in many years.

Mopsie licked his chops and stopped to sniff at the butcher's tent.

"Sorry, pup, I can't afford to buy you a bone today. You've eaten well enough for now." He scratched the dog's ears in compensation for the lack of another treat. As a journeyman magician, he was entitled to a small allowance, payable at the full moon, his portion of the fees paid for services the Commune as a whole gave the public. He'd spent most of his savings on a special crystal for his favorite small wand. Magical tools and healing herbs were the only expenses he should have. The University supplied everything else.

Would he still be a magician come the next full moon and payday?

Mopsie growled a warning. Bessel stopped in his tracks, seeking the source of danger.

Smoke. He smelled fresh hot smoke, uncontrolled and spreading. Where?

Just ahead, thick black smoke roiled out of the carpenter's shop. People gathered to gawk and scream and stand in the way of those who sought to escape the fire.

"Water!" Bessel cried. He grabbed a burly man by the shoulders and shook him out of his staring panic. "Bring water. Form a line with buckets. You know how to do this."

The man blinked his eyes clear of panic and confusion, then nodded his understanding. He grabbed a bucket from the nearby blacksmith and headed for the river. Other men followed. The women brought blankets and soothing salves for the carpenter and his family. Everyone moved quickly, organized—once the trance of panic was broken.

King Quinnault, before these people had made him king, had drilled them in simple ways to defend their homes from attack. Fire had been a favorite weapon during the Great Wars of Disruption.

Bessel took a place in the line of bucket bearers. A team at the river filled any available vessel with water and passed them up the line to the fire.

Three men, garbed in black with trim of bright purple and teal blue, stood to the side watching through hooded eyes. Their dark hair and tanned skin hinted of exotic breeding. Rovers? They leaned casually against the wall of the weaver's shop. But their stance told of wariness.

As one, they heaved themselves away from the wall and approached the carpenter.

Leery of the men's intent, Bessel opened his senses to them. Mopsie crept closer to the men, adding his keener hearing to Bessel's.

"Remember what happens to people who don't pay up," one of the black-clad men whispered to the carpenter.

"The king's guards will protect us," the carpenter protested.

"Who do you think we bribe with your money?" the men replied, laughing. "Spread the word to your neighbors. Ten dragini each moon and we won't burn you out. Another five at quarter day festivals and we keep the tax collector from darkening your door."

"But the tax is only two drageen each quarter day!" the carpenter wailed.

The men just laughed and strolled away.

A chill ran down Bessel's back. He needed to tell someone about this dangerous racket. But who? As a magician, he should report directly to Scarface. The Senior Magician wouldn't listen to him. Nor could Bessel get close to the king. And the king's guards seemed to be in the pay of the extortionists.

Who? Maybe Nimbulan had enough influence to get to the root of the problem. Later. The old man needed and deserved his sleep.

What could he do? Throw a truth spell on the culprits for the name of their leader. But then what? He didn't have the resources to tackle the gang on his own. He also needed time and privacy to work the truth spell. The gaudily clad men wandered through the marketplace, keeping well within the crowds.

Puzzled and wary, Bessel moved along in his quest to get to the library. The locals had the fire well in hand, they didn't need him now.

No one seemed to heed his leaving the line of bucket bearers. As if he'd never been there.

"You'll have to be quiet in the library, Mopsie. We're going to retrieve a couple of forbidden books. I hope they will answer my questions. I need to know more about invisibility spells, and about navigating the Great Bay, as well as more about the plague." He added Rovers to his list of subjects to investigate. If the despised wanderers did lead the extortion racket, how did they get into Coronnan through the magical border and why hadn't they been arrested before this?

Didn't Nimbulan, and therefore, his cousin Lord Balthazaan, have Rover blood in their ancestry? That was how Nimbulan had been able to work Rover magic the season he lived with Televarn's clan. Rumor placed a number of Rover-bred retainers in Balthazaan's entourage. Their magic depended upon a common link in their blood. If a person with Rover blood in his heritage stood on one side of the border, could he link with Rovers on the other side of the magic wall to negate the protective barrier? Bessel filed that idea away for later examination along with the possibility of Rover criminals terrorizing Coronnan City.

Back to his primary concerns. Raanald, the barge pilot, hadn't trusted the depth finder. Either his distrust or a malfunction in the machine had led to disaster. There had to be a better way to navigate the mudflats of the inner bay, even in storms and shifting channels.

Mopsie yipped an agreement with him. He sent Bessel a mind picture of a sleek water dog standing in the prow of a fishing boat again.

"I'm sure you'd have been a big help, Mopsie." Bessel swallowed his chuckle. His image of the long ropes of Mopsie's curls soaked and matted by salt water on the short-legged body didn't quite match the dog's view of himself.

"Dust mop, indeed," Bessel muttered as he noted Mopsie's fur brushing the packed dirt of the road. "You'll need another bath tonight, and every night."

Mopsie tucked his tail between his legs and drooped his floppy ears. Yesterday, Bessel had to carry the dog into the sunken stone bathtub with him. The dog wouldn't go near the water otherwise. "If you hate baths so much, how come you think you belong in a boat on the bay?"

Mopsie just wiggled his entire behind along with his stubby tail.

They crossed the first bridge. Mopsie stopped in the center of the span and looked longingly at the churning River Coronnan below. "Not this time, pup. We haven't time to take a swim today. It isn't warm enough either." Spring might have come, but the river was fed by snow melt deep in the mountains to the West. Bessel only enjoyed swimming in High Summer when the chilly water was a refreshing change from the sultry weather.

As he hopped down the step at the end of the bridge, Bessel fingered the linchpin hidden beneath the railing. In case of invasion, all of the bridges connecting the myriad islands of Coronnan City could be collapsed as the inhabitants retreated inward to the palace and University. Invaders would have to resort to boats to follow them.

This linchpin had been oiled recently. Maintaining the release mechanism was one of the duties of the Guild of Bay Pilots. The Commune made a practice of checking their diligence frequently.

The next bridge showed signs of rust on the linchpins on both ends. Bessel paused to look closer to see how neglected the mechanism was. He didn't pay any attention to the foot traffic going in both directions across the span.

Then Mopsie barked a serious warning. The dog tugged

at the hem of his trews then nipped him lightly on the calf. "What is it, Mopsie?" Bessel glanced up from his inspection, looking for another fire.

The dog kept tugging him away from the bridge.

"I am duty bound to inform you that you die here and now so that you may know I am the instrument of justice!" A black-robed warrior ran toward him, vorpal sword raised.

CHAPTER 26

Early morning, the streets of Coronnan City

Bessel ran. He ducked and dodged through the crowded marketplace. The assassin from Rossemeyer followed close on his heels.

Why was it that when he wanted to be noticed, especially by the Commune, no one seemed to know he was in the room, but now, when he desperately needed to hide, an assassin spotted him easily in this large milling crowd?

People screamed and ran in illogical directions as the assassin cursed and brandished his weapon. Bessel used the confusion to put a human barrier between himself and the black-clad warrior. Desperately, he overturned crates of tubers. The hard vegetable balls scattered and rolled, tripping several of the running cityfolk.

And still the assassin followed, sword raised and ready. Single-minded wild tusker," Bessel mumbled as he ran around a cart piled high with cone roots. He snatched two as he ran and tucked them away for a snack later. He'd need the sugars to replace energy depleted by running and any magic he had to throw to save himself.

At the candle maker's booth, a little girl stood in the middle of the path, frozen in place. She screamed her fear. Bessel stumbled to avoid bowling her over.

The assassin gained three paces before Bessel recovered his balance. The point of the man's sword slashed the back of Bessel's tunic.

Fear gave him new energy and a burst of speed. He reached the next bridge. Without thinking of the consequences, he pulled the linchpin the moment he and Mopsie cleared the last span. The bridge collapsed into the river.

The warrior had magnificent reflexes. He clung to the

handrail, pulling himself along it until he reached the ropes that remained connected to the support posts on Bessel's end of the bridge. Then he proceeded to shinny up the rope, the sword now clutched in his teeth.

"Stargods, even the river doesn't slow him down." Bessel took off again. He had to cross only two more bridges to reach University Isle. He'd find refuge there. No one, not even an assassin from Rossemeyer, would follow a magician into the enclave of the Commune.

All Bessel needed was one other magician within reach. Once they made physical contact, the magic within both of them would amplify and grow. They could erect defensive spells to repel the warrior and his lethal sword.

If he reached the University in time.

Alone, he didn't have a chance of gathering enough magic to throw an effective spell.

Before Bessel had run one hundred paces, the warrior regained solid ground. Water dripped from his heavy robes. He grabbed them with his free hand, keeping the wet cloth from tangling his legs.

Mopsie yipped from the doorway of a ramshackle tavern. Safety? Bessel followed his familiar, trusting him with his life.

The dimly lit common room was nearly empty at this time of day. A dozen plank tables stretched the length and breadth of the open space, with little room to walk between.

Mopsie scooted beneath them, toward the back corner. Bessel dropped to all fours and followed. Deep in the shadowy corner a small metal grate was set into the wall next to the floor. Most of the older buildings on the islands had these primitive drainage gates. In Winter and in times of high water, they were shuttered both inside and out. In Summer, open grates offered some air circulation. After a flood, the grate would allow water to drain from the building. Some industrious city dwellers used the grates as a drain after washing slate or tile floors.

The tavern owner had unlatched the grate and swept refuse through it into the common midden in the back alley. He hadn't refastened the bolts. A buildup of rust on the latches would make locking them difficult.

Mopsie paused only long enough for Bessel to push the grate up. The dog darted through just as the assassin entered the tavern. Bessel didn't linger.

Rusty latches scraped his arms as he wiggled and twisted through the small opening. His slashed tunic caught on imperfections in the metal frame. He heard it rip more as he squeezed his shoulders into the open.

His butt stuck. Curse those extra portions of sweet yampion pie and candied cone roots Guillia heaped on hungry magicians.

Someone clamped a heavy hand on Bessel's boot. He didn't wait to see who. Ignoring scrapes and bruises, he pushed through the opening, leaving his boot behind.

Limping, Bessel sprinted to the next bridge, collapsed it before crossing, and ran for a different one half an island away. He didn't wait to see if the assassin fell for his decoy.

His detour took him onto Palace Isle. He aimed for the palace gate, hoping the guards would protect him. Today was open petitions in court. Anyone could walk into or out of the Great Hall without notice. All of the guards were inside. He didn't have time to dive into the crowds and demand protection from King Quinnault.

And the king might have decided to bow to diplomatic pressure from Rossemeyer and declare him guilty.

Bessel cursed his ill luck and continued to the old causeway. Centuries of high tides and Winter storms had almost completed the work of separating Palace Isle from University Isle. Mopsie leaped across the first break in the stepping stones with no hesitation. Bessel followed his familiar, again trusting the dog's instincts for good footing. Jagged rocks cut his bare foot, but he continued on, knowing his only refuge from the assassin was with the Commune.

Shouts and hurried footsteps told him the warrior with the drawn sword hadn't been fooled by the decoy for long.

"Help me!" Bessel cried, panting for breath as he jumped the last few feet onto University Isle. "Masters of the Commune, help me. Help a fellow magician!" He added a little magic to speed his cry to the proper ears. His talent barely responded. All of his energy went into running for the safety of the buildings.

Scarface stepped into the main entryway, arms crossed, face grim, eyes nearly closed with some carefully contained emotion. "What are you doing here?" he asked.

"An assassin from Rossemeyer is after me. I need your protection," Bessel panted as he skidded to a halt in front of the Senior Magician. He bent double trying to catch his breath.

"You were told to stay with Nimbulan." Scarface made a solid barrier in front of the door and sanctuary.

"I forgot some of my things." Bessel looked anxiously over his shoulder. The assassin stalked across the new bridge that connected University Isle to the Palace. He carried his sword lightly. A triumphant smile split his dark face.

"I'm a member of the Commune. You must protect me, Senior Magician Aaddler!"

"You are but a journeyman, not a full member of the Commune. I have decreed you exiled from the Commune until the issue of your use of rogue magic is resolved. Protect yourself." Scarface whirled and slammed the door in Bessel's face.

* * *

Palace Reveta Tristile courtyard, early morning

"May I help you mount your steed, Your Grace?" King Quinnault asked his queen, tugging his forelock and bowing deeply, like any of the stable hands who might have offered the same service.

"What do you think you are doing, Scarecrow?" Katie whispered to him. She tugged on his cupped hands, trying to get him to stand upright.

"I'm helping my wife mount her steed. And a noble steed it is, even if it is barely big enough to mount a child," he replied with a grin. The king's matching white steed stood nearby, head and shoulders taller than the queen's mount.

"But you're dressed for riding. And Buan is saddled and anxious for a hard run." She eyed the beast's restless feet, as big as dinner platters and unmindful of any human appendage that might get beneath him.

"I'm going with you, love."

"Please don't do this to me, Scarecrow. You've got to stay and find a solution to Lady Rosselaara's demands. And . . . and we can't leave Marilell alone. I don't trust anyone."

"I'm only going as far as Myrilandel's house with you.

Then I'll come back and search the laws and old treaties for a precedent that will placate the widow. And I'm bringing the baby with me." He gestured at the maid who stood near the doorway with the squirming princess firmly clasped in her arms. A full escort of guards waited beside her, also ready to ride.

"I can't take all those guards with me. I need secrecy. You know what my father is like, what technology he controls. We can't let these men see it."

Quinnault's face took on the closed, emotionless look she knew too well. His stubborn face. No sense in arguing with him. Short of a full-scale invasion within the next ten minutes, he'd not change his mind. She couldn't change it for him, even if she used her telepathy.

"Maarie Kaathliin, the absence of an armed escort while you ride about the country is a clear signal that something special occurs. I won't let you go alone."

"I'm going for a ride with friends. I don't need an armed escort when I have a magician with me. They will interfere with my mission."

"The armed escort has orders to stay well behind you. They are sworn to secrecy. They have proved their loyalty time and again. I trust them with my life, so should you."

Katie bit her lip. She couldn't think of a single argument to sway him.

"I thought I was meeting Nimbulan, Myri, and Bessel here." Only the two steeds stood in the forecourt. She had expected to have to walk to the mainland stable rather than have the mounts ready for her less than an hour after her interview with Nimbulan and Scarface.

"We'll meet them at their home on the way out of the city. South, you said?" Quinnault bent once more, holding out cupped hands to assist Katie into the saddle.

She placed her left foot into his palms as she grabbed the saddlehorn. She barely had time to swing her right leg over the steed's back to keep from plummeting over it and onto the cobblestones on the other side.

"Easy, Scarecrow!" she gasped as she fought for balance.

"Sorry, love. Your steed is a lot shorter than I'm used to." His grin didn't reach his eyes.

"And I'm shorter than an adolescent child!" Back home, small stature and efficient metabolism were assets in a resource-deprived culture. Here, those qualities made her the butt of many jokes.

But the easy banter didn't break the tension she sensed in him.

"Quinnault, I need to do this privately. My father is dangerous. If your escort even glimpses the nature of his vessel, everything will change . . . for the worse."

He turned to mount Buan in one swift movement, ignoring her comments. Then he reached down to take Marilell from the maid. When the baby sat before him in the saddle, happily cooing, he spoke. "I changed my mind. I'm going with you. We'll leave the baby with Amaranth and her nanny for the day. Safer, I think, than the palace today. You think your father left his conveyance to the South of here?"

"Scarecrow, stay here, please!"

His stubborn face became more intense.

Katie heaved a sigh of resignation. "The land is more wooded and hilly. He'll want to keep his ship hidden. The land North and East of the city is open fields. To the West is open river plains." Shuttle design hadn't changed enough in the last seven hundred years to make the vessel substantially different from the paintings and tapestries depicting the Stargods descending from the heavens in a cloud of silver flame.

If anyone ever associated Kinnsell and his miracle machines with the beloved Stargods, no one would reject Kinnsell's bid for political and economic power through mechanization. And with mechanization would come colonists from the Terran Empire.

The plague would follow in short order. If it hadn't come already. Most of the plague reports originated in mining villages. Were coal dust and iron filings enough pollution to give the microbe a breeding ground?

She wished she could do this alone. But the medieval culture that didn't depend upon technology and therefore didn't develop a plague breeding ground, demanded that neither she nor Quinnault step beyond the privacy of their bedchamber without an escort.

"Ship? Wouldn't he be on the bay?" Quinnault asked.

"A different kind of ship than you've ever seen before, Quinnault. It sails through air, not water. And it contains many wonders that mimic magic and go beyond. I'll use those wonders to send a summons spell of sorts to my brothers. They are the only ones who might persuade Kinnsell to leave here before he changes our lives and our culture irrevocably." Hopefully, Jamie Patrick was either aboard or carried communications to the crew of the mother ship. With any luck at all, her two younger brothers might have returned from Terra as well.

Katie dug her heels decisively into the steed's flanks. It fairly leaped forward, speeding through the palace gates.

Quinnault followed close on her heels.

No route through Coronnan City was direct. For reasons of defense, the bridges rarely lined up and never connected three islands directly. Crowded streets on market day presented numerous delays to foot and mounted traffic alike.

"What is that?" Kate pointed to the smoke-blackened remains of a shop that had once had a dwelling above it. Both halves had been gutted. People stood before it, looking lost and bewildered, including a family of five draped in blankets. The father had lost his eyebrows in the fire. The three children sniveled quietly, noses running, eyes blinking rapidly, too cowed by disaster to cry out loud. The mother huddled beneath her blanket, staring blankly, heedless of her husband and children.

"Fire. Happens too often in the city. Wooden buildings, dry thatch, all crowded too close. We're lucky it didn't spread and take out the entire island," Quinnault replied.

Katie bit her lip, needing to stop and comfort the victims. But she didn't have time. Neighbors seemed to have the matter in hand.

"Remind me to send a basket of food and clothing when we return." She looked anxiously at Quinnault.

He nodded abruptly, eyes fixed on something in the burned-out ruins.

"What is it, Quinnault." Then she saw it. A sigil of warning painted in blood red on the side wall of the building. Soot couldn't obliterate it.

With a gesture, Quinnault sent one of the guards to investigate. "I want a full report when we return. I expect answers and the name of a suspect. This has happened too often," he commanded. "And send the family food, blankets, clothing, whatever they need to get them through until they rebuild." Then he turned his attention back to Katie and his daughter. "Not much farther, love. Nimbulan and Myri live only two isles away."

"Who is sabotaging our city, Quinnault?" But Katie did not need an answer. Only Kinnsell could be so devious. He wanted control of Coronnan even if it meant deposing his own daughter and son-in-law. She couldn't waste any more time finding his shuttle and stopping his campaign. Kinnsell had had most of yesterday and all morning to work his mischief and move his ship.

By the time Katie and Quinnault negotiated the narrow streets, nearly an hour had passed since they'd left the palace. They reined in their steeds before the narrow row house occupied by Ambassador Myrilandel of the Dragon Nimbus and Nimbulan, her consort.

"Where is Bessel?" Katie asked as they reined in before the ambassador's house.

"I haven't seen him all morning," Nimbulan replied. "At first, I thought he'd only taken the dog for a walk but he hasn't returned."

"He and his familiar ate and left early," Myri said, eyeing the large hired steed her husband held for her. "I heard him say something about the library."

"We don't have time to go all the way back to University Isle," Katie fretted. But she needed the magician. Kinnsell would know how to break through any mundane force field she set up around the shuttle to keep him out. She needed Bessel to set a psychic barrier until the O'Hara brothers arrived and removed their father from Kardia Hodos.

"We'll manage without the boy," Nimbulan said, urging Myri toward her mount. "He'll be safe in the library. Even Scarface wouldn't forbid him access to the library."

"I'd rather walk," Myri said with a disdainful look at the hired steed her husband held for her. He hugged her close, and whispered something in her ear.

"You'll be safe. This steed will not throw you."

Myrilandel's hands moved to her belly in an age-old protective gesture.

Could she be . . . ?

No. Nimbulan would have said something in their earlier interview.

"We have to move fast. You won't be able to keep up,"

Katie said, still eyeing her friend for subtle signs of change in her face and physique.

"Not be able to keep up?" Myri cocked one eyebrow. A grin of mischief twinkled in her eyes. "I have friends in high places, remember?" She cast her gaze upward.

Nimbulan and Quinnault also looked up, scanning for the presence of a dragon.

"Will your dragons help us search?" Katie asked. Her mind kept jerking away from her immediate surroundings, back to her father.

What was Kinnsell up to? Who were his allies? She really needed Bessel's magic to keep Kinnsell from fleeing on the shuttle to someplace neither she nor the dragons could find.

She prayed her brothers would come quickly. Any brother would do who would haul Kinnsell back to the mother ship and home. Preferably Sean Michael. The middle brother showed more responsibility and logic than the other two siblings combined.

"Picture carefully, in full detail, what you search for," Myri instructed. "Rouussin is cruising the bay and is willing to indulge us." Humor made her mouth twitch. Dragon moods were always unpredictable. Rouussin, the aging red-tipped dragon, tended to view humans as children he could spoil with treasures and treats even though he rarely understood the purposes behind their requests.

Katie sensed the dragon's feather-light mind touch. (*I am with you, Little One.*)

Carefully, Katie built a picture in her memory of a sleek shuttlecraft like the one that had brought her to Coronnan last year. As long as two dragons, but no higher than one. Stubby wings, pointed nose with a band of windows, like six eyes, above. Tail fins surrounded the engine ports. Last, she remembered to add a silvery metal sheath covered in translucent porcelain scales.

(*That is a strange dragon, indeed, Little One,*) Rouussin chuckled.

A dragon that threatens to go rogue. If we do not find it soon, dragons will no longer have a home on Kardia Hodos. My father will see to that.

CHAPTER 27

Near noon two days after the dark of the moon, Bay Hag Inn, on the South shore of Coronnan City

Kinnsell stuffed wads of coarse linen sheet over his ears to block out the noise. An obnoxious bird announced the morning repeatedly. Each crow call grew louder than the last. The bird kept blaring his greeting to the sun with no signs of tiring of his duty.

He'd wakened and dozed a number of times only to be roused again, most rudely, by the bird.

A civilized world would have alarm clocks that beeped gently or played soothing music to bring the sleeper gradually to wakefulness. Or a man as politically powerful and wealthy as Kinnsell O'Hara would hire a valet to wake him at a civilized hour.

Dawn was not a civilized hour.

The light filtering through the shuttered window seemed too bright for dawn. What time was it anyway?

Kinnsell rolled over on the lumpy bed, refusing to open his eyes. The other side of the narrow straw-stuffed mattress was empty. Barely wider than a ship's berth, the cot still had plenty of room to share with an intimate friend when neither one required privacy and touching delighted rather than offended.

Where was Maia? She had promised to join him when she finished with the innkeeper.

He glared at the smooth layer of blankets beside him! Then he threw the covers off the bed and stood up. None of last night's fatigue and heaviness in his chest lingered. He needed a good breakfast and a hot shower with real water, not the sonic sprays required during space travel.

Then he'd deal with Maia and her disloyalty. If he didn't need the woman as hostage for the bush lord's loyalty, he'd dump her here within easy distance of the capital for the magicians to find her again.

But the bushie was tricky enough to hold Marilell, Kinnsell's granddaughter, hostage as well as his loyalty in return for Maia.

"I should have kidnapped the child myself, rather than trusting any local." But Katie's servants had been on the alert for him. He'd not sneak into or out of the palace easily, where Lord Balthazaan and his wife had free passage through the place.

"Ah, you have arisen at last, Master Kinnsell," Maia said, entering the room with a cloth-covered tray in her hands. She fairly bounced as she walked, and her black eyes sparkled.

"I thought I locked that door," Kinnsell snapped at her.

"You did. But you opened it again for me when I returned to you at midnight. As I promised." Her eyes narrowed seductively. "Then we broke our fast together and you slept again while I moved about the inn, asking questions. I have learned a great deal."

"I bet you have." Kinnsell glanced at the bed. She hadn't slept there. Her scent didn't linger on the sheets, nor were there any stains left by sex. She lied. He gnashed his teeth, wishing he could leave her here. Not yet. But soon, she'd know his revenge.

"I have ordered a hot bath for you, Master Kinnsell. You slept through the one I offered yesterday. It will be ready for you by the time you break your fast." She whipped the cloth off the tray to reveal fresh bread, hot from the oven, salted fish, creamy cheese, and a bowl full of berries that had been dried and reconstituted in a rich sauce that smelled of wine and cloves. His mouth watered.

"Peasant food," he sneered.

Yesterday? Had he slept through an entire day and two nights? Not likely.

His stomach growled its emptiness and then twisted into an acidic rejection of any food. How long since he'd eaten? A day and two nights?

He couldn't think of food. He had to know how he had

lost so much time to sleep. But it smelled delicious, and his stomach grumbled again with hunger.

" 'Tis the same meal ordered every morning by Master Magician Nimbulan and he comes from the most aristocratic of families. He's first cousin to Lord Balthazaan," Maia protested. She stared at the food and then looked up to Kinnsell with troubled eyes. All trace of pleasure left her expression.

"Does everyone on this planet—er, in this country—eat such coarse bread? Can't you mill finer flour than that." Kinnsell wanted to make her squirm under his displeasure even though he longed to grab huge bites of the stuff.

" 'Tis the spent wheat from brewing ale. The king considers this bread a delicacy!" A fat tear rolled down her cheek. She pouted, pursing her lips forward in invitation for him to kiss away her sadness.

Recognizing the ploy of women everywhere—with or without the spell of allure from psi powers—Kinnsell obeyed. Just this once he'd allow her to believe herself in control of their relationship. He brushed away the tear with his fingers and kissed the corner of her mouth. He dropped a second kiss on the enticing mole just to the right of her mouth, then another and another. . . .

Stop this! he ordered himself. "If the king eats this bread, then I will, too," he said breathlessly, wanting to taste more of her. But he must regain control of himself and of her. "See if you can hurry the bath. We must leave as soon as possible," he added less gently.

Maia rewarded him with a brilliant smile. "Soon I will be home, among my own people, and you will be hailed a hero for rescuing me." She kissed him soundly. "I will wash your back," she said with a new huskiness in her voice. "And your front."

Kinnsell swallowed his desire. He hadn't time to linger this morning. He'd lost too much time already. Katie must be frantic over the loss of her daughter.

He wouldn't take Maia to the bushie lord until he'd satiated the burning ache of desire in his gut. His granddaughter was safe. Even the conniving members of the king's Council wouldn't hurt the child, a mere baby and a girl. Now, if Katie had had the good sense to give birth to a son first, the child would be heir and therefore a threat to the rebellious lords.

The bread tasted nutty with a delightful complexity. It satisfied his hunger and settled the too-hungry-sick feeling quite readily. Kinnsell pushed aside the fish. The cheese would have to suffice for protein. Normally he wouldn't eat milk products, but the meal contained no legumes to complete the amino acid chain. The flavor burst on his tongue, promising new delights. The berries in their wine sauce were worthy of a royal banquet back home.

Maybe he'd linger on this planet a little longer, sample the delights of its cuisine—so much better than ship rations and tanked food. Fresh food was, after all, the primary reason for nurturing this planet. He'd also indulge himself with Maia for as long as he wanted. No need to hurry back to Terra and his cold and unloving but politically powerful wife until he'd secured a power base on Kardia Hodos. But he had to check in with the mother ship soon, or they'd send a search party. He didn't need any of his crew—especially his sons—questioning or sabotaging his work to bring this planet back under Terra's influence. Sean Michael and Liam Francis were due back any time now. The boys might even rescue Marilell from Balthazaan before Kinnsell reclaimed her.

He hurried through the bath despite Maia's attempts to climb into the little tub with him. The water didn't stay hot long and the heaviness threatened to return to his chest.

By the time Kinnsell and Maia walked out of the Bay Hag Inn, the sun rode high and raised steam on the damp cobblestones. A spring returned to his step that he hadn't felt in many years. Maia kept up with him, prattling stories about great adventures of the road. Most of her stories centered around the mysterious Televarn, chief of her clan. He tuned her out and concentrated on what to tell the bushie lord and when.

After about two kilometers, they reached the cutoff from the Great South Road. Kinnsell eagerly turned West. "Not far now, my dear," he said with a smile. Within half an hour he'd be back in his shuttle, an island of civilization on this planet of chaos.

Maia stopped abruptly, pressing her temples with anxious fingertips.

"We must go this way." She took two hesitant steps on the Great South Road. "We must hurry. They need us." She dropped her hands and stared blankly toward the South. Her eyes glazed over as if blinded by a trance.

Kinnsell had seen similar reactions to hypnosis. What kind of latent suggestion had the magicians put upon her?

"The clan of Televarn needs us," she chanted. "Televarn is dead. Long live the clan." Two more steps and she fell to her knees.

"Noooooo!" she wailed, pressing her hands to her temples once more. "He can't be dead. If Televarn is dead, then who has been inside my head this year and more? Who directs me?" She cried and tore her hair, still kneeling in the road. "I didn't believe them when the magicians told me Televarn died. I didn't dare believe them because his voice was still inside my head. He murdered the Kaalipha. I saw him do it. I saw him twist the poisoned knife in Yaassima's gut. He has to be alive!"

Kinnsell stared at her gape-mouthed as she pounded the ground with her fists. She stumbled to her feet and started running.

"That is not what happened," Kinnsell grabbed her shoulders, ready to shake some sense into her. He tried to remember the details of the tales told about the events in Hanassa when he'd first brought Katie here a year and a half ago. "Yaassima turned the knife in time and killed Televarn. Yaasaima died later. Now come along, this way," He tried to lift her to her feet. A deep cough made him release her.

"Follow me. We have to go West. We have to get to my ship." The cough passed. Kinnsell grabbed her around the waist and lifted her to her feet. She kicked his shins and bit at his restraining hands, never ceasing her wails and moans of distress.

"Televarn can't be dead! I know they lie to me!"

"Where do we have to go in such a hurry, Maia? Tell me where, and I will take you there in an instant," Kinnsell soothed. He couldn't let her escape now. Not when he was so close to commanding the full loyalty of the bush lords.

"You know the secret of the transport spell?" Maia ceased her struggles so suddenly Kinnsell almost fell forward, on top of her.

He shifted his balance and loosened his hold a little. The spurt of activity renewed the tightness in his chest. He held his breath a moment to control the cough. He'd be comfortable and warm as soon as he reached the shuttle. Then the cough would go away. He only felt overheated and chilled at the same time because this damned planet was so bloody cold, without the slightest knowledge of climate control.

"Not a transport spell," he replied when he controlled his breathing once more. He sought a metaphor the woman would understand. "I control a dragon. A very special dragon that lets me hide inside her. She will take us wherever you want to go. But first we have to get to her."

"A dragon!" Maia crossed her wrists, right over left, and flapped her hands in the bizarre ward against evil. Her eyes grew wide with respect and . . . and terror. "You control the renegade dragon, Hanassa?"

"Whatever. Now come along this side path. We have to get to my dragon before she flies away on her own." He doubted Jamie Patrick would order the shuttle returned to the mother ship by remote, but he never knew what his sons might do. One day soon he'd have to beat some discipline into them—as he should have when they were little, but he was too busy courting political favor to bother with children then.

He kept his arm around Maia's waist as they returned the few steps to the barely maintained side path. Deep shadows from overhanging trees cloaked them. Kinnsell shuddered in atavistic fear of the unknown darkness. He kept up a prattle of words to mask his uneasiness. "My dragon will shelter us and give us hot food and drink and comfortable beds until dark. Then she will fly away with us. Anywhere you want to go." *As long as it's to the castle of my bushie lord. Once I show you to him, I'll control the majority of King Quinnault's Council and the king's daughter. I'll direct when and where technology is introduced. And I'll collect tithes from these bushies as well as the rewards of bringing this world back into the fold of Terra's Empire. None of my relatives stand a chance of winning the election as emperor once I bring this planet back into the fold.*

"I have never touched a dragon before. But I have seen one," Maia said, caressing his face with gentle fingers. "I did not trust the dragon. I could not penetrate her thoughts.

But she touched mine. She blocked out Televarn's voice, and I did not know what to do without him." Her wonderful hands slid down his back. "You can replace Televarn in my mind. Your talent is strong, Master Kinnsell. You can replace Televarn in the minds of all the Rovers. Your control of the Rovers can extend to all those who have even a trace of Rover blood in their veins, like Nimbulan and Lord Balthazaan."

Heat flooded Kinnsell's veins wherever she touched him. He recognized the subtle psi power and allowed himself to enjoy her for a moment. Her words brought a smile to his face as well. His family enjoyed a similar mind-to-mind contact. But the O'Hara clan had better control, no one person could remain in the mind of another without permission. These Rovers needed a leader to direct them. Kinnsell was willing to employ them if they bent to his control as easily as the rest of this planet. He lengthened his stride.

"You will not be able to penetrate my dragon's thoughts. Only I can do that," he said, warming to his story. Cyber controls could be defined as a form of mind-to-mind contact.

The nagging cough returned.

Maia touched his temple with the fingertips of her right hand and his chest with the flat of her left hand. Heat radiated from the points of contact. An electric buzz shot through his veins. The cough eased. She lingered, not releasing her healing touch. His vision narrowed, blotting out all but Maia. His thoughts focused on her bright beauty.

He raised his hand from her waist to the swell of her breast. She didn't pull away. He risked opening his palm to cup her fullness. Her nipple budded tight beneath his fingertips. His heart beat loudly within his ears, pounding out a staccato rhythm.

He turned her within his arms and kissed her deeply. She opened to him, moaning her pleasure. This trip did have some benefits, after all.

He stepped off the path into the dense underbrush. They could linger a while. No one would find his ship. They had plenty of time before they had to meet the lords at sunset.

"This way!" a feminine voice shouted over the sound of many steeds' hooves pounding the packed dirt of the road. His passion had deafened him to their approach.

Not just any feminine voice commanded this small cavalcade. His daughter, Mary Kathleen O'Hara, led the charge. Led them straight past him along the path that ran only to his shuttle.

* * *

Late morning, University Isle, Coronnan City

Bessel wasted one heartbeat of time staring at the door Scarface had just slammed in his face.

The assassin roared in triumph as he dashed across the bridge, sword raised.

"C'mon Mopsie. Let's see if you are truly a water dog." Bessel ran for the nearest river access and dove in.

Mopsie ran for the assassin, growling.

Bessel caught a brief glimpse of the little dog leaping for the man's sword hand. His teeth latched onto the wrist, forcing the assassin to drop his weapon.

Then cold, muddy waters closed over Bessel's head. The swift current pulled him down, down, down.

Bessel let the river current carry him as he swam upward. He shook water from his eyes while he kept his hands and feet moving. He heard another splash and looked back toward the bridge. Mopsie landed in the water in a great spray that dampened the assassin on the bridge.

"Good boy, Mopsie," Bessel called to his familiar. "You gave me time to escape."

The bedraggled dog paddled strongly toward Bessel. He yipped a greeting and aimed to intercept his master.

"You are the most pathetic looking mutt." Bessel couldn't help grinning broadly at the sight of all that soaking fur streaked with mud. No wonder the dog had looked so forlorn and lost when they first found each other on the docks. Mopsie had been swimming in the bay while Bessel had tried to rescue the ambassador.

"Maybe you are a water dog after all, pup." With determined strokes, Bessel set out for the mainland to the South of the city.

Mopsie growled a warning. Bessel looked about him for signs of the assassin. He saw the black-clad warrior on the bridge of University Isle shaking his fist at Bessel. Then the warrior scrambled toward the nearby dock where the University kept several boats tied.

Bessel swam with long strokes away from the continuing menace. The river offered hundreds of hiding places but few landings big enough for a boat. He knew he could escape the assassin as long as he stayed in the river.

Already the cold water sapped his strength and set his teeth chattering. He had to find shelter quickly. He headed for a series of aits hidden behind University Isle. Some of the tiny, temporary islands had withstood the river and the weather long enough to grow tall grasses and scrubby trees. He might not be able to build a fire to warm and dry himself and the dog for several hours yet. But he'd be able to get out of the water and probably out of the wind.

Mopsie barked again.

"What?" he asked the dog, treading water. He had to work at staying in one place in the strong current, but he didn't dare proceed until he knew the next danger.

Two quick barks. Bessel automatically looked left. He dove down and away from a heavy tree branch before it connected with his head.

"Thanks, Mopsie," he said when he resurfaced beside his new friend. He took a moment to scratch the dog's ears. "Now how did I know that two yips means left? And I suppose one means right?"

Mopsie barked once in agreement.

"Do you know any fishermen we can hide out with until it's safe to go back to Master Nimbulan?"

The dog barked one more time.

CHAPTER 28

Late morning, side trail off the Great South Road

Katie dug her heels into her steed's flanks. "We can't be late," she mumbled to herself. "We can't be late." Her words took on the rhythm of hooves striking the roadway.

She yanked the reins for the animal to turn left along the side path. Roussin told her the path had been widened from a deer trail by Rovers who used to camp in the clearing where Kinnsell had landed his shuttle.

Foam flecked her steed's mouth around the bit. Sweat gleamed along its neck. But its breathing and cadence remained steady. She'd driven the steed hard since Roussin had shown Myri the location of the bizarre dragon in a small clearing South and West of the city.

Quinnault led the way through this wilderness. Nimbulan and Myri kept up with them, through Myri looked decidedly green at the corners of her mouth and the edges of her pinched nose. Their mounts showed similar signs of fatigue. The guards lagged behind, but they kept her within sight until just before she turned off the main road.

Deep shadows darkened her vision the moment they left the road for the woods. She clung to the reins, praying the steed sensed the trail better than she.

She should have come yesterday, or the day before when Kinnsell first made his threats to bring technology to Kardia Hodos, when she'd first thought Kinnsell might own the ring that choked Marilell. But then Ambassador Jorghe-Rosse had died and caused a diplomatic crisis. By the time she and Quinnault had dismissed the emergency Council meeting, dawn of the next day hovered on the horizon.

Then they had spent an entire day hearing conflicting testimony and weighing evidence.

Anxiety gnawed at her. Rouussin said the shuttle was still in the clearing. Where was Kinnsell, and what was he up to?

Katie couldn't tell what or who lurked beneath the thick tree canopy. Just enough light filtered through the interwoven branches overhead to allow undergrowth to flourish.

No time to give in to her fears now. Nimbulan and Myrilandel and Quinnault were behind her. Quinnault rode ahead, slashing at encroaching branches and vines. They would protect her from the childhood monsters that leaped from her imagination into the trees. That wasn't really a Sasquatch and its mate beneath that oak. The last of the legendary pairs of Bigfoot had been captured and held in a protective zoo just after the first atmosphere domes had been constructed. The pair had failed to breed in captivity so none could have been transplanted to Kardia Hodos with the first terraforming project.

The shadows were just shadows.

They pelted up the narrow track for another kilometer—she had to think in miles she reminded herself. They traveled less than a mile. The dense forest opened. More light came through the canopy. The trees were younger, farther apart. Saber ferns and brambleberry bushes filled in the blanks between trunks. The rich scent of thick humus and fresh leaves about to burst forth from Winter's sleep filled Katie's senses. She slowed the steed.

Her companions slowed, too. Not far now. Katie searched for signs of the shuttle's passage through the trees.

A path of singed branches led the way better than the track they followed. Only a shuttle's engine could have burned its way through the trees at that level, along that trajectory. Kinnsell hadn't been careful about damaging the forest when he landed.

Marsh plants dominated the foliage. Underground springs softened the soil. The steed slowed more on its own, picking its way carefully around treacherous mud.

A glint of silver caught Katie's eye. She kneed the horse forward, too anxious to worry about the footing.

Two tall Tambootie trees, stripped of their leaf buds, formed an archway to a wide clearing. A small pool reflected green light onto the side of the sleek shuttle. The landing pods had sunk deep into the soft ground. Sunk so deep Kinnsell would burn twice the normal amount of fuel breaking free.

The soft red glow of the alarm light blinked steadily beneath the hatch keypad. No one was within the shuttle. Kinnsell's footprints had been obscured by rain and the passage of wild animals at least two full days ago.

"Leave it to Kinnsell to choose his landing for convenience rather than safety." She almost laughed in relief.

"Watch the mud, Katie," Quinnault warned, dismounting before she could.

"This is indeed a strange dragon," Myri gasped. She crossed herself, paused, then made the more ancient ward of flapping hands over crossed wrists.

"But this dragon does not breathe and has no mind of its own," Katie replied. "It presents no danger until a human enters it and starts the engines. It is but a machine."

The wind and rain and natural cleansing agents in the environment could cope with the pollution left behind by one shuttle. But when the populace learned of the miracles of technology represented by those who flew shuttles, they always wanted more. The people wanted to control the forces of nature with technology. They didn't want to leave such powers only to magicians. Technology made mundanes the equals of magicians. Technology led to pollution. Bodies adapted to pollution, built up toxins in their body. The plague virus ate pollution in the air, the water, and inside human bodies. When it ran out of toxins, it ate living tissues and spread to the next host with minimal contact.

Kinnsell had to be stopped before he contaminated the entire world.

"I hope he hasn't changed the security codes," she said, marching toward the craft. Quinnault surveyed around the shuttle. Myri and Nimbulan came right behind her, holding hands like young lovers. Myri blushed and cupped her belly protectively again.

Before Katie reached the hatch, her boots sank into the soft mud. She lifted one foot carefully, wondering where to step next. The hatch and its keypad lock had sunk to a level she could easily reach, if she could get to it.

"We need solid ground," Katie looked around for inspiration.

"Branches," Nimbulan said. "We'll cut some of those

everblue boughs and lay them across the path. That should secure Katie's footing. She weighs the least of any of us. I've only my short sword with me. It will have to do." He unsheathed his basic weapon/tool. Quinnault did the same.

"My dagger is sharp. I'll help." Myri pulled her own blade out of her hip sheath.

In short order they laid a dozen branches across the mud. Nimbulan breathed heavily, strain showed around his eyes, and his skin looked waxy pale from the small exertion.

Katie looked to Myrilandel to see if she noticed the undue fatigue in the older man. Her friend already placed her hand upon her husband's chest. A faint eldritch glow of blue healing connected them.

Nimbulan pushed her hand away after only a moment. The blue light lingered, stretched thin, still connecting them. They both stared at her hand in silence for a long moment. "You can't, love. Not now. 'Tis too dangerous for you to use your magic."

She glared at him with a determined set to her chin. Then Nimbulan nodded his head in acceptance. She raised her hand again but held it several finger-lengths away from his chest. The light blazed again, then died gradually. Nimbulan's face remained quite pale, but his breathing came easier.

Katie turned her attention back to the shuttle. If anyone could keep Nimbulan healthy, it was Myrilandel. She'd brought him back to life before.

There was only one reason why Nimbulan would not wish her to use her healing talent. She must be newly pregnant and feared to hurt the baby's development.

The fanning twigs of the cut branches with their blue needles spread out in front of Katie's feet and wove together in a blanket only a little paler than a clear Summer sky. Katie stepped gingerly on the thickest portion of the branches. They sank a little into the mud, but held before her boots suffered any more damage.

She reached up and touched the flat keypad. Seven, one, eight, two, seven, two, eight, one. A soft whirring sound signaled the hatch opening to her command.

A blast of stale air greeted her. She wrinkled her nose at the slightly metallic, almost chemical scent of recycled air. The smell of home.

"Isn't that the same smell Shayla gave us in her dragon dream?" Nimbulan asked, holding a hand over his mouth and nose.

"Yes," Katie agreed, startled by the revelation. Quickly, she placed a fold of her heavy riding skirt across her face, then jabbed the close command on the hatch. The smell had become so ingrained in her memories of home, she had hardly noticed it in the dream. Now that she had inhaled nothing but the fresh air of Kardia Hodos she recognized the truth. This recycled air contained the scent of the plague.

"We have to leave right now. I can't risk contaminating myself or you with any more exposure." Katie gulped back her tears of fear and disappointment.

* * *

Near noon, side trail off the Great South Road

Kinnsell watched Katie and her entourage ride back down the path toward the road. Katie sobbed quietly.

What had happened to upset Katie so? She never gave way to her true emotions in public. Always, *always,* she found a way to convert a bad situation into laughter. In all her twenty-five years, Kinnsell had only caught his daughter crying once. The day he divorced her mother and married his pregnant mistress.

"We'll bring incendiary materials back to cleanse us of that . . . that . . ." the older man in the party said. His shoulders slumped in defeat. Nimbulan, the trusted magician who deceived the lot of them by claiming he'd lost his magic. Psi powers didn't get lost. But sometimes they hid for a while.

Nimbulan's skin looked waxy with a blue tinge around his lips. His fingers had swollen where he gripped the reins tightly. Probably just a heart condition. It had to be just a heart condition and not the first symptoms of the plague. Ill health would mask psi powers. The magician had lost his psi powers over a year ago. The length of the illness suggested a heart condition. The plague didn't linger that long once it chose a victim. Usually.

But the unpredictability of the plague and its mutations often devastated entire city domes before the first diagnosis.

"I will prepare a cleansing ritual for all of us before we destroy that renegade dragon you call a shuttle, Katie," said the tall blonde woman who always clung to Nimbulan's side. Myrilandel, rumored to be half dragon. "Meet me by the mainland stand of Tambootie trees. South of the first bridge." She kneed her steed and galloped ahead of the rest. No expression animated her face. Only the defiant stiffness of her very erect spine suggested any emotion at all.

A few more paces took the mounted party out of sight and out of earshot. Kinnsell stood up, brushing dead leaves and dirt off his brocade tunic and plush trews.

"Come, Maia. We have to hurry." So much for his plans to lie with the sultry woman before taking off. He had no intention of being anywhere in the vicinity when his treacherous daughter returned with the materials to torch the shuttle.

Katie's party and their steeds had churned the muddy path into a sopping mire. Kinnsell picked his way carefully along the sides until he reached the clearing. If these stupid bush dwellers had the sense to install climate control, he wouldn't have to ruin a decent set of boots!

He held his breath against a new round of coughing as the mud seeped through to his socks and chilled his feet and legs.

"Stargods protect me!" Maia exclaimed. She stared straight ahead, eyes wide. Over and over she crossed herself, followed by the bizarre gesture of crossed wrists and flapping hands.

Kinnsell followed her stunned gaze. He saw the shuttle where he'd parked it, settled only slightly deeper in the mud than he remembered. Weak sunlight sparkled on the silvery tiles of the hull. The glare made him squint and lower his gaze.

"What is your problem, woman?" He faced Maia, hands on hips, aggravation and unease making him snap his words.

Maia pointed at the shuttle. Her mouth formed the word "dragon" but no sound emerged.

"That is my ship. I told you it is a kind of a dragon."

"A . . . a . . . atop the silver thing," she choked.

Kinnsell glanced again in the direction she pointed. Then he looked away again quickly. The glare hurt. "The sunlight reflects the silver skin, makes it brighter, just like sunlight on water."

"Not that. A real dragon. A real dragon is perched atop the silver one!"

Maia backed up as if she wanted to flee but didn't dare take her eyes off the thing that frightened her.

"Nonsense. There are no real dragons. Only my mechanical one." Kinnsell tried again to look at the shuttle.

This time a slight shift of the sparkling light made it a little easier to observe more closely. Something big did indeed perch atop the shuttle. Something almost transparent but with just a hint of silver revealing the massive bulk. Bright red outlined the extended wings and claws.

Then the standing dragon opened its mouth and roared. Flames burst forth from behind teeth as long as daggers.

Kinnsell almost wet his pants as he ran back down the path toward the road.

CHAPTER 29

Late Morning, Kaalipha's Palace, city of Hanassa

Powwell ignored the sounds of Yaala vomiting out in the corridor. He thought she'd would have grown used to this sort of thing by now.

But did anyone ever get used to violent and bloody death?

Rollett didn't look any better than Yaala, but at least he kept his breakfast down. "They were my men. They depended on me, and I failed them." Rollett swallowed nervously.

"They chose to live in Hanassa, a city of murderers, thieves, extortionists, rapists, and every other kind of criminal you can name. They came here because they couldn't, or wouldn't obey the laws of the outside world. As long as they lived here, they couldn't hope for a clean death in old age," Powwell reminded him.

"Not all of them. Some of them came here as slaves—like you. They didn't have a choice. They relied on *me!*"

"I haven't time to hold your hand, Rollett, and make you feel better about yourself." Powwell resolutely swallowed his revulsion and stepped into the Justice Hall, senses alert to any danger or presence.

His resources had worn thin again. He pushed the limits of his magic for his own safety.

When he was certain no one hid in or around the huge room, Powwell crept forward. He clung to the shadows as long as possible. Thorny gibbered in his pocket. The hedgehog didn't like the smell of blood. They needed to scuttle away in the dark tunnels and hide.

Powwell hushed his familiar. He didn't like the smell of blood and fear either. But he had to find Kalen—or rather

Kalen's body. The wraith was the only thing left of his sister. He had to use his magic to help Kalen regain her body. She couldn't do it alone. The blood on the altar could give him valuable information.

At last he took the remaining four long strides between the back wall and the raised altar below the dais.

"How'd they raise this stone without 'motes?" he asked. "There's a lot of blood on the manacles, so they managed to open and close them, too."

Rollett shrugged. Yaala wept silently in the corridor.

Powwell screwed up his courage and touched the coagulating blood with sensitive fingertips.

Power jolted up his hand and into his arm as if he had touched a ley line. He sucked up the energy greedily. And with the power came knowledge. The last moments of the dead man's life flashed across his mind.

Pain, humiliation, fear. Accelerated heartbeat. Quivering panic. Then a sharp agony in the back of his neck. Sharp awareness that this was the end. Almost a sense of relief. A flash of bright light and sudden awareness . . . Blackness.

Powwell lived through the shaking limbs and cold sweat only slightly distanced from the events. When his heartbeat returned to normal, he replayed the events through his memory, watching for glimpses of the people around the execution. He recognized Piedro standing on the dais as he passed judgment for treachery. The Kaaliph hadn't changed much since he'd helped Televarn kidnap Powwell, Myri, and Kalen a year and a half ago.

Powwell watched through the dead man's memories an entire clan of Rovers dancing around the altar stone in a stylized ritual. The magical power they generated from the dance raised the altar stone. Rough hands from behind forced his hands into the manacles at one end. His partner faced him at the other end, equally afraid, mumbling prayers to a dozen different gods. Then he shared the sensation of the cold stone on his throat as the outlaw was forced to bend over the substitute executioner's block.

But when he tried to focus on the figure beside the new Kaaliph of Hanassa, his eyes slid up, down, and sideways. He couldn't examine any feature of the vaguely feminine creature. As if Kalen had merged with a dragon!

A sharp pricking pain in his chest brought him back to

the reality of the deserted Justice Hall. Thorny wiggled uncomfortably in his pocket. Fully extended spines threatened to rip holes in the sturdy cloth of Powwell's tunic. Something akin to a sob of grief shook both of them.

Powwell jerked his hand away from the altar. Blood still dripped from his fingertips. Power continued to tingle through him. He hated the thought that he gained from the terror of a man's death. He'd only known one Bloodmage. The thrill of harvesting power from pain and terror had driven that man to insane abuses of his magic.

"Thanks for reminding me, Thorny. Keep reminding me of the cost of this power." He caressed his familiar through his pocket until the hedgehog relaxed his spines and Powwell could safely pet him directly.

"What did you learn?" Rollett asked from the shadowed doorway.

Yaala remained in the corridor. Her squeamishness at the grisly deaths encouraged Powwell that she would not revert to her mother's cruel methods. Or Hanassa's—whoever had governed the Kaalipha's body.

"I'm not sure," he replied to his fellow magician. "The images are complex and distorted. I need time to sort through them. Let's scout the royal suite through Yaala's back door. I think we need to concentrate on Piedro and his consort. They have to have a weakness." He stalled.

He couldn't reveal all that he'd learned—the wraith would take the knowledge and try to regain her body alone. She wouldn't succeed and might kill herself with the effort. Nor could he let the others know that he was now in full possession of his magic. He wasn't even sure he could force himself to use this magic since it was powered by blood.

He wanted to run away from the power and curl up into a tight ball, just like Thorny. He didn't dare.

"I don't think you are going to spy on anyone, young magician," a man snarled from the back of the dais. Piedro stepped through the waterfall tapestry. "You escaped my slave pens once before. You'll not live long enough to do so again."

Two dozen Rover guards crowded into the room from the main doorway, swords, arrows, and 'mote wands aimed at his heart.

Then Powwell saw the consort standing next to Piedro.

Black SeLenese lace of finest silk covered her from head to toe. A shift in the open pattern of the lace revealed her gray eyes and the ferret familiar draped across her left shoulder.

The wraith howled and dove for the consort. Hanassa, within Kalen's body raised her right hand within the lace veil and wiggled her fingers in a mocking shooing gesture.

The wraith screamed in agony and scuttled through the exit, back toward the pit and safety.

Powwell wanted to run after her, but found his feet unable to move, pinned by magic.

The consort laughed hysterically at his predicament.

Now, big brother, we are together again, Kalen's voice, but darker, throatier, penetrated his mind like iced water.

You aren't my sister!

* * *

Justice Hall, city of Hanassa.

"Run!" Yaala screamed. "Move, Powwell, move *s'murghit!*" She hit every 'mote secreted upon her person in hopes one would respond.

The altar rumbled as it slowly lowered, stone scraping stone. Lights exploded on and off around the room. The dais retreated and advanced in random jerks. The waterfall tapestry fluttered.

She backed into the corridor, still slamming her fingers against the various 'motes. She couldn't see a thing. The bright lights continued flashing before her eyes, even when they plunged the Justice Hall into darkness. But she had to make room for Powwell and Rollett to get through the narrow back door.

Two bodies brushed past her. She prayed they were her two friends.

A large hand grabbed her left arm and propelled her backward. Every dragon instinct bred into her demanded she fight the man who held her. A deeper emotion knew that Rollett protected her, keeping his body between her and the advancing Rovers.

He'd do the same for any of his men.

She had to trust his magic senses to get them back to the pit and safety. Her eyes hadn't adjusted yet.

"Powwell?" she asked breathlessly when they had turned two corners and the corridor was beginning to come into focus.

"Here," the young man replied from right beside her. "Your screams helped me break the enthrallment." She heard a high-pitched chatter above the sound of their footfalls and her heart pounding in her ears. Thorny told her that he, too, accompanied them.

"We're all together," Rollett reassured her. He shifted position, dragging her in his wake rather than pushing her. "Get ready to open the gate in a hurry. We won't have much time to get through to safety."

Yaala pulled two 'motes from her left pocket. Which one operated the gate? She couldn't remember. Maybe it was one of the three black boxes in her right pocket. Or the two tucked into her breast band. They all looked alike.

"Catch!" She tossed 'motes to each of her friends. "Push every button you can until the gate opens."

Rollett let go her arm to grab two small black boxes out of the air. Yaala felt an immediate chill from the loss of his touch. That frightened her almost as much as the sight of Rover guards brandishing wands that she thought only she could control.

Yaala pushed buttons frantically as the gate came into view. Her feet slid on the loose sand of the corridor. She struggled to maintain her balance while continuing to push buttons.

At last the gate creaked open.

Powwell drew alongside her, 'mote pointed directly at the gate. He must have the proper one.

No time to think, only to escape to the other side of the gate.

"I will protect you, men, from the wraith. Don't let the gate stop you," Piedro called from behind the refugees.

Rollett reached the crossed iron bars first. He grabbed the gate, ready to slam it closed as soon as Yaala and Powwell passed through.

Powwell skidded on the sand, sliding out of control. He slammed into the bars, in the far corner away from the opening. He dropped the 'mote.

The guards pelted forward, barely ten paces away.

Yaala grabbed Powwell's tunic and dragged him through the gateway. Without thinking, she scooped up the black box and aimed it at the lock.

"Stargods, I hope it's not broken," she prayed.

Rollett slammed the gate closed, pressing all of his weight against it.

Archers followed the initial wave of guards. The nearest Rover raised his belt knife ready to throw it the last three paces into Rollett's back.

She turned off the lights.

Three very long heartbeats later, Yaala heard the lock snick tight.

Then they were off again, deep into the labyrinth of caverns. As they passed through the living cavern, the sounds of pursuit died down. At least the gate had slowed the Rovers.

"We've got to keep moving. I don't trust that lock," Rollett panted. He bent over, hands clasping his knees as he tried to ease his breathing. "Piedro is a very powerful magician. I felt his spells all around me. My armor almost collapsed under his assault."

"The lock will hold," Yaala reassured him. Still she headed toward the caverns where her machines resided.

"We're too late. We can't hide anywhere, and your cursed machines won't help." Powwell stared blankly toward the gate and the clang of wands against the metal bars. "The consort is too strong. She overpowered my blood magic to hold me in thrall. She's even corrupted Kalen's ferret familiar. That takes more magic than any one of us could dream of. Nothing will stop the renegade dragon from killing all of us. Not 'tricity, not magic, nothing."

CHAPTER 30

Early afternoon, the Northern edge of the River Coronnan near the Great Bay, outside Coronnan City

Bessel hauled himself out of the river near the confluence with the Great Bay. He'd run out of islands. The assassin had kept the stolen boat within sight for most of the length of the river. When Bessel managed to get out of sight of the warrior and crawl out of the water, the islands around him were flat, low, and lacking enough vegetation to hide him.

The coast North of the city offered him better refuge than any of the temporary aits. Here, at least, he could find shelter from the rising wind under a tree or behind a sand dune.

Mopsie trudged out of the water beside him. He hung his head tiredly for a few moments before shaking. Bessel was too tired and cold to duck the spray. What was a little more water when half the river weighed down his clothes.

The other half of the river matted Mopsie's long ropes of fur.

Bessel followed the dog's example and wrung some of the dripping water from his tunic. He shed his socks and twisted them somewhat drier. He looked at his cold-reddened toes mournfully. "I'd better let the socks dry a bit before putting them back on. Stargods only know where my other boot ended up."

A muddy and rocky beach stretched before them, separating the bay from the land. A few gentle grass-covered hills marked the end of farmland and the beginning of the mudflats.

"Where to now, Mopsie?" Bessel asked, looking over his shoulder for traces of the assassin or of habitation.

Mopsie yipped once and trotted forward, angling to the right. After half a dozen paces, he stopped again to shake. The other half of the river burst free of his fur.

"You still look a mess, pup." Bessel ducked the spray this time. When the dog had finished and trotted forward again, Bessel shared a sense of lightness and freedom with the dog. "Is that what a familiar does, Mopsie, shares everything, the good and the bad?"

Mopsie grinned his agreement, his little pink tongue making a bright splash in the middle of the muddy white fur. The dog continued along the beach, looking back expectantly. Bessel followed, trusting his familiar as he had trusted few human beings except Master Nimbulan.

Shortly the dog's ears perked up a bit, and he raised his nose to sniff the wind. Bessel did, too. Woodsmoke drifted gently toward his nose. Woodsmoke permeated with salt and . . . and fish! Mopsie yipped happily and bounded forward.

Bessel's stomach growled, so he followed.

Along the beach a short distance and deep in one of the numerous coves on the uneven coastline, a group of three fishermen huddled around a small driftwood fire. The men had hauled their small boat above the ebbing tide line and turned it over to keep the interior dry. Bessel sensed rain on the wind and shivered anew.

Three sleek, long-legged dogs raised their heads from their paws, eyes and ears alert, but not menacing.

"Have you enough fish to share with a stranger?" Bessel asked politely. He stopped well away from the fire. Mopsie hung behind him rather than challenge the larger dogs.

"Looks like you're as much flotsam as man," one of the men laughed. Deep lines creased his face around the eyes from a lifetime of peering closely at the water in all weathers. A broken tooth showed when he grinned. Otherwise he looked healthy, reasonably well fed, and no more ragged than any other man of his profession.

"I feel like a piece of waterlogged driftwood," Bessel replied.

"Then come, sit by the fire, and warm yourself a bit. There's fish aplenty if you don't mind picking out the bones," the fisherman said. He gestured Bessel closer. The dogs lowered their heads but kept their eyes and ears on Bessel and Mopsie.

"Well, hello, pup!" a second fisherman greeted Mopsie. He held out a hand for the dog to sniff. "Where you been hiding these last few days?"

"Mopsie adopted me two days ago," Bessel said. He plunked down next to the second man. "Do you know where my fam . . . dog came from?"

"Them Guild of Bay Pilots turned out all their dogs when they got that fancy machine. Said they didn't need dogs to sense the currents anymore." The first fisherman spat into the mud in disgust. "Name's Leauman, and this here's Aguiir and Waaterrsoon." He gestured right and left to indicate his companions.

"I'm Bessel, and I'm very interested in learning more about your dogs." As if on cue, the three large dogs rocked and stretched onto their feet, then ambled over to sniff Mopsie.

Nose to nose, nose to tail, they introduced themselves. When Mopsie had been approved, they all wrestled a few moments, tugging on ears and nipping tails. But then they settled around the fire, each dog at the feet of his master.

"I don't understand. Can dogs smell underwater?" Bessel mused. He rested his elbow on one knee and propped up his suddenly heavy head with his hand.

Mopsie stretched and shifted, edging marginally closer to the fire and the fish cooking on a spit above it. Leauman smiled at the dog and then at Bessel. One of the dogs growled low in his throat at Mopsie. The little dog gazed back with wide innocent eyes and dropped his head onto his paws. A moment later he repeated the maneuver. This time the warning growls were louder. Mopsie had the grace to look guilty, but he didn't back away from his intended prize.

"What's to understand about Mopplewoggers? The dogs stand in the bow of the boat and yip once for starboard, twice for port. We follow the dogs and never run aground. Ignore the dogs and you run afoul of a sandbar or flotsam, just like that stupid pilot, Raanald, two days ago. If he'd kept his dog and not bothered with the machine, he wouldn't have lost his passenger and brought this country to the brink of war." Aguiir hawked and spat again.

Bessel cringed a little, not knowing if he should mention that he had ridden on the barge with Raanald two days ago.

"Mopsie doesn't look like a Mopplewogger," Bessel said, caressing his familiar's silky ears in an attempt to keep him from creeping closer to the fire and their dinner.

"Yeah, he was a surprise all right," Leauman laughed. "One of the pilot's dogs was in heat when she got turned loose. She must have mated with half a dozen strays around the port. Every pup came out different."

"Is one of your dogs Mopsie's dam?" Bessel inspected each of the lounging animals for any trace of resemblance to his dog.

"Naw," Waaterrsoon spoke for the first time. "My Swabby brought the bitch home with him. She's heavy with pups again. This time I made sure she only mated with Swabby." He petted his dog vigorously, possessively.

"What about Mopsie?" Bessel asked. "Why was he running loose on the docks eager to follow anyone home?"

Not just anyone! They all looked at him strangely, their thoughts as clear in Bessel's mind as if they had shouted them aloud.

"If you don't know why you've been claimed by a Mopplewogger, then you aren't ready to partner one," Leauman stated. He abruptly ended the conversation by reaching for one of the fish spitted above the flames. The sweet meat nearly fell from the bones. He cupped a hand beneath it, to keep the flesh from dropping into the flames. Gently he blew on it to cool it, then fed a morsel to his dog before eating himself.

The other two fishermen did the same. Only then did Bessel take his own fish. Mopsie sat up, brushing his tail rapidly in the mud. By this time his fur was more black than white. Like the others, Bessel fed the dog first, recognizing the importance of a familiar in his life.

Mopsie had found him when he most needed a friend and defender. Could the dog sense the future? Maybe he just sensed emotions and recognized in Bessel similar needs to his own.

These men and their dogs had welcomed him, fed him, and offered the warmth of their fire; more consideration than Scarface and the Commune of Magicians had offered one of their own.

"If Raanald had kept his dog on board the barge, then he wouldn't have relied on the confused readings of the depth finder. If he had listened to a dog, he probably would have avoided grounding on the sandbar, Jorghe-Rosse wouldn't have fallen into the bay, I wouldn't have had to resort to rogue magic to rescue him, and I'd still be a part of the Commune," Bessel sorted the chain of events out loud, no longer caring who heard and who didn't.

"But if it had happened that way, you wouldn't have needed Mopsie and he wouldn't have found you," Leauman added.

"I think all of Coronnan needs to know more about the bay fishermen and their dogs," Bessel said. Surely one of the many books in the library discussed the unique relationship.

Probably one of the books Scarface had locked away.

"No one but us needed to know before this," Aguiir said.

"But we never had to choose between faithful dogs and machines before," Bessel added. "We never had the Commune declare certain knowledge forbidden to everyone, including magicians, before." Without that knowledge, the plague could come to Coronnan and they'd have no defense against it.

"I've got to go back and save those books. We can't afford to let Scarface lock them away forever."

"Someone chased you and Mopsie into the river, boy. Whatever you're running from is still waiting for you in the city," Leauman warned.

"I know. I have to accept that risk. The books are more important. Protecting Coronnan from men like Scarface and Raanald is more important. If I'd had time to investigate invisibility spells, this would be a lot easier."

* * *

Noon, shuttle clearing off the Great South Road

"Stop, Master Kinnsell, the dragon can't hurt you," Maia called.

Kinnsell slowed his steps as he moved away from the

shuttle. He looked all around him very carefully before coming to a complete stop.

His lungs burned from his sudden burst of speed. He dragged in air, trying desperately not to cough. Cold sweat beaded on his skin and his knees shook so badly that he almost couldn't stand.

"It's only a little dragon. It won't hurt you," Maia reassured him again.

Rational thought began to filter back into his brain. "It looked mighty big and dangerous to me." Kinnsell felt his forehead. Perhaps his coughing bouts had induced a temporary fever. He had to have imagined the beast sitting atop his shuttle. Dragons did not exist.

"Certainly, dragons look dangerous," Maia laughed. "But they are oath-bound to protect humans. That is part of their covenant with the magicians."

Then Maia had seen the beast, too. Had one of Katie's companions left a post-hypnotic suggestion on them so they'd stay away from the shuttle?

Kinnsell relaxed a little, content with his logical explanation for the sight of the silver-and-red monster with fiery breath. He turned back toward the clearing.

"You're right, Maia. The dragon can't hurt us." It didn't exist. "But it might tell my daughter that you and I escaped, so perhaps we'd best begin our journey." He held out his arms to escort her back to the shuttle.

Fortunately the draconic illusion had disappeared by the time they entered the clearing again. Kinnsell marched up to the shuttle hatch, resolved to be on his way within moments.

He ran his fingers over the lock keypad. It did not respond to his usual codes. Eight-one-seven-two-seven-two-eight-one. He'd used the same code for years. Why didn't the bloody hatch open? He drummed his fingers on the metal/ceramic alloy of the hull. What random numbers would Katie use to reset the lock? He tried her birthday, his code backward, the coordinates for Earth, the coordinates for Kardia Hodos—he had to try those twice before he got the numbers right—and a straightforward one, two, three, four, five, six. Nothing worked.

"Dammit!" He kicked the hatch.

"Perhaps I can decipher her spell," Maia suggested, quietly. "A woman knows another woman's mind."

"Go ahead and try. But Katie is devious in her logic. There are thousands of combinations she could have chosen." He stepped aside while the dark-eyed woman stared at the numbered keys.

She stared a long time. Finally, she looked away rubbing her eyes and shifting her feet up and down in the mud. "Piedro says he cannot channel magic through me unless there is a second Rover with me. Piedro has replaced Televarn as head of the clan. I do not like him as well as Televarn, but he is satisfactory as a lover and his voice is strong in my head." She closed her eyes and looked off into the distance.

Lover? Had Maia slept with every man on the planet? He frowned, wanting to push her aside and handle the lock himself. He also wanted to drag her down in the mud and prove that he was a better lover than the Rover trash who invaded her mind.

"Tonight we will be together, King Kinnsell." Maia caressed his face. Then she abruptly returned her attention to the lock.

She lied. He knew she had no intention of willingly sharing a bed with him, no matter what she promised. Kinnsell realized Maia would never tell the truth if a lie sounded better, and she would not tell the whole truth if she must tell any of it.

She stared hard at the keypad for a long moment. "I cannot see the heat of Her Grace's hand on the puzzle. Your heat has masked it."

Kinnsell slammed his fist into the hatch. The first assault of pain turned into a numbing ache. The clamminess returned to his skin. He jerked his hand away and sucked on his abused knuckles. They looked alarmingly swollen.

"There are other ways of unraveling a puzzle, though." Maia flashed a radiant smile at him.

Kinnsell forgot the pain in his fist, the growing anxiety inside his gut, and the pressure in his chest. He forgot her lies and deceit. "Tonight, my dear. Get that hatch open, and tonight we will celebrate in safe comfort."

"Yes. Tonight Piedro will reward you for returning me to the clan. Tonight we will celebrate in Hanassa."

"Just open the hatch, and I will command this dragon to fly us to safety." He couldn't remember if the bushie lord had named his castle Hanassa or something else. Many small details eluded him. Had he remembered the right codes for the lock? No matter. He would pilot the shuttle and take her where he wanted to go and nowhere else. Maia had no say in their destination.

Maia concentrated on the keypad one more time. This time she held her palm in front of it, a hair's breadth away. Her eyes rolled up and her expression went blank.

Then she reached her other hand inside her bodice, deep into her cleavage and out again so quickly Kinnsell almost didn't see her gesture.

But he followed her swift movements closely.

Still gazing at the lock in a trancelike state, Maia pulled a small twist of wire free of her garments. She inserted the tool into the very narrow crack that defined the doorway. A few seconds later the hatch clicked and slid open.

If he hadn't known better, Kinnsell would not have seen her pick the lock. But . . . "Electronic locks can't be picked," he gasped.

"A lock is a lock, and all locks can be picked." Maia giggled in triumph. "Now show me this wondrous dragon, Lord Kinnsell. I would make friends with the strange beast."

"Why not?" Kinnsell gestured Maia into the shuttle while suppressing a new bout of coughing. His lungs had been quiet for hours. Why now? Probably the molds and other nasty fungi growing in the mud had triggered an allergic reaction.

The warm, slightly metallic tasting air rushed to envelop him in familiarity. It smelled of home and comfort and safety. He drank deeply of it as he stepped through the portal into the passenger cabin.

Maia stopped short just inside the door. She stared at the comfortable blue upholstered benches that converted to beds, the softly blinking lights of the electronic readers and game boards, the food synthesizer that converted any vegetable matter into tasty dishes.

"What sort of magic do you wield, Master Kinnsell?" she whispered, too awestruck to move.

"The magic of technology," he replied seductively into

her ear. "Settle in one of the benches and fasten the restraints. We'll take off in a minute."

"Don't leave me alone inside this strange monster, Master Kinnsell." Maia's eyes remained wide open. Her pupils contracted in terror, leaving the liquid brown iris to plead with him.

"Very well, my dear." Kinnsell patted her hand and drew her forward into the bridge area. "Sit there." He motioned her to the copilot's seat. She couldn't inadvertently change any of the controls unless he turned them over to her by voice command to the computer. A copilot could take control if the biosensors determined the pilot was dead or unconscious, but that wouldn't happen on the quick hop to the bush lord's castle.

Kinnsell drew the safety strap over his head and shoulders, fastening it on the clip between his legs. Maia mimicked his actions, hiking up her skirts and petticoats to reveal most of her trim thighs. Kinnsell had to gulp back his desire once again. His eyes did not want to return to the control board.

Finally he remembered what he needed to do. He cleared the viewscreen so that they could look out and see the real-time scene around them. Then he ran his fingers over the touchpads and began the firing sequence. Automatically he set his destination coordinates into the auto pilot. No need for the cyber-control headset. They were only going a short distance and not nearing a suborbital altitude. Almost instantly, the atmosphere jets roared to life.

Maia reared back in surprise. But when Kinnsell proceeded calmly with the launch sequence, she relaxed, studying everything. He knew she'd never figure out the complexities of flying the shuttle. She couldn't even read, let alone understand the mathematics of navigation.

He fondled the joystick lovingly. Certainly he could use the touchpads to fly the shuttle. Most pilots did or they used the supersensitive cyber controls. But his family had always had an affinity for the joystick, preferring to sense the craft's movements and vibrations through the palm of their hand and the seat of their pants rather than the technological array before their eyes.

Kinnsell monitored the gauges. When the engines had enough power and fuel, he eased the joystick back. The engines roared again, straining to respond. He looked at the surrounding trees through the viewscreen. The craft did not move.

"What?" he asked the computer.

The displays told him that the weight of the mud on the stabilizing feet of the shuttle trapped them.

He eased the stick back again while rocking it side to side. The trees seemed to shift and waver in front of him. Like riding on a teeter-totter. The shuttle jerked back and forth but still did not lift. The engines continued straining. He burned fuel at an enormous rate.

Pressure built in Kinnsell's chest. His head seemed detached from his body. He had trouble focusing his eyes.

Still, he continued rocking the craft to loosen the cursed mud. Another reason to erect climate control on this planet—or at least construct decent landing pads.

"Perhaps the dragon is back. If it is sitting atop your dragon, the extra weight would make flight difficult," Maia suggested.

"There are no such things as dragons," Kinnsell asserted through gritted teeth. He continued rocking the craft. Seesaw. The trees swayed before his eyes.

Was that a tiny bit of lift?

Yes, he was breaking free. He wasted more fuel compensating for the planet's gravity. He eased the shuttle up to treetop level. The shuttle remained unsteady, shaking as badly as his hands. He ignored the weakness and the need to cough and the sweat pouring into his eyes.

When he had finally cleared the trees, he looked for his compass and couldn't find it. The array of lights and numbers on the control panel blurred and doubled and redoubled. He closed his eyes hard, and blinked several times.

"Wake up, Master Kinnsell. Wake up. You are losing control of the dragon!" Maia screamed in his ear.

Kinnsell roused slightly, shaking his head to clear it. Chills racked his body suddenly. His eyes blurred again.

"Autopilot. Set autopilot," he said. To his own ears each forced word took on new shades of meaning. Had he really told Maia to set the autopilot or had he named the colors of dragon wingtips? No, he had named each of his four children by wife number one and their three half siblings by numbers two and three. Number four, Marjorie, didn't like children.

Seesaw Marjorie Daw.

"Master Kinnsell!" Maia screeched again. "You must control the dragon, we are going to crash!"

CHAPTER 31

Noon, the pit beneath the city of Hanassa

Rollett watched Powwell walk resolutely toward the cavern he said housed the dragongate. Depression weighed heavily on the boy's shoulders. His skin looked waxy and pale in the unnatural light.

That strange misty aura still clung to Powwell's silhouette. Suddenly Rollett knew that Kalen had become the wraith while Hanassa inhabited her body. Now she kept close to her brother, demanding his help.

"Can we force Hanassa to relinquish Kalen's body?" Rollett asked, determined to push the boy into action. He couldn't allow one setback to force him to give up. If he'd done that, he'd have committed suicide a year and a half ago. But now he was out of resources. The city was out of time. They had to act.

Powwell shrugged, studying the bloody stains on his fingers. The dried blood looked black against his increasingly pale skin. He kept his back to Yaala and Rollett. But he tilted his head much as Myrilandel did when she listened to dragons. Did the wraith whisper to Powwell?

"We haven't time for arguing over spells and joined spirits," Yaala reminded them as she peered back along their escape routes. "The food in the living cavern will slow the guards down a little, but if Hanassa rules the consort's—Kalen's—body, then she'll drive the Rovers deeper and deeper until they find us. Hanassa knows these passageways better than I do."

"Does Hanassa know the dragongate?" Powwell whirled to confront them. Hope animated his eyes and his posture.

"He/she must if she's been down here for centuries," Rollett said.

"But does Hanassa *understand* the dragongate?" A wide grin split Powwell's face—a grin that spoke more of malice than of mirth.

"Can anyone understand it?" Yaala returned. "It changed and doesn't work like it used to. Who knows when it will open again, or change again?" She fell into step beside Powwell as they headed into the large cavern with the broken generator named Old Bertha.

Rollett followed the others, needing to stay with them lest he become lost and fall victim to the Rovers who searched for them. Escape was within his grasp only if he stayed with Yaala and Powwell.

Hope. He felt it in his bones.

Freedom. He tasted it in the air.

A haunting song almost within hearing drew him into the cavern more than the presence of his comrades.

Powwell stood in the opening of a small tunnel off the huge cavern. He braced his arms against the sides of the archway, staring into the blackness beyond. A bright flare of red from deep within the tunnel as well as the increased heat told Rollett that they neared the lava core—and the elusive dragongate. The song intensified. If only he could remember it, all of his questions would be answered.

"That's not the way to the dragongate," Yaala called to Powwell. She remained next to the vast hulk of the dead generator, touching it, as a mother caressed a wayward toddler.

Rollett gulped back a sudden surge of desire. The image of Yaala touching a child—his child—filled his imagination with longing.

No. She wanted to stay in Hanassa and rule it. He needed to go home. But he'd come back for his men, make sure they had the option of escape.

Yaala rested her head on the dead hulk of the machine. He wanted to reach out to her, let her grieve for the loss of the machine. Jerking himself back three steps from her, he forced his hands to his sides. He didn't know Yaala, didn't dare trust her with his fragile emotions. He hadn't known a woman's companionship during this entire long year and a half in Hanassa. The only women available were either hardened outlaws or disease-ridden prostitutes. He wouldn't touch either, no matter how much he longed to.

Now Yaala enticed him, probably because she was clean, vulnerable, and lovely.

"This isn't the way we came through the dragongate this last time." Powwell's statement dragged Rollett's attention away from his momentary desire and back to the problem at hand.

"We came through that tunnel." Yaala pointed to a smaller opening adjacent to the one Powwell stared into. "I remember landing in that puddle near the broken pipe."

"But this is the way we left Hanassa last year." Powwell gestured toward the tunnel he leaned into. "I didn't recognize it before because of the partial collapse of the opening."

Yaala looked back and forth between the tunnel openings, confusion written all over her face.

Rollett examined both openings minutely and saw little difference other than the position in relation to Old Bertha.

"Look, the gate is opening!" Powwell called as he dived into the tunnel.

"Opening?" Rollett gasped. "We can escape right now?" His heart pounded in his ears. He plunged into the passage right behind Powwell, ahead of Yaala. "Home. I need to go home." If the opening led to home, then he could come back for his men. He could attack Piedro later, with refreshed magic and reinforcements from the Commune.

He smelled cool dampness. The hot red flares from the lava core swirled into a myriad of colors muted by a soft, soothing blue-white and deep gray. The song that called him grew louder.

"Not yet!" Powwell blocked his path with his staff.

Desperate to be gone from Hanassa and the men who pursued him, Rollett whipped his own staff around to confront Powwell in a fighting stance. "Out of my way, boy!" A red haze of anger blinded him to all but the need to escape.

"We don't leave without my sister!" Powwell snarled.

"Stop it, both of you!" Yaala warned in a hissing whisper. "Hanassa will hear you. Besides, that scene is resolving into . . . into, Stargods, it's underwater! Look at that bemouth. It will eat us alive." She backed out of the tunnel, hands crossed in front of her face, protecting herself from sprays of salt water.

Powwell shifted his stance just enough to see the watery

blue landscape behind him while also keeping Rollett from charging past. "Deep water," he said succinctly. "We have to wait for the right scene. We have to wait for Kalen."

"Does this mean the dragongate isn't broken?" Yaala edged up behind Rollett, but she didn't try to come between the two men who remained ready to swing their staffs at each other.

Her warmth filled Rollett's back with comfort. He relaxed his stance a fraction. Some of the desperate need to escape dribbled out of him. He could go on a little longer. He needed to help Yaala depose Piedro so that he could rescue his men.

"It means the gate has changed. It opens to different locations than before," Powwell replied. "Maybe none of them are safe."

"This way!" A Rover-accented voice yelled from across the large cavern. "They're hiding in that tunnel."

"Keep them away from the dragongate," Piedro called back.

Rollett turned quickly, keeping his staff at the ready. Trapped! They were trapped in the tiny tunnel, barely wide enough to wield his staff. And Powwell just stood there with a feral snarl of satisfaction on his face.

Anger and frustration boiled up within Rollett. The only escape seemed to be the mysterious dragongate behind them. But one wrong step would put them into the lava core.

Powwell moved up beside him, shoving Yaala against the wall and out of their way. He held up his bloody right hand in a spell gesture. The hedgehog familiar keened an ear-piercing wail and dived deep into Powwell's pocket, his spines fully erect.

The entire tunnel smelled of old blood and fear. Powwell's skin grew paler yet. A blue tinge developed around his lips and the edges of his nose. He started to sweat heavily.

Powwell drew his strength from blood magic!

Rollett swallowed heavily, convulsively to keep his bile in his stomach where it belonged. He'd had more than enough experience with the Bloodmage Moncriith. The thought of drawing power from the blood, pain, and fear of another living being revolted him physically and emotionally.

But he recognized that they had few other choices. If blood magic would keep Piedro and the consort at bay until they could step through the dragongate to safety, then so be it.

Powwell began chanting under his breath.

Always sensitive to music, Rollett listened hard to the spell.

"What are you doing, Powwell? You're enticing them this way!"

CHAPTER 32

Afternoon, the pit beneath the city of Hanassa

"Send the consort to me," Powwell called to the Rovers gathering in the large cavern. "My death will not appease Simurge unless it is the consort herself who kills me. She must taste my blood!"

Inside his pocket, Thorny hunched and bristled his spines as far out as he could. The sharp tips penetrated Powwell's tunic, pricking his skin. Powwell inhaled sharply at the ache in his heart and the sensitivity of his skin. But no blood flowed from the tiny wounds.

That's right, Thorny, he whispered with his mind to his familiar. *Just the way we rehearsed it.*

"What are you doing?" Rollett and Yaala each grabbed one of Powwell's arms, dragging him back. Back toward the dragongate.

Powwell smiled inwardly as he caught a glimpse of the reds and black of the desert scene forming within the portal—so very similar to the scene the other gate had taken him and Yaala to, but different. This one opened into the same time as where he stood. The other one had drifted in time, taking Powwell and Yaala to Hanassa of many aeons ago.

Both deserts would not support human life for long. And if the dragongate held true to its previous patterns, it would cycle through many inhospitable locations before opening into someplace green—maybe Coronnan, maybe someplace else.

At the mouth of the tunnel, a black-veiled figure emerged into the uncertain light.

"Is that what you really want, Powwell?" the consort asked. Her voice grated harshly in the confines of the tunnel. Kalen's voice, but not her voice, deeper, harsher. "Do you want your sister to be the one to consign you to your next existence in the most unpleasant way I can think of?"

Slowly, the girl/woman removed the black lace veil. She dropped the priceless silk on the rough floor. It rippled as it fell, like cool water over a waterfall. Gravel and sand snagged the fine threads.

Powwell looked into his sister's gray eyes, so like his own and yet . . .

Wiggles, Kalen's ferret familiar remained draped across her left shoulder, unmoving. Powwell lifted one eyebrow at it.

"You killed the ferret and stuffed it because it would not stay with Hanassa, the renegade dragon. You are not as powerful as you want others to believe. Does the wraith haunt you? Does she keep you awake at night whispering of aching emptiness at the death of Wiggles?" He took another step back, pushing Yaala and Rollett against the wall. Only he stood between the consort and the dragongate.

Hot wind shot through the gate, caressing Powwell's skin with the enticement of escape.

He shut his mind to the need to turn and run through the opening, no matter where it took him. But he noticed Yaala and Rollett edging closer and closer to the inhospitable scene.

"Kalen died, leaving her body behind for me. I am Hanassa. I have always been Hanassa!" the consort proclaimed. She lifted her arms, palm outward as if embracing the entire volcano.

"Then, Hanassa, you will have to come get me. You won't be satisfied until you have my blood on your hands and in your mouth!"

She took four long paces closer to Powwell, not enough.

Thorny squirmed and pressed himself closer to Powwell's chest. A tiny drop of blood trickled down Powwell's chest, over his heart. The sharp lance of pain, brief though it was, sent power singing through his veins, enhancing the fading energy he'd gathered from the severed heads.

"Come and get me, Kalen. Join me in the pit of hell!" Powwell teetered on the edge of the pit. Boiling rock flared upward. The heat nearly seared his back. Sweat poured down his face and made his palms slick.

"Powwell, stop this. I beg you," Yaala tried to pull him away from the edge. "You're my only friend, I can't let you do this."

Powwell closed his eyes rather than look at her. He knew if he saw tears in her eyes—tears in the eyes of a woman who never cried, who had survived horrors he could only imagine—he'd throw away his carefully laid plans.

"It's the only way to save Kalen, Yaala. If this doesn't work, stay with Rollett. You can trust him."

"Thanks, but no thanks," Rollett said, stepping beside him. "I'll help you, but I'm taking the next portal through the dragongate."

Powwell smiled his acknowledgment as he opened his mind a fraction to allow Rollett a brief glimpse of his plan.

"Do you have a death wish, boy?" Rollett raised his dark eyebrows.

"He must. He asked me to kill him," the consort said, only three paces away. "Give me your sword, Piedro. I shall execute this intruder myself."

"Aren't you going to rip out my throat with your bare hands? That's the way a dragon kills," Powwell taunted. "And you are a dragon in spirit, Hanassa. The purple-tipped dragon instincts still drive you. You hunger for fresh meat, cooked by your own flames."

Hanassa licked her lips. A drop of drool trickled from the corner of her mouth. She swallowed heavily as if tasting sweet, fresh meat. Kalen's features twisted into something alien and ugly. Any trace of the little girl had vanished beneath Hanassa's lusts.

"But you'll never have your own dragon flames again," Powwell continued. He and Rollett eased aside just a little, offering Hanassa a tantalizing glimpse of the scene beyond the dragongate. "The real dragon nimbus won't let you have a dragon body again. They won't let you fly out of this hellhole that is your prison. Your only escape is to steal a human body and walk out of here. But the humans won't let you live among them as long as you drink their blood."

Hanassa edged closer. Her nose worked as if scenting freedom in the desert on the other side of the dragongate.

The hot wind died. The gate began to close.

"You're more a prisoner here than we are, Hanassa,"

Rollett added his taunts to Powwell's. "We can step through the dragongate anytime we wish. Can you?"

"It's closing!" Hanassa wailed. She dashed toward them just as the red and black of the desert swirled into a myriad other colors.

"Not again!" Kalen screamed as her body hurtled over the edge of the pit.

A white mist enveloped her mundane body.

"Now!" Powwell commanded as he wrapped a magic net around his sister. "Grab her."

He sensed Rollett's diminished magic reaching to ensnare the young girl before she fell into the boiling lava a thousand feet below. Tendrils of power snaked and looped together, the dark red and deep sea-blue knots of Rollett's magic cradled one side of Kalen. Powwell's red and sparkling black held the other in a net of energy.

Powwell had to open his mind further so that he and Rollett could work together. Every instinct inside him shouted to keep his secrets, keep this other man from learning how much he had enjoyed gathering blood magic.

"Help me, Powwell!" Kalen, the true Kalen, screamed. "Don't let me die in the pit again."

Powwell closed his eyes and gritted his teeth. He sought closer contact with Rollett's mind. Their thoughts mingled, settled on a common need. Together they strained to haul Kalen back to the safety of the ledge.

At last Powwell held Kalen in his arms and opened his eyes. His sister. The only family he had left. The child/woman who completed his every thought and made sense of his ragged emotions.

She turned to him, opening wide gray eyes to him in gratitude.

Don't let it get control of me, she pleaded. Her mental voice blended sweetly with his thoughts, filling a void that had existed since he'd been forced to leave her behind in this very tunnel over a year ago.

"Thank you," she said in Hanassa's harsh voice several tones deeper than Kalen's. The white mist separated from her body once more. The wraith sobbed her disappointment.

Powwell's heart nearly broke in grief.

A self-satisfied smirk replaced the gratitude in Hanassa's

expression. "I read your mind, Powwell." She caressed his face with long, talonlike nails that raked his skin but did not draw blood. "I knew what you planned the moment you shared your thoughts with Rollett. I let Kalen have her body for a few moments, so you would rescue her. Then I took it back. Now you are truly my prisoner, and I shall execute you properly."

CHAPTER 33

Afternoon, a stand of the Tambootie trees, South of First Bridge, on the mainland near Coronnan City

Katie breathed deeply of the redolent smoke from the Tambootie wood fire. The queen, Nimbulan, and Myri stood in a circle around a small campfire deep in the woods South and West of the city. Their escort stood well back from this stand of Tambootie trees, backs turned to avoid breathing any of the smoke.

Across the fire from her, Nimbulan swayed under the hallucinogens in the wood sap. Flame released those chemicals in uneven doses. They had no way of controlling how much each of them breathed in. But they needed Tambootie in their systems to combat the plague virus they might have inhaled. Katie didn't have time to distill proper and controlled doses and then return to the shuttle before Kinnsell departed with it.

Nimbulan's face grew paler as Myri's flushed with heat and distorted perceptions. Quinnault seemingly remained impervious to the hallucinogens in the smoke. He'd endured this before, when progressing from apprentice to journeyman in his priestly studies. Or maybe he simply knew how to flow with changes. Katie stopped fighting the splotches of improbable colors that filled her vision. She allowed the smoke to infiltrate her every pore and corpuscle.

The world spun around her. She lost contact with her feet. Her arms rose level with her shoulders. She turned her palms up to embrace the sky. She could almost reach out and touch the clouds. Dense air seemed to enclose her in a vortex of color, lifting her higher above the others.

Visions of soaring above the clouds of Coronnan layered

over her real-time sight of this mundane clearing and the ritual campfire. Cool air wafted beneath her arms/wings. Warm thermal currents guided her feet/tail. Sparkling crystal outlined all within sight.

Upward she soared, higher and higher toward the bright sun and the blackness of space beyond. The miracle of flight enticed her further and further away from her companions, and yet she did not fear the loneliness of where she traveled.

Suddenly absolute darkness enfolded her. All sensation of flight vanished. Sensory input ceased. Her body disappeared. All she had left was her mind and . . . and the dragons.

A dozen dragon thoughts invaded her mind, whispering secrets of past, present, and future. The meaning of her existence—of all of humanity—seemed just beyond the next confidence.

She listened carefully, certain she would understand soon. Thoughts of her aborted attempt to contact her brothers, her loyalty to her husband and friends, her duty to keep Coronnan and all of Kardia Hodos free of the taint of technology vanished. She had only her mind and the dragons.

(What questions do you bring to the void between the planes of existence?) a voice asked her. It seemed to reverberate and compound into a dozen voices, yet it spoke with the authority of one.

I need—I need to banish all traces of the plague from this world.

(Then you demand the death of one you hold dear.)

Memories of Katie's father arguing before the imperial legislature; Kinnsell ordering the servants; Daddy reprimanding her for some childhood infraction, filled her with a sad bitterness.

I have not loved my father in a long time.

(He is your father.)

His sperm sired me. But he never stayed home long enough to be a father. My mother raised us alone until Kinnsell put her aside for his pregnant mistress. Then my brothers became more father to me than Kinnsell ever was.

(He is your father.)

I wanted to love him. He wouldn't let me. His ambitions and greed got in the way.

(He is your father.)

Every contact with him created greater bitterness between us.

(You cannot love where you do not recognize the truth. He is your father.)

I cannot love him. He won't let me.

(Then you are not ready to recognize the truth.)

With a stomach-wrenching jolt, Katie returned to her body. She swayed on her feet. Gravity weighed too heavily on her limbs after the freedom of flight to the void.

"I have got to sit," she mumbled as her bottom found the ground. Almost sick to her stomach, she dropped her head between her knees, breathing shallowly to keep any more Tambootie smoke from penetrating her lungs.

"Katie!" Quinnault knelt beside her, seemingly unaffected by the smoke. He hugged her close, offering her an anchor to reality.

"What did you see in the smoke?" he asked after a moment of silence.

"Dragons."

"Dragons!" Myrilandel and Nimbulan exclaimed together.

"What have we done to her?" Myrilandel turned stricken eyes on her husband.

"Perhaps we have made a magician of her," Nimbulan said softly, almost below hearing. He didn't move any closer.

"This is what Scarface fears in lighting bonfires of the Tambootie in plague-affected villages," Quinnault added. "The smoke will enhance minor talents, make untrained magicians of minor talents who cannot be controlled."

"We must never mention this again," Katie said fiercely. "Women can only weave rogue magic. I will be condemned by the Council and Commune. I will be forced into exile with my daughter. The people will demand Quinnault marry another." Tears threatened to choke her.

Quinnault gathered her closer in a fierce embrace. "I will never give you up, Katie."

"If we have awakened magical powers within you, Katie, I will give you enough training to hide those powers," Nimbulan said.

Katie looked up at the sadness in his voice. The world spun a moment, then settled. Crystal continued to outline everything she saw. Her eyes focused in sharper detail than she ever thought possible.

Nimbulan moved slowly, almost painfully. The crystal light around the edges of his life flared sharply in orange and black. Blue tinged his lips and spread to his pinched nostrils. He clutched his swollen left hand in the center of his chest. His right arm hung limply by his side.

"Lan!" Myri jumped from her crouched position beside Katie to catch Nimbulan as he crumpled to the ground.

Overhead, Kinnsell's shuttle roared in a low and erratic trajectory.

Katie spared a half glance at the wavering path of the shuttle. The metal/ceramic craft listed to the left and dragged its tail.

"Don't crash, Daddy. I'm not finished with you!" she screamed at him.

Then quite suddenly the jet engines gave way to rockets and the shuttle rose in a new trajectory straight South toward a polar orbit. With the shuttle went her last hope of communicating with her brothers, her last hope of intervening before her father set loose the seeds of the plague on this planet.

She turned her attention back to the people she could help. Nimbulan lay unmoving on the ground. Myri wept silently by his side, holding his limp hand with the blue-tinged fingernails. "I am so sorry, Lan. I dare not help you. The life within me has just begun. We agreed not to taint your son with magic."

Katie realized in that moment that her father also took with him acccss to all of the advanced medical equipment aboard the mother ship—equipment that might save Nimbulan's life.

* * *

Late afternoon, Coronnan City

Bessel crept through the city, Mopsie at his heels. He crossed bridge after bridge, winding among the islands in a convoluted path that confused him as much as anyone who might follow him.

The fishermen had given him dry, mostly clean clothing, but no boots. They usually went barefoot. The yellow tunic and white trews seemed overly bright to Bessel. But the fishermen assured him the clothes represented safety to them. The bright colors were easier to see underwater, should one of them fall overboard. And the colors held no resemblance to the sober blue of the Commune. He'd look like any other fisherman gone to market.

He bypassed the University and its library twice. As long as Scarface ruled that enclave, he'd never be able to delve into the treasure trove of knowledge without help.

As long as Scarface ruled the Commune of Magicians, Bessel would not return, even if invited. He knew the truth now. He was a rogue magician with a familiar. Nimbulan might overlook his crime, but Scarface never would.

Finally, when both he and Mopsie knew that none of the assassins from Rossemeyer had spotted them, he turned toward Ambassador Row. Footsore and exhausted, he limped down several side streets to avoid passing in front of the Rossemeyerian Embassy.

Myrilandel's tall, narrow stone house looked blank and uninviting. The barest flicker of smoke emerged from the tall chimneys at either end of the building, as if all the fires had been banked. Bessel knew that Myrilandel and Nimbulan rarely used the formal rooms at the front of the dwelling. Life centered in the kitchen for them.

Myrilandel should have stoked the kitchen fire by now to prepare the simple evening meal. Unless the family dined at the palace with her brother the king.

Bessel and his familiar scooted down an alley to approach the house from the rear. Closed shutters and a firmly locked door greeted him. Fortunately, he remembered the sequence for opening the lock with magic. Nimbulan had given him that key last night. This was supposed to be his home until the issue of rogue magic and the death of Jorghe-Rosse had been settled.

The settlement meant nothing now.

A chill of unease and stale smoke rippled across Bessel's senses as he stepped down into the kitchen. A mixing bowl and several baking ingredients lay neatly on the worktable, as if set out ahead of time; so, too, were a pile of tubers and cone roots ready for chopping.

But no one greeted him. No one sang while working.

"Anyone here?" he asked the empty room. The fire remained a bank of smoldering coals. The house smelled empty.

Wherever Myrilandel and Nimbulan had gone, they had taken Amaranth with them. Not unusual.

"Well, if we are hungry, Mopsie, I'd best set about fixing something."

"Woof," Mopsie agreed. He waddled over to the pantry door and sniffed eagerly.

"Why did I know you'd be hungry, pup?" Bessel opened the door and followed the dog to the trapdoor leading to the cool cellar. The leftovers of last night's stew should be in the shallow underground room. Mopsie jumped down the four steps and found the covered pot before Bessel could bring a ball of witchlight to his hand for better visibility. Myri had left a bone beside the pot on the shelf, just above Mopsie's reach.

"If I give you the bone, do you promise to be neat with it? I can't have you messing up Myri's kitchen."

Mopsie sat politely and wagged his tail across the stone floor.

"Take it up to the mudroom, then." Bessel handed the bone—longer than the dog's head was wide—to Mopsie. The dog grabbed it with eager teeth and trotted up the stairs.

There he stopped and growled, dropping the bone to bare his teeth in warning.

Bessel set the stew pot back on the shelf very slowly, very quietly. Then he consciously set his magical armor in place. Spells would dissipate before reaching him. Mundane weapons should bounce off him—if he could hold the protection in place long enough. He wasn't used to relying upon ley lines to fuel his spells.

Cautiously, he mounted the first step. The armor sharpened his sight enough to spot the weaknesses in the wooden board that might creak and betray his presence.

His head and shoulders cleared the trapdoor entrance. He searched the pantry with every sense available to him. Once certain that no one had entered the little room and nothing stood between him and an exit, he doused his witchlight and climbed up the remaining three steps.

He paused at the closed door to the kitchen and listened. Someone moved about, restlessly, picking things up and putting them down again.

Who examined the kitchen so precisely?

Then the intruder bumped into the table. He mumbled a curse, barely audible to mundane ears. The wood groaned and a knife clattered against the floor. Four thuds suggested some of the vegetables had followed the knife.

Whoever prowled the room didn't know it well.

Mopsie crawled to the door, belly down, neck fur raised, and teeth bared.

Bessel put aside all of his reticence from invasion of privacy and opened his mind.

"Where have you been, boy?" Lyman angrily threw open the pantry door. "And where are Nimbulan and Myrilandel? The house is as empty and silent as a grave. Do you mind telling me why you and that scruffy mutt are hiding in the pantry like thieves?"

Bessel sagged with relief, leaning against the doorjamb. "I don't know where anyone is, and I was looking for supper when my familiar warned me of an intruder. Why are you here? I didn't think you ever left the library." Certainly he hadn't left it long enough to keep up with current fashion. His knee-length tunics and silk sash were the objects of many apprentice jokes.

"You don't think much, then. I must find Nimbulan. Where could he have gone?"

"I don't know. I left early this morning and haven't been able to get back until now."

Lyman paused to look at Bessel more closely. "Strange garb for a magician."

"But proper garb for a fisherman. The agents of Lady Rosselaara search for a journeyman magician."

"Ah, so they decided to take matters into their own hands." Lyman tapped his lip with his index finger. "I should have suspected as much if my mind had been on this existence."

"This existence!" Alarmed, Bessel grabbed the old man's shoulders. "You can't die and pass on to the next existence yet. The University needs you. The Commune needs you. We have to counter Scarface's fanaticism."

"And you need me to reclaim information in the library. Yes, yes, I read your mind. I couldn't help it when you opened it wide to listen to mine. Well, you'll have to find the books and read them on your own."

"Promise me you aren't dying," Bessel pleaded. He'd had too many upsets in too short a time. Lyman was a permanent fixture at the University. He couldn't contemplate losing his mentor and . . . and friend.

"No, boy, the duty I must perform is much more frightening than mere death. I am destined to plague apprentices with reading assignments for a good long time yet. But for now I haven't time to discuss this. I must . . ." He trailed off as he cocked his head.

"What do you hear?" Bessel whispered.

"Everything and nothing." A typical Lyman answer.

"Steeds, a dozen or more." Bessel heard them, too. "All metal shod, some moving quickly, others plodding at a steady pace. . . ."

Anyone who could afford a steed stabled it on the mainland. The crowded city isle with narrow twisting streets put dwelling space at a premium and made clean up of human waste a big problem; adding steed manure to the compost only made the problem worse.

"I fear we are needed." Lyman turned away abruptly and headed through the house toward the front door. Bessel trailed closely on his heels. Mopsie began whining in distress.

The sound of the moving steeds was cut off abruptly as the elderly librarian thrust open the door. Bessel stopped short at the sight of Nimbulan lying weakly on a litter borne between two placid steeds. His master's tall, imposing presence seemed greatly reduced. He barely breathed, as if the effort of living weighed too heavily on his thin frame.

Myrilandel walked beside him, tears streaming down her face. Something terrible must have happened if Myrilandel, the greatest healer in the kingdom, couldn't cure her husband.

Queen Katie rode just ahead of the litter. Her red-rimmed eyes bore more evidence of tears and disaster.

Another clatter of hooves from the opposite direction

announced King Quinnault's arrival. He reined in his steed sharply. The beast's hooves skidded on the cobblestones, almost throwing the king. But Quinnault mastered his steed and dismounted in front of the queen's procession. Then he retrieved his daughter from the saddle, cradling her easily in one arm.

"Get a healer, Bessel. Hurry. We need the best healers from the Commune now!" Myrilandel burst into tears once more.

"I can't go back to the University. Scarface has forbidden me," Bessel whispered.

"Then I must delay my quest a little longer." Lyman sighed. "I will summon the healers." He took three regulation breaths to trigger a trance and disappeared.

CHAPTER 34

Afternoon, home of Myrilandel, Ambassador from the Nimbus of Dragons, Coronnan City

Bessel sniffed the air around Nimbulan. He reeked of sweet/bitter Tambootie smoke. Tambootie smoke!

The only ritual calling for burning the tree of magic was the coming of age of an apprentice. He remembered his own trial by Tambootie smoke about two moons after he reached puberty. He'd endured two days and three nights in a sealed stone room with only a Tambootie wood fire for heat and light. The smoke had induced visions of drowning and being eaten by a bemouth—one of the monstrous fish that prowled the outer bay. The only predator large enough and fierce enough to hunt a bemouth was a dragon.

Just the memory of those visions sent sharp pains into all of Bessel's joints. He'd been powerless to fight the monster for three days and two nights. Then, finally, when he fell from the monster's jaws, there was nothing left of his body or soul; he'd fled to the sense-depriving blackness of the void.

Moments later Nimbulan had opened the magically sealed door and drawn him back, lovingly, into the protection of his enclave of Battlemages.

Bessel supposed the continued nightmare of the trial that had introduced him to the void, had given him insight into the extent and limitations of his powers. Those limitations had taught him to take responsibility for his actions and never attempt something he couldn't handle alone.

He'd also figured out how to block any magical assault upon his mind or his person.

Two of his classmates had damaged hearts and lungs after their trials and never practiced magic again. They'd had weak talents even before the trial. Tambootie had been proved poisonous to mundanes. Nimbulan had lost his magic a year and a half ago. . . .

The chain of logic rocked Bessel to the core of his being. Only one disaster would require the queen and her two best friends to risk exposing themselves to the Tambootie. That risk was also the only disease Bessel knew for certain Myri couldn't cure with her wonderful talent.

"Does he have the plague?" he whispered to Myri as the royal guards passed them bearing the litter.

Bessel's time sense rocked backward and forward, superimposing the image of Jorghe-Rosse's corpse being carried on a litter before the king.

He pushed aside the memory for more immediate concerns.

"Does he have the plague?" he asked again, a little louder.

Myri shook her head, never taking her eyes off her husband.

"Then why couldn't you cure him?" he asked. A note of desperation crept into his voice. He had nothing left if Nimbulan died. No family, no Commune, not even his friend the librarian . . .

Mopsie pressed himself against Bessel's legs and whimpered. The fishermen had given him more consideration than the Commune. He could build a new family with the hearty seamen and their dogs.

King Quinnault rushed up beside his sister. He thrust the baby into Bessel's arms for safekeeping then hugged Myrilandel's shoulders in comfort. "He asks a valid question, Myri," Quinnault said quietly. "The law against women using magic be damned. Please do not let this great man die if you can do anything to help him."

"Do you think I would willingly watch my beloved die if I could help, law or no law?" Myri shook off the king's embrace angrily. "I am newly pregnant. I can't use my talent lest I harm the baby. He stopped me earlier today when I would have corrected the problem. . . ." She broke into sobs, unable to finish her sentence.

King Quinnault cradled her against his chest, rubbing her back helplessly.

Bessel mimicked the motion with the little princess. He'd had enough practice taking care of his younger siblings back home.

"Does he have the plague?" Bessel insisted, still tending the baby. *The plague kills the old, the young, and pregnant women first,* his aunt had said. He had to get Myrilandel and the princess away from here.

"No, he does not have the plague," Queen Maarie Kaathliin said, entering the room. Shorter than anyone else by at least a head, she still radiated authority and commanded respect simply by being there.

"Are you certain?" King Quinnault asked. Even he, the most powerful man in the land deferred to her.

"Yes, I am certain. The Tambootie smoke would have killed the virus if our brief exposure had infected him."

"His skin is waxy and blue like the dragon dream Powwell shared with me," Bessel argued, desperately needing reassurance and not daring to hope for it. "His breathing is ragged just like my mother's was before she died."

"Your mother had the plague?" King Quinnault swung Bessel around, shaking his shoulders as if he had to force the information from him. "Where? When?" Why wasn't I told!"

"Master Scarface said that only the privations of a long Winter and the aftermath of so many generations of war ravaged Lord Balthazaan's province, especially the mining villages where they grow very little of their own food. But I remembered the smell. Powwell shared the smell with me telepathically when he shared the dragon dream."

"Stargods, the plague is here for certain, not just a 'perhaps' pushed aside for other concerns. How? When?" Quinnault paced the reception hall. He clenched his hands behind his back and hunched his shoulders. With the afternoon sun pouring through the open doorway, he was outlined in red-gold light like the silhouette of a young dragon.

Bessel stepped away from him. Surreptitiously, he crossed himself in a ward against the evils of the unknown.

"My husband's heart is weak from all those years of warfare that left this kingdom teetering on bankruptcy—a bankruptcy of people as well as money. He wore out his heart and himself weaving great magic in battle after battle.

Now he pays the price. Where are the healers? Lyman promised to summon them." Myri ran to the door, looking up and down the street anxiously. Then she rushed back to Nimbulan's side. She knelt beside the litter. The guards had laid the aging man before the unlit hearth.

Bessel forced his mind to light the fire. No other magicians stalked the room; he could use rogue magic for the task—so much easier than the increasingly elusive dragon magic. In a heartbeat the fire leaped high, warming the large room.

A whoosh of displaced air erupted beside Bessel, nearly knocking him into the wall. He clutched the baby tighter to make sure he didn't drop her. As he struggled for balance, Lyman popped into view, much as he had disappeared moments before.

"The healers come," the old librarian announced breathlessly. "Now make yourself useful in the kitchen, Bessel. Kaariin is here to tend the baby. Stay out of sight, and keep your mutt quiet. Scarface is hot on the heels of the medical people. He's angrier than a wet lumbird and looking for a victim." Lyman transferred Princess Marilell to the arms of the breathless maid who dashed up the steps from the street.

"Lyman, how did you do that?" Bessel asked, too amazed to obey. "Dragon magic only allows levitation, not transportation. And no one could transport a living being from place to place even when solitary magic was legal." He dropped his voice as the thought formed into words. The royal couple and their guards were too occupied making Nimbulan comfortable to pay attention to his almost accusation.

"Shhush, boy. The answer is in the timing. And if you ever figure it out, guard the secret with your life. You may need the spell in the days to come, but never use it carelessly. Now I must be off. The dragons call me."

Another whoosh of displaced air and he was gone, almost as if he'd never been there.

"Maybe he only sent an illusion along with a powerful summons," the queen whispered into Bessel's ear.

"Is there anything you don't see or hear, Your Grace?" Bessel asked.

"Very little. Now do as your master says, mull some wine

or prepare snacks, or anything you can think of, in the kitchen and out of sight."

Bessel scuttled down the hall to the back of the house just as he heard Scarface's roar of anger in the street.

CHAPTER 35

The pit, near the dragongate, beneath the city of Hanassa

Yaala whipped her belt knife upward and held it across Hanassa's throat. With her free arm she pinned the consort's arms. Beside her, Rollett drew his own blade and held it up in a fighting stance. Powwell whipped his staff around to fend off any attackers.

"Kill them, kill them all!" Hanassa cried. She held her body tensely, poised for flight at the first sign of weakness in Yaala's grip.

"If I die, you die, too, Hanassa. I've waited a long time to avenge my father's death." Years of anger, frustration, and loneliness concentrated in Yaala's hand, making the knife blade waver up and down across the great vein of life in Hanassa's throat.

Rollett shot her a strange look.

Her determination wavered a moment. If she killed Hanassa, then she condemned Kalen to a ghostly existence as a wraith. Powwell would never forgive her.

If she killed Hanassa solely to exact vengeance, then she succumbed to the renegade dragon's violence. Rollett would never forgive her.

She'd never forgive herself.

But she couldn't let Hanassa go free either. The tyranny had to end.

The Rover guards lowered their sword tips but did not drop their weapons.

"Tell them to throw their swords and clubs into the pool of water beside Old Bertha," Yaala commanded her prisoner, loud enough for the Rovers to hear.

"Never. You must die!"

Yaala nicked Kalen's skin. Three drops of blood trickled onto the blade.

A screech of fear and pain echoed around the caverns. Hanassa hadn't uttered a sound. The wraith had.

The Rovers threw their weapons away. All except Piedro.

Cautiously, Yaala edged forward toward the mouth of the tunnel, keeping her prisoner in front of her, the knife still dangerously close to drawing blood.

Piedro took one step forward, raising his sword. "You haven't the guts to take a life," he sneered.

"Perhaps not. But I do," a solemn voice announced from the main cavern.

All the Rovers fell silent, backing away from the frail old man who stood beside Old Bertha. He wore an old-fashioned blue tunic that hung nearly to his knees, belted with a silk sash. The tunic and trews had been dyed Commune blue. He carried a long staff nearly twice his height. The length of wood was so twisted and gnarled from a lifetime of channeling magic, Yaala couldn't see a pattern in the grain that mimicked the man's magical signature.

"Lyman!" Powwell breathed in relief.

"Iianthe! You cannot still live. I felt you die decades ago." Hanassa struggled in Yaala's arms, ready to break free. She looked right and left, up and down, disregarding the knife at her throat.

"Iianthe, the purple-tipped dragon born your twin, died more than twenty years ago, Hanassa," Lyman replied. He swung his staff in a sweeping circle, moving it so fast it blurred in the dim light. A challenging hum followed its rapid passage through the air. "But since you refused to live out your true destiny, I was forced to assume a human body and finish it for you. Now the dragons have sent me to make certain you do not leave here with the knowledge of the machines and how they work."

"You expect to fight me in that frail old body. I, at least had the good sense to choose someone young and strong." Hanassa broke free of Yaala's grip. She thrust Piedro aside as she marched to meet the old magician's challenge.

Yaala stumbled against Rollett. He steadied her with one hand around her waist, never dropping his confrontational stance before the Rover guards. The warmth of his hand

and the gentle squeeze of his fingers gave her a sense of rightness.

You did right not to kill. His thoughts came to her unbidden. Something lit deep in his eyes. Respect?

Suddenly her previous attraction to Powwell faded. If she ever loved—truly loved—she would love a man like him: mature, decisive, experienced in the ways of the world. Someone to challenge her spirit and her intellect.

"The wraith fights you for control of the body, Hanassa," Lyman reminded his onetime twin. "This body is mine alone." Lyman crouched in a fighting stance, his staff suddenly still. The artificial lights within the cavern highlighted his body in layers of purple-and-crystal light. The strange aura shaped itself into the outline of a dragon.

Yaala shook her head to clear it of the confusing images. Rollett mimicked the motion.

"Stargods preserve us!" Piedro crossed himself several times. He dropped his sword. It clattered against the rock in an ominous chiming.

Hanassa launched Kalen's body at Lyman with fingers arched into talons, teeth bared, and a snarl erupting from her wide mouth.

Lyman blocked her attack with his staff. He swung it down and around, clipping Hanassa on the temple with one end.

Hanassa staggered back. She stumbled against the rusting hulk of Old Bertha.

Yaala winced as pieces of metal crumbled beneath the impact.

"Get out of the cavern!" Lyman called. He pointed the staff at his opponent. A blast of blinding purple-white light shot forth from the staff with a deafening explosion. Hanassa flew backward, into a wall, slamming her head against the rough stones.

Yaala grabbed for the tunnel walls to catch her balance as the magical attack shook the entire system of caves and tunnels. She missed the wall. Rollett caught her against his side. He wrapped one arm around her shoulders, steadying her—steadying them both.

"We've got to get above ground," he said quietly, almost calmly. "He's filled with dragon magic and will stop at nothing to kill Hanassa, regardless of Kalen's spirit."

"Kalen needs that body. I can't let him kill my sister," Powwell cried, dashing forward.

Rollett and Yaala both grabbed their friend. Yaala caught only a handful of cloth near the neck of his tunic. Rollett had better luck, latching onto his arm.

"Lyman will spare Kalen if he can. If anyone can," Yaala soothed Powwell. "He's a Communal Magician, he values life."

Another magical blast sent Hanassa reeling facedown into the pool of hot water. The tunnel shook. Rocks tumbled from the ceiling.

"We have to save ourselves now!" Yaala dragged Powwell out from under the falling rock.

"Kalen!" Powwell screamed. Tears streamed down his face. His tunic tore as he ripped out of Yaala's grasp.

"No, Powwell," Rollett said. "I can't let you do this." He slammed his fist into the boy's jaw.

Yaala braced herself to catch Powwell as he fell backward into her arms.

The next blast of magic knocked the ground from beneath her feet. They both fell. Rollett crashed on top of them followed by a tumble of rocks.

She couldn't breathe. Something hit her head. Starbursts blinded her. Blood clouded her vision.

She fought for consciousness and lost the battle.

* * *

Afternoon, the pit beneath the city of Hanassa

Powwell struggled to push Rollett off his back. "Yaala, are you all right?" He shook his friend, trapped beneath him.

He heard the Rovers tripping over each other in their mad dash to escape the wrath of Hanassa.

Yaala moaned and rolled her head as if in pain. Then she fell silent.

"Get off me, Rollett." Powwell shoved upward with his elbow.

Rollett groaned and rolled drunkenly to one side. "We ga get oot ah here," he slurred, holding his head and shoulder.

"I've got to help Kalen. Take care of Yaala." Powwell drew his knees up under him. The battle still raged around Old Bertha. Lyman crouched on one side of the old generator. Hanassa drew on Kalen's magical talent and created a geyser directly in front of the old librarian.

In fine Battlemage fashion, Lyman channeled the spurt of hot water back into the broken pipe that passed above the lava core. Boiling water built up within the rusted metal, forcing a new opening. Steam shot out of a dozen rust holes in a variety of directions.

Scalding water struck Hanassa in the face as she crept forward. "Yieeee!" she screamed and dodged back behind the shelter of the machine.

Powwell crawled quietly toward her. He winced for her as she pulled her hands away from her face. A long red weal ran from her left temple to the corner of her mouth. Big tears dribbled from her eyes. She blotted them away from the painful burn, crying more at the pain of touching the wound.

Don't hurt my body. I need it back! The wraith added her own mournful cries to the noise.

Powwell needed to go to his little sister. He didn't know how to force Hanassa out of the body and keep her out short of killing the body. Hot moisture prickled the backs of his eyes.

"Leave her, Powwell," Lyman insisted in a ragged whisper. Exhaustion made his eyes droop and his shoulders sag. "You can't win this battle. The only way I can defeat Hanassa is to kill her—if I can. But I do not yet know the cost. Take your friends and get out of here now."

"The dragongate. It'll open soon. We'll go out the dragongate." Powwell looked longingly toward the little tunnel that opened onto the lava core.

"Over my dead body, boy!" Hanassa jumped up in front of him. Her fingers arched and flexed. Her very long nails looked more like dragon talons than human digits.

Powwell didn't doubt she could render his flesh into slender strips with little effort.

Get it out of my body! The wraith pleaded on a sob.

Powwell reached a tentative hand toward the misty form that circled him and Hanassa.

"Powwell, feel the hot wind!" Rollett called. "The gate is opening again. The gate is opening."

"I'll be free at last! You can't stop me. I'll bleed this world dry." Hanassa turned and ran into the little tunnel.

"Stop her. We can't let Hanassa leave this place," Lyman gasped. He wiped his face wearily with a shaking hand.

Powwell scanned his companions. Lyman was exhausted. Rollett tried staggering to his feet and sat back down heavily. No help from either of them. Yaala, his dear friend, lay unconscious, blood trickling from her temple.

Hanassa skidded to a halt at the edge of the pit. The gate swirled in a kaleidoscope of colors. Green dominated the forming image. The green of Coronnan?

"I'm sorry, Kalen, I've got to close the gate forever. Thorny and I have got to close it."

Noooooooooo! The misty form darted after Hanassa at the end of the tunnel.

Thorny hunched and bristled his spines. Powwell couldn't tell if his familiar reacted in gibbering fear or thought this was another setup for blood magic—the only magic left to them.

"No, Powwell. The gate is our only hope of escape from this hell," Rollett reminded him. The older journeyman crawled toward him, holding out his hand in entreaty. "Please, Powwell, in the Stargods' names, I beg you, don't close the gate. That's home out there. We can be home in two moments."

"Yeeees! I'm free," Hanassa screamed in triumph. She looked up at the wraith rather than forward into the gate. The scene solidified (liquefied?) into storm-tossed waves.

Powwell grabbed one of Thorny's dried spines from his pocket and jabbed it hard into his hand. "Yeeow!" He held his yelp of pain deep inside his chest, letting it grow with the flow of blood from the deep wound.

Power grew with the pain. Each drop of blood increased the magic singing in his veins. He knew every grain of dirt and mineral within the cavern. His magic invaded every crack and crevice. His mind flowed outward, melding with the cavern until he couldn't tell where the tunnels ended and he began.

"I'm sorry, Kalen. I'm sorry, but this is the only way

to keep Hanassa or anyone else from controlling you and your destiny."

He sought the weakest point within the tunnel and pulled—

The tunnel collapsed upon Hanassa and his sister, sealing access to the gate forever.

He sensed the weight of the entire cavern system landing on Hanassa's head, splitting it open. Sympathetic pain slammed into his own skull. He fell to the ground, screaming at his physical pain and the emptiness in his heart.

CHAPTER 36

The pit beneath the city of Hanassa

"Wake up. You've got to wake up," Rollett pleaded with her. She moaned slightly but didn't rouse.

"Wake up!" He slapped her face lightly, afraid of hurting her, of breaking those fragile facial bones.

Her eyelids fluttered.

A huge boulder broke loose from the ceiling and landed in the middle of Old Bertha. Powwell had upset the delicate balance within the mountain that supported the caves.

"We've got to get out of here, Yaala." He slapped her a little harder. She moaned and rolled away from him.

Rollett risked a glance toward Powwell. The boy had his hands clutched over his head and had rolled into a fetal ball, sobbing uncontrollably. The little hedgehog poked its nose out of his pocket. It trilled a soothing sound.

Lyman seemed to have disappeared again.

"Stargods, I can't carry you both. I'm sorry, Powwell, I've got to save Yaala. The city needs her." He wouldn't admit that *he* needed her.

Rollett hoisted Yaala onto his shoulder and wove his way out of the deep cavern. The roar of multiple cave-ins thundered against his ears. The opening to the lava core adjacent to the dragongate collapsed. Dust exploded in a huge ball, filling the hot air.

He choked and coughed. With one last look of regret toward Powwell, he increased his speed toward the exit.

His last vestige of hope died along with access to the dragongate. He'd climb out of Hanassa tonight. Demons take Piedro and this cursed city. He hoped Yaala would rouse enough to climb with him. Otherwise he'd have to carry her.

Little Liise, the only operating generator, chugged steadily within a side cavern.

That persistent, unwanted hope flowered once more deep inside his gut. His magic talent stirred in response to the emotion.

He set Yaala down beside Liise. She roused a little, flailing about with both hands clenched into fists.

"Wake up, Yaala. You're all right. Wake up." He shook her gently.

Finally, her eyes flew open and she dragged in a deep breath. She coughed the dust-laden air back out again.

"It's getting hotter in here. The volcano is getting ready to erupt!" She bounced to her feet and staggered back into Liise. "My head . . . what happened?" She touched her temple with delicate fingertips. They came away bloody.

"The lower caverns are collapsing. Powwell destroyed the dragongate. I think he killed Hanassa and Kalen when he did it," Rollett explained as he set about examining the generator with minute care.

Should he take the raw energy as it left Liise headed for a transformer, or take the refined 'tricity after it left the transformer?

He opted for raw power. His body would become the transformer. That's what happened when gathering dragon magic.

Which conduit? He reached out tentatively with his dominant left hand and touched one of the wires. A slight spark made him jerk his hand away. His fingers tingled just as if he had tapped a ley line, but the power he tapped was stronger, more intense.

This was what he needed, a renewal of the magical energy contained within the Kardia.

If either Lyman or Hanassa had reverted to natural dragon form, both he and Powwell could have gathered that magic. Yaala could have gathered power from a purple-tipped dragon—anyone could gather from the rare purple-tips, even mundanes.

Lacking a dragon of any color, Rollett had to find other sources of energy to combat or elude the Rovers who still ruled the city of Hanassa.

He reached again for the wire and the energy he needed.

"No, Rollett," Yaala pleaded. Still clutching her head

with one hand she tried to step between him and the generator. She stumbled.

Rollett shifted his reach to hold her upright. Her body fit nicely against his own. "Soon, we'll be free, Yaala, and I'll be able to hold you as long as we both need."

"It's too dangerous, Rollett. Don't touch the 'tricity."

"I have to. It's the only way I'll have enough power to overcome Piedro and get us out of here. I promise that once we're free, we'll make time to explore this thing between us . . . this 'tricity you and I generate all on our own."

"Please, Rollett. We don't know enough about how 'tricity works. No one has ever tried to use it like magic."

"Not too long ago no one had gathered dragon magic either." Resolutely, he separated from her comforting embrace. Out of long habit he stilled his body to make it receptive to the power, reached out and . . .

Energy coursed through his veins. His body became light as it jerked back and forth. Back and forth. His teeth rattled. Back and forth.

He smelled burning flesh. His own. Pain jolted every joint and nerve ending in his body.

"Rollett! Let go. You've got to stop this. It's hurting you," Yaala cried.

"Don't touch me. It's . . . not . . . supposed . . . to be . . . like . . . this!"

He couldn't let go. He couldn't stop the flow.

He couldn't . . .

CHAPTER 37

Afternoon, home of Myrilandel, Ambassador from the nimbus of dragons, Coronnan City

Katie looked around the entry hall to Myrilandel's home. What could she do to help? Bessel and his mutt were safely out of sight. The healers marched through the doorway. They would repair the initial damage to Nimbulan's heart. Quinnault comforted his sister.

She eyed the line of healers led by Whitehands skeptically.

"I've been breaking rules all my life. Why should I stop now?" Katie rubbed her hands together in anticipation of positive action when she felt so useless to help Nimbulan. "I need your assistance." She snagged a healer journeyman as the procession of gray-clad magicians entered the house.

At least she hoped the gray tunic and blue trews signified a journeyman.

"How may I be of service, Your Grace?" the young man asked warily. His gaze followed the healers into the reception hall, clearly anxious to be close to the center of action.

"Do you know a plant called Fairy Thimbles?" Katie asked him.

His eyes glazed over blankly.

"Broad fuzzy leaves tapering to a point. Tall flower stock filled with purple bells," she described the common *Digitalis purpurea* that had originated on Earth and followed humanity through colonization of a hundred worlds.

"Fairy Bells, sometimes called foxglove," the young man responded, his eyes clearing with enlightenment.

"Yes! Can you recognize the plant this early in the season? Can you bring me a specimen now?"

He nodded enthusiastically. "Do you know a medical use

for the plant? We know it only as a poison—pretty in the garden but dangerous to ingest."

"Yes. Once the healers have stabilized Master Nimbulan, a drug made from the plant can keep his heart beating regularly."

"I shall return in a few moments." The young man's face brightened, and his eyes sparkled. Katie could almost see the ideas churning in his head.

"Take the plant to the kitchen and tell the young man there to begin making a . . . a decoction of the leaves." She didn't dare name the journeyman in the kitchen lest Scarface at the end of the line of healers overhear. "It must be a very mild decoction, no more than one handful to half a pint of water. Simmer it for about one half an hour. No longer. An effective dose is very close to a lethal one. We must start slow and build up by tiny increments to find the right proportions. We'll need more leaves to dry and use in infusions. That is a better remedy, but we don't have time to dry the leaves. I will join you in a moment to help you."

The journeyman dashed around the corner of the building toward the back of the house just as Scarface stormed up the steps.

"Why must you meddle in affairs that do not concern you, Your Grace?" Scarface demanded. The scar across his face whitened and tightened. "You can't help."

How much guilt from his past haunted him so that he could never find peace within himself and therefore couldn't allow it in another?

"Is aiding a dear friend in his struggle for life meddling?" she retorted with a sarcastic half-smile.

"It is if the Stargods have decreed the man's time to pass on to his next existence," Scarface replied. As usual he looked over her shoulder at the wall rather than directly at her.

"Who are we to know the intent of a deity? We are duty bound to use whatever talents and knowledge we have been given. Myrilandel needs her husband, Her babies need a father, King Quinnault still needs his friend, Coronnan desperately needs Nimbulan's wisdom. I will meddle in whatever way I can to help him."

"Perhaps this is the method the Stargods have chosen to tell us that Nimbulan's guidance is no longer needed or wanted."

"Is that the message of the Stargods or of the Senior Magician who replaced Nimbulan but can never truly replace him?"

"That is not for you to question. You are merely a foreign female who barely hides her illegal magical talent!"

"I am your queen."

"For now. But I know you are also a spy for our enemies. You have lied to the king and all of Coronnan. You cannot possibly be who you say you are." Now he looked directly at her, accusing, unforgiving.

Katie swallowed her rush of fear. How much did Scarface know?

"But I am who I say I am. I do not lie," she countered. "The dragons have blessed me as consort to their king. Quinnault rules by the grace of the dragons. Do you care to argue the matter with Shayla and her nimbus?"

"If I must." Scarface maintained his steady gaze into her eyes. "Dragons have many secrets—secret knowledge they deem dangerous to humans. They recognize the value of some secrets. I do not believe they will honor your secrets much longer, unless you have managed to keep information in your mind hidden from their scrutiny. The plague you carry and the cure you keep secret is clear evidence of your evil intent."

"Take your self-righteous anger elsewhere, Master Aaddler. I have never kept the cure for the plague secret. Only the Tambootie can cure the ailment that devastates my people and may be spreading here." Arguing with him was useless. But he commanded a great deal of power—political as well as magical. If she turned her back on him, he'd presume she fled from guilt and weakness. He'd use that against her. She had to stand her ground.

"Tambootie is poison to mundanes and only mundanes are affected by this diseased." Scarface stared back at her, not moving from the doorway of Myrilandel's home. Then he blinked his eyes slowly as if making a decision.

"Terrania, the land you *claim* to hail from is the oldest known country on all of Kardia Hodos. Legend says that men first emerged in that land. But it is now a desert wasteland and has been for many, many centuries. Where do you really come from, wife of my king?"

"We call it Terra now."

"And where is Terra that you and your father can only reach it by flying inside the belly of a mechanical dragon? A mechanical beast that spreads the plague you preach against . . . or have you brought the plague here deliberately to kill us off so you can resettle those who are displaced by the desert sands of Terrania?"

"How dare you!" Katie slapped his face. Red stained his left cheek in the shape of her handprint.

"How dare you!" Scarface raised his right fist as if to slam it into her jaw. "How dare you deceive one and all with your lies, usurping *my* authority by ordering my journeyman to run personal errands when he . . . when none of the Commune even looked to me for confirmation when they received word of *that* man's illness." He pointed to the still form at the center of the healers' circle. "He's not even a magician anymore, and they defer to him in all matters. He steals the respect they owe me."

"Respect has to be earned," Katie held his gaze, daring him to inflict violence upon her. "Nimbulan was your friend. You saved each other's lives numerous times in your escape from Hanassa. Now you wish him and his influence on the kingdom dead."

She didn't know for certain if that last stray thought was her own idea or if Scarface had leaked it to her mind. His ability to guard his psi powers was normally strong.

"Beware of whom you accuse, Your Grace. My magicians may be more concerned with Nimbulan's health than with my permission to leave University Isle, but I can still bring you down and your king with you."

"Scarface!" Quinnault strode to the entry from the reception hall in a few anxious paces. "Why wasn't I told that the plague had already brought Lord Balthazaan's province low?"

"That neglectful lord always loses large numbers of tenants to disease and privation in the Spring." Scarface shrugged off the news. But he shifted his eyes away from his king.

He's lying! He knows something dangerous, Katie thought directly into Quinnault's mind.

"This is more than a lord's neglect," Katie countered, trying to peer into Scarface's mind for the truth. "This is a disease that eats the internal organs until you bleed to death from the inside! Bessel watched his mother die of it. He reported dozens of deaths from the same cause. Didn't you listen to him?"

"Bessel is not a reliable witness."

More lies. What was he hiding?

"Why isn't Bessel reliable? He is your senior journeyman." Quinnault stepped closer to Scarface, towering over him. He looked as if he wanted to beat some sense into the magician as well.

"A familiar has sought out Bessel. Familiars fear dragons and will not come to a magician using dragon energies. Therefore Bessel obviously uses illegal rogue magic regularly. Besides, Bessel has never been *my* journeyman. He belongs to Nimbulan and always has. He defies me at every turn. He is a part of this conspiracy to put Nimbulan back into the Commune as Senior Magician even though he is now mundane. I trust no one who has served my predecessor. The mercenaries of Rossemeyer will serve us all well when they assassinate Bessel since you will not condemn him for the murder of Ambassador Jorghe-Rosse."

Katie and Quinnault looked to each other for explanation. Her husband's thoughts, which she could never fully shut out, rolled in chaos as he sought some kind of logic in the last statement.

Then his mind closed, as if he had slammed a door shut upon Katie's link to him. She recoiled in surprise. Never in the year and a half of their marriage had he denied her access to his most intimate thoughts.

Loneliness nearly overwhelmed her need to remain in this conversation.

"I think you'd best retire to the privacy and security of your apartments in the Commune, Master Aaddler," Quinnault said quietly—too calmly.

Let me into your thoughts, Scarecrow! Katie pleaded with her husband. She tried to hold his hand. He jerked free of her tentative touch.

This terrible aloneness frightened her. Without Quinnault, without her brothers, far from the home of her birth and nurturing, she was lost. She needed to become one with him again.

She used to enjoy being alone when her large family became too intrusive, too boisterous. But she always had familiar surroundings and the knowledge that when she wanted she could reach out and touch one of them with her mind, or her hand.

Her father had always respected her privacy when no one else did. And now her father had been exposed to the plague, possibly carried it to others.

Which others? Lord Balthazaan's province already reeled under the impact of the horrible disease. Lord Balthazaan. Something . . .

"Is that a dismissal, Your Grace?" Scarface backed up a step. Surprise almost masked the new surge of anger in his expression and posture.

"It is." Quinnault remained closed to Katie. The easygoing diplomat, always ready to seek a compromise had disappeared inside his head and behind his clenched fists. "I have lost confidence in you as my chief adviser, Master Aaddler. I will ask the Commune to elect a new Senior, one whom I can trust."

"Then think on this, King Quinnault Darville de Draconis, before you give your trust and confidence to Nimbulan, the man you call friend: The Rover woman, Maia, has escaped. The only way she could have broken through our wards is with help—the help of someone with Rover blood and therefore access to the mind-to-mind link of Rover magic. Nimbulan has Rovers in his ancestry. He has lied to you when he claims to have lost all of his magic. He still has Rover magic. He was also Maia's lover. She bore him a child. Who else in your kingdom would want to help her escape?" Scarface turned on his heel and marched back the way he had come.

"Lord Balthazaan is Nimbulan's cousin, isn't he?" Katie asked, thinking through the convoluted relationships among the nobility of Coronnan. "He would have Rover blood in his ancestry as well. Could an unscrupulous Rover magician manipulate him? We never found Piedro after he escaped, Scarecrow! A Rover helped him escape a magically sealed prison."

"Lord Balthazaan has enjoyed new prosperity of late." Quinnault clasped her hand tightly in his to dispel the lingering nightmare of the night Piedro tried to strangle Katie with the silken tie from Quinnault's robe. "Despite the plague that decimates his population and threatens to close his mines for lack of workers, Lord Balthazaan rides new and expensive steeds. His wife wears the most costly Se-Lenese lace."

"And they both wear a great deal of jewelry," Katie added, thinking again of the Rover ring that Marilell had almost choked on.

"Perhaps Balthazaan's new prosperity results from Rover interference, or possibly your father's manipulation."

"My father carries the plague that has infected Balthazaan's province."

"So is the lord the puppet of your father or of the Rovers?" Quinnault raised one eyebrow. The solid wall that closed his mind cracked a little.

Katie reached in with her own thoughts, sharing every twisted idea surrounding the issue.

"The vandalism, the riot, the ambush of supply caravans, that strange storm that killed Jorghe-Rosse . . . Balthazaan was always the first to accuse you of incompetence or tyranny, Scarecrow. Perhaps he engineered the incidents."

"Or knew of them in advance to prepare his arguments," Quinnault offered. "Perhaps Kinnsell and Balthazaan used each other and the Rovers ride their schemes to further their own ambitions."

"All of them would like to see an end to our reign for different reasons. I think we need to look closer at Balthazaan as a focus for those who oppose you at every turn, Scarecrow."

"The time has come to divide the opposition and thus weaken their resolve."

"But first we must tend to Nimbulan. We need his wisdom now more than ever."

"I hope we are not too late to save him." Quinnault returned to Nimbulan's side, lovingly holding the older man's hand as a bit of color returned to Nimbulan's overly pale face.

"I hope we are not too late to find my father before he infects the entire planet with the plague. There is barely enough Tambootie left to feed the dragons. How can we cure all of our own people without it?" Katie asked herself, the others, and the air.

CHAPTER 38

The pit beneath the city of Hanassa, time undetermined

Without thinking of the consequences, Yaala punched a warning button on Liise's control panel and threw a switch to break the circuit.

The bizarre blue arcing that surrounded Rollett and jerked him back and forth in a dance of death abruptly ceased. He dropped to the ground in a boneless heap.

The overhead lights died, plunging the entire cavern system into darkness. Yaala reeled without a sense of up and down or right and left. Hesitantly, she spread her hands away from her body for balance. Sparks leaped from Liise to her fingers. The residual current needed to complete the circuit. Like a living being, it sought contact rather than die.

She jerked her hand away. At least she knew how far she stood from the machinery. Rollett should be just there. . . .

She bumped against his unmoving body and dropped to her knees. "Rollett, wake up!" she pleaded with him for a sign that he still lived.

He didn't moan. She heard no movement, no rustle of clothing, no scrape of a shoe on rock, no whisper of air entering or exiting a pair of lungs.

"Rollett, don't you dare die on me!" She shook him. Tremors ran through his body.

"I don't know if this will work or not, but Queen Katie says it should." Yaala stuck a finger in his mouth to make certain nothing clogged his air passage. Then she tilted back his head and blew her own breath into his mouth.

"That works better with two people," Old Lyman said from behind her. He held a feeble ball of witchlight in his hand. Powwell staggered beside him, barely outlined in the dim light.

The Kardia continued to rumble around them. Dust filled the air, further dimming the tiny light.

"Help me," Yaala pleaded with them. Tears streaked her cheeks. She dashed them away with her sleeve. There was no time for this weakness.

She sensed the constant shifting of the caverns around her. They didn't have much time. She wouldn't leave Rollett, and she couldn't carry him. His life seemed much more important than all of Hanassa right now.

"Breathe into him on the count of five," Lyman instructed as he knelt beside Rollett's still unmoving form. He passed the witchlight to Powwell. The younger magician looked barely able to hold himself up, let alone maintain the dim glowing ball.

Lyman cupped his hands over Rollett's chest and pressed down. "One, two, three, four, breathe."

Yaala followed his rhythm. Two times, three times, and a fourth they forced Rollett's heart to beat while Yaala breathed for him. On the seventh try, or was it the eleventh, Rollett gasped and coughed. He tried sitting up, but Lyman held him down.

"Rest a moment, boy," Lyman said, holding Rollett down with one finger. "We've brought you back from the dead, don't hasten to return there."

The Kardia shifted beneath Yaala's feet. She braced herself against the rolling motion. "That was stronger than the last one, and closer," she said. "When was the last one?" She realized she'd been so preoccupied with Rollett, she had forgotten the reason for their perilous route to this situation.

"We have to get out of here before—" A crash of falling stone and a shower of dust in the corner of Liise's cavern punctuated her statement.

The cave system had been her refuge from her mother's tyranny for many years before her official banishment. The machines had been her only true friends. She belonged here.

No longer.

Sadness and regret welled up in her throat and dissipated

again as Rollett struggled to his feet. She slid an arm under his shoulders, guiding his rise.

A sense of rightness filled her, replacing the loneliness of many years. She had to find a new family, a new purpose for living. She'd start with these three men.

"This will never be Liise's cavern again. She's dead, and so are all the rest of my machines," she whispered. "No reason to stay."

"Powwell!" Lyman left her to support Rollett alone while he kept Powwell from falling flat on his face.

"What's wrong with him?" Yaala barely spared a backward glance as she half-led and half-carried Rollett up the slope toward the living cavern and the exit.

"I don't think he much cares if he lives or dies," Lyman said, pushing Powwell to follow her. "I know how he feels. We have both lost a sibling today. There is this terrible emptiness." He placed his palm against his chest then resolutely closed his hand into a self-contained fist.

He and Powwell stood together with heads bowed, swaying as they shared the bond of grief.

"I lost my twin centuries ago." Lyman gulped. His voice trailed off and his chin quivered. "I lost Hanassa when he turned renegade, but always I had this faint hope he might be redeemed. Now I have truly lost Hanassa. We will never complete each other again." He bowed his head again, seeming much older than he had when he arrived in the caves.

"I killed her, Yaala," Powwell whispered. "I came here to save Kalen, yet I ended up killing her." Tears streaked his face. The little ball of witchlight flickered, reflecting his waning strength and wandering concentration.

"I'm sorry, Powwell. I'm truly sorry. I know how much you loved Kalen. I know what it is like to lose someone you love dearly, to be helpless as they die before your eyes. But we have to save ourselves now." Yaala led them into the living cavern. They staggered forward. The sounds of collapsing tunnels pursued them the entire distance. The dust grew thicker until they breathed more dirt than air.

For the first time, she became aware of the miles of Kardia that rested above their heads. It could all come tumbling down at any time without warning.

At last the large cavern with tons of stored food lay

before them. The walls seemed more stable here, the air a little cleaner.

Yaala deposited Rollett on a heap of grain sacks next to a barrel full of pickled meat and vegetables. She gave him and Powwell a handful of each. They nibbled halfheartedly. Lyman dug into the supplies with a little more energy.

The pile of stores showed signs of pilferage—torn sacks, open barrels turned on their side—but more than enough remained to fulfill their immediate needs.

"I'll get water for us all," Yaala said retrieving four carry skins.

"Did Kalen as the wraith survive?" Yaala asked as she knelt by the underground stream, letting the natural flow fill the portable bottles. She held her breath, fearing the answer.

"Doubtful," Lyman replied.

"And . . . and is Hanassa truly gone?"

"I cannot sense my twin within this mountain. I haven't the strength to search farther." A set look came over Lyman's face.

"And the dragongate?" Rollett gasped in whispered tones. "Have we totally lost that exit from this hellhole?"

"Yes," Powwell answered. A tiny spark of animation came into his eyes. Or was it merely a reflection from the ball of witchlight? "I fear the false gate that only opens once each moon is gone as well. We must fight our way out of Hanassa now."

"I can't leave as long as Piedro lives," Rollett announced in a stronger, more resolute voice. "The consort might not guide him anymore, but he's still a bloodthirsty tyrant. My men deserve better."

"The people of Hanassa are outlaws—assassins, highwaymen, and murderers," Yaala argued. "They deserve what they allow to happen here." For the first time, she saw the truth surrounding the city she should have inherited from her mother. A new sense of lightness invaded her being. Her spirit had freed itself of Hanassa, even if she physically remained here.

"Not all of the residents are criminals." Rollett shook off her supporting arm and walked weakly to the creek on his own. He drank deeply of the sulfur-laden water, then continued. "Some of them are political fugitives, some merely mercenaries for hire. Some even still hold a tiny glimmer of honor. They deserve better than Piedro's lust for power without the sense to wield it justly."

"Without the dragongate, Piedro is confined to this city. The city will take care of him. Why should we care as long as we get out?" Lyman asked. Craftiness replaced the grief on his face.

"Because the city will starve before they can oust Piedro. He'll deliberately starve my men, my friends, before he allows them to escape." Rollett's knees wobbled as he returned to the food supplies.

Lyman and Powwell looked ashen in the fading glow of witchlight as they struggled once more to their feet, exhausted and burdened by grief. Their skin seemed grayer than just the dust would account for. "All three of you have got to rest a little longer. Drink deeply and eat as much as you can." She seemed to be the only one strong enough to make a decision. But her head ached terribly with every thought and movement. She followed her own advice.

"No time," Powwell ground out between gritted teeth.

She ached to see the bleak expression in his eyes. Thorny seemed strangely quiet within his pocket. They both suffered from the loss of Kalen and the drain of blood magic.

"Piedro is mine. I claim the right to remove his head." Powwell's words filled the suddenly quiet cavern with dread.

"Not if I get to him first," Rollett replied. He kept moving upward toward the iron gate.

The ground shook again, precursor to another larger quake. As one, they hurried up the slope, eating as they walked.

"I claim blood right for revenge." Powwell stopped moving. His stance challenged them all to contradict him. "Kalen was my sister. Her death is a direct result of Rover manipulation. All Kalen wanted out of life was control of her own life. Piedro is only the latest in a long line of people who used her for their own greedy ends. His head is mine."

"Piedro was as much Hanassa's victim as Kalen was," Yaala insisted. "Let's just concentrate on getting out of here alive. All of us, together." She reached out both hands to include all of them.

"Are we certain that Hanassa died?" Rollett asked.

"Yes," Lyman said sadly. "Through all of these centuries of separation I have been aware of his presence in this existence. Always, no matter what form I took, dragon, human, or ghostly guardian of the beginning place, I knew he waited and brooded and plotted escape. And I hoped. . . . Now there is nothing, only an echo of him in the blood of his descendants, those capable of hosting his spirit within their bodies."

"Kalen, my sister, was descended from Hanassa?" Powwell jerked away from the older man. He stepped backward, as if needing to flee into the lower caverns—flee into the death and destruction that hovered there.

"Through her mother, I believe. Not through your common father," Lyman said. He stared directly at Powwell.

"As long as any of his descendants live, then Hanassa has a body to flee to." Rollett searched the shaky cavern with his eyes. His gaze slid over and away from Yaala. "Do we have to hunt them all down and kill them to prevent Hanassa from wreaking havoc all over Kardia Hodos?"

"Possibly." Lyman hung his head sadly. "Hanassa's exile only included himself. His descendants have been able to leave this city and spread their seed far and wide for seven centuries."

"I am directly descended from the renegade dragon, Lyman," Yaala said, her voice as shaky as the Kardia beneath her feet. "Will you kill me for no reason other than that?"

CHAPTER 39

Kaaliph's palace, city of Hanassa

"No, Yaala, that is not what we mean." Powwell stood up a little straighter, shocked out of his lethargy. How could he have considered killing anyone, ever again—even loathsome Piedro? Kalen's death screams lingered, reverberating in his head.

His sister had made one last desperate attempt to regain her body. For one brief second, both Kalen and Hanassa had been joined. And then . . . and then the collapsing tunnel had crushed their skull.

Sympathetic pain still plagued him, nearly blinded him.

Every time he tried to think of something else, remember the happy times with his sister—there had been precious few—her death cry dragged him back to her last agony. If he ever had to kill again, his mind would lock in a loop of reliving Kalen's death.

He clung to his sanity by a slender thread. Thorny wriggled in his pocket as if to remind him of life.

His lust for vengeance against Piedro died. He sagged with relief, knowing he need not follow through with that particular quest.

"Hanassa died with Kalen," he said as he relived the moment of death once more. "My mind was linked to Kalen's at the last moment. They both died. We do not need to kill anyone for fear they will host Hanassa." He looked pointedly at each of his weary companions.

"Are you sure?" Yaala maintained her aggressive stance.

"I'm certain, Yaala."

She turned back toward the exit, spine a fraction less rigid. "Let's get out of here. The city will kill Piedro eventually. We just have to find a way over the crater walls. Lyman, will any of your dragon friends fetch us?"

"I do not know."

"We'll have to climb, then," Rollett said wearily.

Powwell didn't like the color of his skin. A hint of blue still clung to his lips and the edges of his nostrils. He breathed heavily and had to stop often. His hands looked blistered and swollen from the burns. The symptoms resembled the plague, but the smell was missing.

The Rovers had left the iron gate open when they fled the caverns. Yaala sighed her relief. Without Liise generating any 'tricity, the 'motes would not work.

Powwell breathed easier after passing the boundary of the pit. He'd be better yet when he had left the confines of buildings and caves. That moment of oneness with the Kardia just before he collapsed the tunnel on top of Kalen had taught him just how precariously balanced the cave system was. "Stargods, I hope I don't have to go underground again. Ever."

Lyman's steps now seemed a little firmer, too. Rollett still sagged against Yaala for support. She kept her arm around his waist. They fit together as if they had always belonged side by side, two halves of one whole.

Powwell waited for a pang of jealousy. Yaala had been his best friend and constant companion for many moons. At times he had entertained desire for her—when he wasn't consumed by his quest to free Kalen.

His sister had flown free of this existence.

All he had left was Yaala. . . .

No emotion churned within him. He hoped she'd be happy with Rollett.

"Looks as if a lot of people left here in a hurry," Yaala commented as they passed through the corridors of the palace.

Bits and pieces of gilt furniture, costly ornaments, and bolts of silk pilfered from the Kaaliph's stores littered the floor.

"Should we try to rescue the library?" Powwell asked them all. "If Yaala had the right textbooks, she might be able to reconstruct her machines."

"No," Yaala said resolutely. "Queen Katie was right.

Technology has no place in Coronnan. We have magic and the Commune. Machines only breed trouble."

They bypassed the entrance to the secret stair without further comment.

"I wonder if Piedro's followers are deserting him?" Yaala mused, pointing to the debris.

"But they still fear what the Kaaliph of Hanassa represents." Powwell pointed to the hideous pictures of torture and depravity. The first time he'd seen the vivid depictions of perverted sexual intercourse beside the bloody executions, his face had flushed with embarrassment. He'd seen too much since then to feel anything but disgust now. He gingerly lifted the tapestries aside, touching only the blood-red borders, unwilling to be tainted by the pictures. The opening behind the wall hangings allowed them access to the Justice Hall once more.

Only the severed heads of Rollett's friends remained. They seemed to mock the living as they passed in front of the altar. Powwell bowed briefly to the departed spirits in respect for the knowledge and the power they had given him the last time he'd passed this way.

They had almost traversed the room when a thunderous roar shook the entire building.

"That wasn't a kardiaquake," Powwell said, bracing himself for the rolling motion he expected but which didn't come.

"It's coming from outside, not beneath us," Rollett confirmed.

They joined the crush of people in the major corridor exiting the palace. No one seemed to notice four more bodies among the hundreds. Most of the servants, retainers, and guards carried at least one artifact looted from the Kaaliph.

Powwell checked Yaala's reactions to the loss of her inheritance, generations of accumulated wealth. She seemed more concerned with protecting Rollett from the jabbing elbows and careless feet of the fleeing populace. She had never wanted her mother's treasure, only her love. When Yaassima had exiled Yaala to the pit, she had turned to her beloved machines for companionship. Now they, too, were dead. Perhaps she had finally found in Rollett someone who would respect her and maybe eventually love her.

The crowd carried Powwell away from Lyman and the others as they neared the main exit. Everyone in the city seemed to be gathering in the open area in front of the palace. They all stopped in their tracks, astounded as a huge mechanical dragon floated down toward the ground. It spat fire from its hind end rather than its mouth and its wings looked far too short and thin to support the weight of the beast in the air. It listed badly to the left while the nose pointed down.

A mighty roar shook the beast as the fire flared, licking the rooftops of nearby buildings.

People screamed and pressed away from the beast, giving it room to land.

Powwell looked frantically for Lyman. Perhaps the elderly librarian could interpret for the beast. He caught sight of the old man's white hair off to his left. Lyman peered upward, seemingly unafraid of this new dragon.

"Is this Hanassa's new form?" Powwell asked, shoving his way over to Lyman's side.

"Doubtful." Lyman shook his head and shielded his eyes from the bright desert sunshine. "I have never seen a dragon so big or awkward as this. And these human eyes have never seen a true dragon so easily. Our gaze should be sliding around the beast, looking everywhere but directly at it. I do not know what this animal is."

"That isn't a dragon, it's a machine!" Yaala yelped excitedly. She pushed and shoved people out of her path as she made her way to the place where the beast settled into the dust. Rollett limped slowly behind her.

"Yaala, stand back!" Powwell yelled. He reached her side just as a hole slid open in the dragon's side.

Maia, the Rover girl the Commune had held hostage, stepped into the opening. Her face looked pale and bloated with worry and tears—or illness. Dozens of Rover guards reached up to help her down to the ground.

"Piedro, help me please," she wailed. "The queen's father is dead. This beast murdered him."

But the smell of the plague clung to her. He and Yaala stood next to her, breathing the same tainted air.

CHAPTER 40

Midafternoon, city of Hanassa

Joy glowed in Yaala's chest. The Stargods had answered her prayers. They had given her this wonderful mechanical beast to replace the machines she had sacrificed.

She dismissed her first happy reaction to the machine's presence as the Rover woman's words sank in. King Kinnsell lay dead within the machine's belly. The queen's father was a politically powerful man. What repercussions would follow?

She stopped her headlong rush to dive into the rectangular opening where Maia still stood.

"Yaala, don't go near her. She carries the plague!" Powwell screamed at her.

"Plague?" Fear lanced through Yaala. Powwell had related the dragon dream to her in painstaking detail, including the acrid chemical smell generated by the disease.

Yaala stepped back. Rollett's chest stopped her from running away.

"Can you fly that thing out of here?" Rollett asked.

He sounded so hopeful, Yaala hated to disappoint him.

"I'm an engineer. Given a few days of tearing that thing apart, I might be able to tell you how it works, but to fly it is something else entirely."

"That woman landed it. She must have if the pilot is dead. If Powwell and I can access her mind . . ."

Powwell pushed past them and climbed the two steps that folded out of the machine's portal.

"Powwell!" Yaala protested. "The plague."

"Don't worry, Yaala. I should be immune. The Tambootie in my system from the old days is supposed to protect me from any number of ailments." He turned and grinned at her.

Somehow his reassurance fell flat as he muttered, "If Old Lyman's books are accurate."

"Of course my books are accurate," the old man returned indignantly. "Let's see if King Kinnsell is truly dead, or if you can help him. I'll gladly read his mind while he's still unconscious and undefended. He has much to answer for, bringing the plague, sabotaging King Quinnault's authority. . . ." Muttering further descriptions of Kinnsell's crimes, Lyman disappeared into the machine's interior. Maia continued to stand in the doorway, wringing her hands.

A ripple of disturbance in the crowd revealed the presence of Piedro and his Rover guards, six of them. They surged toward Maia. An evil grin split Piedro's face.

"At last, lovely lady, you return to us." Piedro reached up a hand to help Maia descend, as if she were returning royalty instead of the mistress of their former leader—Piedro's now dead rival. "Our group mind has been lacking since your departure. You must have much to tell us."

"Don't even think about moving," Yaala commanded, stepping up beside Piedro. "I won't let you spread that disease to my city!"

"The Kaalipha! Yaassima's daughter, our true Kaalipha!" the people shouted, surging forward dangerously close to the machine and the plague.

Piedro dropped Maia's hand and stared openmouthed at Yaala. His surprise lasted only a moment.

"Seize her, she's one of the traitors!" he screamed. "I thought we left you dead in the pit," he hissed more quietly.

"Long live the Kaalipha returned from the dead!" the people screamed hysterically. The ones closest pushed and jostled, trying to touch Yaala.

"Open the gates to the city, Kaalipha."

"Save us, Kaalipha."

"Feed us, Kaalipha."

They shoved and pushed uncontrollably, separating Yaala from proximity with the Rovers. The steps of the machine dug sharply into her legs. She wanted to run back into the protection and the silence of the pit.

All these people, pushing and demanding her attention.

All these people shouting at her, robbing her of her privacy. She couldn't think, couldn't breathe.

She stumbled against the steps, clutching at the sides of the portal. Air left her lungs. The bitter taste of the plague filled her mouth.

* * *

Midafternoon, home of Myrilandel, ambassador from the Nimbus of Dragons, Coronnan City

"Did you hear the row Scarface just had with the king?" Luucian, a journeyman healer Bessel knew slightly from the old days before dragon magic, rushed into Myrilandel's kitchen. He clutched a pile of greenery against his chest. His breath came in excited gasps.

"I do not indulge in gossip," Bessel said calmly to cover his anxiety. Scarface had been dismissed as chief adviser to the king. His anger could lash out at any moment in any form, catching them all in the backlash.

"But you heard, you were eavesdropping at the servants' door!" Luucian prodded. He dumped his trove of plants on the worktable in the center of the kitchen.

"The kettle is about to boil, there's cheese in the cold cellar, and bread in the pantry. They'll all want nourishment when they're done with the master. Can you handle it?" Bessel marched from his listening post to the outside door.

"Wait a minute, Bessel, where are you going? Didn't you hear that Scarface is out? He's no longer Senior Magician, so you can return to the University. Don't you want to stick around and make sure *they*," Luucian nodded his head toward the interior of the house where master magicians hovered, "remember you are Senior Journeyman, almost ready for elevation for Master status? Promotion is as much politics as merit. You need to keep your face in front of as many masters as possible to get your final quest."

"None of that will matter if Scarface decides to retaliate. Cover for me."

Mopsie pawed at the door, as eager to be gone as Bessel. He whined and yipped anxiously.

"But I've got orders to help Queen Katie prepare the

Fairy Bells into a drug instead of pure poison. I need to know how to do it. You fix the food. I need knowledge to earn my promotion."

"You can handle both, Luucian, I have confidence in you." Bessel didn't wait any longer. He had to follow Scarface now, before he destroyed everything dear to the Commune, and to Coronnan.

Yet he wished he could share the communion of magic with the other magicians one more time—with or without Scarface.

A crowd had gathered in front of Myrilandel's home, the dragon embassy, attracted by the presence of the royal couple and their entourage. Bessel slipped through their ranks, keeping his face averted.

His best and safest route lay in anonymity.

Bessel caught sight of Scarface forcing his way through the crowd like a ship plowing through heavy waves with the wind coming from a cross quarter. The anxious people made way for the Senior Magician with only nominal nods of their heads in respect for his rank, not for the man.

Curious. Last year he had been hailed as a hero and welcomed in the city. Now the populace merely tolerated him.

Scarface passed the Rossemeyerian Embassy. A blackclad mercenary still stood vigil on the front stoop. A bloodred banner drooped above his head, limp from the damp river air. Bessel held his breath as he followed the Senior Magician's path. He willed Mopsie to make himself invisible in the crowd. The assassin had seen the dog with Bessel and might look beyond the common fisherman's clothes to find the man blamed for the death of Ambassador Jorghe-Rosse.

But the mercenary looked right past Bessel toward Nimbulan's and Myrilandel's house, keeping one hand on the hilt of his sword, the other hand fingering some unseen weapon beneath his voluminous robes.

Bessel looked directly at the mercenary. No recognition flickered on the man's face. Bessel smiled to himself. For once he faded into the background when he really wanted to. Had his ordeal in the river settled the skill in his bones as the trial by Tambootie smoke settled a magician's talent?

Once past Embassy Row, Scarface began weaving his

hands in a complicated gesture. Bessel recognized the movement before he sensed the spell that followed. The Senior Magician summoned the Commune to attend him in the tower room. The order contained a subtle, but illegal, compulsion to obey. Only rogue magic could power a compulsion!

In a flash of insight, Bessel knew that this was the spell Scarface had been working yesterday during the storm. The Senior Magician had to tap a ley line in order to compel people to obey him. That was why he'd noticed when Bessel also tapped a ley line.

Bessel erected his armor before Scarface finished the spell. No sense in taking a chance it might work past his natural barriers. He intended to follow Scarface unseen and counter the Senior Magician's plans with any magic available to him.

They neared the open courtyard in front of the University. Bessel ducked into the shadows beneath the last bridge. In his mind he envisioned the dark depths blending with a river fog. He saw no differences in the patterns of light and shadow with his physical eyes, but the apprentices and masters who obeyed Scarface's summons looked right at him without paying him any mind. Even the pesky newcomers who had more curiosity than sense ignored him.

Only Wind-drift looked his way. But he did not linger and did not inform any of the others of Bessel's presence.

For a brief moment, as their eyes locked, Bessel knew the tremendous joy of communal magic at work. Bessel broke the contact, knowing he could not continue within the Commune. Wind-drift shook his head sadly and returned to the summons.

Bessel's heart ached at the separation.

He reasserted the shadows that hid him. He didn't question the source of the energy that fueled his trick. Scarface had exiled him from the Commune. His oath to use only dragon magic had lost validity with that exile. He still served his Commune, Coronnan, and King Quinnault, but he would do so by whatever means he found available against a man who intended to destroy the delicate balance of King, Commune, and Coronnan.

How? What form would Scarface's retaliation take?

Witchlight glowed from the stained-glass windows in the

tower room. Bridge traffic in and out of the University ceased. Bessel crept out of his hiding place, keeping the shadows and mist draped around him like a cloak.

He entered through the library. The slightly musty smell of old books, ink, and parchment reached out to welcome him. He drew the comforting scent deep into his lungs, cherishing his return to the familiar sanctuary of learning.

But he didn't have time to linger here in the great room he'd always thought of as home. Silently he crept up the stairs to the tower room. The stone steps muffled his footsteps. His spell of invisibility muffled the shouts coming from the private enclave of the master magicians. Nothing could block out the intense sound altogether.

"The plague is upon us, masters, apprentices, and journeymen," Scarface intoned, as if preaching to a multitude. "The Tambootie is the only cure to this insidious disease. The Tambootie is reserved for dragons and magicians. If we allow the king to harvest enough of the tree of magic to eradicate the seeds of the plague, there will be none left for the dragons to eat or for the Commune to provide the trial by Tambootie smoke for our apprentices as they approach manhood and promotion to journeyman."

A murmur of protest broke out, mostly young voices, probably the apprentices who saw this as a threat to their careers as magicians.

"If the dragons die or desert Coronnan because we allow the destruction of the Tambootie, then we will have no communal magic to bind this kingdom together. We will have to resort to solitary magic and the chaos it brings." Scarface's authoritative tones allowed for no challenge.

But one master spoke up. Bessel thought it might be Saber Cat, one of the former Battlemages turned mercenary who had escaped from Hanassa shortly after Nimbulan and Scarface had last year. He had very prominent canine teeth that stuck out from his upper lip like the predatory cat's. "Master Aaddler, if we do not allow the Tambootie to be harvested and distilled into the remedy for this plague, then we will die too."

"No, we won't," Scarface countered. "The trial by Tambootie smoke makes us immune. We magicians can survive and use our communal magic to heal those who are worthy of healing without the loss of the precious tree of magic."

"What about the apprentices?" another master asked. Bessel couldn't discern which one.

"I order all of them to undergo an abbreviated Tambootie smoke ritual immediately. By tomorrow morning at dawn they will be ready to assist us in the greater task of preserving the Tambootie."

Bessel sensed the compulsion oozing out of Scarface. Instinctively, he drew on a ley line to refuel his armor before he believed the logic behind the master magician's words.

"How do we save the Tambootie?" many voices asked.

"We must destroy the knowledge that Tambootie is the only cure."

A chill ran down Bessel spine.

"What great magic do you plan, Master Scarface?" Saber Cat asked without hesitation or reservation.

"Wait and see. At dawn we will undertake this great task that will save us."

Bessel drew on every morsel of power he could reach in order to penetrate Scarface's thoughts.

All of the dangerous books in the library will be burned in the central courtyard, above the source of illegal rogue magic. I must control that knowledge to protect myself and the Commune from my enemies. Quinnault, Nimbulan, the Rovers, they all want to kill me because I will not be their tool. I must destroy the knowledge that will give them the power to kill me. Knowledge of solitary magic, Rovers, subverting familiars, and dragon secrets must die forever in the cleansing flames. Then and only then will I be safe.

CHAPTER 41

Afternoon, city of Hanassa

"Don't you dare get sick on me, Yaala. I'll give you up to Rollett, but I'll be damned if I give you up to the plague," Powwell said, dragging her free of the pressing crowd and their incessant demands.

"You can't heal both Yaala and the queen's father," Lyman reminded him. "You have already exhausted your magic talent. I'm surprised you are still walking."

"I'll survive. But we have to know how to fly this thing to get us out of here. Once we are free, we can dose Yaala with Tambootie. Her dragon heritage should protect her from the toxins in the raw leaves." Powwell brushed the hair out of Yaala's eyes. "You'll be all right, sweetheart. I promise."

"Kinnsell lives?" she asked, looking at the supine figure on the floor.

"Barely. I know I can keep him alive a little longer, but I'm not sure I can cure him. He's pretty far gone." Powwell shook his head sadly.

"I'll check out the controls." Yaala touched Powwell's face briefly, affectionately. "You will always be my best friend, Powwell. I trust you."

Brave words from the woman who trusted machines more than people.

Just then, Rollett dove into the shuttle headfirst. He landed awkwardly on the floor. "Shut the door!" That mob is getting angrier by the minute."

Lyman fussed with a series of buttons set beside the door until it whooshed shut. Maia remained outside with her Rover clan.

"They're insane," Rollett muttered as the closing door

muffled the noise. "Maia is telling Piedro that Rovers must start adding the Tambootie to their food to offset the plague. She's planning recipes spiced with timboor—the berries for Stargods' sake—the most toxic part of the entire tree. She'll kill them all."

"They're all magicians," Powwell said. "They'll give each other immunity from the Tambootie through their strange magic."

The muffled shouts of the mob outside continued to filter into the much quieter machine.

"What about the rest of them out there?" Yaala asked. She thrust out her chin, challenging her companions to give her a solution. "Not everyone in Hanassa is a Rover or a magician. A lot of people will die from the plague unless we do something to help."

"Rollett, go forward with Yaala," Powwell said. "Keep her there while I do this."

"You give orders as if you expect to be obeyed. You've grown up, Powwell." Rollett eyed him curiously.

"That happens when you've killed your sister and undertaken your only option for escape, which may just kill us all." Powwell turned his back on the other two magicians. He sought a pulse in the neck of the desperately ill man. A feeble flutter told him the man's heart continued to beat—irregularly.

Decisively, before his fears could stop him, Powwell sat crossed-legged beside Kinnsell. When he was comfortable, he took three deep breaths to trigger a trance. His focus narrowed to himself and Kinnsell. The edges of his vision darkened. His head lightened as if he floated toward the void.

He removed a sheaf of pages torn from one of Lyman's precious books back home and studied them a moment. When he had the ritual memorized, he took one of Thorny's dried spines from his pocket. He examined it closely for the sharpest point. Thorny hunched and protested inside Powwell's pocket. The little hedgehog crawled out of the protective hiding place, digging his claws into Powwell. His gibbering insisted that Powwell stop.

Powwell ignored the advice of his familiar and stabbed his palm deeply, ripping his palm open in a jagged slash with the spine. He squeezed the edges of the wound until it bled freely. He repeated the procedure with Kinnsell's limp hand.

Thorny jumped off Powwell's lap and scurried away.

"No, Powwell! You can't do this. You don't know for sure it will work. Thorny is frightened. Listen to your familiar." Yaala launched herself onto his back, jerking his bloody palm away from contact with Kinnsell.

"I said, keep her up front and don't interfere," Powwell barked.

"I can't let you kill yourself, Powwell. We'll find another way out of Hanassa." Yaala kicked at Rollett as he dragged her away from Powwell.

"I have to do this, Yaala. It's the only way. Comfort Thorny. He likes you."

"But . . ." Her protests died on a sob.

Powwell took three more deep breaths to bring himself completely into his trance. His vision narrowed again. His hand glowed, the blood taking on a luminescence like a ruby in the sunlight. Or a red-tipped dragon soaring across the Great Bay. The void beckoned Powwell to soar with dragons in the vast nothingness between the planes of existence.

He resisted the urge to flee into the blackness and away from his task. Stinging pain in his hand signaled a weakening of his magic and his resolve.

The aura of power shining around his self-inflicted wound extended to Kinnsell's hand. The king's blood didn't shine or reflect light, a sure sign of the advancing disease.

Resolutely, Powwell placed his palm atop Kinnsell's, aligning the wounds perfectly. Lacking a silk scarf to bind the two hands together he signaled Lyman to wrap his old-fashioned sash belt around them. The moment the cool blue fabric touched his skin, he knew it to be silk. Leave it to Lyman's antique wardrobe to cover all contingencies.

"My blood to your blood," Powwell recited the litany of healing he'd stolen from the library. Behind his eyes he "saw" his blood mingling with his patient's. He pushed the residual Tambootie in his blood to the surface, forcing the essence of the tree to flow into Kinnsell.

"My skin becomes your skin." His entire hand burned with the binding.

"My heart beats for your heart." The rhythm of his pulse

stuttered and started up in a new pattern to match Kinnsell's erratic and weak beat.

Slowly Powwell's heart beat stronger, more regularly, forcing healing blood to circulate through Kinnsell, pushing the man's heart to assume a matching rhythm.

Powwell watched his blood seeking out the damage in lungs, heart, liver, and kidneys. At each vital organ he pushed dissolving tissue back into place, binding it to the organs with Tambootie glue and his own healing blood.

Drop by slow drop, Powwell pulled the tainted blood into his own body, replacing it with his own. The Tambootie in his system surrounded the seeds of the disease, making them inert and ineffective. He used every bit of the residual healing properties of the tree of magic and still tainted blood flowed back and forth between his body and Kinnsell's.

The blackness of the void encroached on Powwell's inner vision. He dove deeper into Kinnsell's lungs, desperately trying to repair enough damage for the man to breathe on his own. Powwell's own breathing became ragged, incomplete, clogged with blood. Weakness assailed his heart.

"Powwell, come out of it. You've gone too far," a voice urged him from afar.

Something shook the body he'd left behind on this long journey into another man's life. He didn't care. That body belonged to another existence, another person. He hadn't the strength for anything but to follow the pulses of blood through choked vessels.

* * *

Afternoon, inside Kinnsell's shuttle, city of Hanassa

Rollett watched Kinnsell closely for the first signs of rousing from the coma. When his eyelids fluttered in dream sleep, he allowed Yaala to kneel beside Kinnsell and Powwell's now twitching body.

The younger magician remained unconscious. Rollett hoped they'd get out of here in time to rouse him with Tambootie before the plague damaged him beyond repair.

"Your body is younger than mine, Rollett, your mind more receptive to change," Lyman said. "Perhaps you had best do this, while I keep watch on that mob. They sound ugly, near riot."

Rollett nodded his acceptance. If Yaala failed to absorb enough information, he might be able to fill in the gaps.

"I need to keep one hand on your face here." He placed the fingers of his right hand on Yaala's temple. "The other hand will link me to Kinnsell's mind. But you need to touch my temple the same way. That will link our minds together. I am just the vessel for passing knowledge from him to you. Do you understand, Yaala?"

She nodded mutely, never taking her eyes off Powwell. Her right hand kept reaching toward him, in comfort, in love.

"Concentrate, Yaala." Rollett grabbed her reaching hand and placed it on his own head. "If we are ever going to get out of here and get help for Powwell and all the people Maia has exposed to this plague, then you have to concentrate on learning how to fly this strange dragon out of here."

"For Powwell, for my city." She lifted bewildered eyes to his face. "For us, for this strange 'tricity that flows between us."

Several fists pounded fiercely on the portal to the mechanical dragon. The vessel shook violently.

"We haven't much time," Lyman warned them. He left his post behind Powwell to glance out one of the small round windows. "The crowd is turning violent. The Rovers are retreating into the palace under a rain of stones and offal."

"Feed us! Feed us. Feed us," the people chanted over and over. "Save us from the kardiaquakes!" The muffled voices penetrated the walls of the vessel with increasing intensity.

The dragon trembled under the impact of their blows, much as the Kardia had shaken within the pit.

Rollett drew on his last reserves of physical strength and took himself into a deep trance. Before the void could claim him, he dove into Kinnsell's mind. A wall of armor repelled his first assault. A second and third try weakened the man's natural defenses but still repelled him.

Slowly. Go slowly and ask politely, Powwell told him. His mental voice was weak and distant.

THE RENEGADE DRAGON

Rollett didn't question the boy's instructions. He was linked to Kinnsell in a stronger bond of blood and magic than Rollett could hope to achieve with only a touch.

Please, he asked Kinnsell. *Please let us help you. Show us how to fly this strange dragon back to your daughter and help.*

The wall of resistance dissolved. A flood of bewildering images flowed swiftly past Rollett's mind's eye. He opened his connection to Yaala, finding her easier to reach than anyone he'd ever contacted, except when he worked in concert with Commune Magicians, minds and souls mingling and augmenting each other. He tried to organize the rapid pictures filling his mind and failed miserably.

You don't need to understand this. Just pass it on to me. Yaala almost laughed inside his mind. The happy flow within her thoughts showed him that she understood.

He relaxed his vigil over the images and opened himself like a canal.

Repetition brought some sense of information passing through him. He caught glimpses of the control panel at the front of the vessel. Red lights, green lights, flashing lights, and steady burns imprinted on his memory. A negative aura surrounded the strange crown of more blinking lights. Yaala couldn't use that, it responded only to Kinnsell. Then he saw visions of the entire shuttle—the proper name for the dragon filtered past at some point—flying steadily a hundred dragon lengths above the ground. Air, shimmering with heat, but still colorless, flowed out of the "jet engines" at the rear of the ship. Then he saw a hand passing over the control panel in a new pattern. The engines spat red flame and roared louder than thunder, louder than the largest kardiaquake in the pit. The shuttle turned its nose upward and shot into the heavens almost faster than the eye could follow.

The noise of the crowd outside shook Rollett out of contact with Kinnsell and Yaala. His trance fell to pieces.

They all collapsed into a heap.

"The Rovers have turned the mob against us." Lyman pulled Rollett off of Yaala who lay atop Powwell who lay atop Kinnsell. "They are using metal shovels and rakes as well as spears and pikes against the skin of this dragon. They think we have food in here. Maia is trying to open the door from the outside. I'm overriding her commands from in here. I don't know how much longer I can keep them out."

"Did you get enough information, Yaala?" Rollett shook his head to clear it of the last traces of the trance.

"I think so." Her voice shook and so did her hands. She turned frightened eyes up to Rollett. Her mind remained connected to his.

What he saw there scared him. "Yaala, we need to take the ship to the capital. We have to get help for Powwell and Kinnsell—quickly. They are dying. We can send food and healers back here to help the others."

"Hanassa the city is dying. I can't abandon these people."

"You'll burn out the rockets if you use them to blast a hole through the crater wall." The strange vocabulary flowed out of his mouth as if he'd always known the words for this technology. "We won't be able to fly the shuttle afterward. And there is no guarantee you will succeed. We may be stranded here with this very angry and very hungry mob."

"I have to try. I can't condemn a thousand people to a slow and painful death from starvation. Provided the mountain doesn't collapse on them first. Kinnsell thinks the plague has stopped spreading. It has taken those who are weak and vulnerable, the healthy ones are too healthy for the disease to live inside us. I have to free my people, Rollett. This is my legacy as Kaalipha of Hanassa. I have to help my people in the only way I can. I have to."

CHAPTER 42

Afternoon, home of Myrilandel, ambassador from the Nimbus of Dragons, Coronnan City

Katie watched in amazement as the healers and extra magicians surrounding Nimbulan reared their heads in surprise. The blue glow of their healing spell fizzled and died. Nimbulan lay exposed and vulnerable to his faulty heart once more. Without consulting each other, the magicians rose as one person and walked out the door.

"How dare you desert your patient!" Katie bustled after them. She grabbed the sleeve of the last man in line. He shook off her grip and continued in the wake of his fellows. None of them looked back or heeded her pleas.

"Are you all in a trance?" she yelled at their retreating backs.

"Come back here, every last one of you!" Quinnault ordered in his best parade ground voice.

"I'm sorry, Your Grace, this summons takes precedence. I dare not stay when the others leave," Whitehands said quietly as he trailed after his fellows.

The magicians continued staring straight ahead as they rapidly marched toward the nearest bridge.

"Scarface calls them. They obey a compulsion," Myri said. She looked as if she might also follow the magicians. Then she forced her gaze back to her husband. She sank back onto her heels and lifted his limp hand.

"Compulsion spells are illegal, forbidden by the Commune. Scarface himself wrote that law." Quinnault reached for his short sword. He eased it out of his sheath a few finger-lengths, then rammed it back home. Weapons wouldn't solve this problem.

Katie rushed to kneel beside Myri. "What must we do? We can't leave him like this."

"He breathes on his own. They managed to repair some of the damage to his heart," Myri said listlessly. Her pale blonde hair hung limply about her shoulders. She plucked at Nimbulan's hand with anxious fingers. Lavender circles of exhaustion ringed her eyes.

"You must rest, Myri." Katie wrapped her arms around her friend and helped her stand once more. "You must take care of the new baby. Your neighbors will be bringing Amaranth back here soon." Katie chanced a quick glance to Kaariin, sitting in the corner with Marilell. "Think about your daughter, Myri. Bad enough she see her father so ill, but not you, too."

"I can't. I have to stay with him."

"We will stay for now," Quinnault said. He joined his wife in wrapping his arms around his sister. "Go upstairs and rest. I'll send some of my men to find out what is going on at the Commune. I hope I'm not sorry I relied upon Scarface's honor to step down as Senior Magician." He hugged Myri tightly, released her, and stepped to the front door to address the armed men who still stood guard there.

"Bessel is in the kitchen preparing a drug to help Nimbulan's heart beat regularly," Katie offered. A slight grin tugged at her mouth. "I don't think Bessel will obey Scarface's summons. The boy seems to be immune to outside interference."

"My apprentice has never been disobedient," Nimbulan whispered. He breathed shallowly but regularly. A bit of color had returned to his face and the blue tinge to his nostrils and fingernails had given way to a very pale pink.

Myrilandel pressed her fingertips to his neck pulse. "Too rapid," she said after a few moments. "But strong enough as long as you do not exert yourself."

Katie wondered how she did that without a timepiece to measure the pulse against.

"I fully intend to remain alive long enough to see our son born, beloved." Nimbulan captured Myri's hand with his own and pressed his lips to her palm.

"I do not wish to raise a fatherless child, Lan. You will live a long while yet, and father many more children. Shayla has told me so. Dragons do not lie. But you frightened me for a time." Myri pressed Nimbulan's hand to her cheek and held it there a long moment.

Katie's heart swelled with joy at the evidence of the love between her two friends.

Quinnault came up behind Katie, pulling her tight against his chest. He kissed the top of her head. They cherished the moment of togetherness for as long as they could.

A flurry of movement in the back of the house brought Myri's and Quinnault's heads up in an intense listening posture.

"Nimbulan, Your Grace, we have to stop them. Scarface is going to burn the library!" Bessel skidded to a halt on the slick flagstones just short of colliding with his king.

"Is that why he summoned the entire Commune to attend him?" Quinnault held the breathless boy by the shoulders. The whiteness of his knuckles showed his effort to keep from shaking information out of him.

"Yes." Bessel gulped a huge mouthful of air as he nodded his head. "We have to stop him."

"Why does he take such dire action?" Myri asked the question on all of their minds.

"Because knowledge is power," Katie answered.

"So no one else will know that the Tambootie will cure the plague," Bessel added. "Magicians are immune because the Tambootie remains in their bodies from the trial by smoke when they become journeymen. There isn't enough of the tree of magic to cure all of the people of Coronnan as well as feed the dragons. He's more concerned with his supply of magic than with the people."

"He can't do this. We have to make a cure available to anyone who needs it." Myri stood up in protest. "So many suffer." She clutched her belly protectively. "I have to heal those who suffer, but I can't. . . ."

"We need to consult the dragons," Quinnault added decisively.

"There's more trouble, Your Grace." Bessel gulped air a moment then squared his shoulders. "Rovers in the city are extorting protection money from the merchants. They say they've bribed your guards to help them. They set fire to a carpenter's shop earlier today because he wouldn't pay them protection money. The neighbors put out that fire. Then, on my way back here just now, a band of Rovers were beating up the baker in the next marketplace. I've chased them off for now, but they'll be back."

"How did you chase off a gang of Rovers, young man?" Nimbulan asked, trying to raise himself on one elbow. "They don't frighten easily. Especially in groups."

"I set an ember of witchfire in the seat of the leader's pants. Last I saw of him, he was running for the river with flames shooting out of his bum. The others didn't know what to do without him, so they followed him right into the river."

* * *

Afternoon, Kinnsell's shuttle, city of Hanassa

Yaala ran her fingertips over the touch pads on the control panel. Kinnsell's memories guided her movements. With a few gestures, her muscles knew how to fly this machine as well as her brain did. She wished she had access to the cyber controls. Just thinking what she needed would be easier than using the panel.

Holding her breath in anticipation of flight, she pressed the ignition sequence.

The jets roared to life. The shuttle vibrated with controlled power, suppressed motion. A thrill ran through her. If the engineers of Hanassa had been allowed to experiment and expand the technology of the generators and 'tricity over the last seven hundred years rather than merely patch and repair, they might have developed mechanical flight. Might have . . . Surely the books in the Kaalipha's library would help dreamers expand their knowledge and their technology. But few, if any, had been allowed to learn the arcane art of reading.

She didn't have time for idle speculation. She had the controls of this shuttle now, for however brief a time.

Her stomach bolted toward her throat as the shuttle lifted free of the Kardia. The desperate cries of hunger and anger outside shifted to fear.

"Soon," she promised them. "Soon you will be free."

She closed her ears to their pleas as she rotated the shuttle so that the jets faced the partial tunnel through the crater walls to the outside. Slowly, she backed up so that the engines discharged directly into the excavations Rollett had started.

"You did good work, Rollett. The size of your tunnel is a perfect fit," she told him. "And you were nearly through to the outside. Less than a quarter of the way is left."

"There is still time to fly away. We can send food and healers back from the capital," he reminded her.

"They wouldn't come. Hanassa is a city of outlaws. No one cares about this place except you and me. I've got to do this."

"Yaala," Kinnsell called to her weakly. "It won't work. The shuttle has to be vertical when you fire the rockets. You have to be above the planet's atmosphere."

"I know." She closed her eyes and placed her palm on the clear panel she knew would switch power from jets to rockets.

"Warning, the maneuver you are about to execute does not fall within accepted parameters," a strident female voice proclaimed from the depths of the control panel.

"Retract the wings, Yaala," Rollett said. "If you don't retract the wings, you'll break them off."

"Right," Yaala toggled the wing switch. A grinding noise ran the full length of the shuttle. She looked out the windows to make certain the shuttle remained intact.

"Wings tucked up neatly," Lyman called peering through one of the windows.

Yaala closed her eyes. "Please let this work," she prayed. Then she punched the engage button at the same time slamming the shuttle's flight direction into reverse. The shuttle vaulted backward, slamming into the narrow confines of the tunnel. A great shuddering of the hull and screaming of tortured metal pierced her ears as the shuttle scraped the walls of the tunnel. The engine blast backlashed along the sides of the craft within the narrow confines of the excavation. The temperature gauge crept upward.

"Warning, insufficient altitude for rocket engines. Do not proceed," the unnatural voice ordered.

Yaala pushed more fuel to the roaring engines. The temperature gauge crept higher, pushing against the warning red zone.

"Warning, hull temperatures twenty percent above normal." The strident voice rose in pitch to a tinny whine.

Inch by inch the shuttle crept backward toward the outside world and freedom. A tiny viewscreen on the control panel showed the engines eating away at the blockage within the tunnel.

Some of the flames still washed the hull seeking escape.

"The engines can't take much more of this," Rollett shouted above the thunder that surrounded and filled the shuddering shuttle.

"Warning! Hull temperatures sixty percent above normal. Warning! Warning!" the voice squeaked almost beyond hearing range.

The engine noise grew so loud it blotted out all thought, everything but the need to break free of the rock walls that confined and amplified and reverberated against the shuttle.

Yaala pushed more fuel into the engines. The temperature gauge began blinking red.

"Warrrrnnnning . . ." the voice faded, burned out by the stress.

With a tremendous scream and shudder, the shuttle burst through the rock wall. Momentum shot the vessel across the narrow plateau that ringed the crater's exterior.

Silence descended upon them.

"We're free!" Lyman announced. "We're free of Hanassa."

"The rockets died?" Rollett leaned over Yaala's shoulder examining the control panel with a bewildered look on his face.

"I burned them out and used up all of the fuel. Jets not responding," Yaala replied. Her ears still rang in the aftermath of the noise.

"We're flying! Just like a dragon," Lyman proclaimed. He practically jumped up and down in his excitement.

"We're soaring, without wings to hold us up or steer us," Yaala replied.

"Engage the wings. They'll keep us aloft!" Lyman called.

Yaala flipped the switch for the wings. Nothing happened. "We need fuel to open the wings."

"Manual override," Kinnsell murmured, very quietly.

"What!" Yaala nearly screamed above the ringing in her ears.

"Levers, inside the hidden hatch, both sides of the shuttle. Manual override of wing controls." He closed his eyes, looking exhausted from the small effort of speaking.

Yaala and Rollett leaped to the square indentation on the left side of the shuttle. Lyman examined the companion doorway on the opposite side. The two magicians ran their fingertips around the nearly invisible imperfection in the wall.

"Ah!" Lyman's door popped open first. "Pressure point lower right-hand corner."

Rollett repeated the action and his door flew open as well. Behind the door lay a handle that looked like the handgrip of a walking stick with indentations for the fingers. Above and below the handgrip was a narrow channel.

A sudden lurch downward nearly left Yaala's stomach above her head. "Hurry, Rollett. We're losing altitude."

"Pull the handle out and jiggle it until it engages in the track," Kinnsell whispered.

"Yaala, get back to the controls," Rollett grunted as he followed Kinnsell's instructions. The handle did not want to budge. "Look for some kind of manual rudder. We've got to steer this thing once we get the wings out."

Yaala returned to the cockpit of the shuttle. She searched the control panels for something resembling a handle.

A grinding noise irritated the ringing in her ears. She looked over her shoulder, wincing at the sounds. Rollett heaved all of his weight against the handle. Lyman didn't seem to be having much luck getting his mechanism to engage in the track.

The grinding noise repeated itself. Air caught Rollett's side of the shuttle, dropping Lyman's. Yaala braced herself against the sudden tilt in the floor.

Kinnsell and Powwell rolled on top of each other in the direction of the list.

"Let me." Rollett shoved Lyman out of the way as he staggered toward him. He leaned on the handle. Suddenly the shuttle stopped dropping.

"I hope there is a flat place below where we can land," Yaala said.

"Joystick," Kinnsell gasped.

A sudden image of a short walking staff popped into Yaala's head at the mention of the word. Instantly she knew where to find the instrument and how to use it. She sat hastily in the pilot's chair and reached for the rounded top of the stick.

An updraft caught the left wing; she turned into it and felt a lightness beneath the belly of the shuttle. But it wouldn't last. As soon as the air current changed, they'd lose more altitude.

"It's all mountains, ravines, and ridges for hundreds of miles around here," Rollett said flatly. "Even the dragon that brought Nimbulan and me here last year had trouble finding a place to land."

CHAPTER 43

Home of Myrilandel, ambassador from the Nimbus of Dragons, Coronnan City

"Your Grace, we can deal with the Rovers later. But we have to stop Scarface now, tonight!" Bessel insisted. He couldn't let a few narrow-minded men destroy the precious storehouse of knowledge. Just because they didn't need a piece of information this moment, didn't mean it might not prove useful—essential—later.

And Scarface's comment about familiars— He didn't have time to dwell on that. Any threat to Mopsie was a threat to Bessel now.

"It is not enough that we know a cure for the plague," Nibulan said, trying to rise.

"Don't even think about getting up," Katie and Myri said in unison, pointing warning fingers at him.

Nimbulan meekly lay back down again.

Bessel took a long look at his master and bit his lip in sympathetic pain. Nimbulan's gray face and labored breathing hinted at death stalled, not removed.

Don't you desert me, too, Master. I still need you.

"Our first concern is to save the library." Nibulan held up his left hand, palm outward, fingers slightly curved while he thought out loud. The familiar gesture reassured Bessel a little. "By the law of the Stargods, only magicians, priests, and healers may learn to read. Surely Commune Magicians, who can have no secrets from each other, can be trusted guardians of knowledge before it is lost? We have lost so much through the generations. Communal magic is supposed to replace distrust and the willful hiding of precious information."

"Scarface doesn't trust anyone he can't control," Queen Katie mused, tapping her chin.

"He's also afraid that everyone is out to kill him," Bessel muttered. "He has to control everyone around him to make sure they don't kill him. He's using rogue compulsions to keep their loyalty."

Nimbulan winced at him. "For once, I am grateful I no longer have my magic. In my weakened state, I'm not certain I could resist his compulsion."

"All of us in this room have proved to him time and again that he can't control us," Queen Katie continued. "Scarface knows as well as we do that what we *don't* know can hurt us. He's using the library as leverage to stay in power as Senior Magician."

"The time has come to arrest the man." Quinnault squared his shoulders in determination. But Bessel saw his hands grip the hilt of his short sword too fiercely. He didn't like that option.

"Stop and think a moment, Your Grace," Bessel said cautiously. "If Scarface can control the entire Commune—magicians of great power who in concert could subdue him with a thought—what will he do to the mundane guards you send to arrest him? There isn't a prison cell built that could restrain him. There isn't a sword that can touch him." *If I can't return to the Commune with Mopsie, then I'll remain outside, serving Coronnan and the king in secret. But if we can depose Scarface, there's still a chance for me and for Mopsie.* The instant of oneness he had shared with Wind-drift haunted him.

"He's right, Scarecrow," Queen Katie agreed. "With the Commune backing him, Scarface could manipulate the entire kingdom into deposing you."

"King Kinnsell manipulates the lords of my Council. Scarface misuses the magical power of the Commune. Rovers incite the people to fear me and my men. The provinces are in near revolt over the plague. What happened to the careful balance we built into this government, Nimbulan? What happened to the honor, ethics, and control you built into the Commune?" Quinnault clenched his fists as if needing to slam them into something, preferably Scarface's jaw.

"Scarface believes he is providing unified leadership for

the good of the kingdom," Bessel offered. "I slipped inside his mind. He thinks he's being honorable and ethical in guiding the Commune and therefore, the kingdom." Memory of the twisted loops and dark caverns of Master Aaddler's mind made him shudder.

For half a moment Bessel knew the compulsion to follow Scarface's logic and agree with him. The older magician's memories of atrocities inflicted on him and by him during the Great Wars of Disruption fed his tremendous guilt and his fear of retaliation. Now he saw every person beyond his control as his enemy, determined to murder him for his past activities.

"Stargods preserve us from righteous tyrants!" Nimbulan muttered. He crossed himself then fell silent.

"Our backs are against the wall, Scarecrow. Our options are limited. We may have to resort to trickery to oust Scarface and regain control of the Commune." Queen Katie reached out and clung to her husband's hand.

"I think we can trust Wind-drift and Whitehands," Bessel mused. "They seem to be aware of what Scarface is doing and defying him in subtle ways, but they have to appear to go along with him for their own safety."

"A good piece of information," Nimbulan replied. "We may call upon it later. But right now, we can trust only ourselves."

A long moment of silence stretched out while all of them thought furiously.

"Quinnault, the tunnels beneath the central keep of your palace, is there still access to them?" Nimbulan finally broke the silence. Unsteadily, he attempted to roll to his knees.

Myrilandel urged him back down on his pallet with anxious hands. He shook off her help. Bessel offered his own hand gently under his master's elbow. Nimbulan accepted his silent assistance.

"Can we still get to the tunnels?" he repeated his question as he staggered upright.

"Yes. I have workmen excavating a direct route beneath the river between the palace and the University," Quinnault replied. "If you are thinking of hiding the books down there, the place is much too public at the moment."

"I remember side tunnels and dead ends from the time

you showed me the escape route from the royal apartments to a hidden cove on an adjacent island." Nimbulan's face grayed a moment before returning to a more normal, if somewhat pale, color. He leaned heavily against the chimney but remained standing.

"Yes. We've filled some of those dead ends with dirt and rubble from the excavation, others are tool storage and resting places for the workers." Quinnault began to pace, hands behind his back and shoulders slightly hunched.

"A dead end could be walled off, cloaked in magic so it would be ignored." Queen Katie joined him in his thinking ritual, pacing beside him with one hand looped in the crook of his elbow.

"It will have to be an enduring spell, and a subtle one that misdirects. We can't take a chance on Scarface stumbling on the books because he senses the presence of magic," Nimbulan added.

"We can't hide the books forever, Master," Bessel protested. "The books will have to be found someday. Hiding them forever is as bad as burning them."

"A minor detail. We have to take every precaution. We don't know how long Scarface and his conservative faction will remain in power," Nimbulan dismissed Bessel's suggestion. "When will Scarface burn the books?"

"At dawn," Bessel replied sullenly. He didn't like the shortsightedness of his king and his master. "Scarface wants to make a huge public spectacle of the burning. He's planning a speech that will make it seem as if he's doing everyone a favor."

"But he won't burn all of the books," Katie protested. "I don't want to imagine a life without books."

Nor I, Your Grace, Bessel thought. *When ignorance guides people, the innocent suffer.* As he had suffered as a child because his father believed only myths and legends about magicians rather than looking for the truth.

A pang of regret and loneliness made a knot in his gut. He had to abandon yet another family, the family of the Commune, in order to maintain control of his own destiny.

But he would survive. He would find a new family among the fisherfolk and their dogs.

"Oh, Scarface will keep the volumes he needs or considers 'safe,'" Quinnault reassured her. "He's making a spectacle of the event just to defy me and demonstrate his power and reassert his popularity among the people."

"We'll need help," Nimbulan said. "We might not be able to save all of the books, but we can move a large number from the library between now and dawn. I wish Lyman and Powwell were here. I can trust them to resist Scarface's manipulation."

"I think I know how to keep Scarface busy." Bessel's face brightened.

"How?" Nimbulan raised one eyebrow in query.

"Mopsie and I need to destroy the depth finder."

"The Guild of Bay Pilots will howl mightily in protest." Quinnault grinned mischievously. "They'll run straight to me and to Scarface demanding someone fix it."

"Once the depth finder is disabled, the pilots will need their dogs back. I know some men who would gladly turn large packs of water dogs loose on the docks. Scarface doesn't like dogs, and they don't like him. But the pilots can't afford to let the magicians hurt the dogs. Chaos will reign for a while."

"What do dogs have to do with the pilots?"

"I'll explain later." Bessel grinned widely. "I've got to catch the passenger barge with the depth finder before it sails to the port with the afternoon tide." Bessel scooted out the door. He stopped short before stepping down to the cobblestones.

Two dozen black-robed mercenaries from Rossemeyer stared at him. All of them had covered the lower halves of their faces with turban veils. All had drawn their vorpal blades at first sight of him.

The man who stood in the center of the semicircle stepped forward one pace. "We besiege this house until Journeyman Magician Bessel is turned over to us for justice," he announced.

CHAPTER 44

Inside Kinnsell's shuttle, place and time unknown

Kinnsell dragged his aching body toward the cockpit of the shuttle. "Ignorant bushies," he snarled. Pulling himself hand-over-hand, he managed to struggle into the copilot's seat. He settled into it gratefully as his wobbling knees gave way. "I'll show you real flying." Out of long habit, he hit the mayday button to send a distress signal to the mother ship. He also pocketed a portable communicator—something strictly forbidden by the family covenant. Then he overrode the control panel with the joystick. The shuttle's vibrations communicated to him through the length of his preferred tool.

Gradually, he began to sense the air currents and momentum that kept the vessel floating when, for all he knew, it should be a crumpled heap at the bottom of a trackless ravine.

The terrain whizzed backward past the viewscreen. His perceptions distorted. He needed to turn the shuttle around. The helm resisted his control.

Gradually, he was able to maneuver the vessel into the wind. He gained a little altitude and perspective.

Beside him, Yaala clutched the sides of the pilot's cushioned seat with white-knuckled fists. She stared blankly at the mountainsides skidding past the windows. The young man behind her braced himself against her back and held her shoulders while he too stared at the landscape.

Useless. Both useless. Though he had to admit they'd done an admirable job of getting the shuttle airborne and the wings extended. "You really should have just flown out of that volcanic crater and not wasted a good shuttle on blasting an exit through the crater for the rabble," he muttered. "Totally out of fuel. Rockets burned out. Jets disabled. You barely got the wings out in time. At least I have a rudder to work with."

"The rabble are my people. I had an obligation to free them from their prison and slow starvation. You brought the plague to them. I couldn't abandon them. Once we are safely landed, we can send help. Supplies and medicine can get into Hanassa." Yaala roused a little from her fear-induced catatonia.

"You'd make an admirable ruler, girl. Unfortunately, honor and obligation are only pieces of what keeps a person in power. You also have to balance the political forces. I don't suppose you managed to kill that Rover person who manipulated my Maia like a puppet?"

"If you mean Piedro, the last I saw of him he was leading the mob to kill all of us," the young magician replied.

What was his name? *I should know after that intimate psychic link,* Kinnsell thought. Rollo . . . Rufus . . . Rollett. That was it. Rollett—sounded like a stomach remedy or a chocolate bar. White and dark chocolate in his beard. Good way to remember his name.

Rollett had probed his mind and channeled information to Yaala so she could fly the shuttle. Powwell had been the other one in the link. Powwell, the healer. Powwell had somehow eradicated most of the disease from Kinnsell's body and repaired some of the damage. Some, not all. Enough to keep him alive a while longer.

But Powwell didn't call himself a healer. He thought of himself as a Bloodmage—whatever that was—and hated himself for it.

I can use his self-loathing to make him return to Terra with me. A psychic healer of that strength is worth a fortune in both money and power.

If the boy survived. He'd taken a lot of the plague into his own system and not neutralized all of it. The boy lay unconscious in the cabin, maybe dying prematurely because he had saved Kinnsell.

"I may have done a lot of underhanded things in my life, but I intend to repay my debt to you, Powwell." He fussed with the long-range sensors, seeking a landing place, any landing place.

"I don't think Maia was manipulated by Piedro so much

as she was a willing partner in manipulating you," Yaala said bitterly, returning to the previous conversation. "I know her. She uses men and discards them. Then she blames everyone but herself for the men not returning to her bed when she needs their money, their talents, or their protection. She did it to Nimbulan and to Televarn, the last leader of the Rovers."

"She mentioned Televarn often." Kinnsell wanted to know more, but he needed all of his concentration to get the sensors back on-line. "Lovely woman, but I'm glad she's out of my life."

"My mother killed Televarn with the poisoned knife Televarn used to try and kill her," Yaala explained. "Maia watched her do it. So did I." She fell into a silent reflection.

"Then almost everything she told me was a lie. Or she blocked out the memory." Kinnsell shrugged. "But then, I knew she lied, and I enjoyed her attempts to manipulate me anyway."

The long-range sensors flashed a terrain map into one corner of the viewscreen. "Got it. There's a plateau ahead. A long way without engines, but we may have enough wind to keep us aloft that long."

"How far?" the old man called from the cabin. "Powell's in bad shape. I need a dragon to help him."

"Dragons, bah!" Kinnsell hadn't really seen a dragon sitting on top of this very shuttle. He'd been sick, feverish, hallucinating. "Once we land, I'll show you the miracles of modern medicine. I've got scanners and bonesetters and antibiotics. We'll patch him up almost as good as new. I've also got a stash of Tambootie if nothing else works on the boy."

"Our healers can do as much with dragon magic to fuel them and more healers to amplify the magic," Rollett argued.

"Believe what you will, but shut up now. I need all my concentration to land this without a decent runway."

Kinnsell gritted his teeth and memorized the plateau. Then he closed his eyes and visualized how he had to ease the shuttle down. He shed altitude and dropped the landing gear. The vessel slowed to stall speed, except there were no engines to stall. The control panel beeped at his unusual command. "I suppose you burned out the vocal control?" he asked at the third warning beep."

"The voice in the control panel?" Yaala asked, still gripping her seat with white-knuckled fists. "Yes, it is gone with the rockets, the jets, and the fuel."

"No great loss. My second wife programmed her voice into it years ago. Time to change it anyway. My current wife gets jealous every time she flies with me."

He shed more altitude. The wheels bounced off the rough terrain and hopped back up. Too high. He dipped the nose and felt the first scrape of dirt beneath the cabin.

"Brace yourselves. This is going to be rough!" he shouted, clinging to his own chair with what little strength remained to him.

The shuttle skidded along the narrow ledge. The ceramic/metal alloy screamed in protest as rocks scraped the belly and tree limbs lashed the roof and viewscreen.

Kinnsell ducked instinctively.

With a wild screech, the left wheel snapped off. The heavy tail end of the shuttle skidded around while the nose kept plunging forward.

"Brakes, I need brakes," he yelled at the controls. A confusing array of lights flashed on and off. He couldn't make sense of what worked and what didn't. "How do I stop this damn ship?" he asked the air.

(You must stop now!) A voice sounded inside his head. An alien voice he couldn't recognize.

"Who?" he asked the air. "How?"

Before the words finished echoing in his head, the sound of metal crunching against rock screamed throughout the shuttle.

Yaala and Rollett held their ears. The old man dropped to the floor, bracing his legs against a bulkhead while he draped himself over the still unconscious Powwell.

The sounds of protesting metal wound down to an annoying whine. The shuttle struck some large obstacle. For a moment it hopped back into the air. Three seconds of absolute silence deafened him. All he could see out the front viewscreen were rocks and more rocks. The sensors relayed information too quickly for him to comprehend. Then the shuttle dropped again. Kinnsell's stomach lurched toward his throat. He shuddered with the vessel as it struck ground once more. A great tearing sound ran the length of the cabin. The deck split in the wake of the horrendous noise. The cabin canted sharply backward and to the left. Stopped. Suspended. Where?

Kinnsell unclenched his jaw. He rotated the joints a couple of times, fearing he'd cracked a bone or three. When his chin and cheeks stopped popping, he took a moment to appraise the situation.

His sensors and the view outside the window told him the shuttle was precariously balanced upon the edge of the plateau. A tangle of tree limbs kept the stern of the shuttle from teetering into a steep and broken ravine.

A worse fate awaited him out the front viewscreen.

"Not again," he moaned and buried his head in his hands. When he spread his fingers a little and looked out the broken window, he slammed his eyes shut again. "I have to be feverish. I have to be hallucinating."

A huge dragon eye stared back at him through the cracked window.

* * *

Midafternoon, home of Myrilandel, ambassador from the Nimbus of Dragons, Coronnan City

Bessel slipped up the stairs to his room while the royal couple and their friends made plans. He pulled together a disguise out of odds and ends and returned to the kitchen by the back staircase. Luucian's attention was on the servant's spyhole. Bessel tiptoed around him and opened the kitchen door of Myrilandel's house cautiously. A dozen black-clad mercenaries from Rossemeyer lined the alley. They stood tall and formidable, made more imposing by their voluminous black robes that could hide two dozen weapons, and by their elaborate black turbans with one end draped over their faces. Their black eyes glittered with menace as they surveyed Bessel.

He swallowed his fear and opened the door a little wider. As he took the one step down to the stoop, he held his lower back with one hand and balanced his weight to emphasize the large bulge of a blanket wadded up under one of Myrilandel's maternity gowns. His "pregnancy" was held in place by a wide belt. With a kerchief over his hair, he just might pass for a woman nearing the end of a difficult pregnancy.

Provided Mopsie stayed quiet and didn't squirm around too much within the blanket.

Two of the mercenaries stepped forward, hands on the hilts of their swords.

Bessel waddled up to them, keeping his eyes open and frank. He couldn't betray the truth by even so much as a twitch of fear on his face.

"Allow me to assist you, madama." The mercenary on Bessel's left crooked his arm, ready to take Bessel's weight, should he choose to place his hand there.

Bessel suppressed a grin as he leaned heavily against the man. He placed his other hand, still holding the basket, beneath his tummy bulge and moaned a little.

"I'm off to market for some special herbs to ease the birthing pains," he said in falsetto. "I should ever so much appreciate your company on the journey. One never knows when the babe might burst forth." Bessel clutched his belly again and moaned louder. This time he swayed a little.

"Um . . . um . . . shouldn't you stay home and send someone else to market?" His mercenary escort hesitated. The soldier looked frantically toward his companions for inspiration.

Few men, even healers, were comfortable around women in childbirth. Bessel had learned that much through his mother's numerous pregnancies. At the first sign of a labor pain, all the men in the village found urgent work elsewhere.

"There is no one else. They are all held captive in the street. Can't you hear the commotion? I must go now, I can't delay." Bessel moaned again as he took a few mincing steps down the alley.

"Then I fear you must go alone, madama. We cannot desert our posts." All of the mercenaries bowed low.

Bessel took several more steps—a little longer stride this time while they weren't looking.

"Please stay close. I may need you to boil water and fetch supplies by the time I return." Bessel dismissed them with a wave of his hand. The strangers drifted away from

Myrilandel's kitchen door in an effort to separate themselves from Bessel.

Bessel fought to keep his steps short and awkward until he had rounded the corner into a wider street. A few people passed him without a second glance. Their attention was fastened upon the commotion at the front of the house on Embassy Row.

The crowd milled. Anger dominated the aura of the gathering. But it had no focus.

Suppressing a grin, Bessel shouted above the noise. "I saw one of the blackmailing Rovers with the foreigners. They're in league with the foreigners." The crowd took up the litany, linking their current troubles with the mercenaries from Rossemeyer rather than with the king.

He wanted to join them, but he had an important task.

CHAPTER 45

Inside Kinnsell's shuttle on a plateau deep in the Southern Mountains

Yaala stirred cautiously from beneath a pile of seat cushions and broken equipment. When the shuttle came to a screeching halt, she had been thrown into a bulkhead. She slipped on the sharply canted deck trying to get her feet under her.

The shuttle shifted again. The deck tilted more steeply. She froze in place.

A quick assessment showed Rollett stirring on the other side of the cabin and Kinnsell staring wide-eyed and gaping out the window at the baby dragon peering in through the window. A faint hint of blue along wingtips and horns highlighted the dragon's dark pewter color. Afternoon sunlight glinted off his fur. He appeared about the size of a small pack steed, quite young.

"Don't move, Rollett," she commanded. He froze, much as she had. "We're balanced precariously."

"I think that baby dragon sitting on the nose of the shuttle is all that is keeping us on the ledge," he whispered back, as if afraid that the sound of his voice would upset the balance.

"Can you see Lyman and Powwell?" she asked. Wreckage blocked her view of the central cabin.

"Lyman's legs. Not much else," Rollett replied.

"I'm alive," Lyman whispered back. "Powwell is burning up with fever." Yaala picked out the outline of Lyman's body amid the debris piled around them. He shifted his legs, trying to get his knees under him.

"Don't move," she and Rollett ordered together, much too loud.

The shuttle shifted again.

"I . . . if th . . . that monster is real," Kinnsell stuttered, "can you make it sit on the nose, like a teeter-totter?"

Yaala and Rollett looked at each other and shrugged off the strange words.

"A lever and a fulcrum, dammit! We need a counterbalance on the front to offset the heavy engines in the back." Kinnsell's exasperation broke through his stunned staring.

"Where there is one baby dragon, there will be a dozen more. They don't stray far from the lair at that age. Mama Shayla should be around here somewhere. She'll provide an adequate counterbalance," Lyman said. He lifted his head, cocking it to one side. The gesture was so common to him, Yaala hadn't recognized it as a listening pose until now.

"Do you speak to the dragons, Lyman?" she asked.

"Often. I missed them while I was in Hanassa. The dragons won't let their thoughts penetrate that city," Lyman replied. "The dragonets are too young to communicate with humans. I'm only getting baby screeches from them, no images or words." He tilted his head in the other direction. "Ah, there's Shayla, coming in from a hunt. She understands."

A loud thump vibrated down the length of the shuttle. Metal screeched again as huge talons tore at the strange skin. Then, slowly, the deck straightened.

"She's perched on the roof," Rollett said with a smile. "She wants us to open the hatch and very carefully slide out. The shuttle weighs more than she does, and she can't hold it long."

"I'm not going out there," Kinnsell protested. "I'm not going to become that monster's next meal." He continued to stare at the baby dragon.

Yaala couldn't help giggling. The baby was tiny. Wait until he saw Shayla!

"I—can't—open—the—door!" Lyman said through gritted teeth as he pushed buttons on the control panel and kicked at the hatch.

"There are dragons out there. Can't you gather some magic and force it open?" Yaala asked.

"The air in here is sealed tighter than anything we have encountered before," Lyman reminded her. "The dragon magic can't get in, and I haven't enough reserves to levitate the locking mechanism."

Yaala looked to Rollett for inspiration.

"The engines aren't running. We're going to run out of air very soon," Kinnsell stated calmly.

Yaala wondered if he'd rather suffocate than face the dragons. "Look for a manual override. If the shuttle has them for wings, surely it will have them for the hatch."

They all jerked their heads back to the hatch as a great tearing sound came from the metallic skin of the shuttle. A glimmer of daylight, followed by the tip of a red dragon talon pierced the hatch door.

"I believe rescue is on the way." Lyman grinned.

Seconds later fresh air penetrated the stale chemical tainted odor they'd been breathing since Hanassa. Yaala gulped in the fresh sweet scent of green trees and moisture. Her throat constricted with thirst, reminding her she hadn't drunk in hours—days?

Rollett and Lyman took deep gulps of air. They both sighed in satisfaction.

"Dragon magic!" Rollett opened his arms wide as if to embrace the air. "It's been so long. I didn't think I'd ever fill myself with it again. I didn't think I'd live long enough to find another dragon."

"You can breathe later. We've got to get out of here before the whole shuttle falls into a ravine." Yaala crawled toward the hatch where she could see most of a dark gray dragon paw and some of a red-tipped dragon nose poking through the crack. Blue-tip was still sitting on the nose staring at Kinnsell.

A sudden ripping sound sent the shuttle teetering on the edge again. Back and forth the craft wavered. Up and down.

"Seesaw, Marjorie Daw," Kinnsell singsonged on a giggle. He looked and acted drunk. Or frightened to near insanity.

"We all have to get out now," Yaala said, with all of the authority instilled in her by her mother.

The hatch panel vibrated and split. An inquisitive dragon head poked through the opening. Red-tip scraped his budding spiral horn on the top of the hatch and backed out quickly with an affronted squeak. Yaala held her ears against the high-pitched protest.

The shuttle shuddered and tipped backward again. Everyone froze in place until the rocking ceased.

(Hurry!) a frantic voice pounded into Yaala's head.

Rollett and Lyman dropped to all fours and each grabbed one of Powwell's ankles. They dragged him cautiously toward the gaping hole in the bulkhead, keeping close to the deck. They must have heard the voice as well.

That left Kinnsell. *How can I persuade him to leave the dubious shelter of the shuttle?* Yaala asked herself. His skin had paled again and his eyes looked glassy with fever. Powwell's cure must not have been complete.

"I'm not going to let my best friend sacrifice his life for nothing. You come with me easy, or I knock you out and let the dragons drag you to safety!" She yanked him out of his chair and onto his knees.

"Y . . . you w . . . wouldn't," he protested feebly. His skin turned ashen. He swayed to his feet.

"If Powwell gives up his life to save yours, the least you can do is live." Grabbing him by the collar and the seat of his pants, as if he were a dog or a small child, she propelled him toward the hatch.

At least Lyman had persuaded the baby dragon to back away. He held the creature by the sensitive horn bud and peered directly into its eyes. Shayla lowered her long neck to peer at them closely. Lyman might have been a dragon once, but Shayla obviously wouldn't allow him too many liberties with her babies.

Rollett sat nearby on the ground, cradling Powwell's head in his lap.

The shuttle tipped again. Yaala heard a frantic scrambling of dragon talons on the roof. That decided her. Using every last bit of her strength she kicked Kinnsell's butt. He tumbled out the hatch, landing on the rough plateau facedown. He lifted his head and spat dirt.

"You will regret that, young lady. I am a very powerful man," he sneered at her.

Yaala jumped clear, sprawling next to him. "Out here the only power that counts is friendship with the dragons. You are decidedly powerless," she returned.

Behind her, Shayla screeched and flapped her wings in a

mighty effort to get airborne. The shuttle creaked and teetered on the edge a moment, then tipped. It dropped abruptly down the hundred-foot cliff face, bounced on a lower slope and slid rapidly toward the bottom of a trackless ravine. Huge chunks of dirt and trees broke loose in the wake of the shuttle. Rocks the size of the baby dragons tumbled together in a mighty roar.

Yaala crawled to the cliff edge to watch the shuttle tumble down, down, forever down to the forest below.

Several long moments later, it landed. The rockfall continued, on and on until the wonderful machine disappeared in a cloud of dirt and debris.

"It's gone," she whispered. And with it went the last tangible link to her machines, to Hanassa.

"I flew it once." She smiled. "That's all I really needed." Then she stood up, brushed dirt off her trews, assessed the situation, and began issuing orders.

* * *

Late afternoon, home of Myrilandel, ambassador from the Nimbus of Dragons, Coronnan City

"This is ridiculous!" Katie and Quinnault said in unison. They quirked half smiles at each other. The familiar blending of their minds warmed Katie's heart anew.

"I am king of Coronnan. I will not be imprisoned in the home of my best friends by foreigners who do not like my system of justice." Quinnault marched out the door to confer with his guards. The dozen uniformed men faced twice their number of mercenary soldiers famed for their fierce thoroughness.

"At least you have a system of justice," Katie whispered to him. She sent him that reassurance mentally as well. Then she turned back to their other business.

"Now, while my husband deals with the soldiers outside, I shall tend to your medicine, Nimbulan." Katie rubbed her hands together eagerly. She had something to do.

"You have the gift, Katie." Myri smiled at her. "People jump to your orders and believe themselves blissfully content. When I give an order, servants look at me as if I were talking to air. It's easier to do the work myself."

Katie shrugged off the compliment. She had work to do.

Much to her surprise, the journeyman healer maintained his vigil over the simmering digitalis in the kitchen.

"You didn't succumb to Scarface's compulsion!" She stopped dead in the kitchen doorway.

"Your orders seemed more important. Besides, I'm only a journeyman. The call went out to masters. Some of the apprentices obeyed because they don't know better. I do." The young man shrugged and continued his chores.

"What is your name?" Katie asked. She moved to the open hearth to inspect his procedure.

"Luucian, Your Grace. Journeyman Healer Luucian, at your service." He bowed slightly, then returned to his remedy.

"Journeyman Luucian, you just became the king's personal healer. And I'll do my best to elevate you to Master Healer before the night is finished."

"Thank you, Your Grace, but only the Commune of Magicians can grant me master status." His face fell a little in disappointment.

"By dawn the Commune may undergo a major restructuring. Right now, His Grace, the king, and Master Nimbulan need people around them who are not influenced by a power-mad crusader." Katie ladled a bit of the raw drug into a clay mug. "It's ready. Take this to Master Nimbulan and make certain he takes all of it, even if you have to pinch his nose to make him swallow it."

"Me? You want me to command Master Nimbulan?" Luucian almost stuttered in his awe.

"Yes. That is your job as his healer. When you have seen to his medication, we'll have a job for you to do. We are all going to be very tired by the time this night is through. But you must make certain Nimbulan only supervises. I don't want him lifting anything."

"I'll take the medicine to Lan," Myri said from the doorway. "Shayla just requested a healer. Powwell and Yaala have rescued Rollett and King Kinnsell from Hanassa. They need a healer. Luucian here seems the only one available."

"Me?" Luucian squeaked again.

"What in bloody blazes was my father doing in Hanassa?" Katie asked in bewilderment. Myri had said "rescued." They needed a healer. Her father was alive. She still had a chance to . . . to . . . She didn't know what she needed to do to him, or for him. She was just very grateful he lived.

"Rouussin is waiting for you on Sacred Isle, Luucian," Myri said. "He'll take you to Shayla's lair and your patients. Gather a little of the Tambootie on the island to take with you. I'll dose my husband and make certain he takes all of his medicine." A look of determination settled over her features. She looked very much like Quinnault when he put on his stubborn face.

"How will I get past the mercenaries out the back door?" Luucian asked as he gathered up his black satchel.

"Nimbulan said you should wrap yourself in shadows and divert their attention with a suggestion implanted in their minds." Myri shrugged and returned to the front of the house with the precious dose of digitalis.

"I'll do my best, Your Grace. Do you have any messages for King Kinnsell and the others?"

"What I have to say to my father, I will say in person. He has a lot to answer for."

Luucian bowed to her again and exited, just one more shadow in a sheltered alley.

Shouting from outside drew Katie back to Quinnault and the mercenaries. Her husband stood with his short sword drawn and a phalanx of uniformed guards around him.

CHAPTER 46

Late afternoon, Shayla's lair, deep in the Southern Mountains

Powwell opened his eyes to find an unrecognizable face pressed close to his own. His eyes crossed as he tried to focus. His vision swam, and he lost all definition to the pale blob pierced by two bright blue eyes.

"Who?" he asked through dry and cracked lips. He couldn't move anything more than his mouth. His entire body felt as if his joints had been dislocated one by one and put back together wrong.

"I'm Luucian," the face said. The eyes twinkled momentarily and then relaxed, almost glazed over as if they were the center of the man's exhaustion. "Do you remember me, Powwell?"

"Healer?" Powwell couldn't manage more than a single word at a time. His mouth tasted as if he'd eaten sand. Where had a healer come from? Especially one with a bright blue healing aura?

"Yes, I apprenticed to the healers in Nimbulan's battle enclave about a year before you joined him. We met a few times at the University."

"Water." That seemed more important than the identity of the face. Powwell closed his eyes again; the light around him pierced his vision painfully.

Someone pressed a cup to his mouth and dribbled a few drops of blessedly sweet water onto his tongue. He gulped it greedily. No trace of sulfur marred the taste, so they couldn't be in Hanassa. But then, his mouth was so dry even that rancid water would taste sweet.

"More," he demanded.

"Just a few drops at a time, Powwell. You've had a very

high fever. Your system is still in shock from it," Luucian replied. "But you'll recover rapidly once you start moving around again. Nothing like a little extra Tambootie in your system to restore your internal balance."

Powwell drank a little bit more this time; enough to roll around his mouth before he swallowed. The muscles in his throat ached and didn't want to work. He tried again and managed to get the water down.

"Thorny?"

"Your familiar is distraught, but still with you." Someone guided his hand until it rested upon Thorny's relaxed spines. The little hedgehog didn't hunch and bristle at his touch. Something must be wrong with him.

Powwell tried to open his eyes again and sit up. He had to take care of Thorny.

"Rest, Powwell. Thorny is fine. He's as worried about you as we are," Yaala said. Her cool hand touched his cheek.

He relaxed a little, but kept one hand on Thorny. A sense of well-being thrummed through his system from his point of contact with his familiar.

"Where?"

"We are in Shayla's lair," Yaala reassured him. "The dragons brought a healer to you from the capital. You are going to be fine."

"Hanassa?" he asked on a cough. Yaala pressed the cup to his mouth again. He took a big swallow but rolled it around his mouth, relieving parched tissue while he allowed only a little to trickle down his throat at a time.

"We escaped," Rollett said. His voice grew distant and loud as if he paced away and then turned back.

Powwell risked opening his eyes again. Sure enough, Rollett paced in front of the source of light—a cave opening? Only his silhouette was visible. Was that boulder by the entrance really a baby dragon watching Rollett?

"And the plague?" Powwell's mouth and throat eased enough to allow three words instead of one. He wanted more water, but Luucian held the cup back.

"You gave Kinnsell enough healing and strength to survive. He still needs some rest and recovery, but he'll live long enough to explain himself to his very irate daughter," Luucian told him. "I doused Yaala with the Tambootie.

We don't know if her dragon heritage makes her immune or not. Lyman and Rollett seem to be fine."

When he finished speaking, he lifted the cup to Powwell's mouth again. "Not too much at once. You might bolt it."

Sure enough, the next swallow hit Powwell's stomach like an explosion and threatened to come back up again.

"Did I get the plague?"

"A mild case that I was able to cure," Luucian said. "You went through the trial by Tambootie smoke last Winter, and you'd had a few doses of the raw leaves before Nimbulan discovered dragon magic. There must have been enough of the tree of magic still in your system to keep you alive and to heal King Kinnsell, but since you started as an apprentice after magicians gave up heavy doses of Tambootie, you still succumbed to the disease, probably because you passed so much of your natural immunity to King Kinnsell. It's a nasty one, spreads very rapidly. If Rouussin hadn't brought me here to Shayla's lair when he did, you would have died, Powwell."

Powwell smiled at the thought of Rouussin, the elderly red-tipped dragon who viewed humans as willful children who must be indulged.

He looked around the huge cave a moment. Sure enough a dozen baby dragons perched on various rocks and overhangs. A huge nest of sheep's wool, feathers, and moss dominated a slightly raised section toward the back. If Shayla was around, he couldn't see her.

"The plague in Hanassa? Maia?" he asked.

"We don't know yet. The dragons will scout the area and drop supplies, including some Tambootie wood for fires and timboor to add to their food. We have other issues to settle before we send investigators," Rollett answered, still pacing.

"Actually, the population as a whole is not threatened by the plague," Kinnsell added. He was behind Powwell and out of sight.

"Explain?" Luucian looked up. Curiosity overshadowed his fatigue.

"In my world, a haze of pollution alters the light patterns from the sun." He hesitated as if seeking the proper words. "Our bodies adapt to the changes in light. The poisons in the pollution build up in our bodies, triggering more changes. It is these changes along with the toxins in our bodies that allow the plague to attack us. You don't have the pollution, so only the weak and vulnerable—the old, the very young, and pregnant women—catch the disease. Miners might have a problem from coal dust, but the rest of you should be okay. Powwell caught it because of the direct blood contact. My blood in his system carried food for the plague."

"Interesting. I'll relay that information to the queen," Luucian replied.

"Why did Scarface send a journeyman?" Something nagged at Powwell's mind and wouldn't let him take the rest he so sorely needed.

"Scarface didn't send me. Myrilandel did. The dragons have withdrawn from Scarface and his followers."

Silence followed Luucian's words. Rollett and Yaala stared at him in surprise. Powwell did, too. They all waited for an explanation of this dire situation.

"The dragons have been staying away from the capital for weeks now. But today they have withdrawn their magic entirely from the Commune. Now that I know you and King Kinnsell will recover—he took to the Tambootie as well as any solitary magician I've ever met—I must return to the capital." Luucian stood up and dusted the knees of his trews. "Nimbulan and King Quinnault need me."

"What did Scarface do to earn the wrath of the dragons?" Rollett grabbed Luucian's sleeve, swinging the healer around to face him.

"Scarface wants to burn all of the books that mention anything about solitary magic." Luucian kept his eyes on his knees. "He has compelled all of the Commune to agree with him."

"I knew it! I knew he'd go too far in his need to control everyone and everything around him. But this goes beyond all reason, all rationale." Rollett shook his fists in the direction of the capital city.

"He can't burn the books!" Powwell protested. He remembered the precious information about blood magic he'd gleaned from an ancient text. He'd also learned about Rovers, their mind-to-mind magic and ways to avoid being pulled into their traps. Without those books, he'd never have found access to the dragongate. Never have reached Hanassa. . . .

Oh, Kalen, I've failed you once again.

"Nimbulan has a plan, but he needs help," Luucian replied as he stooped to pick up his healer's satchel.

"Scarface must intend to challenge King Quinnault for more than just those books," Rollett mused. "He wants control. Control over every life he touches, not just the Commune. I've got to go back. We can't let him continue his tyranny over the Commune or anyone else."

"Your help is welcome. The plan requires some interesting magic as well as manual labor. Bessel and I are the only magicians who have resisted Scarface's compulsion that we can be sure of, but Bessel is acting strangely and I'm not certain how valuable he will be. Powwell will be all right with Yaala to nurse him for a few days," Luucian replied.

"I'm not leaving without them." Rollett glanced at Yaala. His eyes caressed her. Yaala returned his gaze frankly. An energy nearly crackled between them. "We've been through a lot together. We stay together until we are all safe back home."

"I'll be all right alone," Powwell insisted. He couldn't stand between Yaala and a man who could love her. A part of Powwell would always separate him from Yaala, the part that belonged to Kalen. Dead Kalen.

He gulped back a sob. "The dragons will take care of me."

"I hate the idea of leaving you alone, Powwell, but we're needed in the capital." Yaala looked truly torn between Rollett and her friendship with Powwell.

"I'll stay with the boy. I can't say I'm looking forward to my daughter's tirade. Though I'd like to retrieve my granddaughter from Lord Balthazaan's custody before Katie tears the kingdom apart looking for her," Kinnsell said from the dim interior of the cave.

"Princess Marilell is safe," Luucian replied. His mouth worked as if he choked back a laugh. "The kidnapping attempt failed. Queen Katie and King Quinnault keep the child very close now."

"You bushies aren't as ignorant and helpless as I first imagined." Kinnsell chuckled. "I owe it to the boy to take care of him until you return. Can't say I want to stay here with these monsters, though. Are you sure they won't eat me for lunch?"

"What do I need other than strength to travel with you? I can eat and drink now, and that will restore a lot of my energy." Powwell struggled to raise himself on his elbows. If he stayed here, he'd wallow in his aching grief and never recover. Nimbulan needed him, needed his magic. He couldn't help Kalen anymore. He might as well give his all to the only man Kalen ever respected.

Suddenly his life had purpose. Kalen had spent her life running away from those who had tried to control her and her magnificent talent. He would honor her memory by challenging all those who would victimize other children before they'd had the chance to learn to control their own destinies.

He'd start with Scarface.

* * *

Late afternoon, Coronnan City

Bessel crossed two bridges and threaded through a number of streets before he slipped into another alley. He faced the wall of a smithy as he removed Mopsie and the blanket from their hiding places.

The little dog yipped his gratitude and squirmed within Bessel's arms, tired of being confined. He licked Bessel's face before jumping to the ground and running three joyous circles around his ankles.

"Yes, yes, I know you are happy, Mopsie, but we have to keep moving. We have to get to the docks before the tide turns and the barge sails. We have to make sure that by the time Raanald gets the barge to the port, he'll mistrust the depth finder so much he'll destroy it himself." He patted his familiar and set about arranging a new disguise.

After removing the dress and kerchief, he folded them into the blanket lengthwise and slung the bundle across his back and over one shoulder. He tucked the loose ends into his belt. Then he snapped his fingers and transported his staff and a metal bowl from his room inside Myrilandel's house. The spell was illegal. Dragon magic only allowed levitation, not transportation. But the men of Rossemeyer would have seen the staff floating through the air and followed it.

King Quinnault had told him to use whatever means possible to destroy the depth finder and create chaos on the docks.

Lastly he smeared dirt on his cheeks and chin in imitation of two days' growth of beard.

With bowl in one hand, held out in a classic beggar's stance, and leaning heavily on the staff, he shuffled out of the alley, just another beggar displaced by the wars.

He progressed to the docks unmolested and richer by seven dragini.

"Dinner," he promised Mopsie as he slipped the coins inside his belt pouch. He tucked the bowl into his makeshift bedroll and wound his way through the confusing array of docks and warehouses under construction.

The elaborate passenger barge he had ridden on—was it just two days ago?—rested against a clean ramp. No one bothered to sweep and scrub the more commercial docks. But this one catered to wealthy and elite passengers. A bevy of colorful canopies and padded benches provided those passengers with a place to await the tide and the whim of the pilot.

If he'd worn his magician's robes, Bessel could have walked directly up to the barge and demanded passage free of charge. Dressed as an ordinary fisherman, accompanied by a scruffy dog—who had gotten very dirty again crossing the city—the stewards and crew wouldn't allow him beyond the velvet ropes that separated the passenger area from the common dockside traffic.

He needed another disguise.

What would get him aboard the ship without question and without having to pay an enormous fee? He couldn't board as an ordinary dockhand, and the uniforms of the Guild of Bay Pilots were custom-made for each individual—no extras. Besides, every man in the Guild knew every other man in the guild.

He'd have to board as a magician needing free passage so he could fulfill some unnamed errand for the Commune. No longer concerned about performing rogue magic, he snapped his fingers again. His formal robe and his best boots from his room in Myrilandel's house landed in a heap at his feet. He ducked behind a pile of crates and rope coils to rearrange himself. The robe covered his ordinary fisherman's clothing. But his bedroll and Mopsie needed a more discreet covering.

He checked the pockets of the robe for his normal assortment of essential equipment. Everything seemed in place.

"With permission to use rogue magic, I can hide the bedroll here and retrieve it later," he whispered to himself and Mopsie. He also needed to change his appearance a little. He didn't want Raanald, the pilot during yesterday's disaster, or any of his crew recognizing him. With just a little magic he made himself appear taller and thinner. The dirt on his face took on a heavier appearance, more like a true beard and mustache.

Mopsie whined in disapproval at the change. "Don't worry, pup, I won't leave you behind. I need you to stand guard while I do what I have to do."

The depth finder was in place. He could see it from here, but he couldn't blast it with magic. That would bring down the wrath of the Guild upon the Commune. He needed to make it look as if the machine were defective—dangerous—so the Guild would cooperate with the Commune in the future, not go to war with each other.

He needed to get closer, close enough to touch the machine. Boldly, he stepped up to the steward standing behind the velvet rope.

"Good man, I travel on business for the Commune of Magicians. I need to interview passengers arriving this evening at the port." Bessel gestured expansively toward the four islands far out in the Great Bay at the beginning of deep water. The steward kept his eyes on Bessel's hands and staff rather than on the dirty mutt who hid beneath the journeyman's robes.

"I need a passport." The steward held out his hand for the bit of slate with symbols scratched on it that outlined Bessel's instructions.

"What you don't know can hurt you," Bessel whispered to himself. He fished in his pocket while murmuring yet another transport spell to bring him the flat scrap of slate he kept with his books. The piece was outdated from his journey to his mother's deathbed. But this man couldn't read—prevented by law from learning the arcane skill.

The steward barely glanced at the passport, then unhitched one of the velvet ropes at the stanchion, allowing

Bessel to pass into the waiting area unhindered. "You may board now, but sit somewhere out of the way. We'll sail with the tide regardless, even if that mob of uppity mercenaries and their lady don't show up on time."

"Mercenaries?" Bessel raised one eyebrow at the man as if the issue were of only moderate interest.

"Yeah. The lady sent word. She's taking the ambassador's body back to Rossemeyer for burial. After she executes that other magician, the one who murdered her husband."

CHAPTER 47

Afternoon, home of Myrilandel, ambassador from the Nimbus of Dragons, Coronnan City

Katie gulped back her immediate fear. Quinnault knew the business end of a sword and how to use it.

So did all of those black-clad mercenaries. But they would not try to find a compromise without violence.

In her fear for Quinnault, the rising noise around them faded from her awareness.

Then she noticed the source of the shouts that had brought her to her husband's side—she must have walked across the cobblestone stoop to stand at his side without being aware of anything but the need to touch his hand and reassure herself he still lived.

Hundreds of people pressed against the foreign mercenaries. They shouted and brandished torches, makeshift clubs, and everyday tools as weapons.

"They're in league with the Rovers," one man shouted. "They steal our money and terrorize our women and children!"

"Kill the Rovers and their helpers!" Another man joined the litany of abuse. "I'll not pay protection money to foreigners."

"Kill all the foreigners!"

"Save the king from the filthy foreigners."

"Stargods bless the king."

The mercenaries looked over their shoulders nervously. They fingered their weapons but kept them sheathed. Their leader, face completely obscured by black veils, backed up two steps. He ran into a solid wall of his own men. They kept pressing forward, away from the murderous crowd. But as they moved away from the crowd, they came closer and closer to Quinnault and his entourage. A few more steps and confrontation was inevitable.

"My people." Quinnault raised his voice above the rabble. He also lifted his hands as a signal for quiet.

The shouts and murmurs stilled closest to Quinnault and spread outward in waves.

"People of Coronnan, listen to me! Once before, you joined to unify against forces that would have destroyed us with civil war. Now I ask you to join me again to save the kingdom. I need your help to unite the crown, the lords, the magicians, and the people. Only you, the people, can bind us together!"

"What do you plan?" Katie whispered. Love and respect flooded her emotions. This medieval man, with a worldview limited by an aristocratic power structure, had just embraced a modern principle of democracy.

He viewed the people as the heart and core of his kingdom.

His mind smiled into hers. She saw his plan. The people would march in triumph to the University and challenge the Commune. Scarface would have to relinquish his hold on the magicians in the face of this determined mob backing their king.

A mighty cheer rose from the throats of the people as they surged forward. The mercenaries looked warily around them. The people pressed against them so tightly they couldn't draw or wield a weapon. Each of the foreigners found himself totally surrounded, cut off from his fellows.

"Hear me, men of Rossemeyer!" Quinnault raised his hands and voice once more. His words echoed in the narrow street. "Honorable warriors, go back to your embassy. Inform Lady Rosselaara that this business is finished. I have investigated and found Ambassador Jorghe-Rosse's death to be an accident. He died honorably fighting the storm and the bay, worthy enemies. No other lives will be forfeited. Take your ambassador home for funeral rites. You are free, all of you, to depart Coronnan with the evening tide."

"And if we doubt your 'investigations'?" the head mercenary asked, fighting to maintain his balance in the midst of the pressing crowd.

"Then your king must send me a new ambassador to

negotiate. Now take Ambassador Jorghe-Rosse's body and Lady Rosselaara home for a proper funeral. Would you like an escort to the docks? I'm certain the people of Coronnan City would be happy to see you safely on your way."

The mercenaries melted away. The people closed ranks, jeering at them. A few cityfolk who carried rocks and tools followed them back toward their embassy.

"And now, my people, we must bring back a balance in our government. The Commune, the Council, and the King must once again hold equal power. No one faction can be allowed to dominate the others." Quinnault forged a path through the throng of eager townspeople. They rushed to walk near him, touch him, bask in his glory.

"Excuse me, Your Grace," Luucian appeared at Katie's elbow.

"Luucian, what are you doing here? You are supposed to be at Shayla's lair," Katie gasped in surprise.

"I've been there and back. The dragons know a few shortcuts. The others are trying to work their way through the crowd."

"My father?"

"Well enough, for the time being. He's in the kitchen, eating and drinking to restore some of his vitality. But, Your Grace, I have a message from Bessel, relayed by the dragons. He said to get these people down to the docks. He needs everyone down on the docks."

Katie stared at the mob encircling Quinnault. They were moving toward University Isle. She'd have to divert them. But first. . . .

"Luucian, go with Master Nimbulan and the others and start moving the books from the library into the tunnels below the palace. Master Nimbulan is to supervise only. He is not to lift a single book." Quickly, she outlined the plan for to him. "While you are doing that, I need my father to find Lord Balthazaan and keep him out of the way and misinformed."

Luucian nodded and melted back into the crowd.

Katie had to fight to stay close to her husband as they swept along the city streets in the direction of University Isle.

"Scarecrow, we're needed at the docks. Bessel sent a message."

Quinnault raised an eyebrow at her.

"I've sent Nimbulan and reinforcements on their errand."

"Reinforcements?"

"I'll explain later.

Quinnault nodded. "How am I going to divert this mob?"

"I'm not sure." Katie bit her lip and glanced around at the volatile crowd.

"Stop!" Five master magicians commanded. They stood in a line across the path of the crowd. They linked hands. A dark green aura of power—Scarface's signature color—surrounded them. "Senior Magician Scarface commands this mob to disperse. We place King Quinnault Darville de Draconis under arrest for interfering with the lawful work of the Commune of Magicians."

* * *

The docks, Coronnan City

Bessel swallowed his apprehension that Lady Rosselaara would recognize him. He had to trust in his disguises and complete his mission. He nodded to the steward and climbed the ramp to the barge. He chose a seat in the back corner beneath the canopy, deep in the shadows. Here he could relax his delusion spell while he studied the depth finder.

Shortly the crew began moving about the deck, coiling lines and performing other chores indicative of imminent launching. A subtle shift of the water's movement beneath the deck told Bessel when the tide turned and began to recede. Just as a crewman prepared to fling the last line aboard from the dock, a long procession of black-clad mercenaries appeared at the velvet ropes.

Deep within their ranks, Lady Rosselaara stood beside her husband's casket, dry-eyed and angry.

The first of the warriors slashed the rope with his sword and kicked it aside. The steward rushed to stop them and demand their passports. They thrust him out of the way as if he were merely another piece of normal dock debris.

Raanald, the pilot and absolute ruler of the barge, stalked to the head of the boarding ramp. He stood firmly blocking the way, hands on hips, feet spread, and a scowl on his face.

"You're late," Raanald spat, not moving out of the way.

The lead mercenary hesitated. They needed the pilot to guide the barge to the port. He couldn't injure the man, and he couldn't get past him without injuring him.

"We are here now. You have not left without us," the warrior replied from behind his turban veil. His voice remained even and remote through the muffling cloth. A pulse pounded visibly in his temple. Politeness was something these men had little time for.

And yet some of them had been quite gentle and caring toward Bessel when he appeared to be a female in distress.

"You may travel with us, but only because it means we're shut of you for good," Raanald replied. "You'd better hurry. Anyone not in place in five minutes has to swim to the port, or walk across the sucking mud." He turned his back on the newcomers and stationed himself by the helmsman on the elevated platform at the rear of the barge.

The Rossemeyerians proceeded to crowd upon the barge in an orderly fashion, despite their rapid pace.

Bessel allowed himself to be edged out of the sheltering shadows to stand next to the depth finder. The warriors seemed to shun it as if it would contaminate them with its arcane magic. Lady Rosselaara claimed most of the covered area for herself, the coffin, two maids, and a few select warriors. The deck of the barge wallowed a little deeper in the water with so many people aboard.

The oarsmen shoved off. Raanald moved back to the depth finder. He stared alternately at the numbers behind the screen and at the water ahead.

Bessel kept his back to the pilot as much as possible, hoping he had the strength to keep up his disguise throughout the entire procedure. Mopsie had crawled under the nearest bench and watched everything through wary eyes.

When the port islands finally appeared as a hazy blur on the horizon and the shore remained within clear view, Bessel edged his foot to touch the base of the depth finder.

He plunged his mind into the guts of the machine and met a solid wall of impenetrable lead. He tried again, probing around the edges, seeking a crack in the mechanism, a seam, any point where he could penetrate. Sharp pain bounced back into his eyes along the line of his magical touch. He grimaced and yanked his foot away from the base as if burned. His entire body tingled with backlashed magic.

Quickly, he looked around to see if any of the many warriors around him noticed his discomfort. They all seemed absorbed in keeping their stomachs intact. Not very good sailors, Bessel surmised. Maybe . . .

He sent his next probe into the bay. The muddy bottom absorbed his magic like a sponge. He tried again, slightly to the left of his original quest for information. A spring bubbled up through the mud. When the tide was completely out, a small freshwater creek would flow away from that spring. Several springs fed the bay in this manner, making for dangerous sucking mud around the source.

This time his probe sounded different within his mind. The fresh water changed the density of the salt water. He checked the numbers on the depth finder. They spun up and back down again quite rapidly. The change in the water had triggered an inaccurate measurement.

Above him, a dragon bellowed as it flew determinedly around the city. The machine numbers fluctuated again, more drastically than it had with the fresh water.

Bessel smiled to himself and edged over to the railing. He searched for the new wood that marked the spot where Jorghe-Rosse had fallen overboard. He spotted the fresh paint showing a stout replacement to the broken pieces. Two paces away the railing paint peeled and the wood looked worn and weak. He stood beside it.

Bessel here. Please, flying dragon, announce your presence again, loudly, clearly, he called to the nearly invisible beast.

(Rouussin,) the dragon introduced himself. Dragon protocol required names. *(What do you wish?)*

Please, Master Rouussin, will you bellow again? I need the sounds to disrupt an evil machine.

(Shayla has shared with us Queen Maarie Kaathliin's dragon dream. We do not like machines that harbor the seeds of disease.)

The dragon bugled loudly. The expanse of the bay picked up the sound, amplified it, and bounced it against the cliff walls farther South.

The passengers held their ears and looked at each other in distressed puzzlement.

The numbers on the machine spun out of control. "Hard a port!" Raanald screamed at the helmsman. Panic widened his eyes.

The helmsman leaned all of his body weight onto the tiller.

The barge swung around. The waves slapped the barge sideways. The helmsman kept pushing the tiller. The spring beneath the barge and the conflicting movement of the water created an undertow. The turning barge caught a rip in the tide, spinning it around so the other side of the barge faced the oncoming waves. Then it grounded on the bar.

"*S'murghin* machine!" Raanald yelled. He grabbed one of the long oars away from his crew and slammed it into the depth finder. The viewscreen split. The numbers died.

Raanald continued pounding the oar into the black casing. The synthetic black shell cracked, but he did not penetrate to the lead core.

Raanald lifted his makeshift club for one last blow. He looked around him, suddenly aware of the crowd that stared at his anger. They all clutched railings or each other to keep them upright on the uncertain deck.

The pilot's gaze landed on Bessel.

"You!" Raanald stared at him, stunned bewilderment clouded his eyes. "What game are you and that bloody Commune of yours playing this time?"

He advanced upon Bessel, oar raised.

"I did nothing to your machine," Bessel replied, calmly. Suddenly his entire future opened before him. He knew what he had to do.

"You destroyed the machine!" Raanald screamed.

"No, you did." Bessel knew everyone aboard heard him. He only needed a little magic to hold their attention, make them understand. "The depth finder deceived you again with invalid numbers. You destroyed it to regain control of this barge. The Guild can no longer rely on the depth finder."

"But we don't know the channels anymore!" Raanald stared at the vast expanse of water between himself and the port islands, at the oarsmen standing bewildered for lack of direction, at the rudder swinging idly awaiting a guiding hand.

"Trust your Mopplewogger as you have for many generations."

Mopsie yipped and danced on his hind legs. He pranced over to the helmsman. He barked once, quick and sharp.

"That means starboard. You have to go to starboard to get off the bar," Bessel reminded Raanald.

"I know what the dog means. But that ain't a Mopplewogger, and you broke my machine."

"Mopsie is a better Mopplewogger than you'll ever know."

"Don't tell me my business, *Magician*," Raanald spat the last word. "I'm a senior member of the Guild of Bay Pilots." He ran the last few steps to where Bessel stood by the railing. He swung the oar with all his might.

Bessel ducked backward. Raanald's blow landed on the railing, splintering the old wood.

Raanald raised the oar again. Bessel braced himself against the damaged railing. The deck shifted under his feet. His balance twisted.

The club clipped his temple.

Starbursts filled his vision. He fell. The railing gave way.

For a moment the weightless sensation of flying cleared his mind.

Then the cold dark waters of the bay closed over his head.

They'll tell everyone I'm dead, he thought as he shucked his boots and formal robe beneath the waves.

Let them believe I'm dead. I have nothing and no one to mourn me.

Above him Mopsie splashed into the water, barking frantically. His cries and whines took on a note of desperation.

Down here, pup. I'm hiding. Meet me ashore. We'll be together. I have you to live for. We are both free now. Free of our pasts and those who judged us. Our destinies are our own to shape and control.

CHAPTER 48

Late afternoon, streets of Coronnan City

"We need to stall Scarface until Bessel finishes his chore," Katie whispered to Quinnault.

He nodded curtly in acknowledgment. His gaze remained upon the five magicians facing him across the street.

"I will deal only with Master Aaddler," he announced. "Since he challenges my authority, he must face me directly."

The magicians looked to each other in a moment of confusion.

Katie caught a drift of their stray thoughts.

Scarface said there would be no resistance.

How do we keep the king and his troops away from the island until dawn?

The dragon magic wanes. The dragons have deserted us! Stargods forgive me. The youngest of the magicians went down on his knees, crossing himself repeatedly.

Katie resisted the urge to mimic the gesture. Instead, she watched the shimmer of green power that connected the magicians fade and break apart.

"What breaks our connection to Scarface?" the senior among the magicians asked aloud.

"Nimbulan's people said that even when the dragons deserted Coronnan last year, they had access to *some* dragon magic for a while," one of his fellows replied.

Sensing confusion and weakness among the magicians, the crowd surged forward, pushing Quinnault and Katie to within a few yards of the opposition.

"Fools! Who gave you permission to drop the barrier spell?" Scarface stalked up behind his magicians. "Link up. Protect University Isle from this mob." His face twisted in anger. The white scar across his brow turned livid, pulsing red.

"Give it up, Master Aaddler," Quinnault called. "You have no authority to arrest me or anyone—*ever.*"

"You can't stop me," Scarface glared at his king.

"Would you care to argue that with my supporters?"

Scarface stared at the dozens, maybe a hundred people, behind the king and queen. They raised their makeshift weapons, shaking them in direct challenge.

"Come," Scarface called to his five compatriots. "We will begin now rather than wait for dawn." He and his magicians backed down the street toward their island.

The crowd became noisy, demanding the end of the Commune's power. They pressed Katie and Quinnault from behind.

"Now what do we do?" Katie asked, fighting to stay afoot. She clung to Quinnault's arm. The dozen armed guards did their best to keep the crowd away.

(Start a fire elsewhere,) a dragon answered out of nowhere.

Shayla circled the crowd low enough for all to see. Then she rose above the city, widening her circle. A moment later she opened her mouth, letting loose a roar followed by a continuous stream of flame. Fire touched the tower roof at the University. The tar holding the slates in place ignited. A second blast of flame exploded the timbers below. Slates flew in all directions becoming deadly missiles.

* * *

Late afternoon, the docks, Coronnan City

Bessel approached the passenger dock from the direction of the fishermen's wharf. He'd exchanged his soaked clothes for a different set of fishermen's togs provided by men who considered him one of them. Raanald and Lady Rosselaara stepped out of a small rowboat within a moment of his arrival.

A dozen boats had been dispatched by royal guards to rescue the passengers from the barge.

"Get me Master Scarface. Now. Bring the interfering bastard here at once!" Raanald shouted above the noise of the curiosity seekers and dock workers.

A dozen or more dogs barked, their excited comments drifting across the bay more clearly than people's voices.

A nice state of chaos ready for the last ingredient.

A new contingent of palace guards appeared on the embankment above the passenger dock. A couple of magicians hovered behind them, but no Scarface. Bessel moved closer to the center of the wordstorm.

Lady Rosselaara looked straight at him without recognition and turned to one of her mercenaries. "Find me another boat. Row it yourself if you have to, but get me out of this city immediately."

"Sometimes hiding in plain sight is more effective than the darkest hidey-hole," Bessel said under his breath as the lady passed him. If she heard, she didn't deign to acknowledge his comment.

He looked up at the line of palace guards arguing fiercely with Raanald and a contingent of magicians. Behind them, King Kinnsell and Lord Balthazaan added their own tirade. Four other finely dressed men followed them meekly.

More dogs crowded onto the docks, barking incessantly.

The babble rose to an uncomfortable crescendo. Confusion reigned, amplifying frustrations and churning anger. But where was Scarface? He needed to be here so that Nimbulan and the others had time to move the books into hiding.

A dragon bellowed from the skies above them. Everyone on the dock ceased speaking and looking up. Bessel could just make out a shimmering outline in a kaleidoscope of all color/no color.

Two dragons in one day? Something wonderful and strange transpired in the city.

A hush fell over the crowd. One of the magicians took an open posture, head turned up, eyes closed. After a few moments of the stillness needed to gather dragon magic, his face crumpled in disappointment. Then he gathered his companions close. They jabbered among themselves and cowered in fear. They kept shifting their gaze between the dragon and back toward the city where a tall column of smoke rose from the vicinity of the University.

Obviously the Commune was out of favor with the dragons if they could not gather precious dragon magic.

Did the smoke have something to do with that?

Shayla! Bessel here, he hailed her.

(Greetings,) the dragon replied. *(Hasten. You are needed. The University burns. The fire will not delay your enemies long.)*

Mopsie nudged him, reminding him of his next chore. "Right, boy. We have to make sure Nimbulan doesn't hide those books permanently."

He whistled sharply. A dozen fishermen looked at him in recognition, then moved to interrupt Lady Rosselaara's tirade. In moments, the diplomatic entourage had been escorted back aboard small fishing boats and headed for the port. Each boat boasted an alert moppelwogger in the bow.

"Coronnan is grateful for your departure, madama," Bessel muttered. "I know I am."

He left the docks whistling. He had his own path to forge; a new destiny to follow. Freedom rode lightly on his shoulders, a comfortable companion.

The magicians turned and hastened back toward the University. The guards ran to follow, Raanald at their heels, still shaking his fist angrily. Kinnsell smiled and followed them more slowly. He kept up a barrage of insults and complaints to the finely dressed men around him. Lord Balthazaan broke off from him to keep up with the magicians. Kinnsell snagged the lord's sleeve, shouting at him and raising his fists. They stood squarely in the path of the mercenaries and dock workers who sought to follow.

The pack of unpartnered water dogs seemed to flow around the obstacle. They nipped at heels as they raced toward this new curiosity.

"We can't delay here any longer, Mopsie. Scarface never showed up. Guess we'll have to try something else to thwart him." Bessel slipped quietly into the crowd, just another anonymous figure watching the antics of the powerful and the angry. But he didn't stay with the throng beyond sight of the docks. As soon as he could, he and Mopsie took off for Palace Isle and the emergency escape tunnels beneath the palace. Mopsie sniffed out shortcuts no human would think to follow.

"Now for the books, pup. We've a lot of magic to weave. Together."

CHAPTER 49

Near sunset, the streets of Coronnan City

"Scarface ain't our king. He's got no right to arrest anyone!" a loud-voiced tradesman bellowed over the noise of city crowd.

Katie squeezed Quinnault's hand. They shared a moment of triumph as the crowd surged along the city streets following in the wake of the fleeing magicians.

"Long live King Quinnault!" a hundred voices picked up the cheer. "Stargods bless our king."

She heard a few angry mumbles about ending the tyranny of tax collectors. But mostly the crowd pressed close in order to keep anyone from menacing their king.

They approached Palace Isle, the last major island before Scarface's refuge on University Isle. Smoke filled the air. Ahead, the now roofless tower continued to burn. Flames shot upward, sending sparks outward in a fountain. Most were extinguished before touching ground or landed in the river.

The crowd increased its speed now that their target was clearly visible.

"Dragons bless us," a woman called above the crowd noise. "The dragons bless us." Everyone looked up to the six shimmering outlines that circled the city.

Two dozen more guards swelled the ranks of the throng. In their midst, Katie saw a few familiar but very grimy faces. They all walked heavily as if very tired.

"Myri!" She waved to her friend, signaling her closer.

Old Lyman plowed a passageway through the crowd for the book rescuers. The crowd made way respectfully for the king's sister and her very dirty entourage.

"Yaala? Is that really you?" Katie grabbed the young

woman in a fierce hug. "I've missed you terribly." A dark-haired young man with blond streaks in his thick beard stayed close behind Yaala, not quite daring to approach the queen but seemingly reluctant to let Yaala out of his sight.

"Your Grace, may I present Rollett, Nimbulan's journeyman, recently freed from Hanassa," Yaala introduced the young man, reaching to hold his hand.

Katie nodded her acknowledgment of the introduction, trying not to raise her eyebrows at the intimate gesture.

"Is Nimbulan all right? What about my father?" she asked anxiously, searching the crowd for signs of the others. Nimbulan walked beside Myri, holding her hand. He looked tired, but not in pain. Powwell walked beside them, pale and sad but staying proudly beside his adoptive parents. Luucian was there, too, keeping an eye on Nimbulan and Powwell.

"Where is King Kinnsell?" Katie demanded.

"With Lord Balthazaan," Myri explained. "He'll join us later."

Just then a pack of dogs began barking nearby. They raced forward to University Isle from an adjacent island. Another throng of people, led by Raanald the bay pilot, came into view. The dogs wove in and out of the crowd yapping louder and louder to be heard above the angry shouts. Raanald kicked at a dog to get it out of the way. Kinnsell yanked the man off-balance and shouted something unintelligible. Lord Balthazaan and a few of his cronies hovered behind Katie's father, looking confused.

"It's useless to talk here." Quinnault shook his head as Katie tried to call to her father. "We'll get the whole story later. Right now, we have to stop Scarface."

And then they faced University Isle. Scarface stood in the center of the courtyard holding a torch aloft. Before him lay a mound of books. Master magicians threw more books out the windows of the adjacent library.

The dogs swarmed over the bridge, baying at the sight of Scarface. They circled him, growling and yapping.

He thrust his torch at them, keeping them at bay.

The dogs backed away, still snarling.

"Hear me, people of Coronnan!" Scarface called. He circled the torch at the dogs, trying to break through their numbers to get to the books. The dogs shifted position, circling but keeping Scarface from his objective.

Finnally one of the dockmen whistled sharply. The dogs backed off.

"Hear me, people of Coronnan!" Scarface repeated.

This time Katie sensed magic behind his words, not a compulsion, but the power to be heard and understood in the farthest reaches of the noisy crowd.

"People of Coronnan, these books harbor evil knowledge. Knowledge of the blood magic and Rovers that brought this land low for three generations of warfare. The books must be purged so that no one can use this knowledge against you ever again."

Murmurs of disquiet rippled through the crowd. They pushed forward to hear more.

Katie found herself and her friends at the edge of the paved courtyard without realizing how rapidly she had been carried forward.

"Stargods, he's going to make the people believe in his madness," Quinnault muttered.

Scarface lowered his torch.

"Who are you to decide what knowledge is evil, which books must be destroyed?" Quinnault screamed.

Scarface hesitated.

"I forbid you to burn any books, Master Aadler," Quinnault said on a calmer note. "I have already dismissed you as my adviser. You cannot be trusted to be impartial."

The magicians gathered around the University courtyard paused to listen. The lords who had gathered behind the magicians looked to Quinnault in puzzlement.

"The art of reading has been forbidden to all but magicians since the coming of the Stargods," Scarface intoned, raising his torch high above his head. "Who else but the Senior Magician can make this decision?" The flickering light cast him in a halo of fire-green light—very close to his signature color of magic.

The crowd of mundane and magician onlookers gasped at the image of sacred blessing he invoked.

"The three brothers who descended upon a cloud of silver flame entrusted a few select, talented people with the forbidden knowledge within these books. As magicians, we carry out that trust by knowing why this knowledge is forbidden to all but us and preventing its use for evil. Rogue magicians who have forsaken the wisdom of the Stargods for personal glory have used it against the good of the common people and the kingdom. We, the guardians of knowledge, decree that the books must be destroyed before more evil is perpetrated by those who refuse the controls of dragon magic and the Commune."

We cannot stop him. Katie moaned to Quinnault. *He doesn't need compulsion anymore. These people will follow him anywhere.*

"How much of our history, philosophy, and law will be lost with those books? That information is as valuable as magic. You can't destroy all of the books just because they might contain information you deem evil," Quinnault protested, as loud and compelling as Scarface's diatribe.

"I can and I will." Scarface lowered his torch to ignite the first books.

"You can't ruin the Commune. I won't let you." A ghostly figure in white trews and yellow shirt launched himself from the edge of the crowd onto Scarface. The two men rolled to the ground. The torch flew out of Scarface's hand onto the paving stone. Silently it rolled toward the books.

"Bessel. The torch!" Powwell bellowed.

"I saw him earlier in the tunnels. He helped move books, but he did it secretly," Yaala added in a quieter tone. "He said he had to disappear. He said . . ."

Rollett dove across the mound of books and grabbed the torch. He thudded into the pavement. Yaala gasped and held her hand to her throat until Rollett rolled to his feet, the torch held away from the precious books.

Beside him Bessel jumped to his feet and disappeared into the shadows. Scarface lay panting where he had fallen.

"Bessel looks more like a ghost than a man," Katie whispered.

"Bessel told me not to believe rumors of his death," Powwell said. He turned a weak smile on his companions. "Has anyone noticed some of the books disappearing from the mound? He's still helping, but I doubt we'll see him do it. Maybe he is a ghost now." He whispered the last.

"Give it up, Scarface. The dragons burned your tower," Quinnault countered. "Surely, if Shayla seeks to destroy your workplace, then she withdraws her covenant and her blessing from you."

"The priests agree with Scarface," Lord Balthazaan shouted above the hushed whispers of the crowd. "He has the blessing of the Stargods to burn these books. I count the Stargods above a murdering dragon any day. Dragons are monsters to be avoided. We can't trust them." The lord clenched his fist and shook it at the skies where the dragons had flown. His fingers looked naked, devoid of the heavy rings he and his wife habitually wore.

A sudden image splashed in front of Katie's vision. Balthazaan should wear a silver ring of entwined strands on his left hand. His wife wore an identical one—the hereditary betrothal bands of their family. One of those two rings had been left in Marilell's crib. The baby had almost choked to death on a ring normally worn by this lord.

Her father might have prompted the attempted kidnapping of her baby, but this man executed the orders—or tried to.

She flashed the information to Quinnault. He reeled under the impact. *How do we prove it?* Quinnault asked her. Anger stained his cheeks red.

I don't know that we can. Balthazaan will side with anyone who opposes you. He will claim our accusations are merely persecution because of his opposition to your politics, Katie thought.

I thought your father tamed him.

My father has his own agenda. Who knows what thoughts and innuendos he planted in that man's mind. We only asked him to keep the lords out of the way while Nimbulan and his friends rescued a few of the books. Now he's disappeared again.

"Balthazaan." Quinnault gathered himself to speak. "Without the dragons, we cannot fight rogue magic. Do you wish to return to the days of civil war when Battlemages led warlords into battle after battle for no reason other than to prove their superiority over another Battlemage?"

Balthazaan reared back as if he'd been slapped.

"By your own argument, King Quinnault, the books must be burned. They contain knowledge of rogue magic. Once they are destroyed, no one will know how to work any magic but that given us by dragons." The Senior Magician dragged himself to his feet. He kept his eyes on the torch Rollett still held out of his reach.

"Master Aaddler," Katie called aloud. "If other lands with Battlemages who use solitary magic attack us, overtly or covertly, how will we know how to counter them unless we have access to the same knowledge they possess?"

"That cannot happen!" Scarface screamed. His scar whitened, and he scrunched up his eyes, making an ugly mask of his face. "There will be no more rogue magic. I cannot allow any more rogue magic!" Scarface raised his hands to the skies and brought forth a huge ball of witchfire. As suddenly as the flames appeared, he launched them into the middle of the mound of books. They exploded in flame.

Wind-drift and Whitehands lunged for him, knocking him back to the pavement once more. The two magicians slammed their fists into Scarface's jaw alternately, repeatedly.

"How dare you!" they screamed.

"How dare you destroy our heritage?" Tears streamed down Wind-drift's face. "I tried to make you see reason. I tried, but you would not listen," he sobbed.

A dozen hands, led by Rollett and Powwell, rushed to douse the flames with water or blankets. The heat of fire in the tower drove them back before they could get close enough to extinguish more than a few sparks.

Katie hid her face against her husband's chest. She bit her fist to keep from crying out. Quinnault held her tightly. His jaw trembled atop her head with suppressed emotions.

Cheers as well as gasps of dismay rose from the throats of all but a few gathered around the courtyard. The common people who watched from the fringes added their voices to the others.

Allow these few books and shadows of books to burn. Your helpers have saved many more of them. A masculine voice Katie did not recognize came into her mind.

Who? She looked up to see if a new dragon had joined Shayla and her consorts who hovered above the fire.

None of them responded.

"I can no longer trust you, Master Aaddler," Quinnault said quietly. "While you remain Senior Magician of the Commune, I cannot trust any member of the Commune, except these two brave souls. You are all forbidden the

Council chamber until another, more moderate man leads you."

"And so the alien queen will be your sole adviser," Scarface sneered.

"I value the advice of my beloved wife. But I also value the wisdom of a magician. I value the balance in my government provided by magicians, lords, and myself. You would upset that balance in your quest for total control of myself and the lords. Master Rollett and Master Lyman will be my chief advisers, with assistance from Masters Wind-drift and Whitehands."

"Rollett is no master! Only I can confirm a journeyman worthy of master status"

"Incorrect," Lyman intervened. He looked exhausted beneath the layer of grime on his face. "Any master may elevate a worthy journeyman. I am the oldest master among the Commune. Rollett has completed his master's quest set for him by Nimbulan, his mentor and the Senior Magician who sent him on that quest."

"I was not informed of this quest!"

"But you were there in Hanassa with us, when I charged him with certain tasks to facilitate our escape a year ago," Nimbulan added. He and Myrilandel stepped up to stand beside their king. "And you made every effort to ensure I left him behind rather than risk *your* chances for escape. He has returned in spite of you, Scarface."

The old man paused to allow his words to penetrate to the farthest reaches of the crowd. "Rollett survived Hanassa the city and aided in the destruction of Hanassa the renegade dragon. He saved the lives of his companions. I deem him worthy and a master," Lyman declared. "Powwell, too, is ready for elevation, but lacks years and book learning. He is a worthy Senior Journeyman."

"It matters not." Scarface grounded his staff and faced Quinnault proudly. His face and posture took on an air of grim determination. "The books burn."

"I'll not have you in Coronnan challenging my every move, Aaddler," Quinnault said, just as sternly. "I banish you to the same monastery you exiled many aging masters too for the simple reason they owed loyalty to Nimbulan. You will be gone from the capital within the hour."

"I command too many master magicians for you to force me to do anything," Scarface sneered.

"We seem to have reached a stalemate," Kinnsell added from the back of the crowd. Katie's three brothers flanked him, holding blaster pistols. And behind them all stood a dozen armed and armored marines from the mother ship.

"Oh, no," Katie moaned.

"The king doesn't trust the magicians, the magicians don't trust the lords, and the lords don't trust the king. Your balance is destroyed. The only solution is for a new, neutral party to step in and take over. I offer my services to one and all." Kinnsell stepped forward, hands open in a gesture of calm reasonableness. "I have the weapons to subdue you all, including the magicians and the dragons." He waved a hand and one of the marines fired his blaster rifle at the bridge connecting Palace Isle to the University. It disappeared in a shower of sparks and thunderous noise.

"Oh, no, you don't, Daddy!" Katie marched up to face him. "You are the renegade here. You and your total disregard for anything but your own selfishness. Go back to Terra now, while you can. We of Coronnan will never succumb to your tyranny." The knot in her mid-region threatened to explode with anger, with loneliness, with grief.

"Come now, Katie. You are one of us. Surely you are tired of all this magic nonsense by now. I'll bring central heating and indoor plumbing to this benighted backwater." Her father reached out to pat the top of her head as if she were no more than a quarrelsome child.

She backed away from him, standing as tall and proud as she could. Majesty came from more than height.

"There are many more important things in life than those conveniences."

"Like what?"

"Like love," Quinnault said.

"And loyalty," Nimbulan added.

"Like honor." Wind-drift shouldered Scarface aside as he added his voice to his king's.

"And justice," Lord Balthazaan remarked.

One by one all those who had been separated by the issue of the book burning banded together to face this new threat.

Only Scarface remained outside the new circle of unified

leaders. A few more books disappeared from the bonfire while everyone was distracted by this new threat.

"You see, Daddy? You'll have to defeat us all to win this war. What will that leave you? A bush world with no one to work the land or mine the resources. Starting up a new colony here will bankrupt you."

Jamie Patrick signaled his brothers to lower their pistols. A smirk brought a twinkle to his eyes. Or was it merely a reflection of the fire that still raged.

"She's right, Pop," he said.

"I'm not actually going to fire on another human being. You said this coup would be bloodless." Sean Michael holstered his weapon.

"Didn't Dad say he saw a dragon?" Liam Francis asked with a mischievous smirk that matched the grin Katie tried to swallow. "When he called the mother ship from his illegal pocket communicator, he said he had flown on a dragon from the mountains to the capital."

"Sounds to me like you are just a little insane, Kinnsell O'Hara," Jamie Patrick agreed. "Let's take him back home for a nice long rest in a secure hospital." The eldest of the siblings clamped a hard hand on his father's shoulder.

"That will take him out of the line of succession. Parliament will never elect him emperor when Gramps dies," Katie reminded them.

"One less to vie for the title." The brothers shrugged in unison. "Two less since you won't be returning with us, Katie."

"Be glad of that, boys. She'd give you all a run for your money if she decided to leave this benighted backwater," Kinnsell said quietly. A half grin tugged at the corners of his mouth.

"I'll miss you." Katie had to blink rapidly to keep back her tears.

"You know us, Katie. We'll be back to check on you."

"No, you won't. You can't." She sobbed briefly, her next words closing her throat. Quinnault touched her hand and she found the courage to speak on, though tears ran down her cheeks. "Coronnan, all of Kardia Hodos must be off-limits to everyone from Terra. Everyone. We can't take a chance that you'll bring a new mutation of the plague, one that we can't combat. We can't take a chance that you will bring technology and pollution that will give the plague a breeding ground."

Her brothers dropped their heads. When Jamie Patrick looked up again, his eyes looked very moist. "We'll miss watching your daughter grow up. We'll miss you, Katie."

"We love you, Sis," Sean Michael said quietly.

Liam Francis looked decidedly rebellious for a moment, then he stepped forward, gathering Katie in a tight hug. "Good-bye, Katie."

Each of them dropped a kiss on Katie's cheek. Then Kinnsell came forward. "You are right, of course. The most sensible one of the lot of you, and she wants to stay here. She'd make the best emperor, boys. Good-bye, Maarie Kaathliin O'Hara de Draconis." He swallowed convulsively and turned to leave, escorted by his three sons.

Kinnsell turned for one last look at Katie. *In time, Daughter, you will appreciate the gift I leave with you. When you could not unite Coronnan and your balanced government looked about to crumble, you all united against me. You'll bicker for a while, but you will settle your differences. Help Quinnault govern with wisdom and raise a healthy horde of grandchildren for me. Teach them well the lessons of love, loyalty, honor, and justice so that they may pass this legacy through the generations of our dynasty.*

Tears came to Katie's eyes as she nodded her acceptance of her father's gift and final farewell.

What happened, Daddy, to change your mind?

I met some locals who took care of me when they should have let me die. I owe them. This is my gift to them, to you, and my grandchildren. I leave you to control your own destinies, free of Terran influence. Free of the Varns at last.

Thank you. Katie swallowed a lump in her throat. She'd never see him again.

Call me renegade if you must, but please, give up this nonsense of magic and dragons. They are all illusions and fever dreams, Kinnsell added.

"Live long and well, Daddy." Katie laughed through her tears. "Someday you will realize that dragons are real and magic works. Even on Terra."

EPILOGUE

Somewhere in Coronnan City, time and date unimportant

There are injustices I must correct as I move through the city like a ghost. I must use my magic sparingly lest the Commune discover my presence.

The Commune still makes rogue magic illegal and maintains the magical border to keep out the unwanted. Winddrift and Rollett will rule them with a more moderate hand than Scarface, but the law was made for a reason and must be enforced.

Mostly, I need to manipulate events only a little to right wrongs perpetuated by those who must control others or destroy them. Whenever possible, I shall eradicate ignorance so that the innocent know their choices. If I have to, I can access the hidden books as well as the magicians' approved library to keep information flowing throughout Coronnan.

Someday I will settle down and make a family of my own among the fisherfolk. Leauman has the most beautiful daughter. Until then, I have a new life among honest boatmen who don't ask about my past. They care only for the strength of my shoulders to haul in nets and the sharp instincts of my Mopplewogger.

Like Hanassa, I have become an exile, a renegade from my own kind. But I choose to work with the dragons and follow the ideals of the Commune, not fight against them just to prove myself in control of my life. I have studied the options, gathered information, and chosen my destiny.

Good-bye, Nimbulan. Good-bye, my friends. You may see me about and we shall each know that the other prospers, but never again will I share with you the incredible intimacy of Communal magic. I miss you.

IRENE RADFORD

GUARDIAN OF THE BALANCE UE2826—$23.95
This first volume of a ground-breaking new series begins in the time of Merlin and Arthur, when the balance of power is shifting between the old gods and their magic, and the new Christian faith. Wren, first in line of Melin's descendants, gifted in the ancient magics, whose rightful place should have been in Avalon, is thrust into the heart of the political and religious struggles of a society on the brink of chaos, and is forced to confront an overwhelming evil which may well destroy Merlin, Arthur, and her entire civilization.

THE DRAGON NIMBUS HISTORY

☐ **THE DRAGON'S TOUCHSTONE** UE2744—$5.99
☐ **THE LAST BATTLEMAGE** UE2774—$6.99

THE DRAGON NIMBUS TRILOGY

☐ **THE GLASS DRAGON** UE2634—$5.99
☐ **THE PERFECT PRINCESS** UE2678—$5.99
☐ **THE LONELIEST MAGICIAN** UE2709—$5.99

Prices slightly higher in Canada **DAW: 188**

Payable in U.S. funds only. No cash/COD accepted. Postage & handling: U.S./CAN. $2.75 for one book, $1.00 for each additional, not to exceed $6.75; Int'l $5.00 for one book, $1.00 each additional. We accept Visa, Amex, MC ($10.00 min.), checks ($15.00 fee for returned checks) and money orders. Call 800-788-6262 or 201-933-9292, fax 201-896-8569; refer to ad #188.

Penguin Putnam Inc.   Bill my: ☐Visa ☐MasterCard ☐Amex_____(expires)
P.O. Box 12289, Dept. B   Card#_____
Newark, NJ 07101-5289

Please allow 4-6 weeks for delivery.   Signature_____
Foreign and Canadian delivery 6-8 weeks.

Bill to: For faster service when ordering by credit card call **1-800-253-6476**

Allow a minimum of 4-6 weeks for delivery. This offer is subject to change without notice.

Name_____
Address_____ City_____
State/ZIP_____
Daytime Phone #_____

Ship to:

Name_____	Book Total	$_____
Address_____	Applicable Sales Tax	$_____
City_____	Postage & Handling	$_____
State/Zip_____	Total Amount Due	$_____

This offer subject to change without notice.

Melanie Rawn

EXILES

☐ **THE RUINS OF AMBRAI: Book 1**   UE2668—$6.99
                             (hardcover)   UE2619—$20.95
☐ **THE MAGEBORN TRAITOR: Book 2**   UE2730—$6.99
                             (hardcover)   UE2731—$23.95

Three Mageborn sisters bound together by ties of their ancient Blood Line are forced to take their stands on opposing sides of a conflict between two powerful schools of magic. Together, the sisters will fight their own private war, and the victors will determine whether or not the Wild Magic and the Wraithenbeasts are once again loosed to wreak havoc upon their world.

THE DRAGON PRINCE NOVELS

☐ **DRAGON PRINCE : Book 1**   UE2450—$6.99
☐ **THE STAR SCROLL: Book 2**   UE2349—$6.99
☐ **SUNRUNNER'S FIRE: Book 3**   UE2403—$6.99

THE DRAGON STAR NOVELS

☐ **STRONGHOLD: Book 1**   UE2482—$6.99
☐ **THE DRAGON TOKEN: Book 2**   UE2542—$6.99
☐ **SKYBOWL: Book 3**   UE2595—$6.99

Prices slightly higher in Canada   **DAW:190**

Payable in U.S. funds only. No cash/COD accepted. Postage & handling: U.S./CAN. $2.75 for one book, $1.00 for each additional, not to exceed $6.75; Int'l $5.00 for one book, $1.00 each additional. We accept Visa, Amex, MC ($10.00 min.), checks ($15.00 fee for returned checks) and money orders. Call 800-788-6262 or 201-933-9292, fax 201-896-8569; refer to ad #120.

Penguin Putnam Inc.   **Bill my:** ☐Visa ☐MasterCard ☐Amex_____ (expires)
P.O. Box 12289, Dept. B   Card#_____
Newark, NJ 07101-5289

Please allow 4-6 weeks for delivery.   Signature_____
Foreign and Canadian delivery 6-8 weeks.

Bill to:

Name_____

Address_____City_____

State/ZIP_____

Daytime Phone #_____

Ship to:

Name_____ Book Total $_____

Address_____ Applicable Sales Tax $_____

City_____ Postage & Handling $_____

State/Zip_____ Total Amount Due $_____

This offer subject to change without notice.

Tanya Huff

☐ **NO QUARTER**	UE2698—$5.99
☐ **FIFTH QUARTER**	UE2651—$5.99
☐ **SING THE FOUR QUARTERS**	UE2628—$5.99
☐ **THE QUARTERED SEA**	UE2839—$6.99

He Sang water more powerfully than any other bard—but could even Benedikt Sing a ship beyond the known world?

☐ **GATE OF DARKNESS, CIRCLE OF LIGHT**	UE2386—$4.50
☐ **THE FIRE'S STONE**	UE2445—$5.99
☐ **SUMMON THE KEEPER**	UE2784—$5.99

VICTORY NELSON, INVESTIGATOR:
Otherworldly Crimes A Specialty

☐ **BLOOD PRICE: Book 1**	UE2471—$5.99
☐ **BLOOD TRAIL: Book 2**	UE2502—$5.99
☐ **BLOOD LINES: Book 3**	UE2530—$5.99
☐ **BLOOD PACT: Book 4**	UE2582—$5.99
☐ **BLOOD DEBT: Book 5**	UE2739—$5.99

Prices slightly higher in Canada   **DAW: 150**

Payable in U.S. funds only. No cash/COD accepted. Postage & handling: U.S./CAN. $2.75 for one book, $1.00 for each additional, not to exceed $6.75; Int'l $5.00 for one book, $1.00 each additional. We accept Visa, Amex, MC ($10.00 min.), checks ($15.00 fee for returned checks) and money orders. Call 800-788-6262 or 201-933-9292, fax 201-896-8569; refer to ad #150.

Penguin Putnam Inc. **Bill my:** ☐Visa ☐MasterCard ☐Amex_____ (expires)
P.O. Box 12289, Dept. B Card#_____
Newark, NJ 07101-5289

Please allow 4-6 weeks for delivery.   Signature_____
Foreign and Canadian delivery 6-8 weeks.

Bill to:

Name_____
Address_____City_____
State/ZIP_____
Daytime Phone #_____

Ship to:

Name_____ Book Total $_____
Address_____ Applicable Sales Tax $_____
City_____ Postage & Handling $_____
State/Zip_____ Total Amount Due $_____

This offer subject to change without notice.